D0548388

Mostly MEN

Lynn Barber

VIKING

For Harry Fieldhouse and Ron Hall

VIKING

Published by the Penguin Group
Penguin Books Ltd, 27 Wrights Lane, London, W8 5TZ, England
Penguin Books USA Inc.
375 Hudson Street, New York, New York 10014, USA
Penguin Books Australia Ltd, Ringwood, Victoria, Australia
Penguin Books Canada Ltd, 2801 John Street, Markham, Ontario, Canada L3R 1B4
Penguin Books (NZ) Ltd, 182–190 Wairau Road, Auckland 10, New Zealand

Penguin Books Ltd, Registered Offices: Harmondsworth, Middlesex, England

This collection first published 1991

10 9 8 7 6 5 4 3 2 1

Set in 12/14 Lasercomp Sabon

Printed in Great Britain by Clays Ltd, St. Ives plc

A CIP catalogue record for this book is available from the British Library

ISBN 0-670-837911

CONTENTS

INTRODUCTION

I am on a train in central Europe in 1939. I am carrying some vital papers which, if I can get them back to Winston Churchill in London, could alter the whole course of the war. But the Nazis are already looking for me, and they will probably stop the train and arrest me at the next station, which is about an hour away. A man sits opposite me in the carriage. I know nothing about him beyond what I can deduce from his appearance. It occurs to me that perhaps I could give him the papers, and he could escape with them to London when I am arrested. But can I trust him? Whose side is he on? Is he brave and resourceful or will he crumble at the first obstacle? I have just an hour, till the next station, to find out. And he must never suspect that I am finding out in case he is The Enemy – we are simply making conversation on a train. And so, casually at first, but with increasing intensity, I start asking him questions – questions on which the fate of nations will depend . . .

Well, yes, there is a huge flaw in this fantasy, quite apart from its essential corniness. Supposing I don't decide to trust him? Then I get arrested and searched at the next station anyway, so the game is up. But the fantasy illustrates what interviewing means to me: an attempt to read someone's character in an indecently short space of time, and as if my life depended on it. I have to believe that it *matters*, although I know in my saner moments that it doesn't.

And time is everything. Time is what outsiders ignore when they say, 'You're so lucky meeting all those famous people.' I am lucky and I hope I never lose that sense of privilege, but while I am doing an interview I am often so conscious of time ticking away that my brain is screaming, 'Can't you talk faster than this? Oh, *please* don't embark on another anecdote.' Time makes me graceless. 'How was your journey?' asks the polite interviewee. 'Fine,' I say, slapping down my tape recorder and getting out my list of questions. Once Julie Andrews was telling me about her children and asked, 'Have you got children?' 'No,' I said, abolishing two daughters without even thinking about it – good heavens, she might start asking me their names and ages and whole minutes could be wasted.

I believe that if you and I were locked in a cell with a famous person (FP – I can't stand the word 'celebrity') for a week each, we would probably both come back with equally perceptive accounts of what they were like. We might differ, but your judgement would be at least as valid as mine. But if we were locked in with the FP for just one hour then my character description would be fuller and sharper than yours. This is simply because I have more experience – it's my job. There's a man who comes to the St Giles Fair in Oxford every year who makes his money by guessing people's ages – you pay him 50p and he tells you your age; if he gets it wrong, he pays you £1. My skill is like that: specific, narrow, almost useless, but very well honed.

FPs are by definition much-interviewed and that, for me, is part of the fun. I take little joy in interviewing 'virgins' – newcomers to the media scene – and none at all in 'real people'. I love stars. I love the tension between the public image and the private person; I like the fact that I don't have to waste time explaining who the subject is; above all, I like and need the competitive edge of going where many journalists have gone before, and trying to do better.

Of course, you never know if you've succeeded. Interviewing is exactly like fishing in that you can come back with a good big fish feeling mighty pleased with yourself, and never know that your fish was actually the smallest in the entire river. Sue Lawley once had the horrendous experience of an uncaught fish climbing out of the water and trumpeting to the world, 'You missed me!' She interviewed the Duchess of York on television one night and the next morning the Duchess announced that she was pregnant – Sue Lawley hadn't asked. But I couldn't participate in the general glee because it could perfectly easily have happened to me. You can cast your hook as often and as widely as you like, but you will still miss things. I suppose a good interviewer is one who doesn't miss too much too often – and above all who doesn't get found out.

Why mostly men? Only because I seem to interview men better, perhaps because I am more curious about them. I was an only child, educated at a girls' school, and hardly met any boys till I went to Oxford. When I did, I was so excited and intrigued I kept a notebook in which I jotted my observations of the species, much as I had kept bird-watching notes as a child. 'Flat back of head, untrustworthy.' 'Says he shaves twice a day – boasting? Implies sexy?' 'They like you to know the names of flowers, not of birds.' (A sad observation, this – all my years of ornithology instantly erased; henceforward I would never admit to knowing the difference between a coot and a moorhen.) I believed that if I studied the species diligently enough I would arrive at useful generalizations on the strength of which I could achieve my then ambition of becoming a *femme fatale*. I never did – but I think the habit of overwrought and slightly dotty observation I established then has stood me in good stead as an interviewer.

When I started in journalism, in the late sixties, interviews were of an extremely high calibre, especially in American magazines like *Esquire*, *Playboy* and the *New Yorker*. Even in this country, they quite frequently ran to 6,000 or even 10,000 words and were as well researched as a biography.

The classic, of course, was and still is Lillian Ross's profile of Hemingway, originally published in the *New Yorker* in 1950. It has never been surpassed.

In the seventies and eighties, interviews seemed to dwindle. They got shorter and lazier and were so manipulated by PRs that they were often indistinguishable from press handouts. In newspaper offices they were known as 'starfucker pieces' and were acknowledged as something you had to have – like a weather map or bridge column – but that no one particularly wanted to be in charge of. But now interviews have regained a little status (as indeed have obituaries, another manifestation of the biographical impulse) but still to nowhere near their former glory. Incidentally, I call my articles interviews, but in America an interview means a question-and-answer dialogue that reads like a playscript. Here, profile and interview are used more or less interchangeably, though a profile can be written without meeting the subject whereas an interview can't. I prefer interview: profile sounds a bit pompous to me.

Outsiders seem to imagine that hours of thought and consultation go into choosing my subjects. Would that it were so. Most of the time it's a scramble. PRs ring up all the time with clients who want to plug something; friends and colleagues make suggestions; once a month I brace myself to write a score of letters (journalists hate writing letters) requesting interviews with the great and the good; occasionally there's an editorial directive – 'You haven't done a woman for months', 'We need someone young in this issue', or the all-out panic of 'We need anyone at all by tomorrow.' I've made various attempts at instituting a system for organizing interviews, but have come to the conclusion that, in journalism, panic *is* the system.

Left to myself, however, I will tend to choose interviewees who are male, older than me, and 'difficult'. I like complex characters, I love temperament. I don't mind if they are vain, egotistical and badly behaved. Journalists on the whole tend to be egalitarian-minded and contemptuous of tall poppies, but I prefer the prima donnas. My father is a noisy eccentric so the sort of scenes from which most English people retreat in embarrassment are familiar and homely to me. Indeed, when an interview becomes a 'scene', I always think 'Yippee – great copy!' I can cope with drunks, eccentrics and people who shout. What I can't cope with is bores, which for me includes most politicians, most businessmen and many members of the acting profession. Another group I avoid, for interviewing purposes, is nice, sane, straightforward people with their feet on the ground. I have interviewed a few – Michael Palin, Julie Andrews, Jane Asher – but never very successfully. I feel as Tolstoy did about happy families – they're too alike. Once you've said they're nice, what else is there to say? Moreover, you can say that someone is nice without particularly bothering to prove it, but if you want to say that they're self-obsessed or vain or rude, you've got to be supremely sure you've got the evidence in your interview to justify it.

This is my answer, incidentally, to people who accuse me of being an aggressive or bitchy interviewer (bitchy enrages me – it's a sexist insult, and implies dishonest and underhand, which I never am; I loathe innuendo). Aggressive? Maybe. It's a quality which in male journalists is admired, after all. But I think it's more that I choose to interview people who are not, by nature, easygoing. My best subjects are the last people on earth you'd want to have to your dinner party.

The interviews that read most entertainingly are not necessarily the ones I'm proudest of because there are some FPs who talk so easily you could practically send a baboon with a tape recorder and get a good interview. Thus, Richard Harris, Zsa Zsa Gabor and Ken Russell in the present volume are all good fun but no particular credit to me; I'm much prouder of, say, Muriel Spark or J. Paul Getty, where to get anything at all is an achievement.

I am nervous of showing how much I care about interviewing. It is only journalism, after all. I don't want to find myself in Pseuds' Corner. But I do care: I am enraged when I do a bad interview, elated when I do a good one. I know I've done a good one when I feel weirdly exhausted afterwards; once or twice, interviewing someone outside London, I've had to park in a lay-by and sleep before I could summon the energy to drive home. It's like an exam: you can prepare as much as you like beforehand (and I do do a lot of preparation, reading all the press cuttings I can find), but ultimately it all either comes together or falls apart on the day, and if it falls apart you feel very sick.

And, as with exams, the best deployment of time is vital. Most FPs are busy people; they rarely agree to be interviewed for much longer than an hour (I always ask for two hours but don't often get it). The old Hollywood stars like Kirk Douglas have an absolutely set routine: the PR tells you that he never gives interviews of more than forty minutes, but 'just this once, for you, Lynn, he's agreed to an hour'. Then at the end of the hour when the PR comes to collect him, he'll say, 'I'm enjoying this interview so much – but my goodness she's giving me a tough time – can we just overrun for another fifteen minutes?' The PR says, 'But the schedule's already very tight.' He says, 'Yeah, but this is important – we're doing a great interview here.' The PR shoots you a look suggesting 'Goodness, you are honoured!' and you are meant to go away feeling incredibly grateful. It is a brilliant routine – except that it is now so hoary that old hands like me will already have written one hour and fifteen minutes in their diary.

I used to kick against this time limitation and howl, 'Oh, if only I could spend longer with the subject, how much better my article would be.' But now I'm not so sure. A couple of years ago, I was stranded with Keith Floyd on a remote Orkney island for five days, but my article was not noticeably richer as a result. If anything, my perceptions became blunted with repetition, and I got lost in the maze of 'on the one hand this, on the other hand that'. I don't think I could ever write a good profile of someone I knew really well.

The fact that time is so tight has all sorts of implications – the most important of which is that any minute when the FP is not talking is a minute wasted. Thus, an interview is not a conversation; it is not even a dialogue; what I hope it will be is a monologue with only minimal questions by way of prompt, and I smile smugly if my FP complains at the end that I've made them hoarse with talking.

An interview should not be a meeting of minds. The good interviewer is faceless, ego-less, devoid of personality (at the interview – the personality can come into the writing), a *tabula rasa* on which the subject writes. Since joining the *Independent on Sunday*, I've noticed that my subjects are sometimes curious about me – presumably from reading my articles – and want to ask me questions. It won't do. It isn't on. It's a handicap. There isn't time for a conversation. I want to get on and do my job.

To me, interviewing is about listening rather than asking questions. Of course you do have to ask questions, but only the bare minimum to get them going. Whereas listening is really important – listening for what they don't say as much as what they do, listening for what they say glibly and what they say awkwardly, listening for the 'charged' bits that touch an emotional nerve. I try never to interrupt when someone is talking but I make mental notes all the time of things to go back to – why has he talked all this time about his father and not mentioned his mother? Why is he so shifty about his brother? I try constantly to turn generalizations into specifics: if someone says they hardly knew their father, it is too vague to convey anything, but if they say they saw their father for perhaps five hours a year, it is vivid and shocking. Often it only takes one tiny detail to bring a picture alive. I remember Jonathan Ross telling me his parents were not well-off, but it was only when he added that sharing a bedroom with his four brothers made masturbation difficult, that the 'not well-off-ness' became evocative.

And since every minute is precious, there is no time for clever questions. Non-journalists imagine newspaper interviews to be like television interviews where the question is often as important and informative as the answer, but my idea of a clever question is the shortest one that will get the

longest, most interesting answer – in practice, usually 'Why?'
I do begin an interview with a long, clever, scripted question
which might go something like 'In 1986 you said in a *Times*
interview that "bla bla bla", whereas in 1988 you told the
Tatler that "bla bla bla". What happened between those dates
to make you change your mind?' The object of this convoluted
codswallop is simply to say, 'Look, I've done a lot of
homework for this interview; I have read all the cuttings; I
expect you to make an effort now I'm here.' There is also a
faint hope that by showing my familiarity with all their
previous interviews, I can prevent them giving me the same
old guff they've given before, though the hope often proves
illusory.

Another key point at the beginning of the interview is The
Plug. Most FPs nowadays only give interviews when they
have something to sell – a new film or a book or whatever –
and they are fretful until they have done it. I therefore let
them do their plug at length and generously at the beginning
of the interview, to get it out of the way. Merely listening to
it doesn't mean that I have to include it in the written article
and I use this time for familiarizing myself with their voice,
their turn of phrase, making mental notes on their appearance
and checking that the tape recorder is working . . .

Oh, the tape recorder! I almost forgot! Yes, I do use a tape
recorder; indeed I am so dependent on it that I couldn't be an
interviewer if it hadn't been invented. I know lots of good
interviewers, like Lynda Lee-Potter and Maureen Cleave, use
shorthand, but I believe that maintaining eye contact is vital
(for the same reason, although I have a list of questions, I
never refer to it – it is there as a comfort blanket). One
disadvantage is that the tape recorder can sometimes make
people self-conscious for the first few minutes, but that time
can be devoted to the plug. A tape recording is also good libel
insurance: I don't want anyone ever to claim that I misquoted
them or 'doctored' a quote. It's fine by me if, like Tony Benn,
they want to tape-record the interview themselves. The more
the merrier. The whole game is getting people to say things,

not making them up. I also transcribe my own tapes, which everyone says is a waste of time, but I value that time for thinking and mulling over the interview.

As I say, I have a list of questions but it is only a prop. I will have read the cuttings beforehand and decided what areas I want to explore and which areas have already been done to death by previous interviewers. Again, because time is precious, I don't want to waste time eliciting facts which could be found from other sources. After the clever question and the plug, I usually move swiftly on to asking about their childhood. Most people talk fairly easily about their childhood – they regard it as a 'safe' subject, safely distant, and they are often quite happy to describe what they were like as children, warts and all, whereas they'd be more wary of describing themselves today. But I believe that if you can understand someone's childhood you're three quarters of the way to understanding them now.

My habit of asking about childhood arose really by accident. I returned to journalism when my children were three and six respectively and at the time I was completely obsessed with sibling rivalry. As an only child myself I'd never even thought about it: now I found it dominated my life. I felt guilty about going back to work at all, so by asking people about their childhood, and especially about their relations with brothers and sisters, I felt I was acquiring useful knowledge which might improve my own performance as a mother and alleviate the guilt of going to work.

Luckily, too, it was faintly appropriate to the job I was supposed to be doing – interviewing people for the *Sunday Express* back-page feature 'Things I Wish I'd Known at Eighteen'. It was a cumbersome format, invariably drawing the answer, 'I wish I'd known how to play the piano', but I found that getting people to describe what they were like at eighteen was very fruitful. And then I would launch into all the sibling stuff that obsessed me: 'Did you think your mother gave you a fair share of attention?' etc., and perhaps the very intensity of my mad curiosity communicated itself to my subjects – at all events, I got some good interviews. It was valuable practice for me, too, doing the same format week after week and trying desperately to vary it – it taught me to look for the differentness of different people, to draw out their most idiosyncratic characteristics.

Even now, no longer obsessed with sibling rivalry, I probably spend as much as half the interview asking people about their childhood. Much of it won't appear in the written article, but it gives me a basic understanding of their character which I don't feel I can get any other way, and it helps them, I think, to shed their selfconsciousness about 'image'. In this phase of the interview, too, I try to establish a sort of ground level of honesty where it just seems pointless to lie and we are both equally committed to finding the truth. I try very hard never to force an interviewee into a position where they have to lie – for instance, by asking about their marriage when it is obviously rocky; or by asking closet homosexuals why they aren't married. I usually say at the beginning of an interview that if there are any of my questions they don't want to answer, they should just shake their head rather than trying to waffle round it. Because if a subject tells one lie they will tell others; I much prefer them to keep silent. Dealing with homosexuals who have not 'come out' is difficult; I don't want to try to force them out, but on the other hand, I don't want to listen to a load of codswallop about how they had a fiancée but she died. But, after all, there are questions like 'How often have you been in love?' which can be answered without giving too much away.

Often looming over the interview is the big awkward question that has to be asked because readers would be disappointed if it wasn't. There is no point in pussyfooting round it or trying to camouflage it in new, subtle disguises. I believe in asking it early and baldly, accepting the answer and then getting on with the interview. The subject's relief at having survived it so quickly and painlessly may pay dividends for the rest of the interview. I was criticized by many readers for asking Sir Jimmy Savile whether he liked little girls, but actually he was glad to have the opportunity to answer that question – he was aware that the rumour existed.

Towards the end of an interview, I try to vary the emotional temperature a bit – perhaps to provoke the subject into anger if we have been unduly cosy hitherto, or to drown them in honey if we have had a rough crossing. At this stage I sometimes give a sort of resumé of what I have concluded about them, for example 'It seems to me you're very arrogant.' It is remarkable how often the response to such an accusation will actually provide the proof that has hitherto been lacking, *vide* my Ben Elton article where I ask if he's self-righteous. I also like to ask questions with a bit of topspin: 'You obviously think you're a pretty wonderful person – why?' This, incidentally, covers the same ground as 'Which of your achievements are you most proud of?' – i.e. it's an invitation for the subject to recount their achievements – but asking it in a 'hostile' form will often elicit a more passionate and actually more sympathetic answer than asking it in its bland form. Interviewees are often much better served by hostile questions than by friendly ones: forced to defend themselves hard, they are far more likely to appeal to the reader. The really deadly questions are the dulcet ones.

I try to attend the photo sesssion after the interview or, if I can't, ask the photographer what transpired, because it is amazing how differently some FPs – especially showbiz stars – behave with photographers. Pavarotti was the most glaring example: he gave me a perfectly pleasant interview, was courteous and helpful throughout, then went off to be photographed and threw a quite horrendous tantrum. I had been warned he was 'funny' with photographers but he practically reduced the photographer to tears.

Immediately after the interview, I write some rough notes of what struck me. How much other work I do before writing the article rather depends on how satisfied I am with the interview. If it has gone well, and if I am confident that I have 'read' the subject's character correctly, I will rely purely on my own instincts. But if I am still unsure, I may phone round their friends and colleagues trying out my hunches and seeing the reaction. People rarely agree 100 per cent, but the relative strength or weakness of their disagreement often tells me whether I'm on the right track.

Of course, it is unfair to write what amounts to a character analysis on the basis of a one-hour meeting. My only defence is that I don't pretend to know the subject any better than I do (I despise those profiles which are written as if from intimate knowledge when they're actually based on rehashed press cuttings). And occasionally my character readings have been confirmed months or even years later by people who know the subject well and say, 'You got him/her to a T' – the most gratifying remark an interviewer can ever hear.

It is wrong to make snap judgements on people's character, but in real life we do it all the time – 'That builder looks honest', 'The new neighbour seems stuck up.' I believe that we actually have more insight into other humans than we normally allow ourselves to use, and that these hunches or intuitions, 'vibes', call them what you will, have some basis in experience. I would never put my hunches in print without proper proof, but in the course of an interview, I will certainly listen to them and follow whatever lines of questioning they suggest. Often the more 'off the wall' the question, the more spot-on it proves to be.

I read books on psychology, of course, but I also read books on palmistry and astrology, not because I believe in the occult, but because the potted character descriptions they give are often rather odd and stimulating – the terrible slow-burning Taurus who never forgets, the fast and flighty Gemini, the slippery, soothing, elusive Pisces. Thus I might think of someone as 'a typical Taurus' irrespective of their birth date, but as a sort of shorthand for their character. I suspect that we know less about character now, in the late twentieth century, than at any previous time in history. It is an unfashionable subject, but I think it's now dangerously neglected. By handing over character analysis entirely to psychoanalysts and psychologists, we neglect the accumulated worldly wisdom of, say, GPs or prostitutes or clergymen, or even, dare I say it, palmists and astrologers, bookies and casino staff (who are often amazingly perceptive), hairdressers and restaurateurs.

What is the character sketch of a good interviewer? First and foremost, curiosity, real nosiness, about other people's lives. If you have never sat on the Tube wondering about that couple opposite – How did they meet? What do they do in bed? At weekends? What music do they listen to? Where do they go for their holidays? – then you are not a potential interviewer. Second, an ability to listen, to be able to let other people talk without wanting to express your own opinion (harder for men than for women, I suspect), an ability to switch off any desire to assert your own ego. And thirdly, a sort of nonconformity or at least a tolerance of difference. People who want to be like other people, to find their points of similarity and say, 'Oh, I'm just the same', on the whole do not make good interviewers; the best interviews – like the best biographies – should sing the strangeness and variety of the human race.

My articles are written with the primary intention of being entertaining and, where possible, funny. Like all journalism, they have to compete with many other distractions, so the opening always has to be attention-grabbing. My first editor, Harry Fieldhouse, gave me some good advice: he said, Write your first paragraph exactly as you would wish it to be, ponder every word, hone every comma, polish it to perfection – and then throw it away and write the article. I have done this ever since and only once, recently with Kirk Douglas, and when I knew Harry was too ill to read it, did I let my first paragraph go to press.

I rather wonder if I should follow Harry's advice and throw this whole introduction away. If the articles don't speak for themselves, they are not worth reading. But I would like to pay tribute to the two people who taught me to write – dear, patient Harry Fieldhouse, who hired me as an absolute beginner on *Penthouse* and spent four years raising me to

competance, and then my editor at the *Sunday Express*
Magazine, Ron Hall, who encouraged me to commit the
journalistic solecism of writing in the first person and thereby
liberated me. I would also like to thank my present editor,
Stephen Glover of the *Independent on Sunday*, and my
colleague Ian Jack, who have both been perennially kind and
generous. My grateful thanks too to my former employers the
Sunday Express and especially Andrew Cameron for allowing
me to reprint these articles. I hope you enjoy them.

RICHARD ADAMS

6 May 1990

A meeting with Richard Adams is not for the socially squeamish or easily embarrassed. Friends who had met him warned that, if he liked me, I would get long excruciating doses of sexual reminiscence, and, if he didn't like me, he would shout and thump the table. Actually, he didn't thump the table at all, and I got off fairly light on the sexual front with only a brief excursion into blue movies and pornography ('It's just something a man needs every six weeks or two months or so. I'm what they call in the trade a "straight", I'm not into domination.')

What nobody had warned me about, or not sufficiently, was the crying. Over and over again, and sometimes seemingly at random, his eyes would fill with tears and he would start talking in a broken voice, gasping between sobs, about the death of a friend or about cruelty to animals. Worst of all was when he got on to the Crucifixion, and howled, tears streaming, 'To think that He suffered for *me*! I don't want Him to suffer for *me*!' His agent later told me that the crying was quite a recent development and seemed to start with the writing of his last novel, *Traveller*, 'but of course he's always been very sensitive and highly strung'.

We talked for a while over madeira in the sitting-room and

then moved to the dining-room for lunch, where his secretary
and her husband, the gardener, joined us. (Incidentally, they
ate pizza while we ate meat pie. I don't know whether this
marked some social nuance.) Thinking he would not like to
cry in front of his employees, I was especially careful to avoid
any potentially tear-provoking subjects, but he, at the first
possible pause in the conversation, and apropos of nothing,
suddenly announced, 'But I don't think you've *realized*, Lynn,
what it meant to me, the death of my friends in the war . . .'
and the tears splashed noisily into his meat pie. I found myself
wanting to bark 'Brace up, man!' or 'Pull yourself together!'
– not phrases that normally spring to my lips. But his rabbit-
like demeanour has a fox-making effect.

Apart from that (but apart from that, Mrs Lincoln, how
did you enjoy the play?) he seems a perfectly sweet old buffer.
He lives on the edge of Whitchurch in Hampshire and is, he
says, well liked by his cronies in the pub. The village is near
Watership Down. I drove up there before I met him, by way
of homage, but he told me: 'You know, my sentimental
feelings about the Down are not as great as people suppose.'
The house is not particularly grand – it is only when he takes
you to the library and starts showing you his first editions or
casually mentions that, to enlarge the garden, they bought the
next-door cottage and knocked it down, that you remember
just how colossal his worldwide royalties from *Watership
Down* must be.

In the eighteen years since publication, it has been translated into twenty languages, and become a bestseller in
countries where they don't even *have* rabbits or downs –
many of the foreign dust-jackets show species of gerbil
cavorting among sand dunes. Much as one relishes Craig
Brown's remark, when told that *Watership Down* was a book
about rabbits written by a civil servant, that he'd rather read
a book about civil servants written by a rabbit, the fact
remains that *Watership Down* will live long after all of us are
forgotten.

None of Adams's subsequent novels has been so successful.

Most have been panned by the critics, and the sexy ones, *The Girl in a Swing* and *Maia*, outraged many of his old rabbit fans. His last novel, *Traveller*, about General Lee's horse in the American Civil War, sank almost without trace. He says one of the hazards of signing sessions – which he enjoys on the whole – is that so many people tell him they loved *Watership Down* and hated *Shardik*. 'What did *you* think, Lynn?'

'Er . . . I loved *Watership Down* and hated *Shardik*.'

Now he has written his autobiography, *The Day Gone By*, which contains truly glorious passages of ecstatic nature writing but loses charm when he gets on to people. It finishes, frustratingly, with his demobilization after the war, and his first meeting with Elizabeth Acland, who became his wife. (She is a ceramics expert, currently engaged in excavating an old china factory in Limehouse.) He says he has no intention of writing a sequel because 'the nearer you come to the present, the more you run the risk of hurting people's feelings and upsetting them'.

Thus one will learn nothing of his famous nervous breakdown at Oxford when he was reputedly found in the Provost of Worcester's study with a note pinned to his chest saying he had committed suicide – he took his finals from the Warneford mental hospital – nor indeed of his twenty-five years in the civil service, though he remembers them with great affection. He was an expert on river flooding in the Department of the Environment and told me that if he had not written *Watership Down*, 'which made my fortune', he might have ended up an undersecretary – though he told someone else that he probably wouldn't have done because he was considered 'unsound'.

He wrote his autobiography in order to commemorate his father, and to record the everyday life of the Berkshire village in which he grew up. His father was the local doctor, as was his father before him, and seems to have been a rather unhappy man – in later life he took to the bottle. There were two much older siblings and then a son who died in infancy before Richard was born; as a consequence, he was enormously spoilt.

His father seems to have been almost obsessively preoccupied with class – perhaps because he himself married a nurse: 'In those days,' Adams explains, 'a nurse was, shall we say, a good cut below a governess and only a little better than a housemaid. So to marry a nurse was little short of a family disgrace.' His mother, Adams concedes, 'adapted well' to her new position in society and was much loved by all who knew her but 'Well . . . she was a very *straightforward* person, she was not a person of trained intellect. My mother had a delightful unselfconsciousness and could get on with shop people and that sort of thing. I mean, it's no good saying there isn't a class system in this country because there is.' Ironically, his own daughter Rosamond became a nurse but gave it up because, according to her father, she said, 'I don't mind being paid peanuts, I don't mind working all the hours there are but I *do* object to being treated like a skivvy.'

Adams claims that he hated snobbery and was the victim of it at school when, for instance, another boy asked him, 'Is it true, Adams, that your mother does the *cooking?*' But his father seems to have endorsed it. 'I'll tell you a little anecdote,' Adams says fondly. 'My sister had a boyfriend at one time who was in the RAF – he was a Squadron Leader. And he was always referred to as "The Squadron Leader" at home – "Oh, the Squadron Leader's coming to lunch today, chaps." And one day my father was talking to the Squadron Leader and the Squadron Leader said, "Pardon, Dr Adams?" Well that finished him, as far as my father was concerned. That was the end of that. He couldn't feel respect for a man who said pardon. That was what it was *like* in those days.'

One of the first things Richard Adams did with the money from *Watership Down* was to get himself a coat of arms. He showed it to me, framed in the hall, three rabbits on a green ground, holding gold pens, and the motto *Adamare Adamanda* – to love passionately those things which ought to be loved passionately. He wears the crest on his signet ring. 'You see so many coats of arms these days that are not genuine, but mine is genuine. You've got to go down and see the people at the College of Arms and convince them that they want to have you as an armigerous person. I think you have to be a little bit distinguished in some way, though it's not my place to say it. Of course you have to pay. And after that, you can have cigarette cases with your arms on and table silver and so on. I don't think there's any *snobbery* about it. It was only a kind of joke, really, but I think my father would have been pleased. A great many of the things I've done and written are because I think my father would have been pleased.'

I mentioned earlier that the autobiography is frustrating because it ends in 1946 — the year of his father's death. It is also frustrating in that it is disingenuously coy on the subject of his psyche, though, having undergone three years of Jungian analysis, he must know it better than most. He seems to expect the reader to understand things without being told: the book is full of odd hints and references. For instance, he mentions one of his earliest memories, when he stole some begonias from the garden and got away with it, and says, 'I believe this was the start of a certain unscrupulous streak in small matters which has remained with me all my life.' Could he expand? 'Oh well, these are things I'm ashamed of and I'd *rather* not go into details if you *don't* mind. The episode of the begonias was the start of an unworthy feeling of "Oo, I can get away with this." You see, it's when the passions are inflamed. The point was not that I'd pinch a peardrop out of a sweetshop bottle — I've never done anything like that, that would be mean and contemptible — but I've always been a very volatile and highly charged person, and the beauty of the begonias simply swept me into a feeling that I must have them at all costs. I don't think I'll say any more than that.'

Another traumatic childhood event was when he went to a children's party and was so frightened by the Punch and Judy that he ran away and hid, causing endless embarrassment to his hosts and to his parents. As so often with Richard Adams, class was a factor – 'It was a very up-market party' – but he also says in the book it was 'the origin of a behaviour pattern of cracking under stress which has remained with me all my life'. When else did it happen? 'Well perhaps,' he finally concedes, 'my joining the Royal Army Service Corps was a case of this. I mean a young gentleman during the war should really have joined a combatant arm, should he not? I mean, only funny fellows, comic men and clowns in private life joined the RASC. But I had one idea at the back of my mind: I knew I was afraid to join the infantry. And I volunteered for the Navy and the Fleet Air Arm, but they were over-subscribed, and I could feel the infantry lapping about my ankles, so I volunteered for the RASC. So I originally joined up in a self-indulgent way. But I later came to my senses and volunteered for airborne service, and it was only the luck of the draw that kept me out of anything serious.' In the RASC he met the fellow officers who became the models for Hazel, Bigwig and Co. in *Watership Down*. He hero-worshipped them all the more because he felt he was a coward himself.

'And that meant,' he said sweepingly, 'that the only possible future for me lay in writing – because there's nothing to run away from in writing.' It took him twenty-five years to do it, but he is now blissfully happy in his status as 'a man of letters', proud of his literary friends, Ruth Rendell, John Wain, Iris Murdoch, and his honorary membership of the Royal Society of Literature. He is extremely well read, quotes reams of poetry by heart, and rejoices in his enormous library, which he converted from the former billiard room, with its shelves of first editions – all of Dr Johnson, the great Victorians, a Shakespeare second folio and a Charles II Bible. At lunch he told me, 'Of course the folio *Hamlet*, with all its cruxes, is a goldmine.' I said sorry, what? and he was suddenly shaking with apopletic fury: 'I think I said cruxes, did I not? Oh come on! You're teasing me. You're playing the *faux naïve*. You *must* know what a crux is.' I assured him I didn't and he then explained it was a bibliophile's term for a disputed point, or where one edition of a book differs from another, but it was a black mark against me, almost on a par with the Squadron Leader saying pardon. Consequently I got a rather abbreviated tour of the library. ('He takes everyone there, even the man who comes to read the electricity meter,' says A. N. Wilson.) It is a *very* grand library, with proper revolving bookstands and library tables, the latter laid out with chess boards and a chess computer, for his various correspondence games in progress. There is also a conspicuous colour photograph of an almost naked girl – actress Meg Tilley, who starred in the film of *Girl in a Swing* – forming an odd contrast to all the family photographs, and rabbit mementoes, and general paraphernalia of what his family calls 'The WFA' (World Famous Author).

After lunch and library, he took me back to the sitting-room for coffee and announced, 'One thing I've tried to put in my book is the appallingly restrictive sexual conventions of the day. I thought you would probably want to talk about that . . .?' Friends had warned me what this could entail. I said that, *actually*, what I really wanted was a cigarette, which I thought would stop him dead in his tracks, but no, off he went to the kitchen for an ashtray, apologized for not having a light, gave himself a good squirt with his asthma inhaler and settled down to tell me about sex. Luckily his secretary, perhaps practised in these occasions, came in with a message almost immediately, but it was a nasty moment.

I liked him better when, by way of farewell, he showed me round his garden, pointing out all the plants and telling me their Latin names. He seemed frail and small walking beside me; he turns seventy this week, and admits to 'an almost Johnsonian fear of death'. He says the worst thing about being old is the physical infirmity, having a false hip and being short of breath. 'It's a great deprivation not to be able to walk because walking in the country used to be two thirds of my life. Elizabeth and I thought nothing of walking fifteen miles a day. And, thanks to my father, I knew the names of all the birds and the flowers. To walk over a meadow or a down, if you do know about flowers, is a delight rather like listening to the first movement of the *Eroica*. But now I can't do it. You know, people say "You can't be seventy!" – head waiters with whom you're being a bit chummy, or publishers, tailors, this kind of person – and I always say "I assure you I *am*!"'

What *is* one to make of Richard Adams? I suspect he is one of those people who put their worst face forwards, and that if you could get over the squirming stickiness of the first meeting – the crying, the boasting, the general excruciating embarrassingness of the man – you could probably grow to like him. His affection for his family, for his comrades in the war and his friends in the civil service; his generosity to animal causes; his touching pride in knowing other authors, all betoken a heart in the right place. His agent, Jacqueline Korn, has known him for seventeen years and says he is one of the kindest, most considerate and appreciative authors she has ever had to deal with – 'He's *not* a monster.' Ruth Rendell also talks of his kindness, his warm-heartedness, and says, 'I'm sorry to use such an awful cliché, but he's the sort of person who simply couldn't do enough for you.'

He seems to get on with women better than men and indeed often falls in love with them. He was so smitten with one lady journalist the other week that he sent her a pearl necklace. (She sent it back.) His relations with men are more touchy, as witness his dealings with fellow-novelist A. N. Wilson. When *Girl on a Swing* came out in 1980, A. N. Wilson wrote a hostile review of it in the *TLS*. Five years later – *five years* – Adams went up to Wilson at a party and asked him to justify it. When Wilson said he couldn't now remember what he'd said, Richard Adams recited the whole review from memory, all 1,000 words of it. He then bombarded Wilson with letters, phone calls, even a tape recording, until eventually Wilson wrote to him and said, 'This has got to stop.' Far from stopping, Adams invited Wilson to supper and Wilson went. Adams lambasted him all through the meal until Mrs Adams begged him to stop, then he took Wilson off to the library, and announced 'As we are both Christians and gentlemen we should be friends. Would you like to shake my hand?' Wilson did ('It was like Fiver offering his paw') and drove off into the night with a signed copy of *Maia*, all sweetness and light. But then, in a round-up of the eighties in the *Telegraph*, Wilson said that Adams had written one good book and no more since, and Adams is back on record again as thinking A. N. Wilson is a shit.

Adams is perfectly well aware that most people loathe him – if anything, he seems to glory in it. It is he, after all, who tells the story about meeting Robert Robinson on the stairs at the Savile Club, and Robinson cutting him dead, whereupon Adams ran after him and said, 'You don't remember me?' and Robinson said firmly, 'Oh, but I *do*,' before going on his way. How can he *bear* to tell this story? How can he bear to recall, in his book, that his brigadier referred to him as 'that awful little shit, Adams' or his headmaster as 'that little beast, Adams'? How can he bear to tell *me* how, in order to get out of beatings at school, he would sob and fling himself to the floor and grovel and beg till the master dismissed him unbeaten. 'Most boys didn't do this,' he adds complacently, 'the convention was you took your beating like a man.' Well, *yes*. He told me that his wife, 'dear Liz', was always telling him he had a very bad self-image and ought to try to lift it up. So why didn't he? The suspicion must be that he enjoys feeling himself reviled. I kept thinking of the old joke: Beat me, says the masochist. No, says the sadist. That is why, though I feel a sneaking admiration for the man, I thought it kinder to suppress it.

Reproduced by permission of the *Independent on Sunday*

MARGARET, DUCHESS OF ARGYLL

17 August 1986

Margaret, Duchess of Argyll, has written a book called
. . . No, we had better leave the question of what it is called
till later. What it is about is entertaining. So she entertained
me to a glass of iced water in her apartment in Grosvenor
House, where she lives with her maid, and her poodle, Louis.

We sat in her study where she keeps the tools of a duchess's
trade – *Debrett's* and *Who's Who*, racks of invitations, boxes
of engraved writing paper, leather-bound dinner-party books,
and boxes and boxes of press cuttings. She keeps them all,
good or bad (and they have been *very* bad in their time), but,
'This interview will be about my *book*,' she had stipulated
beforehand.

The question that puzzled me while reading it was: who is
this book intended *for*? I mean, it tells you how to lay a
table, and not to serve red wine with fish; it advises you
where to seat the Lord Chancellor of England (on your right)
and what to do if your butler gets drunk (ask the guests to
put him to bed); but it fails to tackle the *really* thorny
questions like what to do if your one spare man cancels, or how
to treat gay couples, or what to do with guests (as opposed to
butlers) who get very drunk, or how to cater for the seemingly
ever-increasing number of vegetarians. The Duchess has a

Nelsonian way with all such questions. Vegetarians? 'They eat what they can.' Spare men? 'I always invite three or four extras.' Drunken guests? 'It never happens.' Gays? '*Must* we mention this?'

So who *is* the book intended for? 'I haven't a clue,' said the Duchess, surprised at the question. 'I think some of it will be of interest to very young couples.' I suggested that young couples with butlers were fairly thin on the ground. 'Don't go *on* about butlers!' snapped the Duchess. (I had not mentioned them heretofore.) 'It's so stupid to go on about them. *I* had a butler but it doesn't mean that everyone's got to. But, however simple the dinner may be, *somebody's* got to serve the food. It doesn't have to be the butler. It could be the gardener!' Ah.

The Duchess's priorities for party-giving are people first; drink second; food, decor and everything else, last. She is ruthless in eliminating bores; even when one partner in a couple is riveting and the other boring, she will drop the couple rather than tolerate the bore. 'The people you invite to your parties may not be your dearest *friends*,' she told me. 'You may not even particularly like them, but they're going to add to that party.' But supposing, I said, you had a very dear old friend who was not particularly brilliant/pretty/famous/amusing. 'The old school chum?' drawled the Duchess. 'Invite her to lunch . . . another day.'

I asked if she would ever invite people who were not 'Society' but stars from another world – Luciano Pavarotti, say. 'Oh you wouldn't ask a *dancer*,' she said firmly. 'I mean, he can contribute nothing. All *he* can do is dance.' (I would have thought that any hostess who could offer the sight of Pavarotti dancing would be the toast of London, but still . . .) 'How about Kiri Te Kanawa?' Here the Duchess was on surer ground: 'Yes, she's charming, a very pretty woman. She could contribute a lot.'

Food, for the Duchess's dinner parties, is not a problem. In the old days, when she had a house in Upper Grosvenor Street, the excellent Mrs Duckworth – 'one of the best cooks in London' – spirited up the victuals, and nowadays she gives her parties at 90 Park Lane, the Grosvenor House restaurant. The Duchess herself has never tried to boil an egg or make a cup of tea; she prefers not to enter a kitchen for fear of encountering something unpleasant such as raw meat. Nevertheless, she is aware that some people *do* cook their own dinner parties – indeed she had been to one such last night, given by a young bachelor. Did *he* have a . . .? 'No, but he had two men to serve the food. Don't go *on* about butlers. It's so stupid.'

The Duchess's role in preparing her dinner parties is inviting the guests (three weeks before – 'people in London get *so* booked up'), sending reminder cards a few days beforehand and making sure she spells people's names right. ('It is *amazing* how many people write to me as Argyle. But why don't they look at the map – it's a *county*!')

Then she gets down to the knotty business of *placement* which, she tells me, is not difficult as long as you obey the rules. She still remembers with horror the party at which she put the Lord Chancellor of England below the salt, not knowing at the time that he outranked everyone, including the two ambassadors present. Ambassadors have to be seated according to seniority (length of accreditation), 'which means it's perfectly possible for the American ambassador to be outranked by the Ambassador to Pago Pago, and you just have to understand that'. Titles are seated from duke down to baronet, and if the Duchess ever has any doubts, she telephones the Hon. Diana Makgill at the Foreign Office 'who is the expert – she knows the name of the smallest baronet's smallest son's grandson'.

What if, I asked, you had someone terribly old and terribly distinguished – Graham Greene, say – to dinner, would you really seat him below some junior sprig of a baronet? 'Graham Greene?' The Duchess looked puzzled. 'But he's just a *writer*, isn't he?' (Clearly she would place writers, not only below the salt but preferably below the table.) 'You've got to think of rank as rank. You're thinking of eminence and that is just brains, which is very nice to have, but it doesn't *count.*'

At this point, the Duchess surprised me by asking, 'But why do you keep on about dinner parties? There's a lot more we could talk about.' Oh *right*, goody! Roll on the divorce case, the 'headless man' who featured so prominently therein, the row with her daughter, all the things I had been longing to ask her about all along. I decided to start fairly gently by asking how she retained her amazing looks, although, as everyone knows, her age is . . . 'Everyone does *not* know that, I think it's very rude to mention a woman's age. Now we're supposed to be talking about my book. Please let's keep to the subject. We're *straying.*'

The desire to leap at her throat, hurl my glass of water in her face, and kick her dog was very strong, but I managed to restrain myself.

'Very well. Your book is called *My Dinner Party Book* . . .'

'No it's not.'

I was deprived of speech by now, so I merely handed her an advance copy of the book, open at the title-page. *My Dinner Party Book* by Margaret, Duchess of Argyll. A literary hoax? Another *Hitler's Diaries*?

'But that's the wrong title,' shrieked the Duchess. 'I wanted to call it *Let Me Entertain You.*'

It took several phone calls (and copious apologies from the publisher) to sort out this little contretemps, and when the Duchess returned to me our relationship had subtly changed. Not that the Duchess went so far as to *apologize* but she seemed less anxious to tell me I was stupid.

I asked about her forthcoming role in *Legacy*, an Anglo-American television series which promises to out-*Dynasty Dynasty*. She will, of course, play herself and, according to producer John McLaren, her screen test was brilliant. Then there is her planned second dose of autobiography, though she has not yet got down to writing it. I remarked, nervously, that her first autobiography (*Forget Not*, 1976) was a little on the bland side. 'It was bland, yes. On purpose. I didn't want to stir up any more controversy. It was the truth and nothing but the truth, but I don't say that it was the *whole* truth. This book will be very frank, and absolutely truthful. I think a lot of people might be quite upset by it!'

Any hopes, though, that the book might finally reveal the identity of the 'headless man', whose torso featured so memorably in photographs nos. 54 and 62 of the Duchess's divorce case, were dashed when she said the book would start in 1975 – twelve years after her divorce. '*Why* must the press keep dragging up my divorce – it's so *unnecessary*!' she complained.

According to the Duchess, she has 'only one enemy, and she's almost dead – about time', but the list of her public quarrels is a long one. She has not spoken to her daughter, the Duchess of Rutland, for eighteen years, and her grandchildren by the Duchess do not wish to see her. She has had legal tiffs with her stepson, and with the late Duke's second wife. At the height of the divorce case she sued her own stepmother for alleged adultery with her husband, the Duke – though she later dropped the case and paid £25,000 libel damages.

And just the other day, another quarrel had come to light – with Mrs Betty Kenward, the formidable 'Jennifer' of Jennifer's Diary in *Harpers*. Nigel Dempster reported that the Duchess of Argyll would not be going to Mrs Kenward's eightieth birthday party because she was not invited and quoted her as saying, 'Who wants to go to her eightieth birthday anyway?'

Actually, the Duchess told me she said, 'Who wants to go to *their* eightieth birthday party?' but she wouldn't bother to sue this time, because she quite liked Nigel Dempster. 'Betty Kenward and I were once friends,' she went on, 'but she stopped seeing me when I married Ian Argyll because she didn't think anyone should marry a divorced man. I don't give a damn; I couldn't care less about her.'

So much for Mrs Kenward. Now what about her step-mother (who, incidentally, is two years younger than the Duchess)? 'I adored my father, and there was a row about money, which can happen. But actually we're very close allies now. We were allies over the will.'

Moreover, she said, she had not had a 'row' with her daughter – 'I hate the word row, it sounds so catty.' An estrangement then? The Duchess, for once, faltered and lost her poise. 'As things are now,' she said eventually, 'it stands the same. Actually she, my daughter, *has* been here, in this flat, at the christening of my grandson. I don't say it was a very cosy meeting, but it is not true to say that we have not met for eighteen years. If I were asked to Belvoir' (Castle – the Duchess of Rutland's home) 'well, I would have to think about whether I would go, but it has not arisen and I'm not crying my eyes out about it.'

Finally, I asked her who was the most important person in her life. 'My father,' she said promptly, pointing to the several photographs and portraits of George Whigham in the room. 'I meant alive . . .' There was a long, painful silence. 'Louis,' she said finally, fondling the French poodle on her lap. Then, as an afterthought, 'And my son, of course, though he has his own life to lead.'

However, it would be wrong to leave the Duchess on a note of pathos because she is not in any sense a pathetic figure. She is formidable, occasionally terrifying, sharp, witty, tough, courageous. Admittedly, it is irritating to be treated as an errant housemaid, and wrong-footed at every turn, but once in a while she climbs off her alarming dignity, and lets loose a shaft of pure fun. At one point, I dared to ask whether the reason she had never remarried was because she liked being a duchess. 'Supposing,' I suggested, 'you had fallen in love with a mere viscount, or even a baronet?'

'Actually,' she giggled like a schoolgirl, 'titles don't mean all that much to me. What I *really* wanted was a millionaire!'

Reproduced by permission of the *Sunday Express*

JEFFREY ARCHER

15 December 1985

Poor Jeffrey Archer is beset by knockers. Ever since he became deputy chairman of the Tory Party three months ago, every knocker in Fleet Street has been having a go at him. There was naughty old Nigel Dempster implying he was having an affair with Andrina Colquhoun – but Jeffrey Archer says he hasn't even seen her for eighteen months. The *Telegraph* (the *Telegraph*!) said that Norman Tebbit was so fed up with the way Archer kept putting his foot in it (e.g. by saying that Ian Paisley should be premier of a united Ireland) that he wanted him gagged. Muckrakers with long memories dredged up all the old business of why he had to pay back some expenses to the United Nations Association, and why he sued Humphry Berkeley for libel about it and then, years later, settled out of court and paid all Berkeley's costs.

Feminists howled in horror at the discovery that Jeffrey Archer was going to be one of the judges of the Miss World competition, but Jeffrey Archer said too bad, he was a man who stuck by his commitments. Then unfortunately he had to withdraw when a by-election came along. And still the mail kept flooding in from upset parents who didn't like to hear their unemployed offspring described as 'work-shy'.

So by the time I went to see him at his home at Grant-chester, outside Cambridge, he was feeling badly bruised, and he launched into a tirade about 'all these people whose sole purpose in life is to be unpleasant, and to bring you down'. He was particularly annoyed about the 'being gagged' story, and said he had made forty-six speeches, twelve TV appearances, fourteen radio interviews and a speech in Tebbit's own constituency since that story was published. 'Anyway,' he said, 'here I am, talking to you.'

Yes indeed. Talking to Jeffrey Archer, or at least trying to interview him, is quite an experience. He rattles out answers like a machine-gun, and when he makes a joke he tells you, 'That is a *joke!*' He tells you what you can say, and what you can quote him as saying, and what you can say in your own words but not in his. For instance, he told me that before he was appointed deputy chairman, several MP friends had asked him to speak in their constituencies and word got round the Commons that Jeffrey Archer could be relied on to draw audiences of four hundred upwards – 'You can say that, but not in quotes,' he said. Fancy. We even had to go off the record to discuss whether Somerset Maugham was a great novelist. (We both agreed he wasn't, so what's the big secret?)

Right at the beginning, I took two tape recorders out of my briefcase, placed them on the table in front of him, and read out a prepared question from my notebook. He grumbled about knockers for about ten minutes, then suddenly said: 'You're not recording this, are you? Oh no, this is all off the record. We're just having a chat.' It was all very confusing.

Anyway, let's begin at the beginning. While some parts of Jeffrey Archer's career have been told and retold a thousand times, other parts are curiously obscure – particularly everything that happened before he surfaced at Oxford *circa* 1963. He was born in 1940 near Weston-super-Mare, an only child. His mother was a local Tory councillor and journalist on the *Western Mercury*. His father was a retired professional soldier, who had worked his way up from the ranks in the

First World War and retired, injured, as a major after the Second World War.

He died when Jeffrey was fifteen. 'He just went downhill after the war,' Jeffrey recalls. 'My mother had an awful time trying to make his life bearable and just keep me going along. But I was never aware of any money worries – that's one of the things I always praise my mother for. It was not until I left school that I realized the struggles she must have had. She bluffed and covered it, which is why I hope in later life I've been able to make her life considerably easier.'

'Would it be accurate to describe your family as distressed gentlefolk?' I asked.

'Oh I hate talking about class, don't you?' said Jeffrey Archer. 'Say "struggling middle class".'

Our hero next surfaces as a PE master at Dover College, Kent, a small public school where he taught games for two and a half years. The then headmaster, Mr Tim Cobb, recalls him as 'an extremely good schoolmaster, endowed with great enthusiasm and success – whenever he put in a team for anything, they practically always won. I remember he wore a blazer with some sort of "England" badge on it – I've no idea what for.'

When Jeffrey Archer joined the school, aged twenty, he told Mr Cobb that he had previously taught at a small school in Hampshire and, before that, done a degree at Berkeley in California. (He now says that in fact he only did a short vocational course at Berkeley.) It was Mr Cobb who suggested he should go to Oxford: 'You've obviously got a future, but you'd better get some qualifications,' he told him. So Archer went to the Oxford Institute of Education to take a Dip. Ed. (teaching diploma) course, and while there, somehow attached himself to Brasenose College and gained an athletics Blue for running.

At Oxford, he made friends with Nick Lloyd (subsequently editor of the *News of the World*, now a top Murdoch executive), who was then the Oxford 'stringer' for several Fleet Street papers. It was Nick Lloyd, Archer recalls, who got him going on his next career, as a professional charity fund-raiser. 'Nick egged me on. He'd say, "Here's Brian Epstein's number" – I didn't even know who Brian Epstein was – "why don't you get him to ask the Beatles to come to dinner at Brasenose for Oxfam?" And then "Why don't you ask Harold Macmillan to come too?"' Jeffrey Archer duly did ('That man would have bottled my pee and sold it,' Ringo said afterwards) and Nick Lloyd recorded his exploits for the Fleet Street gossips.

It was Nick Lloyd, too, who introduced Jeffrey Archer to Mary Weeden, who became his wife. While the women in Jeffrey Archer's novels are mainly distinguished by having powerful fathers and 'long silky thighs', Mary Archer is distinguished by any standards you care to name. She gained a first in chemistry at Oxford; she is now a teaching fellow at Newnham College, Cambridge, and a world authority on solar energy. She is also, incidentally, beautiful and quite possibly the possessor of long silky thighs. They both agree that Mary is the brains of the family, and they both happily quote their friend Max Beloff's remark about their first child: 'I hope it will have Mary's looks – and Mary's brains.' Mary lives in Grantchester, teaching at Newnham and bringing up their two sons, thirteen-year-old William and eleven-year-old James. Jeffrey joins her at weekends, but lives in his Thames-side penthouse during the week.

The big testing-period in their marriage – and indeed in Jeffrey Archer's whole life – came when he faced bankruptcy in 1974. Without telling Mary, he had borrowed £427,000 to invest in a company which turned out to be a fraud. 'Everything seemed to be absolutely fine,' he recalls, 'and then in ten minutes it went crash. I was visited by Detective-Inspector Clifford Smith, who said: "I have to tell you, Mr Archer, that you and eighty others have had your money stolen by fraud."' Jeffrey Archer did the honourable thing, and resigned his seat as an MP.

He was determined to pay off his debts, because if he went bankrupt he could never have entered public life again. He did. 'But for three years I was in desperation. It was at least three years. Now, ten years later, people say "He flashed back overnight", but how do they think I wrote *Penny* – in a weekend? It took nine months to complete and two years till it was published. I didn't finally clear the debts – with *Kane and Abel* – for four years. I was slogging away night and day to keep the creditors off and pay the bills. I got physically unfit, I couldn't sleep at night, I dreaded opening the post in the morning because it was all bills. They need only be little bills, £32, but I hadn't got it. I couldn't afford the bus, I noticed that my shoes were getting down at heel but I couldn't afford to have them mended.

'We only had a home because Mary's college offered us a flat. Mary was obviously distressed and showed it. She thought I'd acted foolishly, and she was right. Now, when I go to talk to schoolchildren, I say, "Listen: don't bother with the politics, don't bother with the books. The one thing I want you to remember for the rest of your lives is never to invest more than 5 per cent of what you're worth. Because I went to 200 per cent and that was my downfall."'

He wrote the first book, *Not a Penny More, Not a Penny Less*, 'simply in order to get up in the morning, not to be lazy', and was pleasantly surprised by its success. He is modest about his literary powers, insisting that he is a storyteller and not a writer. (I can't resist here quoting my favourite passage from Jeffrey Archer: 'She looked beautiful in that blue dress. Fantastic creature . . . Why didn't I just take her by the hand into the bedroom and make mad passionate love to her. I would have happily settled for a sandwich. That way we could do what we both want to do and save time and trouble.')

But his stories have to date sold 25 million copies around the world. They have also brought him fans and compliments, and the warm bath of public approval. That is why his return to the political scene has seemed like a blast of icy air, reminding him of all those beastly knockers lying in wait.

Which brings us back to the first point: why do so many

people want to knock Jeffrey Archer? Brian Walden, a keen Archerphile, believes it is because they are all snobs – they turn their noses up at his self-made-gent manner. But journalists aren't usually snobs, whatever their other vices – so why do *journalists* dislike him? Jeffrey Archer believes it because they are all either 'lefties' or failed novelists.

He wasn't sure at first which category I belonged to, though he was sure – even before I opened my mouth – that I was out to knock him. (Was I? Not before I met him, no, though I admit that reading his press cuttings beforehand had not inspired me with much liking.)

Then I mentioned that I lived in Highgate, London, and that clinched it for him: 'Ah, ah, ha. Only *Guardian*-reading Lefties live in Highgate.' I never read the *Guardian*, but let that pass. Then just to please him, I threw in that I was a would-be novelist as well. 'Ah! Then I can hope for no affection in this article at all,' he said, with one of his crocodile smiles.

But come on, Jeffrey, be fair. You almost made me dislike you even before I met you simply by leaving me standing on your doorstep for twenty minutes on a freezing day while you failed to answer your bell. To make up for that, you asked me to stay to lunch, which I thought was terribly kind – except that in the end we went to the pub (you and me, and your wife, and your two children, and your Costa Rican lodger, and the photographer and his assistant) and somehow I paid. 'You can get this on expenses, can't you?' you said, which of course was true – but it made me think I'd hesitate to accept an invitation from you again.

These trivial points would not be worth mentioning – except to illustrate why Jeffrey Archer sometimes seems to attract more criticism than is his due. Jeffrey Archer treads on toes: people dislike that.

Because, of course, the great point about Jeffrey Archer is that he is a man in a hurry. He was a sprinter in his youth, and he has sprinted through his careers as an MP, as a businessman, as a best-selling novelist. Like all people in a hurry, he bruises people who get in his way and, like all people in a hurry, he appears to take a few short cuts.

That is why he will always seem fair game to knockers – and why, ultimately, it doesn't matter. He doesn't *need* praise or encouragement, he functions perfectly well without them. Whereas he does need watching: it does him no harm at all to know that there are enemies out there following his every move and waiting for the one false step.

Jeffrey Archer will keep on running, and the knockers will keep on knocking; and that way, in the end, he might just stay the course and make it a marathon.

He is certainly fun to watch.

Reproduced by permission of the *Sunday Express*

JOHN ASPINALL

28 January 1990

Odd to start an interview by watching your subject being almost killed by elephants. I'd met John Aspinall in London, but he suggested we talk some more and take photographs at his home and zoo, Howletts, in Kent. We went straight out to the elephant enclosure, which Aspinall had chosen as an appropriate setting. The keepers warned him that one of the old cows, Masa, had been behaving oddly, but Aspinall went in and fondled her and played with her trunk and posed between her front legs. Then another elephant came up, and Masa got the needle.

Suddenly Aspinall was on the ground, and the elephants were rolling him between them like a football. Every time he tried to get to his feet, Masa flipped him down again. When he tried to wriggle away, they fielded him with their trunks. One of Aspinall's elephants once killed a keeper by squeezing him against the fence, and it looked for several seconds as though this might be a repeat performance.

Eventually the keepers managed to distract the elephants long enough for Aspinall to make his escape. He was bleeding profusely from cuts on his knees, ankles and face; he was trembling and in shock. He is sixty-three, and has already suffered two strokes. Nevertheless, after five minutes, he insisted on going back in with the elephants 'to show there's no hard feelings'.

Armed this time with a keeper's goad and secateurs, he stood for a few shaky minutes face to face with Masa while the photographer snapped away and honour was satisfied. As a display of courage – or folly – it was breathtaking.

We drove him back to his house for a bath, and he suggested we should leave him for half an hour and go and see the gorillas. To my horror, there was an inert woman's body lying face down in the straw of one of the cages, with various young gorillas romping on top of it. I coughed: 'Ahem . . . are you alive?' The corpse wiggled a finger and we went back to the house relieved.

As we drove back, Lady Sally, Aspinall's wife, followed us in her car and I recognized the body from the gorilla cage. 'I was just saying hello to my babies,' she explained. 'Those are all young gorillas I raised myself.' When a gorilla proves a bad mother, Lady Sally rears the abandoned baby herself, which involves letting it cling to her day and night *for a year*, until it can survive alone. She says she loves doing it and gets broody when there are no abandoned gorillas to hand.

Aspinall was waiting to greet us at the house, newly bathed, changed and only slightly bloodstained. Lady Sally insisted on dabbing witch-hazel on his cuts, but he pooh-poohed any notion of calling a doctor. He said the incident would not leave any scars – although he already has several scars from gorilla bites, tiger scratches and the like. Three keepers have been killed at his zoo, and at least two visitors badly mauled. He regards occasional 'accidents' as a small price to pay for the pleasure of romping with animals.

John Aspinall's friends maintain that he is a man born out of his century. He should have been a Roman emperor or a Whig grandee, or perhaps a Zulu chieftain. Yet in fact he has done very well for himself as a twentieth-century Briton. Born the illegitimate son of an Indian Army officer in 1926, with no inherited money, he has made two great fortunes and kept one of them; he owns a town house in Knightsbridge, two magnificent country houses in Kent, an estate, De Goede Hoop, in South Africa, and two zoos which are the envy of the zoo-keeping world. All this from the fruits of gambling.

He is an extremely genial man to meet – handsome, charming, courteous, friendly. His views, as we shall see, are appalling, but if I had to choose between throwing myself on John Aspinall's mercy or, say, Lord Longford's, I would prefer Aspinall every time.

His employees are entirely devoted to him – despite the rather high death and injury rate among them. His third wife, Lady Sally, the daughter of Earl Howe and widow of the racing driver Piers Courage, is equally charming. He has one son by her, Bassa Wulfhere, seventeen, and two older children, Amanda, thirty-two, and Damian Androcles, thirty, by his first wife. He also had a daughter, Mameena, by his second marriage, but she lived only three-and-a-half months.

Although he is a self-made millionaire, he prefers to portray himself as a dilettante, a gentleman amateur, a member of the idle rich. He boasts often of his inability to get out of bed. Yet he invited me to meet him two hours after landing from a twelve-hour flight from South Africa: he was having a business meeting that evening; and making a film for National Geographic the next day, before flying off for a ten-day holiday at Sir James Goldsmith's estate in Mexico. He does not lack energy.

The two great themes of his life are the love of animals and the love of gambling, and he has always used the latter to finance the former. The attraction of gambling, he once explained in a letter to the *Sunday Times*, was 'the corrosive effect it has on such outdated concepts as the sanctity of money and the dignity of labour'.

He loves magnificence, munificence, outrageously ostentatious consumption. In the hall of Howletts, there are crates upon crates of kumquats, litchis, starfruit, pineapples, mangoes – fruit which most working people in this country (including presumably, his own staff) can rarely afford to taste. They are for his gorillas.

He started gambling seriously as an undergraduate at Oxford; he would have started earlier, but 'you need *money* in order to gamble, and I only had £1 a term pocket money at school [Rugby] and £1 a week in the Marines'. But at Oxford he had an ex-serviceman's grant of £90 a term and he took it straight to the bookmaker.

'There was a horse called Palestine running in the 2,000 Guineas at 7–2 and I put my whole grant on it. The bookmaker said: "What's going to happen if it loses, young man?" but he won by this much [a hand's-breadth]. I've always had the ability to put everything at risk. As a young man I owed half the bookmakers in the ring but I always believed in my star. I often used to go to poker games with no money at all, just hoping to win. I always had an intuition that I would survive somehow: that's part of my character. When I began to be a gambler, I realized that if I failed, I would face disgrace, bankruptcy, ruin and obscurity. And that if I succeeded, life would be pleasurable. So I knew the risks I was taking.'

He feigned illness in his finals, to go to the Ascot Gold Cup. As he later explained to the Master of Jesus, who sent him down in disgrace, he considered it more important for a would-be professional gambler to have a big win than a degree in Eng. Lit. 'I decided to be a gambler because I knew I was unfitted for hierarchical life in any grouping of males where I would have to start at the bottom. Not that I had the *choice* of working for Unilever or whatever: it's not as though I turned down the chance of a glittering career.'

In the fifties he ran a floating chemmy game, exploiting a loophole in the law whereby, if he moved premises constantly, he could not be convicted of running a common gaming house. Eventually, in 1958, the police brought a test case against him, but the judge dismissed the charges. Thereafter the law was changed, explicitly to crush games like Aspinall's. In fact it had the opposite effect: it made London for a while the casino capital of the world, with Aspinall's club, the Clermont, now tethered to Berkeley Square, the jewel in its crown.

In 1972, bored with gambling and eager to devote all his time to his zoo, Aspinall sold the Clermont for £500,000. But the fortune which he thought he had invested so wisely disappeared in the stock-market crash of 1974, and he was forced to start another club – Aspinall's Curzon – to earn his crust again. In 1987 he sold it for £90m, and used the money to endow a charitable foundation to ensure the survival of his two zoos, Howletts and Port Lympne, after his death. (They cost about £3.6m a year to run.) He now has a small bookmaking business in the basement of his town house, but is out of the big casino league, although he still gambles regularly himself.

A love of gambling and a love of animals do not seem, on the face of it, to have much in common, but Aspinall explains that the common denominator, for him, is the sense of risk. He kept ferrets at school 'which I liked because they were *wild*, you know, and quite tricky in that they're likely to nip you. This I find an attractive quality – fear has to be an element in all friendships, I think. I was never attracted to the typically English love of dogs and horses, who you can dominate. That didn't interest me the least bit.' As soon as he made money, in the mid-fifties, he started keeping monkeys and tigers in his Belgravia flat.

But why is he so keen on risk? Why does he need to keep testing his courage? 'Oh gosh. Auto-analysis is so inaccurate and so difficult, because one superimposes one's own romantic conception of oneself over the facts, so that in the end one makes a legend of one's early life in one's own mind. But I suppose it was genetically inspired. Not that my parents were gamblers. My mother subsequently *became* a gambler, both at the casinos and on the horses, but entirely through me.'

For one who talks a lot about breeding, and believes in 'a natural aristocracy', his own family tree is undistinguished. His supposed father was an Indian Army medical officer with not very much money. Aspinall did not realize he was not his real father until he was grown up. 'It was very stupid of me, because Colonel Aspinall of the IMS was rather small and dark, with very black eyes, but it just never occurred to me that he wasn't my father. He showed no affection to me, but then he didn't towards my older brother either, who was his natural son; he was very distant with us both.

'It wasn't until I left Oxford that he told me. I went to meet him at the East India Sports Club in hopes of borrowing £2,000 to pay my debts – it doesn't sound much today, but it was a lot then. He said he couldn't help me. He'd paid for my private school, my public school and Oxford, but now he was finished. And anyway, he said, he wasn't my father.

'That was quite a shock, though not as bad a shock as if we'd been close. He gave me a fiver, which I took, and as the train jingled back to Uckfield, where I lived, I found that my natural optimism started to take over. I thought, "Well, I've obviously *got* a father – what an incredible find! And he might be very rich and powerful and able to help me." I had dreams that he might be anything. But when I told my mother, she broke down. "Oh, the brute! the brute!" she cried. "Why did he tell you?"

'"But, Mama," I said, "I'm not criticizing you, but what was he like?"' And then, still mopping her eyes, she looked at me and said, "Just like you, darling. He had your blue eyes and golden hair and wonderful physique. Just like you, darling. Boo hoo!" So I said, "But, Mama, this is wonderful! Is he still alive? How can I find him?" So she told me his name – Captain McIlree Bruce of the Lincolns – and I went through the army lists till I found him. Didn't look too good; it was not a fashionable regiment and he was a retired major-general in Campden Hill Gardens, which in those days was not a very promising address. None the less, off I went with optimism in my heart, hope at the thought of meeting my father.

'When I got to the flats I saw that they were for retired army officers, which wasn't good. By now I'd abandoned any hope of an immensely rich father who would bail me out of my debts. I just wanted to meet him. It was the most extraordinary moment, probably, of my entire life. I rang the doorbell and there was one of those cloche-shaped lights with a frill round it, and as he stepped forward into the light, I saw myself forty years on. He was then sixty-three or sixty-four, the same age I am now. He looked marvellous, a very nice-looking man. And he said, "Who are you?" I said, "I'm your son," and he grabbed me and pulled me into the light and said "You're Polly's boy, aren't you?" '

His mother subsequently confessed that he was conceived under a tamarisk tree beside a lake in Uttar Pradesh, the night of the regimental ball. 'Unlike me,' says Aspinall, 'my father was a womanizer. He was always knocking girls off wherever he went.' As a money-making venture, his search for his father was a failure: although Major-General Bruce offered to sign all his life savings over to his new-found son, in the end Aspinall found himself supporting him. 'But we did form a relationship; we became good friends for the last five or six years of his life.'

The most important influence of his early life, he says, was reading a book by Rider Haggard called *Nada the Lily* when he was thirteen. It is about an illegitimate Zulu prince, kicked out of his tribe, and forced to live among animals. The boy discovers a rapport with animals and develops 'the heart of a wolf', he becomes a mighty warrior and leader of men. But he is always a solitary, because 'the tree that stands by itself on a plain thinks itself tall and that there is no shade to equal its shade'.

This, then, is how Aspinall sees himself. Like the silverback gorilla, or the Zulu chieftain, he is the patriarch, the provider, the lord of all he surveys. He speaks; you listen. His speech is a heady cocktail of 'dictionary' words, statistics and uncheck-able biological and historical generalizations, designed to impress those less intelligent than himself. He does not brook argument, or even interruption; the role of the interviewer –

especially the female interviewer – is to listen in awe. And indeed, the jaw does drop in amazement when he expatiates on some of his beliefs.

He is happy to be described as to the right of Genghis Khan. He would not say that he regards Hitler *uncritically* – 'some of his ideas were nonsense' – but he approves of Hitler's views on eugenics. Aspinall favours infanticide as a way of disposing of defective babies, and indeed of extraneous babies generally. He also thinks people should be taxed for having children. They could have one free, then pay £500 or so for the second, several thousand for the third, and a million for the fourth, 'so that the most adaptive citizens, the higher-income groups, will have the most children'.

But surely, I tried to argue, rich people aren't necessarily the best? 'Well, it's not a policy of perfection, and of course you can have a completely barmy duke with £20m who is a very bad breeding prospect, weakened by inbreeding; but broadly speaking, the higher-income groups tend to have a better adaptive genetic inheritance than the less successful.'

He does not believe in the sanctity of human life. He hates Judaeo-Christianity because it elevates man at the expense of other animals; he prefers pagan or 'Nordic' or Zulu beliefs. He believes the role of women is to provide sexual pleasure for the males and to produce babies, which they should raise by holding them to the body for at least a year. He believes in a natural élite – the rich man in his castle, the poor man at his gate. It is wrong to imagine he says these things *pour épater les bourgeois*. He enjoys *épater*-ing – but he also means every word.

Somewhere at the core of Aspinall's character there is an odd lacuna. It is any sense of brotherhood or empathy with other members of the human race, Forster's 'only connect'. Aspinall definitely does not connect. Like the Zulu prince in *Nada the Lily* – or like the child whose father is not his real father – he feels himself set apart, 'different', a species of one. When he lists his greatest friends, he mentions some humans (notably Sir James Goldsmith) but many more gorillas and tigers.

He carries friendship to extraordinary extremes, and says quite explicitly in the case of Lord Lucan* that discovering a friend to be a murderer would not alter his affection. But those not his friends are a grey blur, an 'urban biomass', and he cheerfully expects their imminent destruction by a natural holocaust, leaving the world free for gorillas and tigers.

He would like to die like his friend George Adamson, gunned down by poachers while protecting his beloved animals. 'That's a good way to go. The ancient Romans believed that the manner of a man's death is as important as the manner of his life, and I'd like to have a kind of heroic death. But I'll probably die in my bed like any boring old man.' He does not want to be killed by one of his own animals – although if I had to place a bet, that would be my prediction – because people would blame the animal.

He will be buried at the end of the avenue at Howletts together with his mother, his baby daughter and all his favourite primates. Palaeontologists in millennia to come will study this strange ossuary and ponder what manner of species this was.

•

* John Aspinall never normally talks about his friend Lord Lucan, but towards the end of our interview, he did. Lord Lucan, it will be remembered, disappeared in November 1974, after the murder of his children's nanny, Sandra Rivett. The inquest concluded that he murdered her in mistake for his wife. I began by asking Aspinall if he believed Lord Lucan was dead.

JA: Of course, he's at the bottom of the English Channel.
LB: *By his own hand? Suicide? Why are you so sure?*
JA: I'm sure of it.
LB: *Is it true that he told your mother he planned to kill his wife?*

JA: Mm.
LB: *And she didn't try to stop him?*
JA: What was she supposed to do? [*Laughs*]
LB: *And the famous meeting the day after his disappearance when you summoned all his friends to lunch — why did you do that?*
JA: Oh, we wanted to discuss the situation, or how we could help him. That was all. Just how we could help in any way. Pool our knowledge and see how we could help — all friends of his.
LB: *Do you miss him?*
JA: Yes. A lot. Oh yes.
LB: *Because, from all the books about him, he sounds a narrow and horrible man.*
JA: Not at all. He was a charming man. Charming. Really an extraordinarily decent, charming and kindly fellow.
LB: *Was he?*
JA: Yes, of course. And much admired and liked by his circle of friends.
LB: *Do you think it's right for someone to murder his wife?*
JA: Certainly. If she's behaving in a bad way. It depends how badly she behaves. That's all. In the same way as I've no doubt that wives on occasion should murder their husbands. There are times when a woman can provoke a man and give him little alternative.

Women always know the soft spots of their spouses, and even when all love has gone, the knowledge of where you can wound and hurt remains. And if you continually do that — touch those notes on the piano — eventually there's a reaction, and it can be a violent one.
LB: *Do you believe that the female is deadlier than the male?*
JA: No, I don't think so. *Some* women are deadlier than many males, but no, I don't believe that. I *love* women. No problems with women, never had any. I did have some trouble with my first wife, but never had any difficulty with women apart from that.
LB: *Have you seen his children at all?*

JA: Yes. The children are very attractive and sensible and decent.

LB: *And have they talked to you about their father?*

JA: Well, I don't know. I never talk to them about their father.

LB: *But if they wanted to, would you?*

JA: Oh if they wanted to, yes, certainly. But it's not a subject you immediately . . . I mean I don't see them very often. I didn't know them before, hardly. They were very young then. But – from what I'm told – George, the son, is a very stable and worthwhile young man. And there are two daughters as well.

The mother came down here once but I had to tell Lucan that I could only entertain him down here without his wife. Even if you have quarrelled – I occasionally quarrel with my wife, you know, but we keep a united front to strangers and dinner guests, we keep up appearances – I think most people do. It came as no surprise to me that finally he snapped when he didn't get custody of the children.

LB: *Still, you can't just murder people.*

JA: Well, look. You said to me, can you imagine someone murdering their wife? Of course I can, it happens all the time. And I'm sure that sometimes the wife murders the husband. One of them snaps.

Now it's not commendable to snap. It's a lack of emotional control, which is bad. However annoyed with your wife you are, you shouldn't murder her. I accept that. But it's very easy to *say* that.

Women have this amazing gift, haven't they? They *know* what hurts their male because they know him so well. [*Interruption; butler brings tea.*] That's all I'm saying – that of course it's understandable.

LB: *And your feelings about him as a friend were completely unaltered?*

JA: Well, I always think that if someone who has been a great friend is then in a terrible position, you rather feel *more* warmly towards him because that's when you're needed. A friend is *needed* when things are going badly. Anyone can be a friend of a successful man, who's done nothing wrong and is in the New Year Honours. But somebody who's in trouble, who's snapped and done something silly, that's when you *need* your friends.

I'm more of a friend of his after that than I was – though I haven't seen him – because if he wanted me to do something, I'd do it for him. Because he *needs* one and, like everyone else in life, I like to be needed. What's the use of a friend who, because you make one mistake, suddenly . . . I don't believe in that.

LB: *But if a friend does something – you think you know their character and then . . .*

JA: No. Now if he'd defected to Russia and sold a lot of secrets, I wouldn't have had him in the house again, you know? If he'd become a raving communist and joined Scargill, I probably wouldn't have bothered with him any more, because I would have been too irritated to have him around.

LB: *You didn't snap in your first marriage?*

JA: Well, I mean I had, perhaps, a better emotional control than him. You need emotional control, otherwise you land up in real trouble, not just in that, but in anything. You can't go overboard. In gambling, you've got to have a control system whereby if you're losing, you don't go crazy and lose too much, and in argument you have to have a certain control.

I mean, perhaps John Lucan had a less than perfect emotional control system. He must have done. But he did, on this occasion, snap. My sympathies are definitely with him. By the way, my sympathies are entirely with Sandra Rivett. I mean, it's grotesque that *she* should have suffered when the whole thing was a miscarriage of natural justice. He had nothing against his nanny – I mean, that was a *horrible* misfortune.

LB: *If he had successfully murdered his wife, what do you think would have happened?*

JA: I don't know really. I don't know what his plans were.

But he'd decided to do the dreadful deed. And it was all botched up; he killed the nanny; it was terrible – and then he killed himself. No, my sympathies were all with him. Because I didn't *know* the nanny.

LB: And why are you so absolutely sure that he's dead? What do you think he did? Just swam out to sea?

JA: No, no. He was very skilled at motor-boat racing, and I think he had a boat there at Newhaven, where his car was found, and I think he jumped into one of his little motor boats, went out to sea, put a big weight round his body and jumped overboard. And scuttled the boat. That's what happened.

You love this Lucan thing, don't you? You're like every other journalist: all you want to talk about is Lucan. It was fifteen years ago. I've known people who are matricides and uxoricides, and if you know the circumstances of each thing, you can't make blanket judgements right across the whole spectrum of human nature, any more than you can with tiger nature or gorilla nature. You can't say, 'Oh, all wife-killers are automatically bad.'

LB: You seem to carry loyalty to such extremes that there is absolutely nothing a friend could do that would make you . . .

JA: Oh no, I've just explained: if somebody became a raving communist or a traitor, they'd no longer be my friend. Friendship's a very delicate thing to maintain. I have a lot of friends, both male and female, and there's very little I wouldn't do to help them, and I know they'd do the same for me. Do I put a romantic glow on friendship? Yes I do. I put a romantic glow on everything. I mean, that's my nature.

Reproduced by permission of the *Independent on Sunday*

TONY BENN

30 September 1990

In the *Children's Hour* serials of my childhood there was always a character called 'The Professor' or sometimes 'The Boffin' whose role in the story was to answer children's questions and provide esoteric information. He deciphered codes or did experiments, and he smoked a pipe and worked in a den full of dusty tomes and exciting gadgets.

The memory comes back quite overpoweringly on meeting Tony Benn. First the lovely wuffly *Children's Hour* voice and, yes, the pipe, and then, hooray, the den, *exactly* as I had always imagined it − home-made shelves and trestle tables groaning with files, leather-bound tomes, piles of paper, and peculiar gadgets whirring away in the background. The Kensington house upstairs is rather grand, but this basement den could be anywhere: it has the unique squalor you only get from hoarding bits of paper obsessively for decades on end.

Mr Benn gives me a little tour, showing off the kitchenette where he makes his tea (we shall be hearing a lot about tea) and the shelves and shelves of box files that contain the transcripts of his diaries. Every night for an hour he dictates his day's doings into a tape recorder, a secretary transcribes them, an editor winnows them and eventually Hutchinson publishes them. The fourth volume, *Conflicts of Interest 1977–80*, has just come out, and he is already at work on the next.

'You mustn't be *kind* about it,' he insists. 'It isn't an old man reflecting on his great triumphs, quite the opposite. The *Diaries* are a conscious political act.' Rather a peculiar one, if so, because the effect on me of reading about the last days of the last Labour government was to give me a sudden new enthusiasm to vote Tory next time. But Benn argues that it wasn't really a *Labour* government: most of the Cabinet went on to join the SDP. Anyway, at the risk of being kind, I would say the *Diaries* are a surprisingly bright and readable account of a political life. Though gossip is absent – 'I don't want to injure people. A lot of diaries are malice, really' – the characters leap fresh from the page.

He records *everything* and when I produce my tape recorder, he promptly produces his, saying. 'Do you mind? For archival purposes?' Several times in the next two hours, his tape recorder emits loud clicks, whereupon he says, 'I think your tape recorder's just gone off,' and I say, 'No, yours has,' and we both inspect our machines and he agrees that it is his. The Professor on *Children's Hour* was always a bit absent-minded, too.

'Coffee or tea?' he asks, and comes back with the Big Mug which is such an essential accompaniment of his life. 'That's one of the few media myths about me that is absolutely true: I do just adore tea.' He has a pint mug every hour on the hour, he has one first thing in the morning and last thing at night. Once he accidentally dropped his hearing aid in his night tea and it worked much better as a result. His *Diaries* are full of tea references – people presenting him with mugs, with tea sets, the occasional desperate dearth of tea in foreign parts, the packing of the Thermos. Off on a visit to the European capitals as President of the Council of Energy Ministers 'I took my own mug and lots of teabags.' When he collapsed with Guillain-Barré syndrome in 1981 the papers all speculated that maybe it was brought on by excessive tea-drinking, and it was, he says amazingly, the first time he'd learned that tea was a stimulant. Did the doctors advise him then to cut down? 'It wouldn't have made any difference – I'm an addict!'

He has never even tasted alcohol. 'My father was brought up in the East End of London where alcohol was the demon drink and mother's ruin and all that. *His* parents used quite innocently to sing an old temperance hymn which went "The Good Ship Temperance is heading for the port" without ever realizing what it meant. During the war when I was in the Air Force and people did get very tight, I was rather gutless to begin with and used to drink ginger ale in hopes they'd think it was whisky. But then I recovered from such embarrassments and after mess parties, I was the one they always asked: "What really happened?"'

The best Professors always get on well with children because at heart they are still schoolboys themselves. And certainly Benn, even at sixty-five, looks remarkably boyish, with the sort of haircut I thought you could only get at public school. His behaviour is often boyish, too: in the *Diaries* he recounts how in 1977, when deeply upset by the Lib–Lab pact and wondering whether he should resign, he first phones his mother for advice ('Don't resign,' she tells him), and then goes round to Metyclean, an office equipment shop, 'which is one of my favourite ports of call when things are going wrong. I bought myself a Casio quartz clock computer which has the most fantastic facilities – gives you the time, works as a stopwatch and as a calculator, and has four alarms. It weighs four ounces and fits into your pocket. I was thrilled with it.'

His mother, Viscountess Stansgate, is still alive, aged ninety-three, and he visits her often. 'She told me the other day that she could remember when Queen Victoria died – she was three-and-a-half – and her mother cried and she said, "Why do you cry? She never came to visit us."' She is writing her memoirs now and plans to call it *My Exit Visa*. As the daughter, daughter-in-law, wife and mother of MPs, she has a deep insight into politics, but her main interest is theology.

She is a Hebrew and Greek scholar, an honorary fellow of the
Hebrew University, a great believer in Jewish Christian fel-
lowship and a campaigner, since 1919, for the ordination of
women. While her husband was alive, she lived rather in his
shadow (he was twenty years older) but she has blossomed in
widowhood. 'She's a very alert person, terribly frail now but
enormously alert, and when I go and see her I don't go out of
duty, I go for the *fun*.'

Filial piety is one of the great themes of Tony Benn's life.
His father died in 1960 but he still refers to him constantly,
and the *Diaries* are full of remarks like 'I wish Father had
been alive to see this.' He was obviously a remarkable man.
He 'believed that in wartime you served in the services and in
peacetime you served in Parliament': consequently he was a
Liberal and then a Labour MP, Secretary of State for India,
and managed to serve in both world wars – in the second, he
volunteered for air gunnery training, though he was an air
commodore, and flew on missions at the age of sixty-seven.
He was an old father, forty-eight when Tony Benn was born,
but a fond one – he would always greet his sons with a kiss,
which was unusual in that class and generation. Benn's whole
life is moulded on his: 'My father had a study *just* like this,'
he says proudly, and adds that he has copied his father's filing
system, which was a model of the art.

Often in answer to a question such as 'Why are you
teetotal?' Benn will simply say, 'My father was,' as though no
other reason could possibly be required. He says that now he
is older, he finds himself giving the same advice his father
used to give him, adages like 'Never let the sun go down on
your wrath' or 'Don't wrestle with a chimney-sweep' (which
means don't sully yourself by responding to personal attacks
with counter-attacks).

Despite being a grandfather, Tony Benn still seems to think
of himself primarily as a son. He also thinks he is 'very much
a second son. Indeed, I'm the second son of a second son of a
second son, and *my* second son and *his* second son all share
certain characteristics – they're cheeky and ebullient.' Cheeky

and ebullient are not perhaps descriptions of Tony Benn that immediately spring to mind, but they do convey the essential boyishness.

He never, at any stage, tried to shed this son-ship. Most teenagers go through a phase of rejecting their parents and rebelling against them, but he never did. He *always* revered his parents. 'And I think that's quite important because people who sort of rebel against parental authority, it creates a tension in them which I think can affect their judgement adversely.'

The one time he allowed himself to become 'very cross, actually' was when his father accepted a hereditary peerage without consulting him. Attlee needed some Labour peers in 1942, so he asked Benn's father to go to the Lords as Viscount Stansgate. He consulted his elder son, Michael, but Michael was planning to enter the Church, so it didn't bother him. Tony, however, always wanted to go into politics, and his father should perhaps have thought of what would happen if Michael died – which he did, on active service, in 1944.

Thus when Tony Benn (the Hon. Anthony Wedgwood Benn in those days) entered Parliament in 1950, he knew he had a limited life expectancy in the Commons. His father did everything possible to support his campaign to renounce the peerage, but even so the issue was not resolved when he died in 1950, and Benn as Lord Stansgate was barred from the House of Commons for three years while he got the Act of Disclaimer passed (incidentally enabling Alec Douglas-Home to become prime minister).

Benn found the campaign to renounce his title a bitter one, and says that if he'd been a dustman who was trying to prove he was a peer, they would have treated him with more respect. He wanted to extinguish the title entirely but Garter King of Arms wouldn't allow it, because, he said, 'Imagine what would happen if a duke renounced his title. It would mean social demolition for the duchess.' In consequence, when Benn dies, his son Stephen can, if he likes, revive the title and become Viscount Stansgate. Will he? 'Well, I don't

know. I don't want to have any *post mortem* influence so I've
left a letter saying "Do what you think is right."'

Benn is clearly, from the *Diaries*, a doting father. He has
three sons, Stephen, Hilary and Joshua, and one daughter,
Melissa, all now in their thirties. 'So much of their life was
scarred by my work,' he says, recounting how, as children,
they often had to run the gauntlet of hostile journalists on
their way to school. Yet neither his wife nor any of his
children has ever suggested he should tone down his views in
order to spare them. At one point in the latest diary, his
daughter Melissa, a feminist, puts posters all round the house
saying 'End sexism in the Benn family' and he promptly cleans
the house from top to bottom and does all the washing – an
isolated gesture, it turns out, but an amiable one. He is
devoted to his family and says feelingly, 'I couldn't have
survived if it hadn't been a very tight happy family unit.'

Thus far my conversation with Mr Benn has been entirely
friendly. However, at the first whiff of a critical question from
me, his manner suddenly changes. The question is apropos a
point in the *Diaries* where an MP says something about his
aristocratic origins, and Benn assures him that he is not an
aristocrat – that his father was a Labour MP who got a
peerage 'like George Brown or Fenner Brockway'. This is true
– but also slightly misleading. His father was not some horny-
handed son of toil; he was the younger son of a baronet, with
a comfortable private income. Wasn't it a little disingenuous
to compare him to George Brown? 'No. This theory that I
come from a long line of aristocrats is a media story designed
on the whole to separate you from the people you're trying to
represent. I'm not pretending anything, but I think the idea
that I'm a belted earl who's gone funny is just inaccurate,
that's all. There are various lines, you know – that you're a
hypocrite, you're mad, you're an aristocrat, you're dangerous,
you're a red, and so on – but you have to recognize that those
are weapons that are used politically.'

In his diary, Benn tells himself, 'I mustn't get obsessive

about the press, like Harold Wilson, or paranoid'; nevertheless he often refers to the press as a 'flame-thrower' apparently
wielded by the henchmen of 'the Golden Triangle' (the City,
Westminster, Whitehall) to discredit him. And now that I
have called him disingenuous, I am The Enemy and his
manner henceforward is no longer avuncular and Professorial
but wary and suspicious. Even a perfectly innocent question
about how intelligent he is is taken as some terrible smear,
though not in the usual direction: 'No, I'm not an intellectual
at all.' But he went to Westminster and New College, Oxford?
'Well, it was nothing very much. I don't really think my
formal education has played much part in my thoughts. I got
a totally fraudulent degree because at the end of the war they
were so keen to get you through university that if you'd been
a sergeant for more than six months they credited you with
moral philosophy without taking the exam. So I'm not an
intellectual, never pretended to be. I tried to learn from my
experience. Although I have a high regard – possibly an undue
regard – for intellectuals, I think they can also take you off
the course of common sense.'

He believes, with some justice, that the tabloid press has
tried to discredit his arguments by making out that he is mad.
And of course, as soon as he starts talking about it, he begins
to *look* mad, with staring eyes and straining neck muscles, his
normal pleasant wuffly voice taking on the fanatic's drone.
He recounts how once the *News of the World* paid Debrett's
£10,000 to go into his ancestry and they came up with an
incident in 1883 when his great-great-uncle (who, incidentally, was Margaret Rutherford's father) murdered his father
by striking him with a chamber-pot. 'So all the papers had
stories on Benn's mad ancestry. Now that was used politically
to try and undermine what I was saying.

'I'll give you another example, just for amusement's sake.
When I was ill in 1981 I had a thing called Guillain-Barré
syndrome which affects the sensory nerves in your hands and
legs. Now the papers described that as a *nervous* disease –
but you know there is a difference between sensory nerves

and "nerves". They do it all the time – I mean, it's happening to Arthur Scargill now. I know what it's like to have that sort of flame-thrower turned on you, and you come through it – it's like being tested, like steel, like tempered steel . . . I used to think it was personal and that *was* unpleasant, then I realized it wasn't personal but political. If I'd joined the SDP you'd never have heard any of those arguments mentioned again.'

This may well be true, but the trouble is that he interprets almost *any* question about his character as politically motivated. 'Character assassination,' he says, 'is about the destruction of someone's credibility by raising questions about madness, senility, hypocrisy, ambition and so on which are used to destroy an argument.' Moreover, he adds, 'it produces, of course, a mass of death threats because people read it and write, "We're going to kill you" – which is not very pleasant for the family or for yourself.'

Thus if I ask what, to me, are normal questions about whether he is ambitious and so on, the suggestion is that I will be to blame for his getting death threats. This is an absurdly heavy guilt trip to try to lay on anyone, and my reaction is to wonder if perhaps he really *is* mad. He certainly seems to have a deep vein of paranoia.

However, the question that *really* gets him mad is, oddly enough, a quite innocuous one about whether he is lonely. He almost explodes with anger: 'Don't you think I haven't got thousands and thousands of friends? Who tell me what's what and encourage me? Do you *really* imagine this is a lonely position? It's not lonely at all. This idea that you're just a difficult customer, a bad colleague, a *loner* – I just think it's wrong. I don't accept the idea of loneliness at all. Now the other day on the National Executive I moved an amendment on the Gulf and Dennis Skinner and I were the only ones who voted for it, we were defeated 16 to 2. Now that, I suppose, in that particular context, is a lonely position, but then you come back here and read all your mail about the Gulf, all supporting you, and then you don't feel alone. You couldn't *survive* in this job if you were really alone. I mean, I'd be *destroyed* if I really thought for a moment that there weren't people whose views I was representing.'

All right, all right, not lonely – but constituents or political allies are not the same as *friends*. He almost doesn't seem to understand the meaning of the word. In the first volume of *Diaries* (admittedly when he was out of Parliament and therefore less busy) he and his wife seemed to go to lots of parties and to have many friends, but in the latest volume there is almost no social life at all. And when Tony Crosland dies, who *had* been one of his closest friends, his grief seems perfunctory – he turns almost immediately to the question of who will be the next Foreign Secretary. He and Crosland, of course, had had their political differences and there was an odd business when Susan Crosland wrote a profile of him and he *hated* it (thought it seemed perfectly anodyne), but one would expect those disagreements to be erased by death. The trouble is he seems to believe that anyone who is not 100 per cent for him is against him.

Michael Foot once called him self-righteous and talked of his 'halo of martyrdom'. Certainly he is profoundly unclubbable, and proud of it. When he was talking about his addiction to tea, he told me how Harold Wilson, after Cabinet, would order brandy and cigars – which of course he didn't want. So once Wilson secretly sent his car round to Benn's ministry to collect his Big Mug so he could have his proper tea when the others had brandy. A kind gesture, you might think, but not if you were Benn: 'I knew then that he was trying to buy me. Every man has his price and if I was ever corrupted it wouldn't be by the usual things – it would be by someone offering me a mug of tea when I really needed it.'

Prime Minister Callaghan once called him 'devious'. Is he? On the face of it he is very straightforward, and prides himself on always saying the same to everyone, in every context, which is rare for a politician. But there is an odd inconsistency in the latest volume of *Diaries* on the question of his ambition. Right at the beginning, in 1977, he tells Frances Morrell that he is not ambitious and has seen many lives ruined by ambition. But when Labour is defeated, in 1980, and the search for a new leader is on, he promptly photocopies a list of Labour MPs, cuts it up and sticks it on a board on his wall, planning to 'have a word' with each of them in turn. What is this if not campaigning? But he never seems to ask himself: does this mean I am ambitious after all? The *Diaries* are curiously devoid of introspection. He punctiliously records everything he does, but not why he does it. And this studious refusal to examine his motives makes it easy for him to be self-deceiving – which in turn can make him devious in others' eyes.

At one point in the *Diaries*, his associate Frances Morrell tells him he is thought to be fanatical and humourless and he 'must be more human and more relaxed'. He strives valiantly and goes to collect a Golden Joker Award from the Cartoonists' Club and, though he is uneasy about going, decides afterwards: 'Appearing in a human guise from time to time is quite useful.' Well, yes indeed – but useful for what? And what on earth is he when *not* in human guise?

The notion of relaxation just doesn't come in. His life, according to the *Diaries*, is all work and no play. He doesn't have any vices, or even any foibles, apart from tea; he hardly ever seems to read, or go to the cinema, or listen to music. Was that accurate? Oh no, he said, he was very interested in music, especially this case of the conductor who was sacked for refusing to play 'Land of Hope and Glory' – 'I recorded *that* in my diary, and that's a musical *point*.'

'No, it's not, it's a political point.'

'Well, politics covers everything, you see.'

The fact that his father, his father's father and his mother's father were all in politics gives him, he believes, an unusually long political perspective: 'One of the effects of growing up in a political family – and I think my children would say the same – is that your political *understanding* goes back to a much earlier part of your life. I mean, I was taken to see Mr

Gandhi when I was six and I remember it vividly. I remember I met Ramsay MacDonald in 1930 at the Trooping of the Colour. At home we discussed the Japanese attack on Manchuria [in 1931], so you see I have the memory of someone perhaps twenty years older, and that gives you a certain – I don't know how to put it – *confidence* in dealing with the material. You don't start with today's headlines.'

Indeed Benn's political perspectives are quite exceptionally long. He says that Harold Wilson's remark that 'A week is a long time in politics' was one of the silliest ever made: he was much more impressed with Mao's answer, when asked about the impact of the French Revolution: 'It's a bit too soon to say.' He would say the same about his own effect on politics: history will decide, and he is not talking about next year or even next generation but centuries hence.

In many ways he is more like a religious leader than a politician, perhaps more like his mother, the theologian, than his father, the MP. He sees himself as a runner in a relay race, a carrier of the pure flame of socialism from his father's and grandfather's generation to his son's and grandson's. 'You have to take a long sweep of history. And after all if you look at the Gulf: is this the Crusades coming back? Is this Christianity arming itself to destroy Islam? I think if you are serious about politics you have to be serious about history. I mean, what *is* the footprint left on the sands of time?'

Reproduced by permission of the *Independent on Sunday*

THE BEVERLEY SISTERS

15 May 1988

When I first walked into the dark bar at London's Hippodrome, I couldn't see anyone, but there was this odd sort of cooing noise which gradually rose to a hum, and suddenly three middle-aged women in luminous Mickey Mouse T-shirts were sashaying down a flight of stairs towards me, going, 'Mmmmm ho-ow-ow *much* is that doggie in the window?'

Then the big one, Joy, stopped singing and cried, 'Don't mind us, Lynn.' And they all ran down the stairs and kissed me. Peck peck. Peck peck. Peck peck. It was like being nibbled to death by gerbils. Then they all flung themselves on to a sofa in their approved interview mode – Joy in the middle, twins Babs and Teddie on each side, and all started talking at once.

They *loved* the Hippodrome, they explained, because that was where it all began: the Comeback. It was three years ago. They'd been huge stars in the fifties and sixties – 'Joy doesn't like me saying we were megastars,' said one of the twins, 'but we were, Lynn – we were *big*.'

But they gave it all up to raise families (in fact, only two of them, Joy and Teddie, have children but they all talk about 'our children') and for eighteen years were north London housewives. But one day Joy, going upstairs, heard 'the voices of angels' – it was her daughters Vicky and Sasha and Teddie's Babette singing in harmony.

The daughters formed themselves into a group called The Foxes. And one night their mothers went to see them at the Hippodrome.

'We *crept* in . . .' 'wearing black suits . . .' 'and sat at the back because we didn't want anyone to notice us.' 'But at the end Peter Stringfellow, the owner, grabbed us and said, "I've had the daughters, now I want the mothers. Name your price."' And they all said no, but eventually they all agreed, and duly unveiled themselves in see-through dresses and false eyelashes for Gay Night at the Hippodrome.

They brought the house down. 'We thought it would be just a one-off, a flash in the pan, but the bookings just keep coming in.'

'The one bitter sweet in our return,' says Joy, 'is that we *wish* it were happening to the girls.'

'Joy!' screams Teddie, 'Don't *say* that. It *is* happening to the girls.'

Aha. I am beginning to get the hang of sorting them out. Joy is the indiscreet one; Teddie is the one who keeps them all in line; Babs is the quieter twin who often echoes what Teddie says. But when I ask them if perhaps they could say their names as they speak so that later, listening to the tape, I will be able to recognize who says what, they all shriek, 'But it doesn't *matter*. We all say the same.' And indeed, when they phone me, they say, 'This is one of the Beverley Sisters,' and seem surprised that I should want to know which one. Their interchangeability produces some mind-boggling effects. One of them gave me a long account of how their feelings changed with motherhood – but it was Babs, the childless one.

Most families, I said, have some private consensus that this child is the clever one and this is the pretty one, and so on. 'Oh no!' cried Teddie, shocked. 'We don't have *anything* like that. Our mother's the pretty one.'

'Our mother' features a great deal in their conversation. She is a widow of ninety and lives a mile from them and every day they take her for a drive – a drive to the pub, it later emerged. She and her husband were music hall stars, Coram and Mills. 'An angel came to earth – our mother,' said Joy. 'Oh it's wonderful, her spirit and vitality. I just wonder, how did God spare such a wonderful person to live such a long life?' Since Teddie (or was it Babs?) had raised the subject, I asked them, as tactfully as I could, what would happen when their mother died. Six eyes promptly filled with tears.

'We'll never be the same again.'

'We'll suddenly be old.'

Their mother always disapproved of vanity. 'Because our mother is a very beautiful woman,' (Teddie). 'Oh, glorious,' (Babs). 'She never needed to be vain, did she? Because she's got everything,' (Teddie). 'I'd say – ' this is Joy – ' "Oh Mum, I must wash my hair," and she'd say, "Why? Are you working?" '

Teddie: 'That was her answer. You mustn't think about yourself.'

Joy: 'I remember once when we were teenagers and going on television, I must have looked at myself in the mirror a bit too long and our mother said, "Who's going to look at *you*?" – only three million viewers!'

Their mother's childhood motto was: 'A little less I, a little more we.' She dressed them identically and trained them not to compete. Teddie explained: 'We weren't to compete with each other. Our job in life was to compete with the rest of the world, to make something out of ourselves.'

All right, so officially they are all the same. Nevertheless they have had quite different life stories. Joy, for instance, is the non-twin and in their childhood was three years older than the twins – though, confusingly, she now says she's three years *younger*. (It is very hard to get a fix on their ages, but the twins seem ready to admit to fifty-seven. Joy, however, is not sixty and never will be.)

During their childhood, in the East End of London and

then as evacuees during the war, Joy was the big sister and babysitter to the twins. She remembers taking them for their first day at school, crossing the road with a twin holding each hand; she remembers at night when their parents were out working, 'and I had to answer the phone, and if I made them a booking I got a shilling – which was a lot of money'.

It was Joy who first started singing, and told the twins to sing harmony to her melody, and taught them how to do it. 'Oh she's the musical one,' the others agree. 'She can hear one wrong note in a fifty-five-piece orchestra.'

Sometime in her late teens (again it is hard to be precise about dates) Joy was briefly married and had a son, Vince. 'I did that on my own. All I cared about was having a child. I would never have married if I couldn't have had a child. I felt that until I had a child I hadn't lived.' Their mother looked after the baby while the Sisters built up their career, and Joy recalls making long train journeys in the middle of the night from wherever the Sisters were singing, in order to get back to the East End to see her baby. Vince was twelve when Joy married Billy Wright in 1958.

'So he must be forty-two now?' I asked.

'Oh no, *nothing* like that. Maybe thirty-six – say thirty.'

Teddie showed signs of distress at all this talk about Joy's son and suddenly pointed across the room. 'Look at that chair! Doesn't it remind you, girls?' The girls looked fairly nonplussed, but Teddie pushed and prompted them into an anecdote about how as children they had tried to clean one of their chairs at home and when their mother sat on it, the colour stained her dress.

'You've changed the subject,' said Joy reproachfully.

'A little less I, a little more we,' said Teddie.

But where was I? In 1958 Joy married the England football captain Billy Wright (the papers then gave her age as thirty-four) and has been happily married to him ever since. I asked how Billy Wright coped with 'all three of you', and Joy said stoutly, 'He doesn't have to cope with all three of us: he copes with me.' The twins agreed that when he came home at weekends – he works in Birmingham as Controller of Sport for Central TV – they made themselves scarce. They are all very proud of Joy's husband, whom they invariably refer to as 'England captain Billy Wright'.

Teddie, the younger twin, says, 'I'm the one nobody recognizes. They never remember my name, except once in the lift in the London Clinic a man said, "I know you, you're Teddie. You sing low. I know that because I sing low too."' In fact, she says, she and Babs have identical voices, but when they first started harmonizing together they tossed a coin for who would sing high and who low, 'and I've been stuck with the low voice ever since'.

Teddie has a daughter, who with Joy's two make up The Foxes, and she was married twice, briefly. Were they happy marriages? 'I'd say they were happy enough. I don't think you can look for perfection; you look for moments of happiness.'

Babs struck me as the prettiest one, and the most serene. But she has had, they all agree, the unluckiest life. She remained a virgin till she was thirty-two – 'In those days you could have wonderful romance and love, without the sex act – ' and then married a dentist, but the marriage lasted only a few weeks. She also suffered a long series of illnesses and accidents; she was in hospital in America for a year, then broke her back in a riding accident, fractured her skull in a car crash – 'So that probably contributed to my not having children, because I spent so much time being ill.' Teddie: 'It was unlucky for me, too, because I was paying the bills.'

I asked Babs if she had ever had a happy relationship with a man, and she said, 'Mm, yes, I think so. Briefly.' Joy butted in, 'We always say Babs is going to write a book about her love life . . .' 'Go on! go on!' screamed the twins, falling about – this is obviously a well-loved family joke – 'Only it won't be a book: it'll be more of a *pamphlet!*'

The longest they have ever been apart is six weeks and even then they talked every day on the phone. When both her sisters were married, Babs lived with their mother, but only a mile or two from the others. Now they all live in three identical next-door houses in north London: Joy and Billy in one, the twins in the second and the daughters in the third. Before that they lived in grand mansions, but the daughters didn't like it . . .

'They didn't like being fetched from school in the Rolls-Royce; they didn't like the opulence.' 'Let me just explain,' says Teddie, taking over, 'that in those days, if you'd been a success, you showed it. You had mink coats and Rolls-Royces and indoor swimming-pools and quadrophonic sound. You had butlers and staff.' 'But the butlers were so *bossy*, they used to tell us what time we could finish dinner.' 'So our daughters persuaded us we should live somewhere less ostentatious.' 'I was horrified at first,' said Joy. 'I thought, God, I'll never move.' But she did.

They spend their spare time reading biographies – I suspect they are curious about how non-Sisters live. They asked me a lot about myself, about my mother and my daughters: they never once asked about my husband or father. At one point they all leapt up in unison and started stroking my cheeks. 'I do believe she's not wearing a shred of make-up.' 'But she's got quite a lot of colour.' They went on exclaiming about my non-made-up face for ages, like a troop of Martians discovering their first Earthling.

It is almost impossible for any of them to talk for more than two minutes without the others interrupting. At one point, Teddie was in the middle of a long disquisition about violence, and how civilization is a very thin veneer. 'I always say to Babs, "If Waitrose were to close next week, we'd be in there scratching people's eyes out for food for our children."' Suddenly Joy interrupted, '*I* wouldn't. I've got loads.' Babs turned on her, 'What – rhubarb?' 'Yes,' said Joy, 'I could feed us all for three months.'

I must say they seem to have terrific fun, teasing each other and chattering away non-stop. And they are all highly delighted with the Comeback because: 'It's a bonus. We were at the top for a long time and we thought we'd had our innings – we're just so lucky.'

So do they feel they have missed out on anything? '*I* don't,' says Joy. 'Count your blessings,' says Teddie. 'Mmmm,' says Babs. And then all three leap up simultaneously and whisk into their mink coats.

Kiss kiss. Kiss kiss.

Kiss kiss.

Reproduced by permission of the *Sunday Express*

RONALD BIGGS

25 November 1984

Ronald Biggs fixed me with a stern eye over the lobster salad and said, 'You know, you were very lucky to get me through the Mousetraps. Otherwise I would have tried to sucker you for $500 at least – and that's my off-season rate.'

It was true and I knew it. If it hadn't been for the Mousetraps (equals Japs in rhyming slang) I wouldn't have met Biggs at all. I had gone to Rio de Janeiro on holiday: no instructions to see Ronald Biggs and certainly not to pay him anything. He is, after all, a convicted criminal with a thirty-year prison sentence still hanging over him for his part in the Great Train Robbery of 1963. His part, he always claimed was a small one ('I was the tea boy to the Train Gang'); nevertheless, he shared the £2½ million haul and he also shared responsibility for the coshing of the train-driver.

And yet, and yet . . . It is almost unbearable for a journalist to go to Rio and return to Fleet Street *without* seeing Ronald Biggs. He is one of the sights of the city, like Sugar Loaf Mountain or Copacabana Beach. So as soon as I arrived, I started putting it about that I wanted to meet Biggs, and numerous people promised that they would get his phone number for me tomorrow. But the days went by, and no phone number materialized, and even the reporters on O

Globo, the leading newspaper, admitted that they had temporarily lost touch with Biggs, because he had moved house. And as everyone, even taxi-drivers, knew, his minimum price for an interview was $500. So then I gave up thinking about Ronald Biggs and flew off to Iguacu to admire the waterfalls.

When I got back to my hotel two days later I found the lobby knee-deep in Japanese. 'Lynn BlaBla? Lynn BlaBla?' they all twittered when they saw me. One of them, who spoke English, introduced himself as Mr Wakamiya and said he had been looking for me all day. He was here with a film crew from Nippon TV making a documentary about Ronald Biggs's life. They needed English tourists to play English tourists in the film. He knew that I wanted to meet Biggs so could we come to an agleement?

The agleement took hours of bargaining but eventually it was this: Nippon TV would let me have Ronald Biggs and their photographer, at no charge, for a Night Out on Friday. In return, I would deliver a minimum of six English tourists to act in the film on Saturday morning. When they had completed the scene to the director's satisfaction, the photographer would hand over his film of me and Biggs.

It sounded good, but I insisted that I should speak to Biggs on the phone beforehand to confirm it. After about twenty phone calls, I finally got him – a surprisingly flat, frail, old man's voice saying there was a problem. (I had suspected there would be.) The problem was that his ten-year-old son Mike, who is a pop star in Brazil, was going to be on television on Friday and he wanted to stay in to watch him. So would I mind doing a night in, instead of a night out, and then maybe we'd have dinner afterwards? Yes, I said – anything.

Meanwhile I trundled up and down the Sugar Loaf and Corcovado in search of English tourists. They had vanished from the face of the earth. By Friday morning I was getting really desperate but then, stepping off the cable-car below the statue of Christ, I saw a cluster of pastel shades that could *only* come from Marks & Spencer. 'Are you English? Do you want to meet Ronnie Biggs? Are you free to be in a film tomorrow morning?' I gabbled, and much to my relief they all chorused yes. So that was all right.

Friday evening I took a taxi round to the address Biggs had given me, which turned out to be a smart apartment block near the airport. A wonderfully warm tigerish-looking woman greeted me in English and said she was Ulla and Ron had phoned and said sorry, he would be a bit late, but meanwhile I was to come in and sit down. So we sat on the long leather sofa in the narrow sitting-room and made conversation – strained on my part, because I was desperately trying to work out who she was. It turned out that she is Biggs's long-standing girlfriend: they have been together for ten years, virtually since Mike was born.

She told me about Biggs's life today: he is under a peculiar form of Brazilian detention which means he has to sign on at the police station twice a week (the policemen all call him 'O Big-gish'); he is not allowed to work or to marry, and he is not allowed to leave Brazil. 'Still,' Ulla said, 'it's a beautiful prison, and a big one.' He no longer misses England; if anything, he misses Australia more, where he lived after his escape from Wandsworth; but he is content to remain in Brazil.

As we were talking, Ulla suddenly leaned over impulsively and clutched my hand. 'My dear, I must tell you: you must never, never wear a ring like that [my engagement ring] in Rio. The thieves here are terrible. They would cut off your finger to get it. And there are thieves everywhere in Rio.'

At that point, the door opened and the most famous thief in Rio walked in – Ronald Biggs, together with his ten-year-old son Mike, the pop singer, and several Japanese. He hugged Ulla, shook hands with me, and apologized for his dirty clothes – 'The Mousetraps have had me filming in this filthy dump, supposed to be the place I lived in when I first came to Brazil. I'm poorer now than I was then but I don't live in a *slum*! Still, they're paying me $8,000 for eight days' work so I'm not complaining. Money for old rope!' Again, I was struck by how weak and frail his voice seemed, especially coming from such a huge figure of a man. He is fifty-five but looks younger, though his hair is grey. He kept hugging Mike and hugging Ulla: I felt rather keen to be hugged myself. He was trying to go to the bedroom to change, but the phone kept ringing with the conversations going on in Japanese, Portuguese, English.

I meanwhile asked Mr Wakamiya when my photographer was due to arrive. He denied all knowledge of a photographer and seemed prepared to karate-chop me when I said, 'But you promised.' 'Are you impugning my honour?' he thundered in suddenly perfect English, and I found myself cowering behind the reassuring bulk of Biggs. Biggs took my side. 'Why don't you phone your photographer and get him over here?' and after a certain amount of Japanese head-banging Mr Wakamiya did just that. Suddenly Mike, who was hovering over the television set, gave a great wail and Biggs shouted, 'Shut up, everyone. I want to watch my offspring in action.'

The programme was a lavish one-hour special featuring Magic Balloon, the teeny-boppers' group of which Mike is a member. It was surprisingly enjoyable. As we watched, Mike made comments to his father in Portuguese (he understands English, but rarely speaks it), while Biggs made comments to him, and explained the action to me, in English. At the end Biggs shouted, 'Well done, Mikey, well *done!*' The bond between them is touching to behold: Biggs brought him up single-handed from a baby and is now over the moon at his success.

For the past two years his life has been that of a showbiz parent, chaperoning Mike and travelling around on the Magic Balloon bus. 'The other parents spend all their time fighting – it's real pandemonium. I act as peacemaker.' There is now a chance that Magic Balloon might come to Britain, but Biggs, of course, will not be with them.

The programme lasted an hour but there were lots of commercial breaks when everyone chatted. Mr Wakamiya asked me if I knew who he was ('Er, no'). 'I am the velly

famous journalist who witnessed the assassination of Benigno
Aquino at Manila Airport in 1983. I saw the man who fired
the fatal bullet. I could recognize him again.' Ulla said, 'There
was something about the Philippines on the news tonight.
Street fighting again.'

'Oh,' said Mr Wakamiya, leaping up, 'my life is in danger!
They know I know the guilty man! I must return to Japan! I
must have a gun! I need a machine-gun!' and he strode up
and down the room, apparently in search of spare machine-
guns.

'Is he for real?' I asked Biggs. 'Don't ask – he's paying the
$8,000.' Then the programme started again and Biggs
shouted, 'Sit down and shut up,' and Mr Wakamiya did, the
machine-gun forgotten. At the end of the show, we all
congratulated Mikey, and he started playing it again on the
video.

Meanwhile, the Japanese photographer had arrived and Mr
Wakamiya signalled me to come outside the door. 'Velly
famous photographer,' he said. 'How much you pay him?'
'You said there would be no charge' – and Mr Wakamiya did
his kung-fu face again and started howling about his honour,
so I handed over $100 and we all trooped back into the flat
and took some photos of Biggs and Mike watching the
television replay. Then Biggs went off to change and
reappeared looking very elegant in dark trousers and sweater
and we set off to dinner. Except that he kept popping back
for things he'd forgotten. 'He's always like this,' Ulla murmured, 'he can't bear to leave anywhere.' It seemed strange
that he had managed to make so many successful escapes. But
finally Ulla bundled him out of the door and I managed to
grab the photographer just as he was escaping, and we all set
off in a taxi to the Meridien Hotel.

This, he told me *en route*, was 'the place to go for a bit of
decent nosh' – also, incidentally, Rio's most expensive restaurant. The *maître d'hôtel* greeted Biggs effusively, and the
elderly pianist came over and talked to Biggs in Portuguese.
'He's saying he'll play my old favourite tune. Trouble is,

neither of us can remember what it was. I'm getting old. Oh yes, "East of the Sun".' So the pianist played that and then "London Bridge is Falling Down" and "We'll Gather Lilacs" and "In an English Country Garden". 'Does it make you feel nostalgic for England?' I asked. 'No,' said Biggs, 'but I did have quite an emotional experience today. The Mousetraps showed me a video they'd done with Paul Seabourne, the friend I escaped from Wandsworth with. He looks good, he's still got his hair. I've many many times thought about Paul. When I was in Australia I used to get the *Daily Mirror* and from time to time Paul was in it, doing another four years or seven years for attacking an armoured car or whatever. He says on the video he'd like to come to Brazil, all he needs is the fare, and I'd surely send it him if I had it.'

The waiter came to take our order, which was no easy feat, since the menu was in French. I translated it into English for Biggs and he translated it into Portuguese for the waiter; then we all stared at the photographer, who spoke only Japanese. 'You want some Lilian Gish?' (fish), Biggs asked helpfully, but the photographer only bowed and handed over his roll of film and went away.

Biggs meanwhile embarked on the narrative of his vastly eventful life. He is still bitter about the plastic surgery he had in Paris after his prison escape – 'I paid for the best and got a complete novice.' It went on bleeding for years afterwards and he still has to shave behind his ears because his skin is so skewed round. Actually, despite the scars and a lopsided crease down one cheek, his only really unattractive features are his cold fishy eyes, and the fact that he rarely looks at you while talking, but keeps his head down and talks out of the side of his mouth.

He kept mentioning his luck: he believes that his life has been a run of incredibly lucky coincidences. This seems a rather perverse way of looking at it – it was surely very *bad* luck that, having gone straight for three years, he happened to ring Bruce Reynolds just when the Train Robbery was being planned. But still, it was an amazing piece of luck that

Raimunda, his Brazilian girlfriend, was pregnant when Slipper
of the Yard finally caught up with him in 1974, because that
saved him from deportation. In fact, he confided, Raimunda
had already had two abortions and was planning another, so
it was a close shave all round.

After Mike was born, Raimunda pushed off to Switzerland
to be a stripper, and Biggs was left holding the baby. He was
really on his uppers, behind with the rent and borrowing
money from friends (mainly Ulla) to pay for nappies when
'suddenly these Argentinian journalists turned up and offered
me $200 for an interview, and somehow that cracked it and I
didn't look back'. He charged for interviews, charged for
autographs, and even had T-shirts printed ('Rio – a great
place to escape to') which he sold to tourists on the beach.
But by 1979 these various wheezes were running a bit thin.
Suddenly the next big 'luck' happened: he was kidnapped to
Barbados by a gang of British mercenaries: 'That put me back
in the headlines!' he said with satisfaction.

'So was the kidnapping a put-up job?' I asked, and Biggs
shot me a very hard look. 'I wouldn't say that,' he said
warningly, and I readily conceded that I wouldn't dream of
it. Anyway, while he was in Barbados, Mike was invited to
appear on Brazilian television to appeal for his father's return,
and the head of CBS records was so charmed by Mike's
appearance that he had a contract drawn up to put him in a
pop group by the time Biggs got back. So that was 'Biggsie's
luck' again.

I suggested, rather nervously, that some people might say
he was exploiting Mike, and that the child might suffer when,
inevitably, the Magic Balloon bubble burst. But Biggs took
the question in his stride: 'Mike's all right. He knows this
caper can't last for ever – CBS give it another three years. He
knows he's not good enough to be a singer, though he might
make it as an actor. One thing he's definitely not going to be
is a crook. We always say in interviews that he's going to be
a politician because he talks so much and so convincingly and
he's an outrageous liar – which he gets from me, of course.

The judge described me as "a specious and facile liar". But when you go to court and they start asking you if you were at Leatherslade Farm, you're not going to tell the *truth*, are you? Well, *are* you, Lynn?'

He seemed seriously to expect an answer so I murmured something about honesty being the best policy and he jumped down my throat. 'It's all right for people like you' (he meant middle-class people), 'you've no need to be dishonest. But if you're poor it's a different matter. I remember as a child the big thing in my life was to have a three-wheel bike and it was the standing yearly promise and it never happened. That's what criminality is all about – the burning desire for something that you can't afford, that you can see far, far away. If you're a sheep, you knuckle down and accept your lot, but if you're a freethinker like I am, like I *was*, and the opportunity comes along, you grab it. There's no way of knowing how my life would have turned out if I'd hung on there as a carpenter, going straight. I really was a tiger for work when I was young. I loved to let loose with a hammer and nails, I worked very very happily. But it was frustrating money-wise.

'But Mikey will be honest, because he has no *need* to be dishonest. I really do see it as a medium-sized miracle – the fact that Mikey is achieving all this success when his old man is nothing more than a crook, or ex-crook shall we say.'

At this point I asked the inevitable question: 'If you had your life all over again . . .' but he interrupted before I had even said it. 'Yes! Of course I'd do it over again! I've had a good life. I've really enjoyed myself and now the icing is coming on the cake with the acting bit and making a few bob out of movies. People sometimes ask whether I'm hoping for a royal pardon, but what would I do with a pardon? Stop being Biggsie? You must be joking!'

It was 2 a.m. by the time we left, but Copacabana was still buzzing with cars and streetwalkers and Biggs insisted on walking me back to my hotel. 'Very dangerous, Rio, there are thieves all over the place.' I asked if he was armed. 'Ooo no. Don't like arms. If someone comes at me and says he wants my money, I hand it over, no question. You know, when I first got over the wall, the newspaper line was "This man is armed and will shoot on sight." Then, as the years went by and I achieved a kind of ragged fame, they started saying "Good old Ronnie." Funny business, journalism.' Then we reached the Copacabana Palace and he gave me a big hug and walked off into the night.

Next morning, I rounded up my English tourists for the Mousetraps. The filming was great fun. We were re-enacting a scene from Biggs's middle Brazilian period when he sold T-shirts on the beach. We each had to buy a T-shirt and get him to autograph it (he wrote on mine 'Crime doesn't pay – not much!'). He confided between takes that the Mousetraps had double-crossed him: they told him they were making the film only for Japan and now he found they were selling it world-wide.

'There's a lot of dishonesty in the world, Lynn,' he said soberly.

'There is indeed, Biggsie,' I agreed.

Reproduced by permission of the *Sunday Express*

PETER BOGDANOVICH

25 November 1990

Whooo, but Peter Bogdanovich is *weird*, and like all the most seriously weird people he looks perfectly ordinary. You would take him for, say, a successful private dentist – sharp Italian shoes, gold bracelet, blow-wave hair, possibly a hint of ManTan. He has completely dead eyes, and looks at you with all the human warmth of one deciding how much he can sting you for your bridgework. It is not clear whether he regards doing this interview as torture or just ineffably boring. His voice is weary, he is jet-lagged, and he makes a point of conspicuously consulting his watch every few minutes.

He is in London (from his home in Los Angeles) for the London Film Festival showing of his new film, *Texasville*. It is a sequel to the 1971 film that made his name, *The Last Picture Show*, and has the same stars, Jeff Bridges and Cybill Shepherd, playing the same characters thirty years on. In America it has had a disastrous reception at the box office, and the whisper among British critics is not promising. It is less engaging than *The Last Picture Show*, perhaps because it is in colour, perhaps because it is a sequel, or perhaps just because it is a story of middle age. All the actors, Bogdanovich says, 'agreed to look lousy and to look older, to be lit unattractively, to use lenses and lighting that would not be flattering – just the opposite of what you'd normally do'. This is particularly hard on Cybill Shepherd – all the characters in the film keep commenting on how she's lost her looks – but Bogdanovich insists that she was 'very good about it'. She was Bogdanovich's girlfriend for many years – they fell in love while filming *The Last Picture Show* – so the making of the new picture must have been fraught with strange resonances.

Texasville is supposed to be Bogdanovich's comeback, and he needs it desperately. His reputation has been at a nadir throughout the eighties and this may be the last chance of his career.

Like François Truffaut and many of the French *nouvelle vague* directors, he started as a film critic and was by all accounts a very good one, writing mainly for *Esquire*. He was obsessed with film: Cybill Shepherd said that when they lived together they used to watch 'at least 1,000 films a year'. He kept notes about them all on file cards – when he'd seen them and what he'd thought of them, with cross-references to his files of cast lists and bibliography. 'It was a way of teaching myself about film,' he says, and he did it for thirteen years. When he stopped, in 1970, he had between 7,000 and 8,000 cards.

He stopped simply because he was finally making films himself. Roger Corman gave him a tiny budget to make his first film, *Targets*, with the unusual brief that he must use Boris Karloff (who owed Corman a favour) and include eighteen minutes of out-takes from a previous Karloff film. Bogdanovich carried it off with aplomb and then got the backing to make *The Last Picture Show*, which was a huge success. His first wife, Polly Platt, had been his producer and helpmeet so far, but he now broke with her to fall in love with Cybill Shepherd, his star. He 'discovered' her on the cover of *Glamour* magazine – she had never acted before – and they lived together for eight years. (Polly Platt went on to become a successful producer in her own right.) Bogdanovich had further sucesses with *What's Up, Doc?* and *Paper Moon* – and then a string of expensive failures, *Daisy Miller, At Long Last Love, Nickelodeon*.

He made one more good film, *Saint Jack*, before his career, and his personal life, plummeted to the depths. Cybill Shepherd left him and he fell in love with another blonde beauty queen, Dorothy Stratten, the *Playboy* 1980 'Playmate of the Year'. He put her in a film, *They All Laughed*, and spoke of marrying her when she divorced her husband, a pimp called Paul Snider. On 14 August 1980, Snider tied her into a 'bondage machine' of his own devising, raped her, sodomized her, shot her head off, raped her again and then killed himself.

Bogdanovich's career virtually stopped while he buried himself in mourning: 'I felt in the early eighties that I didn't really care to make pictures any more. I went through a very strong period of disillusionment with the whole thing.' In 1985 he bought the Stratten film back from the distributors, tried to market it himself and went bankrupt to the tune of $6.6m (£3.4m). He became a director for hire, but some of his subsequent films were so bad that they were never released, and this month he was 'taken off' his latest directing job, *Another You*, which is now the subject of legal action. He says, not very convincingly, that he has 'lots of projects' in mind, including a vehicle for Cybill Shepherd and Michael Caine, and 'I want to make pictures very much – it's the only thing I really know how to do and I enjoy shooting – if I don't feel like I'm a slave.' But his chances of rising above slavery now hang on *Texasville*. It will have to do outstandingly well in Europe, to make up for its box-office failure in America, if he is ever to be 'bankable' again.

Why did it happen? Why such swift success, such catastrophic failure? Bogdanovich has various excuses, mostly involving blame of other people. He told *Esquire*: 'My pictures were destroyed largely in post-production – by lack of encouragement, by pressure to open the picture, and by misadvice in terms of what to take out and what to leave in.'

   He also blames his relationship with Cybill Shepherd: 'Here
I was, a young, reasonably attractive director with three
successful pictures in a row and a cover-girl girlfriend ten,
eleven years younger than me – kind of the all-American
dream, both of us flaunting the fact that we're not married –
we were the first to advertise it – and not being overly modest.
I mean, how could you *not* hate us?' Yes indeed – and
especially when he adds, as he did to me, that it was really all
Cybill's fault, that it was she who flaunted their non-marriage
and got up people's noses.
   Then again, he said, he suffered from his eagerness to give
credit away. This seems improbable – he does not strike one
as a generous person – but he explains: 'All my early films I
said were my *hommage* to so-and-so or so-and-so, Ford or
Hitchcock or Cukor or Hawks. It was not entirely true, but
they were people I admired greatly – and they couldn't get a
job. I was this hot-shot, you know, and getting jobs over
them. So I liked to get their names in the paper as a way of
giving credit away. But it backfired on me because critics
began to assume that everything I did in a picture was an
hommage to someone else, and they couldn't see the forest
for the trees. I stopped all that with *Nickelodeon*. I got fed up
with that "movie buff" monicker being stuck on me.'
   Unfortunately, the recipients of the *hommages* weren't
always terribly grateful. Billy Wilder said: 'There's a canard
that the Hollywood community is full of bitterness, dissen-
sion, envy and hostility. It's just not true. I've lived here forty
years and I can tell you it took just one simple event to bring
all the factions together – a flop by Peter Bogdanovich.
Champagne corks were popping, flags were waving. The guru
laid an egg and Hollywood was united.'
   Bogdanovich and Shepherd were the most hated couple in
Hollywood, mainly because they were perceived as arrogant
and bratty. Bogdanovich explains: 'I was probably a bit
defensive, and that manifested itself as arrogance.' Is he less
arrogant now? 'I don't know. I think so. I think life has a way
of knocking the foundations out from under you, and you

realize you're less in control of your life than you think you are when you're younger.'

Of course, it is harder to be arrogant when you are not a success – but there is a fairly long roster of people who swear they will never work with him again, headed by Burt Reynolds, who starred in *At Long Last Love*, and Cher, who starred in *Mask*. Of Cher, he says: 'She makes it seem worse than it was. It was fairly normal. She didn't know what I was doing, not having done a lot of movies, and we had some misunderstandings early on, really caused by the studio insisting on testing her, which I knew would put her off. Plus she doesn't like male authority. Lionel Barrymore, you know, said the best directors are the ones that manage to convince the actor he did it all by himself. And Cher was trying to convince everybody that she did it all by herself. She wanted to indicate that I hadn't directed her, which is a lie but, poor woman, that's her insecurity.' I think you can see why people don't like him: he is not very likeable.

What knocked the foundations out from under him was the death of Dorothy Stratten. I thought it might be difficult to raise the subject, but actually he couldn't wait to get started. All the time he was talking about films he was bored and looking at his watch, but as soon as he got on to Dorothy Stratten the words came tumbling out. He met her in 1979 when he was forty and she just nineteen. She was from Vancouver, Canada, where she had worked at the local Dairy Queen restaurant (there are endless shots of a Dairy Queen in *Texasville*), then she was 'discovered' by the local pimp, Paul Snider, who persuaded her to pose for nude photographs which he sent to *Playboy*. When Bogdanovich met her she was staying with Hugh Hefner at the Playboy Mansion and being groomed to become the 'Playmate of the Year'.

What was Dorothy like? Bogdanovich wrote a book about her after her death, *The Killing of the Unicorn*, but it is pure hagiography: 'Kind, selfless, and good-natured, Dorothy was an angel in the shape of Aphrodite.' Although he met her at the Playboy Mansion, where most of the girls were 'available' to VIPs like himself, he was a painfully slow wooer. He 'dated' her for months before he dared ask for a kiss; he serenaded her with love songs and she wrote him poems, an awful lot of which are reproduced in his memoir. For instance:

> The dissolution of a raindrop evolves
> Into the creation of a rainbow –
> The mystery of nature:
> A seed giving birth to life,
> A word giving birth to love.

Dorothy and Bogdanovich would spend the evening holding hands, reading poetry and looking at the moon, maybe occasionally building up to a kiss, then she would clamber into her bunny ears and bobtail and scuttle back to the Playboy Mansion to watch non-stop porn films and take part in orgies. Bogdanovich was an *habitué* of Playboy Mansion himself, so he knew what went on. Reading between the lines of his memoir, her motive seems to have been a fairly predictable desire to get into films: his was to enshrine her as a 'maiden in distress', a unicorn (symbol of purity) caught in the thickets of sin.

He met her only ten months before she was murdered, and was her lover for only five. In fact they spent barely more than a few weeks together, because they were both busy with their careers. But there are hints in the book that he believes he knew her in a previous life – he told her that he could tell from the lines of her palms that she was an 'old soul'. And he told me that 'She didn't have the experience of someone older – not in this lifetime – but she seemed to have that sense of vast resources of reasoning and understanding.' He persuaded her to initiate divorce proceedings against her husband, though he never actually promised to marry her. And meanwhile she went on seeing Snider. Indeed, she crept out of Bogdanovich's house secretly to visit Snider on the day she was murdered. Hugh Hefner broke the news to Bogdanovich.

*

After her death, Bogdanovich became a virtual recluse and spent the next four years writing *The Killing of the Unicorn*, watching her film over and over, and pursuing a vendetta against Hugh Hefner, whom he blamed for her murder.

How long did his mourning last? 'I don't know. A while. A long time. Years. I read somewhere that, going through grief, the fifth year is the most difficult, and it was true – that fifth year, 1985, was the worst. You know, it's very difficult to understand unless you've experienced it – and I wouldn't wish it on my worst enemy. So to you maybe it seems morbid, to live with a memory for five years, but she's somebody I *loved* and will love all my life. You don't get over something like that in five years, even in fifty. And, you know, *murder* – it's such an unnatural act, so sudden, so horrible, you don't recover from it, you just don't. Sharon Tate's mother runs an organization called Families of Victims of Violent Crime and I've spoken to her about it. You are never the same again. I mean some people develop a twitch. I know a guy who saw his parents kill each other and his eyes, from that moment on, flickered like this – I can't even do it – back and forth all the time. Everybody has a different reaction to that kind of violent removal of life. It's unreal, it's unnatural, everything you are *not* ready for. And so when it happens, it's a little bit like an A-bomb went off at your feet and somehow you're still alive.'

For the first time he seems human – but also desperately lost. The blankness in his eyes is pure pain. When does the grieving finish? Obviously never. And the search to find a means of carrying on with life has led him down some strange paths – writing his weird book, harrying Hefner, keeping the flowers fresh on Dorothy's grave – and finally marrying her sister.

Dorothy's sister Louise (or 'L B', as Bogdanovich calls her) was twelve when Dorothy died. She had stayed with Dorothy at Bogdanovich's house, and had played with Bogdanovich's daughters. After Dorothy's death, Bogdanovich paid for Louise to go to private school, bought her her first car, and

had her and her mother to stay for holidays. The first person
to suggest that there might be something unfatherly in his
motives was Hugh Hefner. In 1984, when Bogdanovich
published *The Killing of the Unicorn*, with its devastating
indictment of the whole seedy Playboy Mansion milieu,
Hefner gave a press conference to deny the charges. In the
course of it he said that Bogdanovich had seduced Louise
when she was thirteen and planned to marry her when she
was grown up. Bogdanovich claims that no such thought had
ever crossed his mind, and he threatened to sue Hefner for
saying it – though he later dropped the suit.

So when *did* it first occur to him that he might marry
Louise? 'I don't know. I mean, obviously when Hefner
mentioned it it was *there*, so I must have thought about it,
but it seemed absurd. In fact when he brought it up she was
going with a guy she was hoping to marry – she was sixteen,
she was in love with this guy in Canada, you know, one of
those tough teenage romances and it was a big thing in her
life. So when it all hit the papers, she was *horrified*, because
all her friends at school said, "What is this? I thought you
were going with Tony." And she *was* – she had a boyfriend.
So it was horrible. It was just garbage.'

But he had no girlfriends between Dorothy and Louise: 'I
dated a little bit, but just old friends. I hadn't really gotten
involved in anything serious. It wasn't a romantic period of
my life.' So he was available when she grew up, and married
her in 1988. Her mother was distraught: 'I've lost another
daughter. I had one with her head blown off and now I'm
gonna have another.'

There is a line in *Texasville*: 'The ones that are alive carry
the lives of the one that died.' Was that what he hoped – that
Louise would somehow incorporate Dorothy? 'No, I don't
believe . . . They share a common goodness and a common
kindness and sensitivity, which is unique in my experience, a
quality that they both have. And strength, too. But it isn't a
question of trying to synthesize them. Dorothy is a very
separate person in our minds.' The problem really is whether

Louise is a very separate person in his mind. It is striking that every time I ask him about Louise, he starts talking about Dorothy. He and Louise lay flowers on her grave on her birthday and the anniversary of her death. No doubt they talk about her, too – I got the impression that Bogdanovich would happily talk about Dorothy all day.

Asked by *Esquire* why he married Louise, he explained, 'The thing about marrying Dorothy's sister – I mean, that's not an unusual story. Somebody dies violently and then the person – her lover – marries the sister, that's not so unusual ... You've heard the expression, "Are there any more at home like you?"' As it happens, Louise is not very much like Dorothy (they had different fathers) and her looks are not of the Playmate variety. But she looks more like Dorothy now than she did as a child because Bogdanovich paid to have her jaw reset. He denies that this had any cosmetic or Dorothy-imitating motive, and goes into extraordinary detail and length explaining Louise's maxillary problems, her overbite or underbite, and why the orthodontistry was necessary. But the effect was to make her face look different, and more like Dorothy's – so much so indeed that some friends thought she had had a nose job. And there is something unconvincing when he adds: 'Actually, Dorothy put money in a fund for LB's teeth, she was saving up to have the operation done when she died.' It is as though everything he does has to be sanctioned by a higher authority, 'Dorothy', of which he is custodian and arch-priest.

The prevailing Hollywood theory is that Bogdanovich went mad when Dorothy died. I wonder if he actually went mad a couple of years before, when Cybill Shepherd left him? His career was foundering and his mother died about the same time.

He says in the book that when Cybill left him 'I felt adrift and rudderless . . . There followed more than a year of devastating promiscuity, which left me exhausted and miserable, hoping for an enduring bond that would never lose its strength or magic.' Thus he was looking for a Dorothy before he found her, and when he *did* find her he was determined to put her on a pedestal. There is a telling moment in *The Killing of the Unicorn* when Dorothy insists on showing him her 'Playmate of the Year' photographs and lingers on the most gynaecologically explicit shot. It's as though she is trying to say: Look, this is what I'm really like. But Bogdanovich turns away in disgust. He wanted her to feel ashamed of her *Playboy* exposure but she insisted, 'I'm not a hypocrite. I did it, didn't I?'

Did he really love Dorothy Stratten, or only a Gatsbyish myth of his own devising? Obviously *now* he loves her, now that she is no longer flesh and blood, but in the book he describes how, at one stage in their courtship, she had to have a minor operation to remove a tiny growth from her cheek. 'Disfigurement. Would it, honestly, or would it not, affect my love for her? Was love irretrievably bound to outward appearances? . . . I think I knew that my passion for Dorothy and my empathy with her was far too strong to be lessened by a change in her physical appearance.'

Well, that must have been a relief. But Dorothy was sensible enough to have realized that a man who wondered whether he could still love her if she had a small scar on her cheek was not exactly husband material. What about stretch marks, what about wrinkles, what about ageing? Cybill Shepherd had left him because he wouldn't give her a child: no doubt he was afraid it would ruin her looks. There is something profoundly unadult in all Bogdanovich's descriptions of women. They are cut-outs, they are pin-ups, on to which he projects his own fantasies. Nowadays he speaks the rhetoric of New Manhood, and claims to have put *Playboy* behind him, but he still seems to have trouble believing that women are people. For instance, to prove to me that he liked strong women, he said: 'One day Cybill was obviously holding something in and I said, "Yell it out. Go on. Tell me." And she yelled, and I said, "There. Now just do that all the time."' This is proof of her *strength* – that she is capable of yelling at him when he gives her permission? It is like the man who pays a Miss Whiplash to beat him and fools himself that he is being dominated.

He claims that strength was the common characteristic of all the women in his life. 'The big misapprehension people have about me and the women I've known is that the women were weak and malleable victims and I was like this manipulating, calculating Mesmer or Svengali – that I made them do things and they couldn't do a thing without me. It's all bullshit. I like strong women. My mother was strong, she kept my father going. And Dorothy was anything but a malleable, weak person. She was just the opposite. People say "dumb blonde". To tell you the truth, I've never met a blonde who was dumb. Women are very smart. They sometimes *play* dumb.'

Still, these women, these non-dumb blondes, were all terribly young when he got involved – his tastes seem to have stuck at twenty-year-olds, though he is now fifty-one. His explanation is simple and breathtaking: 'You see, I had a very young mother. She was twenty years younger than my father – I've just figured this out recently – and she was about twenty-one when she had me. So it may be for *that* reason I have tended to gravitate towards younger women. Because the first woman I ever knew was twenty when I met her – a very young mother.'

Whooooooo. Do I need to point the Freudian morals here? Do I need to say that most people's mothers are young when they are born? But that it is – gulp – *unusual* to identify mother and girlfriends quite so overtly? The Hollywood producer Harry Gittes once said of Bogdanovich: 'The whole woman side of his life is a disaster area. He's a man dealing with a lot of life trauma.'

But wait – it gets weirder. Dorothy, he says, was the *mother* of the Stratten family: 'There's a famous story – famous in the family – about Dorothy and her mother and brother walking down the street. Dorothy was three, and her brother John a year and a half. And John said, "Oh look – I want that candy bar," and Dorothy said, "No, don't say that. Mom doesn't have the money – don't depress her." And her sister

L B, who is my wife now, I mean – Dorothy was her mother. Dorothy taught her how to fix her lisp, Dorothy taught her how to tie her shoes. Dorothy taught her *everything*. In a funny way she was the mother figure – even to her own mother. I've got letters from Dorothy to her mother in which she says, "Now I want you to do this, be sure to do that, don't do this" – amazing. But this is very hard for people to understand.'

Indeed. So, to recap, Dorothy is like *his* mother, but not like *her* mother, who was more like Dorothy's daughter. Where does that leave Louise? Bogdanovich clearly regards her as Dorothy's daughter – indeed, in a classic Freudian slip, he actually called her her daughter – so he has married, wait for it, the 'daughter' of a woman he identifies with his mother – i.e. his sister.

I am struggling to digest all this when Bogdanovich thrusts a slim green volume into my hand. It is called *A Year and a Day Calendar*, text by Crescent Moon Productions, illustrations by White Magic Productions, and 'A portion of the proceeds from this book will go toward the planting of trees in North America.' He produced it, he says in the foreword 'in memory of a dear friend who first asked me if I thought the Unicorn was real', i.e. Dorothy Stratten. It is based on Robert Graves's *The White Goddess* and he proudly shows me how it all works, the thirteen months named after trees, the useful charts correlating to palmistry, to Irish tree names, classical Greek rulers and Pelasgian-Greek rulers, Biblical jewels and Hebrew tribes.

Do you really believe all this? I ask him. 'Oh yes! You should use it,' he tells me eagerly. 'It's thirteen months of twenty-eight days, so you see it's especially useful.'

Why? (A dim question.) 'Well, you know, for women . . . because of your, you know, *menstruation*.' He whispers the word excitedly. I say goodbye very fast. There are species of weirdness that are too weird even for me.

Reproduced by permission of the *Independent on Sunday*

MELVYN BRAGG

17 June 1990

Melvyn Bragg has an awful lot of friends, and I seemed to bump into dozens of them while writing this article. One after another, they all said the same thing: 'I hear you're doing Melvyn. You've got to like him, haven't you?' It was posed as a rhetorical question, but often it seemed to be followed by a quivering space for an answer, and so I found myself asking, 'Why? Why has anyone *got* to like Melvyn?' After all, no one says you've *got* to like David Frost or Robert Kilroy-Silk or Terry Wogan or Sue Lawley or Robert Robinson – you *might*, but there again, you might not. Why is Melvyn Bragg somehow sacred, like the Queen Mother?

A colleague quite seriously suggested that it was because he was working-class and (can I have got this right?) that attacking him would somehow be indicative of snobbery. No, I *can't* have got this right. It's true that he supports the Labour Party, but he sends his children to private schools, owns a million-pound house in Hampstead and is a member of a syndicate at Lloyd's; I think the working classes can survive without him. Someone else said I should be kind because he'd had a lot of tragedy in his life – a reference to his first wife's suicide – but that happened almost twenty years ago, and since then his life appears to have been blessed with continuous good fortune.

The commonest argument for why one should like Melvyn is that he does such sterling service for the arts, and this is undeniable – he is head of arts for LWT and not only presents *Start the Week* and *The South Bank Show* but is now producing a new books programme for Channel 4 which will go out next year. He is a genuine popularizer and regularly attracts more than two million viewers to *The South Bank Show*, which means he draws viewers who would not normally watch arts programmes. The other week he was awarded the Royal Television Society's gold medal in token of these achievements. He is a tireless campaigner for the arts; he lunches with Maurice Saatchi, weekends with Andrew Lloyd Webber; he is a great wheeler-dealer in the corridors of power. He does less glamorous things too, like supporting the recent Hay-on-Wye Readers' Festival, or attending obscure Workers' Educational Association lectures in Cumbrian town halls, which tends to vitiate the argument that promotion of the arts can sometimes seem indistinguishable from promotion of Melvyn Bragg.

Personally, though I pay lip-service to the excellence of *The South Bank Show* along with everyone else, I actually find it almost unbearable to watch precisely because it has Melvyn Bragg on it. Smiling, simpering, giggling, looking down at his nails when he is supposed to be asking questions, exuding his awful smug matey blokiness ('Look! I have the common touch!') he makes me almost weep with longing for Russell Harty. He insists that he, too, hates all those 'reaction shots' of Melvyn giggling on the sofa, but claims they are necessary to cover editing cuts – however, they never seem to occur so conspicuously or so interminably in anyone else's programmes.

For years I thought Melvyn Bragg was far too boring and transparent to interview, and that what you saw on television was what you got. Then, a few weeks ago, I met a woman at a party who had worked for him, and she said that everyone at LWT was completely obsessed by him, spent their whole time exchanging Melvyn anecdotes and, even after years of working with him, found him an enigma. I duly beat a path to his door.

His door is opened by his friendly, charming wife, Cate Haste, a television producer. The children are playing in the garden with their friends, and shout cheerful greetings to their father when he arrives; the whole scene could be transposed directly into one of those Happy Families ads for life insurance. Though he has come straight from work, through horrendous traffic jams, he looks as fresh as a daisy. He is fifty but could pass for forty; he looks like what he is – a man who jogs.

Cate brings him tea and me wine, and he explains that for the past five years he has made it a habit to forgo alcohol for the first week of every month; not that he is a lush, but he works in a profession where alcoholism is almost an occupational hazard, so this rule is a precaution. And here, already, I find myself lost in wonder. Can you think of *any* more punishing regime? One month a year, one day a week, or, surely, complete abstinence would be easier; his rule seems designed to demand the maximum degree of self-discipline.

The next thing that strikes me is that he is quite peculiarly, unexpectedly nervous; he keeps writhing in his chair and squeezing his arms down between his legs – not at all the bland, sunny soul he appears on television. He keeps saying this is because he is shy of interviews, but he is not exactly new to the sport, nor did I have to twist his arm to get him. On the contrary, when I had to cancel my appointment, it was he who rang the next day to set a new date.

But this real-life, twitchy, neurotic Melvyn is in my view infinitely more interesting than the smug bit of thinking woman's crumpet that fronts *The South Bank Show*. Is he vain? As soon as I mention his looks, he becomes defensive: 'First of all – I know this is hopeless to say – I have got no opinion of the way I look at all and that's the truth. I actually think that people who are plain have a better time on television, because more people sympathize with them, and identification is everything. But there you are, you can say what you like, but that's the truth, and I think you'll find that everyone who knows me will agree . . .' But I *did* ask someone who knew him and he laughed, 'Is Melvyn vain? Is the Pope Catholic?' Of course he is vain. He wears his trouser belt too tight and tries to remember to hold his tummy in. When he went to look up someone's phone number for me, he couldn't see to read, but he still preferred not to put his glasses on. Interestingly, a friend who knew him at Oxford said he was not good-looking as a young man; he had greasy hair and glasses.

He certainly worries about his image. Whenever a piece appears about him in the press, he buttonholes all his friends to ask what they thought about it, whether it gave a good impression. He phoned several people about this interview, asking whether he should do it, what I was like, what I thought about him, whether, afterwards, I'd said anything about the interview and if so, what. His friend and colleague Nick Elliot, controller of drama of LWT, who has worked with him closely for twelve years and inhabits the next-door office, explains, 'He has this obsessiveness about himself and how he's seen in the world – which is true of many television presenters, of course. The only coiled-in bit is there's a determination about achieving. I don't mean that his image is *false*, but the thing about Melvyn – I'm choosing my words carefully here – is that there is an exterior, and people like that protect themselves behind a sort of wall. And of course he's very concerned about how this book is going to be seen.'

He may well be concerned about how this book – *A Time to Dance*, Hodder & Stoughton – is going to be seen, because it is an extremely, explicitly erotic account of a middle-aged man's affair with an eighteen-year-old girl. Melvyn himself said he felt embarrassed about writing the sexy bits: 'It was very difficult for somebody of my sort of background. I had to take a very deep breath before starting. And when I'd finished, I didn't quite know what to think. I waited for what

Cate had to say, and Ion Trewin, my editor.' Apparently they gave him the go-ahead, and indeed the book has had several favourable reviews, but *Private Eye* summed it up accurately, in my view: 'The book is one long, bragging contact ad. It's a book by a man about how right women are to adore him.'

He claims to be surprised that everyone keeps asking whether he *really* had an affair with a much younger girl, but I don't think anyone could read *A Time to Dance* without assuming that he had. This is not because it is a good novel, but because it is a bad one: it feels like a confession unsuccessfully disguised as fiction rather than a creative task successfully achieved. The fact that he alludes to *Lolita* in his opening chapter and throws in lots of stuff about Hazlitt is just plain cheeky; there is *no* comparison between Nabokov or Hazlitt and Bragg. Of course he denies that it is based on any real-life affair, but one is inclined to echo Mandy Rice-Davis – 'well, he would, wouldn't he?' Despite being married, he has never seemed averse to being thought a ladies' man.

When I asked what we were meant to think of his hero – whether we were meant to admire him or consider him a bit of a shit – he seemed amazed that anyone could think he was a shit. But the supposed moral dilemma of the novel is nugatory: the man is married to an invalid wife, he takes her breakfast and twenty minutes' conversation a day and seems to feel that this proves his devotion; when he falls in love with the girl, he has no qualms about leaving his wife, beyond a slight concern about the loss of his respectability; his wife then develops cancer and he stays with her until she dies. This latter fact is meant to prove his decency, his essential moral goodness, but it is still hard to see him as anything other than a shallow adulterer suffering a belated mid-life crisis.

The book raises yet again the question always asked about Melvyn Bragg: why does he bother to write novels? The critical response is generally underwhelming; even his friends tend to snigger when you ask if they've read them; and the money is negligible. The biggest advance he received for any of his first eleven novels was £7,500. He changed publishers for *The Maid of Buttermere* and upped it to £20,000, but still, it is peanuts compared to what he can earn from television or any other form of writing. His biography of Richard Burton, *Rich*, earned huge royalties and became an international bestseller, but that was a special case (and an excellent book).

So why does he write? 'I don't know. Since I was twenty I've been writing fiction and I just can't imagine not. I like writing. I don't mean that I always like what I write – I'd like to be better at it – but I like the *activity* of writing. I like being on my own and making things up.' On the other hand, he admits that he went through a bad patch in the seventies when 'I wrote too much and it wasn't as good as I would like it to have been. In the seventies I was so knocked sideways one way and another that writing became a great relief, a consolation – just like when I was a teenager, being on my own and working in my own room, it helped. Unfortunately I published – I don't want to say I regret writing those books because I'm not ashamed of them, but I didn't progress at all, in fact I may have gone backwards. And I was so locked into myself that I missed things that were going on. I didn't understand properly, say, the feminist movement – I mean I was blocking too much out and that is maybe why the books are static or even regressive.'

The trauma of the seventies was his first wife's mental illness and eventual suicide. He met Lisa Roche while he was an undergraduate, reading history at Oxford; she was the daughter of the director of the Sorbonne. According to a friend, she was 'beautiful, intelligent and slightly frightening'. He married her as soon as he graduated in 1961, when he was twenty-one and just setting out on a BBC traineeship. Almost immediately, 'something happened that I just couldn't understand' and her parents revealed that she had suffered mental illness. She also suffered from severe asthma and, later, back problems, and 'I just became a nurse. There were moments which were wonderful, just marvellous, but there was this . . . business . . . going on, and after a while I couldn't take it. I began to go down and down, just trying to survive.'

Mistakenly, in retrospect, he gave up his graduate traineeship at the BBC so that he could stay at home and look after Lisa and write novels. But being cooped up in a small house in Kew, with few outside distractions, they dragged each other down. Lisa had psychoanalysis and her analyst suggested Melvyn should have it, too – he resisted the idea for a long time, but eventually started. Then Lisa committed suicide in 1971, and he stopped. He is awkward talking about this, wanting to protect his daughter by that marriage, twenty-four-year-old Marie-Elsa; it is a tragedy that casts a long shadow over his life.

He married Cate Haste in 1973, started a new family (Alice and Tom, now twelve and ten) and attained a new happiness. He also went back into television, starting the much admired paperback-book programme *Read All About It* and then *The South Bank Show*. Christopher Booker once said that Melvyn Bragg was made for television; and so indeed he seems. He has the requisite common touch; he is a genuine popularizer; he is good-looking whether he worries about it or not; he has just enough of a regional accent for credibility, without being incomprehensible. And he *likes* television; he likes the teamwork, the gregariousness. He told me: 'Actually I found arriving at the BBC [as a graduate trainee straight from Oxford in 1961] was like arriving home. Certain aspects of Oxford I'd enjoyed a lot, but almost after ten minutes at the BBC I thought: "This is terrific." It was a job I knew I wanted to do.'

But even so, even while forging an ambitious and successful career in television, he persisted in writing novels, and he believes his 1987 novel, *The Maid of Buttermere*, marked a turning-point: 'In the eighties something started to open up, and I felt tremendously released in *The Maid of Buttermere* – perhaps because of the disguise, the camouflage of an historical setting. It enabled me to let loose in a way that I hadn't been able to before. I think there was some kind of progression.' It is interesting that he talks about the need for camouflage, disguise; it fits in with what Nick Elliott says about his exterior wall.

His friend Phillip Whitehead, the former MP, once complained that 'his novels have yet to distil the more profound experiences of his own life', but in *The Maid of Buttermere* he was able to talk about some of his own feelings, and especially his teenage angst. An only child, he grew up in Wigton, Cumbria, where his parents kept a pub; he still goes back there often and has many friends in the town. On the face of it, his childhood was happy and successful: he went to grammar school and eventually won a scholarship to Oxford. But he was unhappy as a teenager. 'There was a time between the age of thirteen and fifteen or sixteen when I had a sort of nervous breakdown, unacknowledged by myself or anyone else. It was a particular sort of private, locked-in desperation, and the next time I encountered it was about fifteen years later [when his wife committed suicide] and I never want to go through it again. It wasn't depression, it was *fear*: it was something that scared the living daylights out of me, and I'm still nervous sometimes that it will come back. I had these out-of-body experiences where something would slip out of my head and go up into the corner of the room – it sounds ridiculous but this is as accurate as I can make it – and hover there, and I knew that that was *me*. And unless I stayed absolutely still, it would go away – *I* would go away. It scared me to an extent I can't tell you. And it began to happen an awful lot, I mean night after night for two or three years. I didn't know what to do about it – I couldn't tell anybody because I just couldn't.'

The only thing that cured it, or kept the fear at bay, was doing things, and it was at this period that he established the habit of relentless busyness that is still such a feature of his life. 'You become very refined at trying to find strategies to stop it happening – you make yourself very tired so that you go to sleep right away, you find certain noises that will stop you thinking it could happen – because if you were at home and you started thinking it might happen, it *would* happen.

Praying a lot, if you want to know the truth, because I was a very keen churchgoer in those days. But the main thing was just to keep *doing* a lot of things – schoolwork, acting, choir, sports, anything, so that activities blocked out this . . . *panic*, really. It was quite disturbing being brought up over a pub, especially at weekends, with all the sounds, sometimes violence. I don't want to exaggerate the violence, but it could be quite rough, now and then. And although I didn't like it, there was also a sort of excitement, so that was disturbing as well. It was as if I had two parallel lives – almost like a Thermos, the inside and the outside. On the outside, I had a very cheerful time, I did lots of things and had friends and went to dances and played rugby and worked hard at school and did acting; but on the inside, you'd go to bed and this thing would just slip, or you'd look in the mirror and it would slip, and you'd actually think, "How can I put myself together again?" '

He described this sensation in *The Maid of Buttermere* because, he said, it helped to explain how the hero, Hatfield, became 'such an impersonator – it enabled him to have this split'. But in fact – although he seems to have forgotten it – the theme is also present in his first novel, *For Want of a Nail*, published when he was twenty-five. The novel describes a boy, Tom, growing up in Cumbria; we first meet him when he is ten and follow him through to eighteen, when he leaves home to go to Oxford. The prevailing impression of the early childhood is one of fear; the boy is aware of tension between his parents; his relationship with his father is happy and uncomplicated, but his father is weak; his mother is more problematic. Tom adores her (she is very beautiful, far more beautiful than other boys' mothers), but she is ungiving: 'She was a blackness which smothered him whenever she wished, and an enigma in whom he could discover and confirm nothing.' She never tells her son anything, never kisses him; she seems permanently angry, burning with a bitter resentment. Gradually, as the boy grows older and picks up hints here and there, he realizes that his mother is unfaithful and that his father is not his father. He survives the trauma of this revelation by burying himself in religion and then schoolwork, but at tremendous cost to his psyche: 'He had eaten away his own guts in an attempt to preserve he knew not what. For he had no aim. He could ride on whatever impulse or circumstance presented itself . . . but he would do all this in no other capacity than that of a man who clings to activity to hide his own stagnation from himself and others. The world was a husk – and he had eaten its kernel.' He has achieved sanity, but only by means of constant denial and self-control: 'He saw how straitened his feelings and attitudes were. He knew that many things affected and moved him which he could not acknowledge, for fear of their consequences. He wanted nothing to be dependent on that which he could not control.'

His present novel, written twenty-five years later, deals with what happens when control slips. The hero is, on the face of it, a careful diligent, respectable, uxorious bank manager, but inwardly seething with passion for an eighteen-year-old girl. Bragg claims not to know where the idea came from, but 'I remember being unnerved by *The Blue Angel* many years ago – the idea of the German professor, the perfectly controlled man, polite and precise, becoming completely intoxicated by this nightclub singer, so that he is utterly humiliated by her and ends up on stage crowing like a cock. What interested me was the idea of someone who was totally controlled being taken over by something that destroyed his self-control in every way – that obviously stuck with me in some way.'

Is this how Bragg sees himself? As someone who has constructed a totally artificial personality, a fragile and immaculate shell which is constantly endangered by the almost uncontrollable passions within? Or his own image of the Thermos: the cool outside, the heat inside? Does he see himself as an impostor and fear that one day people will 'see through him' and be shocked? In his novels he keeps offering little glimpses of his real self, but in interviews he stresses that 'the novels are *fiction*, I make things *up*'. Of course he does, but one nevertheless feels that he is writing from some private compulsion which is not strictly literary.

It may seem unfair to go on about Melvyn Bragg having written a bad novel, and if *A Time to Dance* were the only book of his I'd read, I wouldn't persist. But *For Want of a Nail* was a revelation. It is an *extremely* good novel; critics at the time compared it to D. H. Lawrence and Hardy and even now, twenty-five years later, those comparisons stand. No *wonder* the Melvyn Bragg who wrote that book took himself seriously as a novelist: he was absolutely right to do so. So the question is not exactly why does Melvyn Bragg bother to write novels but why, having once been so good a writer, is he now so bad?

Obviously, the answer is television, and simply time. His friend Phillip Whitehead pinpointed the difficulty ten years ago, when he said, 'Personally, I don't think he can write decent books by jotting down chapter headings on a transatlantic jet.' He worked five years on *For Want of a Nail*; he wrote *A Time to Dance* 'in convulsions' over nine months, whenever he could clear his diary for a few days.

As late as 1980, Melvyn Bragg was still describing himself as 'a novelist who makes television programmes'. Nowadays he describes himself as 'a novelist and broadcaster' and no doubt in time he will admit what is already the truth: that he is a broadcaster who also writes novels in his spare time. Why should we condemn him for that? His contributions to radio and television are valuable and popular: it is snobbish to argue that it is *necessarily* better to write novels than to make television programmes. But having read *For Want of a Nail*, I can only mourn a great novelist lost. And I suspect that, in his heart of hearts, Melvyn Bragg does too.

Reproduced by permission of the *Independent on Sunday*

ROALD DAHL

24 September 1989

Will he be a BFG – a Big Friendly Giant – or a fee-fi-fo-fum one? Roald Dahl is certainly a giant – six foot six tall, with legs like tree trunks. But it is hard, at first, to discover whether he is friendly. One *hopes* his bark is worse than his bite, because his bark is jolly alarming.

'You're wrong!' he shouts, if you dare to disagree with him. 'You're absolutely wrong and I am right. Do you understand now? I am right and you are *wrong*.' At one heart-stopping moment I muddled up the characters in two of his books, and his snort of scorn echoed round the house. 'Hurrumph! Not very clued up, are you? Not very *with it*.'

We are in a magical, low-beamed house on the side of a hill in Buckinghamshire, where he has lived for the past forty years. Inside are treasures – paintings by Francis Bacon and Matthew Smith and Malevich – and wonderful antique furniture, but the effect is modest, not grand.

I found him in the kitchen with his secretary, Wendy. He gets hundreds of letters from children every week and replies to them all, often with a poem. Today he is replying to a junior-school class:

My teacher wasn't half as nice
As yours seems to be.

His name was Mr Unsworth,
And he taught us history.
And when you didn't know a date
He'd get you by the ear
And start to twist, while there
you sat
Quite paralysed with fear.
He'd twist and twist your ear
And twist it more and more
Until at last the ear came off
And landed on the floor . . .

'There,' he tells Wendy, 'and start the letter "Hello, Gorgeous." The teacher's probably some middle-aged woman with a bun, so I like to think of her reading that out to the class. Ha!'

Then he turns to me and asks, 'Got children, have you? Good. Names? Ages? Read, do they? Read me? Good.' Of course my children read Roald Dahl. Is there any child in the country who doesn't? His latest book, *Matilda*, sold 160,000 in hardback in the UK alone, and when *Charlie and the Chocolate Factory* was published in China, it had an initial print run of two million – possibly the biggest printing of any book ever. Moreover, although he is now seventy-two, Dahl seems to be becoming more, not less, prolific. Three of his very best books, *The Witches*, *The BFG* and *Boy*, were written in a great burst of genius in his late sixties.

However, I must confess to some qualms about *Matilda*, which goes into paperback this week. Matilda, the heroine, is a nasty little prig who despises her mother for having bleached blonde hair and playing bingo. She is, in short, a snob. But will I have the courage to say this to Dahl and risk provoking an outburst? Deep breath. Here goes . . .

'Rubbish! Absolute tosh. Matilda isn't snobbish at all. Her mother is just a boring, foul woman. You don't understand that, in writing for children, you have to exaggerate a million times in order to ram the point home. *I* understand, which is

why, if I may say so, I am a *very* successful children's writer.
Why else do you think *Matilda* sold 160,000? Children
absolutely love it. No. You are simply wrong. So snubs to
you.'

That seems to be that, but Dahl keeps on returning to the
theme, like a dog with a bone. When his daughter Ophelia
comes into the room, he tells her, 'D'you know, this woman
has the nerve to say there's snobbism in *Matilda*. Never
heard such balls in my life.' Ophelia looks understandably
nervous.

'The trouble is people *look* for bad things in his books,' she
explains quietly. 'Sexism, or racism, or snobbery or whatever.
And of course I can see what they mean. But you must
understand he's from a completely different era. He doesn't
intend it.'

Dahl himself is quite happy shouting at me and, once I get
the hang of it, I am quite happy too. I feel like a child being
cheeky to a schoolteacher; exhilarated at plucking up the
courage to be rude – then waiting for the explosions. Ophelia,
hovering in the background, is clearly upset. 'You really
mustn't think he is arrogant,' she tells me. 'He is one of the
most humble people I know. Really.'

Really? His ex-wife, Patricia Neal, said in her autobiography that he believed life was a two-way street – in which he
had right of way. That seems pretty accurate. 'It's true I don't
suffer fools gladly,' he concedes, 'and that is a fault. A big
fault. But nowadays I'm always admitting I'm wrong.'
(Really?) 'Couldn't do it at thirty, even at forty. But when
you're as old as me you get to this sort of plateau where you
don't have that awful pride and conceit, and it's lovely.'

In truth, Roald Dahl is a very kind man (he does an
enormous amount for charity on the quiet) but he doesn't
realize quite how intimidating and overbearing he appears. It
is hard to have an adult conversation with him because any
hint of disagreement is his cue to start shouting, and soon
there is a table-thumping crescendo of 'I'm right and you're
wrong.' So it is easier to approach him as a child would a

crusty old eccentric schoolteacher, which is amusing, if rather limiting.

He used to write for adults (his *Tales of the Unexpected* have recently been revived on television) but it is unlikely that his adult stories will be remembered as his children's books most certainly will. He says he loves children because they are 'sexually innocent'. He knows that children are cruel, but then adults are, too, and less forgivably so. 'Your average human being is really a very revolting creature.'

He has said, many times, that his books have no moral. He isn't trying to preach to children, but only to seduce them into reading by giving them jokes and terrors and excitement to keep them on the edge of their seat from page to page. And of course, in that, he's been astonishingly successful.

But his books, even if they have no moral, do have a constant theme, which is revenge – the revenge of a child against the wicked adults who oppress him.

'I *know* what it was bloody well like being a child,' he insists, 'and most people, even the mothers, have forgotten. You're surrounded by all these giants and the giants, basically, are your enemies. Even if they're your parents and you love them. Because they're trying to force you to do things you don't want to do. You want to eat with your fingers, but they force you to eat with a spoon. Children very much resent these giants giving orders, so if I take the mickey out of them, children love it.'

Like all the best children's writers, Dahl would seem to have some pretty murky corners in his psychic cupboard. His childhood autobiography, *Boy*, recounts at excessive length the beatings he received at school. The headmaster who administered them, Cosmo Lang, went on to become Archbishop of Canterbury, and Dahl claims he lost whatever Christian faith he might have had as a result.

His father died when he was three, and he was brought up by his Norwegian mother in England, wrote to her every week when he was away and lived with her until he married at thirty-eight. His second volume of autobiography, *Going*

Solo, on his wartime exploits, finishes with him rushing back
to his mother's arms.

As an adult he suffered far more than his fair share of
tragedies. His only son, Theo, was injured as a baby and left
permanently brain-damaged. Then his eldest daughter, Olivia,
died of measles. And his beautiful film-star wife, Patricia
Neal, suffered a series of strokes. He bullied her back to
health but then suddenly left her for another woman, Felicity,
known as 'Liccy', about eight years ago.

Patricia Neal published an autobiography last year which
must have hurt him dreadfully, revealing the most intimate
secrets of their marriage. 'I won't talk about it. She's a good
woman and I saved her life and all the rest of it, and she
didn't have any right to write a book like that. But I'll refrain
from comment. Better. More dignified.'

His daughter, Tessa, also published a book last year which
must have rankled. Ostensibly a novel, *Working for Love*
recounts all the family tragedies and the marriage break-up,
with Dahl very much the villain.

Ophelia, it seems, is the 'good' daughter: the one who stays at
home when strangers are coming, to keep him sweet. She shares
his addiction to gambling, and takes him off to the Curzon
Club two or three nights a week to play blackjack. 'Of course,
she always loses, whereas I always win,' he explains. Of course.

We adjourn for lunch in the garden, where an array of
exquisite salads awaits us under the vine trellis. It is all very
elegant – until we come to pudding. Pudding is a Tupperware
box full of chocolate bars.

'Help yourself. There's Twix, Crunchie, Mars, Maltesers,
KitKat – which do you like? These are the great chocolate
classics, and most of them were invented in the thirties.

'That was an astonishing period, rather like the Italian
Renaissance. John Forrest Mars was the Leonardo. His father
had a little chocolate factory in Chicago and invented Milky
Way, but he told his son, "There's no room here for both of
us", so John went off to England.

'He experimented with putting soft toffee on the Milky Way and then chocolate on top of that. Jolly difficult to make it stick. Cadbury's tried with the Curly Wurly and failed. But John Forrest Mars got the chocolate to stick to the caramel and so invented the Mars Bar. Tremendous breakthrough! Marvellous! And then three years later, in 1935, he got a bit of malted dough, exploded it inside a vacuum and created the Malteser! He called the thing Energy Balls at first but everyone laughed like hell.'

He knows all about chocolates, he says, 'because I love them. Simple as that.' In his study, he keeps a silver ball, the size of a tennis ball but twenty times as heavy, made by packing together all the silver paper from all the bars of chocolate he ate as a young man. And then, in his fifties, he wrote out his childhood fantasy of having all the chocolate he could ever possibly want, in *Charlie and the Chocolate Factory*.

Extraordinary, in view of this addiction, that he is so thin. But he has a thing about fat people. Patricia Neal claims that his first words to her, ever, were 'I'd rather be dead than fat, wouldn't you?' He drinks hefty quantities of gin and smokes, but – despite a whole string of spine operations and hip replacements, and a stomach operation that almost killed him – he looks remarkably fit.

After lunch, Ophelia takes me to see his hut, a horribly comfortless, nicotine-stained shack in the garden, where he has written all his books. There are photographs of his children and their mother, and a table of mementoes – the silver chocolate-paper ball, and his two arthritic hip bones, his various slipped discs and a motto from Degas: 'Art is a lie to which one gives the accent of truth.'

Ophelia shows me the writing board and the yellow notebooks, and the sleeping-bag he puts his feet in when it is cold. It seems creepy, looking round this private holy of holies without its occupant, as if Dahl himself is already dead and this is a museum exhibit.

'You will be kind about him, won't you?' she asks. 'He

really *is* a good man.' I'd go much further – he is a truly great man, and I'll be boasting to my grandchildren in years to come that I met Roald Dahl.

Why hasn't he been honoured – knighted at the very least? I think a grateful nation should be beating a path to his door. Great children's writers are very rare – the fact that he's also a difficult bugger is neither here nor there . . .

Reproduced by permission of the *Sunday Express*

KIRK DOUGLAS
14 October 1990

Let us assume that we are members of the Indipi tribe
and our traditional grazing lands are being devastated by a
giant armadillo. The armadillo does not intend any harm but
it goes trampling round very slowly, flattening all our crops,
and we will starve if we don't kill it. Our only weapons are
our little blowpipes, and it is a *very* large armadillo. So all we
can do is lie in the long grass and wait for the armadillo to
trundle past and fire our darts and hope that one day one of
them will land in the interstices between the armadillo's body-
plates and kill it. But gosh, it is a long, boring wait, here on
the hot savannah. It takes hours for the armadillo even to
come within firing range, and then invariably the darts bounce
off its thick armour, which means lying around for several
more hours till it comes within range again. This is by way of
explaining what it feels like to interview Kirk Douglas.

It isn't as if he's particularly, preternaturally boring. I mean
probably by the standards of veteran Hollywood stars, he's
in the upper percentile of interest. It is just that he suffers
from anecdotage, the terrible brain rot that overcomes elderly
people who have spent a large portion of their lives on chat
shows. When you ask him a question he quickly scans it for a
cue word, feeds the cue word into his memory files, and then,

zap, brings out an anecdote that has the cue word in it. Being an actor, he of course delivers his anecdote with every possible nuance of expression, animation, funny voices, gestures, pauses for suspense, which makes it take about an hour longer than it's worth. And as the armadillo lumbers off into the distance, you can only whimper, *But that wasn't the question, Kirk.* He shrugs impatiently. Questions, she wants, questions, you think at my age I should waste my time answering questions? Look, I'm giving you material. Johnny Carson loved it. Questions already!

We are having lunch together at the Berkeley Hotel, so that he can plug his new novel, *Dance with the Devil.* He is already hoarse, having been up since dawn spouting the same hoary anecdotes to breakfast television, breakfast radio, trade press, foreign press, women's magazines, national newspapers. Later, I will watch him on Wogan and watch him on Hunniford, and there will be whole chunks I can recite from memory. Gloria Hunniford cosied him and made out she found him irresistibly attractive, which was more than I could bring myself to do – my admiration for her grows by the week. Wogan as usual revealed his frolicsome refusal to do any homework whatsoever, and seemed to think Kirk had written a novel about Hollywood. Oh I don't *want* to be blasé! Believe me, I do appreciate how incredibly lucky I am to have my job and to be able to meet interesting people and ask them nosy questions, but there is a downside too and this is it.

Now he's started on the What John Wayne said to me about playing Van Gogh story. I'll just lie here in the long grass and have a little zzz till it's over ... 'Wayne said: "Christ, Kirk! How can you play a part like that? There's so goddam few of us left. We got to play strong, tough characters. Not those weak queers." So *I* said, "Hey, John, I'm an actor. I like to play interesting roles. It's all make-believe. You're not really John Wayne, you know." '

... Zzz, where was I? Oh yes, sitting opposite Kirk

Douglas. I suppose he looks all right if your tastes happen to run to septuagenarians with blow-waves and funny stretch-marks round the ears. Like many film stars, he is weirdly proportioned – huge head, quarterback's shoulders, dainty waist, tiny hips, bandy legs and almost invisible little twinkle toes. Anyway, he 'keeps in shape' as he puts it, telling me about ninety times that he always walks up and down to his fifth-floor suite instead of taking the lift, and that at home he works out in a gym for fifteen minutes every day. And of course he is on a diet, which means that we are doomed to sit in one of the best restaurants in London picking at salads. (Later, out of sheer malice, I recommend the bread-and-butter pudding. 'What's it made of?' he asks me.[!] 'Currants,' I tell him. He eats it, looking surprised.) He is famously vain, with a penchant for baring his chest at every possible opportunity, though I am spared. These days he admits to his age (seventy-four) and has let his hair go white, but for years he dyed it. 'I used to lie about my age so much I got confused because I had to take a few years off of Michael's age and Joel's age. And then when Michael got famous, for godssake, and started telling people how old he was, everyone said, "But Kirk said you were twenty-nine." Jeez, I'm not that good at arithmetic and it got so complicated.'

He still thinks of himself as an actor first and foremost, and embarks on the plot of a new film he is making called *Veraz*. 'It's more of a romantic thing about this guy who falls in love with this girl and through her love he learns to love what she loves – the trees, the animals, the forest . . .'

Zzz . . . Why am I here? Now there's a question. Guilt says I'm here because I was lazy one day and said 'Yes' to a PR who phoned and now I am being punished. But that's unfair because I wanted to meet him ever since I read his autobiography, *The Ragman's Son*. It's a good book – a rags-to-riches story, but well told, about his parents' escape from the ghettos of Russia to the slums of America, and his gruellingly poor childhood in Albany, New York State, where his father worked as a rag-picker and his mother – who never learned to read and write – struggled to bring up her one son and six daughters. Kirk was unofficially adopted by a schoolmistress – who also seduced him – and he worked his way through college and was the first Jew ever to be elected students' leader. Then he managed to get into drama school – again working at nights to pay for his keep – and finally Hollywood, where, as he would put it, 'the rest is history'.

In case it isn't, I should gloss: he is one of those actors who has made a lot of films but few good ones. In his early days he specialized in loincloth parts (*Spartacus, The Vikings*) and was always baring his well-oiled biceps and rowing somewhere in a galley under the lash of a black slave master, presumably for the delectation of closet queens with mild s-m predilections. Later, he made some good films, especially *Paths of Glory* and his own favourite, *Lonely are the Brave*; he is also proud of his portrayal of Van Gogh in *Lust for Life*. He became an independent producer, long before it was normal for actors to do so, and struggled unsuccessfully for years to make *One Flew Over the Cuckoo's Nest*. His son Michael eventually produced it – and cast Jack Nicholson in the part Kirk had set his heart on. His relationship with Michael Douglas, the eldest of his four sons, is a bit of a Kingsley-and-Martin-Amis one, alternately envious and proud. Michael has already won two Oscars to Kirk's none, and the latter ruefully recognizes that to the younger generation his main claim to fame is that he is Michael Douglas's father.

Kirk, of course, was not born Kirk; he was born Issur Danielovitch, and I find it interesting that he should have chosen a stage name meaning a Christian church. The hero of *Dance with the Devil* refuses to admit he is Jewish, and actually spouts anti-Semitic remarks to put people off the scent, but even he doesn't go so far as to call himself Kirk. Kirk himself says that 'the only advantage I have found to being Jewish is that I can be openly anti-Semitic'. He has never gone to synagogue but nowadays, he says, 'I've become more aware of the heritage of being a Jew.' In fact, his speech rhythms are so entirely Jewish he must be a better actor than one suspected to have played so many gentiles.

Dance with the Devil is his first novel (though he is already at work on a second, and under contract for a third), and it is by no means bad. On the face of it, it's the predictable sex 'n' violence airport tome, laced with forays into paedophilia, incest, troilism and homosexuality. The hero, Danny, bears an uncanny resemblance to Kirk Douglas, and there's the nail-biting suspense of will he/won't he get to sleep with the mother and daughter both, and will he/won't he dare to go to bed with a boy. (No and yes, respectively.) The homosexual scene is a real surprise and Kirk says he's taken a lot of stick for it. 'But you know what? I'm always surprised when a *man* is too shocked by that scene. For instance, if I were a young man sent to prison for twenty years, no women around and a nice young pretty boy comes in . . . Yeah, I can imagine that. I think that's normal, not abnormal. People says, "So did it happen to you, Kirk?" and I say, "Well if it did, you'd be the last to know." And after all, the book is fiction. Not everything is based on fact.'

But underlying all the sexual shenanigans, the novel also contains a very interesting theme about – don't snigger – Art. The hero falls in love with movies as a child and eventually struggles out of the gutter to become a film director. But the films he makes, though successful, are rubbish, and he knows it. He dreams of making a serious film, an 'art' film, and eventually, after many sexual vicissitudes, does so. But it is a flop. Why? Because he is still 'living a lie', denying his Jewish birth. Now this is a valuable idea, about how creativity has to be rooted in honesty and self-knowledge, and next time the armadillo lumbers into range from one of his anecdotal excursions, I raise it. This time he hears the question. 'You know what? I wrote a goddamn good novel. Because if I were just a hack writer, I'd have made that movie a success. But I didn't try to just be slick, I tried to *deal* with some issues.'

At this point a group of perfectly ordinary businessmen come

into the restaurant and Kirk is distracted: 'Jeez! This looks like
such a distinguished group of people! I tell you this is a really
classy place!' What on earth . . .? It turns out he is waiting for
them to recognize him and eventually they do, much to his
gratification, but meanwhile his ideas on art and truth have
reminded him of another anecdote. Back to the long grass.

How about a full frontal attack? Why don't I just run straight
up to the armadillo and stick a dart in his face? Mid-anecdote
and à *propos* of nothing, I do it. 'How would you feel, Kirk, if
one of your sons told you he was gay?' His surprise at the
question is absolutely nothing compared to my surprise at the
answer: 'I would love him like any of my sons. I think sexuality
and religion are personal property. I could never reject him.
People who feel that way don't love their children.'

Well, at least now I have his attention. Let us deal with the
question of his notoriously Neanderthal attitude to women.
In *The Ragman's Son* he recounts how, when he left home to
go to college, his mother said to him, in Yiddish, 'A boy is a
boy, but a girl is *drek* [shit].' This was a mother of six
daughters. No *wonder* he has a funny attitude to women. He
says even he was shocked by her words. 'But I myself don't
feel that way. You see, people have no conception of my
attitude to women. I *like* women. Women have always played
an important part in my life. I've always liked capable women.
I've always liked intelligent women. I have never met an
intelligent woman who wasn't sexy – because sex takes
imagination. I like capable women and my wife, Anne, is very
capable. She's the *president* of my company. When we take a
whole group of people out to dinner and the cheque comes,
my wife takes care of it. She takes care of all my business
affairs. She's *better* at it than I. But she didn't write my books,
she didn't choose the scripts to make into movies, she didn't
teach me about acting. And most of the time she's not very
generous in her praise of what I do. But I admire what she
does. I'm not stoopid.'

And yet in his autobiography he recounts an occasion when
he was filming abroad and a woman rang his hotel suite and

described herself and he went haring round to her flat – a woman he hadn't even *seen* . . . 'Yeah, but you forget how much older I am than you. Of course anyone who did that now would be *crazy* but I'm talking about a time when no one had even heard of Aids. And you see, my weakness was always I was swept away – it's snowing, her voice is low, Tchaikovsky's music is playing in the background. It's a *romantic* interlude. I mean, yeah, I'm guilty of those things.'

Was he married at the time? 'I might have been. I might not have been. I'm not *talking* about that aspect of it. Hey listen. I've been married thirty-six years and Anne my wife is very happy. And if anyone who's been married thirty-six years – especially a man who's been around a lot – tells me that he hasn't strayed somewhere along the line, I don't believe him. These things happen.'

'So maybe your wife is even at this moment up in your suite taking a phone call from an unknown man with a deep voice, Tchaikovsky playing, and preparing to . . .'

'Why do you have to ask these difficult questions? For godssakes, Lynn, why can't you just be a nice girl and ask nice questions and we can have a nice lunch and you can have a nice interview? Because there's a double standard, dummy. And I'll tell you *why* there's a double standard. Because women, basically, equate sex with emotion. A man is able to have a sexual diversion without an emotional attachment, but, generally speaking, for a woman that's more difficult. See? Now don't keep asking me such tough questions.'

He must know a *bit* about women because he grew up with six sisters. What happened to them? He hardly mentions them in his autobiography, and never in interviews. Does he still see them? 'I love my sisters, but I'm not close to them, not *very* close, because their affection is overwhelming. But a couple of months ago I went down to Albany and had a whole bunch of them in. They wanted to bring all their in-laws but I said, "No. Just my sisters and their husbands. I don't even want to see their kids." All those nieces and nephews, too goddamn many of them – it's a mob, how can you deal with it? See, why I love my sisters and why I feel grateful to them, the same way I felt grateful to my mother, is: they let me go. They could easily have said, "Hey, you're the only man in the house. We need you here." But they let me go. This is the greatest love, not the selfish love but someone who loves you so much that they're willing to let go because that is best for *you*. Real love means being concerned for the spiritual growth of that person.'

The great theme of his autobiography is his rage and resentment against his father, who never gave him the love and comradeship he craved. He grew up in a house full of women, and the one other male he *should* have identified with was off in the boozer with his mates ignoring him – hence no doubt his need to be so tiresomely virile. Kirk never forgave his father, even when he was dying. He went to see him on his deathbed but only to tell him he couldn't stay, he was a busy man. It is this anger, this seething quality, that has always distinguished Kirk Douglas as an actor, and that gives his autobiography its savour. He says even he was surprised, when he reread the book, to find just how angry he was.

I used the word resentment, but Kirk said that what he felt for his father was 'never resentment; just a *hunger* for some kind of contact. If they ever made a movie of *The Ragman's Son*, to me the most poignant scene would be the son, the successful movie star, going to the saloon to see his father. "Hi pa. You know I made a movie?" "Yep." "Did you see it, pa?" "Yep." "Did you like it?" "Yep." And the son goes out destroyed. Because he didn't get the pat on the back from his father, that's all. It would even make me angry when people would say, "Kirk, you know your father was so *proud* of you," and I'd say, "Yeah? He never said that to *me*. Cut it out." But if they *were* doing a movie of it, I would want to play my father. Because I feel that now, having vented my anger, my weakness, my desperate need to get a pat on the back, I would like to show why he was incapable of giving the son that he loved – because I know he loved me – why he could never say it.'

And will one of his sons one day write an autobiography saying how they suffered from this terrible dominating father who was such a hard man he could never show his love? 'Let me tell you. I have several times said to Michael: you ought to start writing your autobiography now. I'd like to read it. And it's a catharsis. Because I'm *cured*. And from the point of view of my kids, yes, they might have grievances against me. I think that's very possible. And I'd like to be alive to see it. You know, to be a parent is a terribly difficult thing. And to be a so-called movie star parent is incredibly difficult. Now I have four sons and the test is: do they function? Yes they do, so I must have done *something* right.' (All four sons are in movies – Joel runs the studio which Michael owns in Nice; Peter is scriptwriter; and Eric, the youngest, is an actor – 'he's the most mercurial, the one who drives me crazy because he's most like me, very complicated.')

Kirk has stopped being an anecdotal armadillo and has become rather a likeable human being, eager to talk about his sons and their successes. He shows a most unactorish interest in the outside world, talking about politics and the media, the way fiction and reality seem to be becoming blurred so that news stories are often hyped like novels. But then he folds his napkin and says firmly, 'Now I don't want you beginning to think I'm an intellectual. You're going to destroy my image. I don't want *that*.'

What's so great about his image? Crummy old sexist dinosaur, why doesn't he jettison the boring thing and start talking sense? He *does* talk sense when he lets himself. Once he drops all the chat-show blether, he's intelligent, observant, goodhearted, a proper Jewish paterfamilias. But for interview purposes he prefers to present a Neanderthal face and swagger around in his boring old loincloth. Why? 'Well, I tell you, Lynn, the one thing I hate, more than anything in the world, is pretension. I would rather bore my ass off than be in something pretentious, whether it's a book or a movie.' A pity, say I.

Reproduced by permission of the *Independent on Sunday*

PRINCE EDWARD

22 November 1987

Funny feeling, doing a Royal interview in a publisher's office. I wish it could be in the Palace. The interview is set for 10 a.m. but, of course, I am there at 9.30, biting my nails, and photographer Tim Graham is already setting up his lights. Tim photographed Prince Edward for his eighteenth birthday and again for his twenty-first, so he knows the form. 'Call him Your Royal Highness the first time,' he tells me, 'and Sir thereafter. He's very nice . . . you'll find him easy to talk to.'

A tall, distinguished-looking man comes in to say hello – an equerry, Lord Chamberlain or something? No, it's the Prince's detective. He seems satisfied that I haven't got a bomb in my handbag and he drifts off again. Ten o'clock comes and goes, 10.10, 10.15 – whatever happened to the politeness of princes, I wonder?

At 10.20 the door opens and there he is – *far* handsomer than I expected, with beautiful long-lashed eyes. Most press photographs hitherto have shown him in silly costumes doing amateur theatricals: in a suit he looks fine. The only obviously royal bit is the gold E signet ring on his little finger, and the fact that he is about a million times better tailored than your average twenty-three-year-old. He sits behind the office desk and starts talking about the book: *Knockout, the Grand Charity Tournament* (Collins).

'We thought a lot of people would probably like a record of the event and I tried to give as much help as I possibly could, both by filling in some of the background, and also setting the right sort of tone. We wanted it to be lighthearted and, you know, enjoyable. I hope you read it?'

Read it? I practically memorized it. It is not a bad book at all, a running narrative of the Royal Knockout contest held in June this year, with contributions by many of the participants. The introductory chapter by Prince Edward shows real writing talent. I asked him whether he used a word processor – 'No, I used a very ancient form of technology called a pen.'

He explained, at rather inordinate length, about how the proceeds from the book would go to make up the million pounds that the Royal Knockout raised for four charities: the Save the Children Fund, World Wildlife Fund, the Duke of Edinburgh's Award International Project and International Year of Shelter for the Homeless. These charities received £450,000 within three weeks of the event, and will have received the full million by the end of the year. He said they were printing 10,000 copies of the *Knockout* book and 'We'd be over the moon if we sold all 10,000.'

Then he added, engagingly, 'I must confess, as it's my first connection with the publishing world, I've no idea whether 10,000 is an enormous number or not. Is it?' I said I thought it was a moderately enormous number (actually it is quite small) and he seemed content with this.

From the book, the Knockout contest all sounds like a jolly romp, but of course it required an extraordinarily complex degree of planning and organization. Prince Edward, as overall producer, had the sticky task of phoning round all the international showbiz and sporting celebrities, asking them to take part. Nobody actually *said* they didn't believe him, 'but you knew damn well that every alarm bell was ringing. And it *is* very difficult to convince people who you are.'

Since many of the stars they wanted were in America,

Prince Edward and his assistants regularly worked till nine or
ten at night, making transatlantic phone calls. How, I asked,
did he get all the celebrities' phone numbers? 'I'm not telling
you *that!*' he laughed. 'I'm not going to give away trade
secrets!'

This was the first of several occasions in the course of the
interview when he refused to answer a question, and I must
say he did it very charmingly each time. Many people resort
to waffle or bluster, but the Prince simply smiled and shook
his head.

For instance, me: 'Do you know what you'll be doing in
1988?'

Prince Edward (with grin): 'Yes.'

Me: 'A job prospect?'

(Broad grin, silence.)

'You're not saying?'

Prince Edward: 'I'm not saying, no. I'll only say when I am
ready to say it.'

I thought sometimes that he was being over-cautious in his
answers, looking for potential pitfalls that weren't really
there. But there was one eye-opening moment which made
me realize just how cautious he is trained to be. The Prince
was talking to me, while Tim Graham was photographing
him over my shoulder. Suddenly the Prince broke off mid-
sentence, and said, 'Hey, I suddenly thought – what books
are there in the background? Because last time I did photographs like this was at Cambridge, in the library, and I
realized afterwards that there were rows of books on Nazism
and the rise of Hitler in the background.'

So then we all stopped and carefully scanned the bookshelves behind Prince Edward's chair, and agreed that they
were harmless. But I suppose we *could* have caused a scandal
if Collins' office bookshelves had happened to be stocked
with National Front tracts.

While Tim clicked away, the Prince confided, 'Funnily
enough, I find a stills camera much more intrusive than a
television camera.'

'Yes,' said Tim (click), 'because it makes a noise' (click).

'I remember so vividly at Badminton,' said the Prince, 'and at the Montreal Olympics, when Princess Anne was showjumping. Every time she came to a jump, the clatter of cameras went round the entire stadium.' For a twelve-year-old boy, as he was then, anxiously watching his favourite sibling compete, it must have been frightening. He must have hated the cameramen.

The Prince seemed happy reminiscing about Knockout and the weeks of planning that went into it, but when I asked if he had ever, at any point, regretted his decision to do it, he turned sour.

'No. Funnily enough. It may seem odd. I mean, there were people who were just out to make it as difficult as possible. But on the whole there were more people giving us encouragement.'

The 'difficult' people he meant were obviously the press with whom he had a row at the end of the Knockout day. I wasn't there but I have talked to reporters who were. They were cooped up in a marquee all day, frustrated at their lack of access to any stories, so when Prince Edward strode in afterwards and said, 'I only hope you have enjoyed yourselves – have you?' he was met by silence. He then said angrily, 'Great. Thanks for sounding so bloody enthusiastic,' and stormed out.

Understandably, Prince Edward looked weary when I raised the subject. 'I didn't have a "row" with the press. They were just very hostile and I didn't have the patience at that particular time to sit down and be all conciliatory. Everybody was very tired. We'd been working *so* hard, living on remarkably little sleep and virtually no food at all. So at that particular moment in time I wasn't really interested in having a battle.'

But, as I understood it, the reporters weren't looking for a battle. 'They were fed up and frustrated but they weren't out to lynch you.'

'Well, that's what they *did*!' the Prince retorted. 'I thought

I asked a perfectly reasonable question: had they enjoyed themselves? I mean, they could have said no. They could have said anything they liked, but *they didn't say a thing.*'

Perhaps they were shy, I suggested, and Prince Edward erupted. 'Oh *please*! That lot shy! Come off it! No, there was a combination of factors and it ended the day on a pretty sour note.'

Having opened this particular can of worms, I plunged on to ask him about the (almost unanimously unfavourable) reviews of the television programme. '*Any* excuse to lay into a person, as far as I can see,' the Prince said bitterly. 'They'd never been particularly enthusiastic about the event in the first place, so it didn't come as a great surprise. But yes, I was annoyed that I had given them the opportunity to get their knives in.

'The fact is, 18.25 million people watched the programme and thoroughly enjoyed it and, as far as I'm concerned, what the press says doesn't worry me. They didn't lay into the charities, or the other participants, so if someone was going to be sacrificed for the sake of their circulation wars, at least it was only me.'

This excuse about 'circulation wars' is getting a lot of airing at the moment, but the truth is there have been circulation wars as long as there have been newspapers so the situation is nothing new. What *is* new is the degree of disrespect that has recently crept into Royal reporting. But many old Fleet Street hands would argue that this is precisely because of events like Knockout: if the young royals carry on like showbiz stars they must expect to be treated like showbiz stars, as media playthings.

I put this argument to the Prince – that Knockout had diminished the Royal Family's dignity. 'But presumably you, Sir, don't believe that that's true?'

'Oh I do believe that's true. It was an experiment and a lot of people have learned a lot from it. I don't think it's done an enormous amount of harm, and it's done an awful lot of good

many areas and there was a blur of – how shall I put it? –
identity. I got my hands dirty with the production but I
thoroughly enjoyed doing it, and I learned a lot.

'I suppose if I'd wanted to, I could have done something
commercially and made myself lots of money, but in fact I
made a million for charity and probably lost quite a lot
because I had to cover my expenses. So I seem to have lost
everything, and gained very little.'

That seems an unnecessarily black view of the situation.
True, Prince Edward has had a very bumpy year, starting
with his decision to leave the Royal Marines, and going on to
Knockout. But the public will respect him for his admission
that he has learned from his mistakes; the damage to the
Royal Family can be repaired; and the press is always happy,
where the Royal Family is concerned, to kiss and make up.

Reproduced by permission of the *Sunday Express*

BEN ELTON

3 June 1990

Ben Elton is not ashamed to admit that he *cries* when newspapers say nasty things about him, and it was unfortunate that I met him the day after Peter McKay had written a bitchy paragraph about him in the London *Evening Standard*. He claimed not to have read the piece, though he kept referring to it, so finally I offered to show it him – 'I've got it here in my briefcase.' He recoiled as if I were trying to hand him a dead rat. Thereafter, whenever the conversation became remotely sticky, I noticed his eyes flickering nervously to my briefcase.

We met at the Theatre Royal, Haymarket, where his new play, *Gasping*, opens this week, and I couldn't understand why he kept shouting at me. We were sitting in the green room only a few feet apart, but his voice was pitched to carry between fishing trawlers in high seas. Later, much later, he mentioned that when he started in comedy, he used to shout all the time and talk very fast because he was so nervous. Now, he claims, he's learned to slow down a bit and to smile ('Remember to smile, Ben. Try hard to look relaxed') but he still hasn't mastered the volume control. There is a character in his stand-up routine called Captain Paranoia, who sits on his shoulder whispering new anxieties into his ear, and

Captain Paranoia was on full alert at our meeting. Ben Elton is not a relaxed or relaxing person.

Why should he be, though? It is a cliché – but none the less true – that comedians tend to be tortured souls. And if you doubt that Ben Elton is a comic writer of genius, compare the first series of *Blackadder*, which he had no part in, with any of the subsequent series which he co-wrote. *Blackadder* is probably the most generally liked of his achievements, but the others are by no means negligible – scripting *The Young Ones*, compering *Saturday* and *Friday Night Live*, hosting *Wogan* infinitely better than Wogan, writing a novel, *Stark*, and now the play *Gasping* – all this before we get to his one-man show, which in its most recent incarnation, *The Man from Auntie*, a few weeks ago (especially in the third programme, about emptying the kitchen bin) was as breathtakingly exhilarating as the best of *Fawlty Towers*.

And he is only thirty-one. He actually looks about twenty-one, or even younger, in his little jeans jacket (no, he doesn't wear his awful glittery stage suit in real life); he looks like the sort of bloke you might find sitting opposite you on the Tube, and indeed you might, because although he owns a car he never uses it in London. He has a flat in South Kensington, though nowadays, he says, he leads 'a rather transworld lifestyle' because his girlfriend, Sophie, is Australian and he often goes over there to see her. She will be coming to join him for the first night of *Gasping*, and then he will go to Australia with her to write his second novel. They've been going out for three years and 'Yes, marriage is a possibility but I think I'll discuss that with her first, if you don't mind, rather than the readers of the *Independent on Sunday*.'

Gasping is his first play in the West End, but he has written dozens before – he wrote his first comedy at fifteen. As a schoolboy in the London suburbs, he was obsessed with Noël Coward and determined to be like him, though *now*, he says, he prefers Alan Ayckbourn. He took part in amateur dramatics ('My Artful Dodger is still remembered in Guildford') and begged his parents to let him leave school and be a stagedoor keeper; they compromised by sending him to a college of further education where he could do an A-level in theatre studies along with his ordinary A-levels, and then he went to Manchester University to read drama. At Manchester he met Rik Mayall and wrote scripts for him; later, when Mayall was invited to make a television series, he enlisted Ben Elton to write the script which became *The Young Ones*. By then he had written twenty-odd plays which had been performed in student productions and the Edinburgh Fringe.

He works hard as a writer, sweating all day at his computer, polishing lines until the rhythm is perfect. He talks about the agony of hearing an actor insert a word that was not in the script and quotes Coward's putdown to Edith Evans, when she kept saying, in *Hay Fever*, 'On a very clear day you can see Marlow': 'Edith dear, the line is "On a clear day you can see Marlow". On a *very* clear day you can see Marlowe and Beaumont and Fletcher.' When he was a child, his parents worried that he only read comics, which he bought by the box at jumble sales, so his father brought him a book of P. G. Wodehouse short stories: 'The idea was to encourage me to read more books, but all it did was encourage me to read more Wodehouse and for two years I read nothing else.' Another early love was Morecambe and Wise – 'Script by Eddie Braben, and a great script, but only Eric could say [putting on the voice, perfectly] "Little Ern sat at home washing his money . . ." Chaplin, of course, is a big hero and if there are any people out there who still think it's clever to say "Of course Buster Keaton was the real genius" – it's *not*. They were both geniuses.'

When he talks about comedy, he is confident and knowledgeable and relaxed: the mood changes when I ask about Captain Paranoia, and whether his obsessive preoccupation with checking gas taps and plugs is Ben Elton's own. 'Oh God,' he groans, 'that's all for real. Have you checked the gas taps? Better look again. Are the lights off? Is the fire out? Is that creak a mad axeman coming in through the window? I *am* a bit of an obsessive. It irritates my girlfriend sometimes.

On occasion I get silly.'

Oddly, he only worries about small things – 'gas taps and dinner parties' – rather than about his work. 'I have my work in perspective – I'm pretty healthy about that.' But the thought that he might have left a light bulb burning can drive him demented. Why? 'Because,' he explains, as if to a dim toddler, 'it's *important* not to leave lights on all day. I mean what a silly thing to do. The world's in an energy crisis. I was brought up to turn out lights – weren't you? Do you leave *your* lights on when you leave the house?' I nod Yes, and he looks at me as if I have just confessed to some wild affectation like bathing in champagne or lighting my cigarette with rolled £10 notes: he seriously doubts my sanity.

But what is the fear if you *don't* turn lights out? What is supposed to happen? 'Well I could give you all sorts of energy-saving arguments, but the *real* thing is that any power is a fire risk. That is why I check all the plugs. I don't pull them out any more, because I've learned that that is actually more dangerous because you degrade the plug, but you make sure it's all turned off. All my life I've been laughed at for worrying that a light bulb might spontaneously combust, jump across the room, land on that inflammable cushion and before you know it, a conflagration ensues. And my worry is that I might be responsible for something that might hurt someone else, you know? I don't mind me dying in a fire, but what about the neighbours? I think we've gone a bit far with this . . . let's change the subject.'

Wholehearted 'Yes', but now Captain Paranoia is up and running with the ball he won't easily let it go, and somehow every conversational gambit seems to lead back to light bulbs. The crux of the argument is: can a light bulb really start a fire? He insists that it can: 'I was on tour last year and my stage manager in one of the dressing-rooms hung a shirt over the light fitting – this was during the day and the light was off, but later someone came in and switched the light on and there was this shirt on the bulb and next thing we knew it burst into flames and we had a dressing-room fire. One day, a bit of paper might be close to a bulb . . . All I'm saying is: I'm very paranoid. I feel great responsibility. I pick up litter. I think society is about being responsible – it's all down to good manners really.'

Why do people dislike Ben Elton? Having met him, I'm prepared to swear that he's a thoroughly decent bloke who struggles constantly to be considerate and kind and good and to make the world a better place. Yet he obviously gets up people's noses – most visibly Sir Robin Day's on *Aspel* the other week, when Day actually batted him to shut him up. Many people find him brattish, loud-mouthed, opinionated and frankly insufferable. It's true that he does talk too much, too loudly and too fast. He is the youngest of four children and perhaps at home had to shout to get his word in. One of his favourite expressions is 'I hasten to add' and he *does* hasten to add, all the time, going on, on and on, repeating, revising, making absolutely sure that you cannot possibly have misunderstood one atom of what he has said. He recalls his first girlfriend once going berserk because he interrupted her with: 'I know what you're going to say' and so he has trained himself never to do that, but he is still guilty of ending perfectly comprehensible sentences with 'Know what I mean?'

He tries, he really tries, not to needle people, to respect their rights, not to intrude on their space. He is genuinely, totally non-racist, non-sexist, non-workerist – any time he says he works hard he always hastens to add that of course he works no harder than a checkout girl in Sainsbury's or even, by some bizarre bit of right-on logic, than the unemployed.

But the *real* problem, the almost insurmountable nose-getting-up problem is his self-righteousness. Why does he have to say he checks all the lights and everything because he doesn't want the house to burn down *and burn the neighbours?* Why can't he just say he doesn't want the house to burn down? He gives a sort of moan of pain at the question and whimpers a bit before answering: 'Because, I tell you, it's an honest fact that I feel connected to other people. That's not being self-righteous, that's being whingeing and paranoid and overly anxious. *Now* of course I wish I hadn't said it; I think that's about the most horrible thing I've ever been accused of – it makes me shiver to think of it – but it's fair, it's fair and I thank you for saying it.'

He insists that he is not self-righteous, not a martyr. 'I don't *martyr* myself. I don't give *all* my money away – I give *some* of it away, but if we had a proper welfare state I wouldn't have to. If I say I would prefer to be taxed at a higher level, some people find that irritating and Jesuitical: I say it's an extremely logical, selfish stance because I am not bettered by beggars accosting me in Tube stations. I'm not bettered by people who have nothing to lose breaking into my flat and stealing all my possessions. That might sound self-righteous, but I'm thinking about me and my girlfriend and being able to walk safe in the streets.'

Notice that even while he is denying he is self-righteous, he has leapt nimbly up to the moral high ground and delivered yet another sermon. He is *always* higher up the moral high ground than you are, he is waving down from the summit of K9 while you are still plodding into the foothills. And he has that fatal urge to *teach* (his mother is a schoolteacher, his father a university professor) which is particularly nose-get-upping for older people. It is as if he has spent his life surrounded by people less intelligent and less caring than himself. But has he? Unlikely. He went to university, but he doesn't strike me as a really impressive intellect like, say, Stephen Fry. Could it be a pedagogic habit caught from his parents or his older siblings? I picture the Eltons as a hyper-articulate family all having intellectual arguments the whole time and shouting little Benjie down. This is pure guesswork: he won't talk about his family because, he says, they don't enjoy the *benefits* of celebrity so why should they suffer the downside – the loss of privacy? He did remark in passing, though, that his mother got fed up with people telling her she must be proud of her Ben, because, she said, she was equally proud of all her children – an unnecessarily pi remark in my view and therefore highly reminiscent of Ben Elton's own style.

After every interview, Ben Elton says he worries, 'Oh I *hope* I presented myself properly. I'm sure I sounded like a complete tosser.' And when he says he *worries*, you can bet he worries and worries and worries and drives his friends mad talking about it. There was a review once of his live show which started: 'No one, not even Mr Elton's parents, could find anything remotely redeeming to say about him,' and even now, as he quotes the words, he turns white with shock. There have been hundreds of good reviews since which he has forgotten, but that one sentence is engraved on his heart.

However successful he is, however many Bafta awards he wins, 'I still don't *feel* successful. That's what the Peter McKays and people don't understand – he probably thinks I'm so successful and so cocky he can pour whatever shit he likes on me and I won't notice, but it's so untrue. Often, when I get all whingey and stupid and start crying about being misrepresented in the press, someone like John Lloyd [*Blackadder* producer] will say, "Oh come on, Ben. Your friends love you, you've achieved all this, don't worry," and I think that's a lovely thing to say and I'm terribly pleased he feels like that but I do not feel my achievements protect me from being deeply hurt. I'm *hurt*.'

Reproduced by permission of the *Independent on Sunday*

STEPHEN FRY

22 April 1990

The magazine *GQ* managed to have a whole cover story on Stephen Fry without once mentioning his sex life. This is a feat I shall not try to emulate. His personality – which includes his childhood kleptomania, youthful homosexuality and present celibacy – remains a challenge to amateur psychologists everywhere. And knowing that he was once jailed for stealing credit cards adds incomparably to one's enjoyment of his role in the Alliance & Leicester Building Society TV commercials.

By rights, Stephen Fry should be blubbing on a psychiatrist's couch somewhere, irreparably damaged by all his adolescent traumas, but in fact he is popping up almost every time you turn on the television. In the last six months, he's appeared in *Blackadder Goes Forth*, in *Whose Line Is It Anyway?*, in his own *Fry and Laurie* comedy series with Hugh Laurie, and now in the new LWT series *Jeeves and Wooster*. He has also just opened in the new Michael Frayn play *Look Look*. He is beginning to seem a possible successor to John Cleese – the comedian he most admires.

Cleese once propounded the theory that every comedian's comic character was based on the person he would have become if he had not been blessed with a sense of humour. In

Fry's case this means, generally, a bland old Establishment
buffer somewhat in the Willie Whitelaw mould – portly,
public-schooly, philistine – but with a hint of sadism behind
the eyes. Fry himself comes from a straightforwardly middle-
class background in Norfolk. His father is an electronics
inventor with his own business, a remote descendant of the
Quaker Frys who spawned so many Victorian social reform-
ers; his mother is from a cosmopolitan Viennese Jewish
family. Unfashionably, Fry plays his public-school accent up
rather than down (he went to Uppingham, Leicestershire); he
also goes to some lengths to acquire his quintessentially
tweedy English wardrobe – buying it all at Brooks Brothers
in New York. He is huge (six foot four), imposing, and looks
considerably older than his real age, which is thirty-three.

Where he differs from his screen persona is that he is much
kinder and more likeable than you expect: he is also much
less confident, more neurotic. He occasionally breaks into
quite bad stuttering and wrings his hands. But the most
striking difference is that as soon as he starts talking, you are
struck and then awed by his intelligence: despite expulsion
from school and a prison record, he still won a scholarship to
Cambridge. As a child he learned a whole *Guinness Book of
Records* by heart; he took his O-levels at thirteen; at school
he could do the *Times* crossword in under fifteen minutes.
(One of the few prison memories that still makes him weep is
the thought of his mother turning up at visiting time with
three months' worth of *Times* crosswords neatly cut out for
him.) Although he strives valiantly to suffer fools gladly, he
can never quite repress the impatient, hypercritical, fretful
brain gnawing away in the background, and he often interrupts his own flow of thought with critical comments on his
choice of words or syntax.

He looks tired, as well as he might: he went from the
Sunday night cast party for *Blackadder*, which finished at
2 a.m., to start filming *Jeeves and Wooster* four hours later;
wrote *Fry and Laurie* (with Hugh Laurie) between *Jeeves*
scenes, filmed it, and went straight into rehearsals for *Look*

Look. He admits to being a workaholic: he gets bored when he's not working and never takes a holiday voluntarily. His partner, Hugh Laurie, also works hard, but he doesn't cram in all the extra jobs, such as organizing fund-raising concerts for the Terrence Higgins Trust or acting in live theatre, that Fry does: 'Hugh's not as *driven* as me. He has a family.'

Now, embarking on the Michael Frayn play, Fry half-dreads, half-welcomes the enforced monotony of doing the same thing every day for six months. It will certainly make a change because 'for the last few years I've been completely irregular in almost everything from the bowels upwards'. He plans to exploit the regularity by having piano lessons two days a week, and going to a gym three days a week – the latter, a very new, and, for him, alarming, departure – his first-ever attempt at physical exercise.

And, oh yes, he remembers, he also has to finish his novel. He wrote 60,000 words earlier this year but then had to put it aside, and although he meant to think about it while he was filming, of course he didn't: 'I'm not the sort of person who *can* think about things. If I have a bone, I eat it; I don't bury it in the garden. I can't hoard anything, and that includes thoughts. I spend – thoughts, money, myself. I can't save and conserve anything.'

He can afford to be insouciant about money because since 1984 he has enjoyed an extraordinary windfall: he was asked to rewrite the book of the old Cockney musical *Me and My Girl*, and has received 3 per cent of its hefty worldwide box office ever since. This is in addition to the £100,000 or more he earns from television and advertising work. Consequently, he owns large houses in Islington and Norfolk, and is able to indulge his taste for expensive technology – five state-of-the-art Mackintosh computers, several fast cars including an Aston Martin, an MG and an Austin Healey (at one point he had ten but 'decided to rationalize the fleet' when he lost his driving licence), and a stunt plane which he bought for his brother-in-law, a pilot, to use. He also has a magic Yamaha piano that plays itself, and a stuffed cat in his window which he occasionally kicks *pour épater* the passers-by.

So he lives comfortably, and has no particular need to work. But he is, as he admits, 'driven' – partly because he believes his current fame can't last and he must capitalize on it while he can, but also because he just is. He himself finds it mysterious: 'One *assumes*, just from observing other people, that various hungers will drop away – hungers such as the wanting to say "Yes", the wanting to be on television, the wanting to do another play. Because if you talk to say your John Cleeses or your Alan Bennetts, it's quite obvious that their appetite has gone for the whole scene, because they have no need to prove themselves. Whereas I still have the appetite – for being in the world of doing it all the time, and knowing the latest gossip about everybody. I mean, you talk to Cleese and he won't even know who the controller of Channel Two is, or who's bought which theatre, but I just *love* being involved with that whole world, gossiping in Joe Allen's with a load of silly old actors about what's going on, and generally being right inside the whole thing. It's partly to do with not having a family so I've got no home to go to, as it were. But I'm sure it will change. I mean, that seems to be what happens to people – just as one knows that one's hair won't always be this colour, but will go grey. It's not the age thing exactly, it's the bourgeoisification that worries me.'

While most of his friends and fellow comedians – Ben Elton, Rowan Atkinson & Co. – are now in the thick of marriage and babies, Fry sees no immediate prospect of that happening to him. At school and university, he was 'about 90 per cent gay'; for the last eight years he has been celibate. It all came out simply because a television interviewer once asked him, and since then he finds himself endlessly rung up to appear for gay causes or to contribute to gay debates. 'It's rather ironic, when I'm actually celibate, that I seem to be far more "out" than many fully-fledged, highly practising, not to mention promiscuous, gay actors who prefer not to talk about it. But I'm quite happy to speak up for gay causes and demonstrate my complete unembarrassed belief in people's right to choose to go to bed with whomever they wish to.'

Or, in his case, their right to choose not to go to bed with anyone at all. Although he makes a joke of it, his distaste for sex is very strong. He talks of the sudden realization, at parties, that someone in the room would like to go to bed with him, and the horror of imagining 'God, they'd be there in the *morning*, and I'd have to *talk* to them, and – aagh, no! But celibacy is just great. I have many good friends whom I love dearly and couldn't bear to be without; I just don't want to rub the wet slimy bits of my body all over them. It seems perfectly reasonable. I would have thought I was doing them a *favour*. I mean, who *wants* to have their bellies slapping together in a great sea of mucus? It's an *awful* idea, sex, don't you think?' He says this lightly, but he means it seriously: I noticed that he awaited my answer with real curiosity and was disappointed when I said 'No.'

He would like to have children, but recognizes that it is unlikely to happen. His dream would be to go home and find a wife and children already installed: it is the preliminaries, like courtship, that put him off. 'I can't bear *relationships*.' In any case, he says, he never seems to fall in love, either with men or with women. 'Perhaps it's because I'm selfish and think only of myself?' – but this is belied by his very large circle of friends, who are all devoted to him.

He *did* fall in love with a slightly younger boy at school 'and that's obviously a knockout thing, your first adolescent experience of love. It's not deeply *erotic*; it's more platonic and romantic – and so mockable, that strange public-school world of romantic crushes that then develop into some goaty old writer living in Morocco with seven houseboys.' Perhaps this is the explanation: that when he saw he was homosexual, he also saw that he didn't want to end up like that and so renounced sexuality altogether.

How seriously screwed up is he? 'Well, I don't think one ever becomes completely unscrewed, but – I don't mean this in a smug way at all – I'm reasonably cheerful with myself. I mean, I don't contemplate suicide or anything like that. I wouldn't tempt Providence by using words like "happy", but I am reasonably content and I've no cause to complain. If I was a lonely, sad figure living in damp cardboard at Waterloo, then I would say something somewhere went wrong. And if I was weak – which I would be – I would blame either my parents or my genes or some part of my background. But I'm rather intolerant, or impatient, with people who take that line. And I'm not a *completely* unravelled human being.'

At first glance, he's not unravelled at all, but he gets odder as he goes on. If you met him, for instance, on a train, you could probably talk to him for hours without thinking him anything other than a very intelligent, pleasant, charming chap – unless the conversation turned to sex, or to his childhood. As a child, he seems to have been quite spectacularly screwed up. He 'half-inched' things and shoplifted; he ran away from school and got himself expelled; he was so frightened of his father, his voice changed to a squeak when he spoke to him. He was also freakishly tall, but useless on the games field, and seriously asthmatic, which created its own problems: 'An asthmatic can become a bit of an onlooker, which can make you quite unpopular,' he explains. 'I used to try hard not to be asthmatic, but I used to take advantage when it was convenient . . . My asthma was never really severe. I was just a mixed-up adolescent who didn't know what he wanted to do.'

The mixed-up-ness reached its peak when he was seventeen and stole a man's coat from a coat hook in a pub (he stole it simply because he was cold) but then found a wallet full of credit cards in the pocket, and decided to go on the run. For three months he travelled round the country, staying at hotels and buying goods with his stolen credit cards. He never rang his parents. Finally, in Swindon, the police caught up with him, and he spent three months on remand at Pucklechurch (where he was known as 'The Professor' because he read books and played the piano in chapel), followed by two years' probation. Prison, he believes, 'was the making of me. I have absolutely no doubt that if I'd had a normal childhood and done what the school expected me to do, I would have gone on the rocks at university or in my mid-twenties. I was lucky to have gone wrong so disastrously at an age when it was possible to put it right.'

He put it right by taking his A-levels and going on to Cambridge – but why did he have to go wrong so disastrously first? What was his *problem*? Fry remains silent for a long time, which is unusual for him, then explains: 'Archbishop Ramsey was once asked to define wisdom and he said, "Oh I don't know – the ability to *cope*," and I think that's a very good definition. That's why I was so silly – I couldn't *cope* ... And that finished when I was in prison. I suddenly realized that I was able to concentrate and do things, to use my mind properly.'

Stephen is the middle child: he has an elder brother, and a younger sister who works as his assistant. The brother, who now works for their father, was 'a perfect public-school citizen, head boy and very good at everything' – which Stephen believes gives the lie to any notion that his upbringing might be to blame for his own difficulties. His relationship with his mother was happy and uncomplicated: she always believed that he would turn out all right.

His father, Alan Fry, was more doubtful. Stephen told the *Sunday Times* a few months ago, 'I lived in fear of my father until I was about eighteen, fear of the eyebrow and the sniff ... It was very hard to prove myself because he did tend to frown at anything I did with any degree of competence.' His father rather confirmed this by saying that Stephen 'spends a lot of energy doing things that aren't worthy of him'. He, the father, also said, 'At an early age one puts one's father on a pedestal; it's not until much later on that one discovers what feet of clay the old fellow really has. Stephen was perhaps a little slower in his disillusionment than he ought to have been.' He describes their relationship as 'turbulent' and apparently still thinks of his son as a bit of a wastrel. Stephen

Fry seems to agree with this assessment, saying that he feels 'guilty that the rewards for what I do are so much greater than his, and I'm aware of the absurdity of the recognition for flinging your face around like some whore'. He adds, 'I hope he derives some enjoyment from my work. Our relationship is still spiky enough for me not to get many signs that he does.'

When Stephen was fourteen, his parents were sufficiently worried to send him to a psychiatrist, but it didn't do any good. The psychiatrist decided that he must come from a family that constantly moved house, diplomats perhaps or armed services, and that his kleptomania (he tended to bury the things he stole) was nest-building. But, like so many good theories, it was destroyed by the facts: the family was actually perfectly immobile in Norfolk. As a result, Stephen is contemptuous of psychiatry, explaining that 'psychiatrists just don't recognize the diagnosis A Bad Lot – which is what I was'. John Cleese and other friends have extolled the advantages of adult psychotherapy but he has never been tempted, partly because he doubts he could ever find a psychiatrist as intelligent as himself and partly, I suspect, because psychiatry usually entails some notion of disloyalty to, or criticism of, one's parents, which he would find unacceptable. In so far as he has a counsellor, it is Hugh Laurie's wife.

In any case, he points out, therapy is only another word for healing and he prefers to find his healing through religion. 'With psychiatry, you have to believe in a psyche, and I've no particular evidence in my life to make me believe in one, but there's a lot of evidence to believe in a *soul*. And if the soul is in bits, that means that someone with experience of coping with a soul in bits, such as an intelligent, wise priest, might actually be able to do a lot more to help.'

He still thinks that doing comedy is only a temporary hiccup in his life and imagines that he will end up either as a teacher 'or a priest, preferably Archbishop of Canterbury'. I assumed at first he was joking, but he talked quite seriously about how, when the call came, he would go to ACCM (the Advisory Council for the Church's Ministry) and test his vocation. But did he, does he, believe in God? 'I believe in the importance of the *idea* of God, and giving it a name, the principle that somehow causes things to get better. I think it's very good for people to have a spiritual or theological outlook on the world rather than a moral one.' He says he has a 'very powerful' religious sense but 'not a *faith* – this is the difficulty. In a sense my religion now is humanism, and I wish people would realize that humanism is not just atheism – it's something much more positive. It only takes one difference to make a humanist into a religious person and that is faith in some kind of outside power or eternity of spirit. And I don't really have that – but I'm not closed to the possibility.

'You know, someone once asked Archbishop Ramsey what was the purpose of Christianity, and he said, "Well, one of the reasons, which is so easily overlooked, is to be good." And, he said, "I don't know that I want to be good, but I know that I want to *want* to be good." And I recognize that in myself: I want to want to be good, I want to want to have faith. And I think one should have the courage, in the face of what is a very atheistic and sceptical age, to realize that if it were to come, some kind of call, that it could be embraced to advantage . . . Besides, I just think I would make a *bloody* good bishop!'

Reproduced by permission of the *Independent on Sunday*

ZSA ZSA GABOR

19 October 1986

There were ten of us present for Miss Gabor's photo session. First, Zsa Zsa (or Princess Frederick von Anhalt, as we must now learn to call her) and her husband the Prince. Then the photographer Clive Arrowsmith and his assistant; hairdresser Ricci Burns (who *always* does Miss Gabor's hair when she's in London) and his assistant; Celia Hunter, the make-up artiste; a bodyguard; Michael Lewis, a thirty-one-year-old interior designer and friend of Miss Gabor's; and me.

Zsa Zsa erupted from the dressing-room in a whirlwind of pink flounces. "Ow do I look?' she cried, pirouetting about. 'Wonderful, wonderful, darling,' chorused Michael and Ricci and the make-up girl and the hair assistant while Prince Frederick looked on impassively, and I mentally revised all my homework and decided she couldn't *possibly* be sixty-six, could she?

'Not too much boobs?' called Zsa Zsa as she threw herself on the bed, and the make-up girl dabbed powder in her cleavage and Ricci did some final flicks with the comb. 'I look better with the camera higher up,' said Miss Gabor, and Clive Arrowsmith duly raised his tripod. Never let us forget that Miss Gabor is a veteran of forty films.

At one point Clive asked the Prince to pose with his wife. 'Put your arm round her, look at her,' he ordered, and the Prince slowly winched his arm a few inches upwards and creaked his head round ten degrees. His expression never altered – a small, ambiguous smile, polite but not friendly. While Zsa Zsa and Ricci and Michael shrieked and giggled, he stood like a hat rack expressing nothing at all.

I asked Michael Lewis what he was doing there and he said he was 'a friend of Zsa Zsa's – *unfortunately!*' (shriek). 'I stay with her when I'm in Los Angeles, and we have breakfast in bed together – but only when she's between husbands, darling!' In return, he acts as her major-domo when she's in England.

I asked him about his clothes because they were the sort it would have been impolite to ignore. '*Well,*' he explained happily, 'the suit is by Tommy Nutter, to my own design. The tie is Hermès – can you spell that, darling? – but again to my own design. Shoes by Manolo Blahnik and socks by Versace. This pocket watch,' an enormous gong featuring a spoon, for stirring coffee, one supposes, 'is by Tom Binns and it goes with these cufflinks,' shaped like two outstretched hands.

Since I was getting all this sartorial education I asked him why Ricci Burns, the hairdresser, was wearing such very short trousers, exposing a good two inches of sock. Did they shrink at the cleaners, perhaps? 'Well *no*, darling,' Michael said, shocked. 'That is Ricci's new look.'

Poor Prince Frederick didn't seem to be in on the new look because he was wearing a very square double-breasted suit with turn-ups. He stood around being the strong silent type and everyone ignored him. Michael whispered to me loud enough for him to hear: 'Zsa Zsa said to me, "But dahlink, I love him, I must marry him." And I told her, "Darling, you love your dogs but you don't want to marry them!"'

Feeling rather sorry for the Prince in the circumstances, I went to ask him how he was enjoying his first months of marriage. He manoeuvred his head a few inches in my direction but spoke to the space above my left shoulder. 'I am not used to all this showbiz,' he complained in a strong German accent. 'Sometimes I don't like it. It is not my profession.' What is his profession? 'I own a champagne vineyard in Reims. I own the only Rolls-Royce in Munich.'

Marrying Miss Gabor, he told me in well-rehearsed PR-ese, was the culmination of a lifetime's dream. 'I fall in love with Zsa Zsa many years ago when I see her in *Moulin Rouge.*' (Many many years ago, actually: it came out in 1952, and remains the only memorable Zsa Zsa Gabor film.) 'I keep her photographs by my bed always. I say, "Zis is ze woman I want to marry."'

It is a romantic story, the idea of this devoted man waiting years to meet and then marry the woman of his dreams. Except that he didn't wait – he married one or two others first. How many exactly? 'Six,' said the Prince. 'Are you *sure?*' I squeaked (press reports hitherto have always said two or three) and held six fingers up to his eyeline and wiggled them about. 'Yes, six,' said the Prince. 'They all wanted my title.'

Ah yes, his title. It dates from 4 March 1980, when he was officially adopted by the eighty-one-year-old Princess von Anhalt, last surviving granddaughter of the last German Kaiser. Before that, he was plain Robert Lichtenberg, a struggling wine merchant. Quite why the Princess decided to adopt him remains a mystery and is currently the subject of a forty-million-dollar libel suit brought by the Prince against the *National Enquirer* magazine.

I put it to him that six marriages in six years seemed a bit hasty, and the Prince readily agreed. 'I marry them all after two weeks. I make many mistakes. Some women are very good actresses, and then they change after marriage. They think they can be the quiet housewife and that I don't need. All the women I meet before are very boring but Hungarians are full of life. She is full of life,' he said, tilting his head a fraction towards Zsa Zsa, who was still cavorting on the bed.

But the subject of lively Hungarians reminded me of

another delicate matter: the seventeen-year-old Miss Hungary, Andrea Molnar, who committed suicide in July by swallowing snake poison, while allegedly pregnant by the Prince. The Prince looked mildly irritated when I mentioned her: 'I met her on a TV show in Germany and she came to my house in Munich and we had a good time together. After two weeks she found she was pregnant.' (Shrug.) 'These things happen. I always told her I planned to marry Zsa Zsa.' So much for the late Miss Hungary.

I asked why he was on a TV show in Germany (because, as far as I knew, he was not famous until he became the eighth Mr Gabor). 'I am *very* famous in Germany,' he assured me. 'Everyone knows me.' As what? 'Business, political things.' (Shrug.) 'In 1976 I save the life of a boy from drowning. I see him fall in and I just jump in after. I break my arm but still I do it. I win a Gold Medal.'

At this point Zsa Zsa emerged from the dressing-room dressed in her street clothes — suede poncho, high-heeled boots tufted with fur and feathers, white trousers, deep cleavage. 'We go eat! Frederick, come! Dahlink' — this to me — 'ask me questions, anything you like, I tell you about my horse Silver Fox, I rode him in the Olympics with your Prince Philip, in America he is more famous than me, worth a million dollars but I never sell him because I loff him, he is my son. No! I tell you about my latest film *Johann Strauss* I make in Germany behind the Wall it is farbulous, dahlink, simply farbulous, I play the Baroness Rothschild. I forget who plays Strauss. He is very handsome actor you know him dahlink he is in *The Stud*, he is *farbulous* . . .'

All this while barrelling down the corridor clickety-click on her high-heeled boots, with me panting in her wake and the Prince, Michael Lewis and her bodyguard bringing up the rear. We were supposed to be going to lunch in Chelsea but suddenly she spotted the studio canteen: 'Spaghetti! We eat here!' she cried, and Michael was dispatched to fetch food. A young English girl in a long skirt and cardigan was passing

by and Zsa Zsa suddenly called to her, 'I see you in the nude!
I saw the movie! I saw you undressed in the movie!'

It was Helena Bonham-Carter, star of *A Room with a
View*. 'Oh she's so cute,' Zsa Zsa went on to me, 'so adorable
and such a good actress' – the first time I have ever heard an
older actress praising a younger and prettier one, and worth
putting on record for that reason.

I kept thinking that any minute Zsa Zsa would let me ask
a question but she never did. She maintained a constant
stream of chatter in her bubbly Hungarian accent, switching
through her childhood in Hungary, her schooling in Switzerland, her first marriage in Turkey, her seven subsequent
marriages, her films, her house in Bel Air, her horses, her
sisters Magda and Eva, her mother Jolie, 'the most beautiful
woman in Hungary' (still alive and Zsa Zsa phones her every
day), her grandmother, 'the most beautiful woman in Europe'
who was shot by the Russians, her parents' escape from
Hungary, her father's return to Hungary and his second
marriage to his secretary. 'Father was my love. Conrad Hilton
[second husband] looked exactly like him.'

Names, facts, dates (especially dates) tend to blur incom-
prehensibly in the kaleidoscope of her talk. I knew there was
no point in even asking her her age but I thought I might at
least try to establish the Prince's – he had told me he was
forty-three, but I was doubtful. Zsa Zsa said: 'The press say
he's forty-one. Actually, dahlink,' she confided, 'I think he's
forty-six. Just nine years younger than me.' She managed to
say this with a perfectly straight face. But she had told me
(and many other journalists before me) about her meetings
with Kemal Ataturk while she was married to her first
husband, the Turkish Minister for Propaganda. Kemal Ataturk died in 1938. Which, if she were fifty-five, would make
her seven at the time of her first marriage.

However, the most intriguing lapse over numbers occurred
when we were talking about the Prince (in his absence) and
Zsa Zsa said he had been married three times. 'Oh that's
funny,' I said, 'he told me six times.' Zsa Zsa whirled round

in her seat towards Michael and they both goggled at each other. 'He didn't tell *you* that, did he?' Michael asked Zsa Zsa, and it was painfully obvious that he hadn't.

I put it to her that, although it must be good fun to be married eight times, it is not really a recipe for happiness. 'Boy, you're so *right!*' she sighed. 'But you see the Turk [husband number one] was forty-two years older and I only married him to get out of Hungary. Hilton [number two] was too busy with his hotels. George Sanders [number three] was just right for me but he was unfaithful all the time.'

She dismisses husbands four, five, six and seven with a shrug, though number seven (her divorce lawyer Michael O'Hara) distinguished himself by being the worst. And husband number seven-and-a-half, the Duke of Alba, whom she 'married' while still married to O'Hara, was 'just a joke'.

The only one whose photograph she still keeps is George Sanders, the English actor: 'He was not just my husband, he was my father, my brother, my pal.' But he was unfaithful and she left him for Porfirio Rubirosa, a playboy who bewitched her with sex. 'His lovemaking was like a drug, I couldn't give it up. George wasn't interested in sex, his lovemaking was nothing. But Rubirosa was a man no woman could resist. He was the best . . . But Prince Frederick is better,' she remembered.

Where was the Prince, by the way? We all looked around vaguely to see if he was lurking among the hat racks, but he had disappeared. Oh well, shrug. I told Zsa Zsa, in a spirit of motherly advice (she has that effect on one), that it was very silly of her to go dragging her new husband around like a piece of luggage.

'He wants it, dahlink, I know he does. He wants to be in the photos. Yes, he is getting impatient. I watch him today and I see it, too. But he knew when he married me that I was not a housewife or a little girl. I always work very hard because I have at least $25,000 a month expenses. I will do my best to be a good wife. I am a good cook and a good provider. I think this marriage has a very big chance, I really do.'

But Michael Lewis didn't agree. As we were leaving the studio, he suddenly grabbed Zsa Zsa and said, 'Did you hear what he [the Prince] said to the photographer? He said, "Maybe we can use this photograph for our Christmas card!" Darling, he won't *still* be around at Christmas, will he?'

Oh poor Zsa Zsa. With friends like that, who needs enemies? George Sanders once said of her, 'She is perhaps the most misunderstood woman of our time – she is guileless.' I agree. She struck me as entirely warm-hearted, generous, trusting, sweet – and almost fatally naïve.

'Yes,' she agreed, 'I am very naïve, and I intend to stay naïve. I hate wise asses.'

Reproduced by permission of the *Sunday Express*

J. PAUL GETTY II

5 July 1987

Last month J. Paul Getty II, KBE, was supposed to go
out. He was to attend a dinner at the Savoy hosted by the
National Art Collections Fund at which he would receive a
special award as 'Arts Benefactor of the Year'. The Prince of
Wales would present it.

Those who knew their Getty – a small group which by then
included me – greeted the news with some scepticism. Would
Getty really go *out*, in *public*, when he knew that press
photographers would be present?

Well, he said he would go. He went on saying he would go
until just forty-five minutes before he was due to arrive, when
his friend Christopher Gibbs rang the organizers and said Mr
Getty wouldn't go after all. He had toothache. He sent his
son, nineteen-year-old Tara Gabriel Galaxy Gramaphone
Getty, to receive the award in his place.

J. Paul Getty II has lived in the heart of London since 1972
and yet has remained almost completely invisible. He fled
here, aged forty, when his second wife Talitha Pol died of a
drugs overdose in Rome. Getty himself was a heroin addict at
the time and in no condition to deal with police inquiries. He
holed up in a house in Cheyne Walk, Chelsea, and effectively
disappeared for a decade.

Rumours accrued around the house and its mysterious occupant: it was said that a doctor arrived by Rolls-Royce every morning to administer Getty's heroin injection; that a Mercedes collected Getty after midnight every night, and brought him back shortly before dawn; that uninvited visitors to the house were greeted by a gorilla who said, 'Watch my belt', and then flashed open the buckle to reveal the words 'F— off'.

Getty even managed to remain invisible throughout the trauma of his son's kidnapping in 1973. Paul Getty III was sixteen and living with his mother (Getty's first wife, Gail) in Rome when he was abducted. The ransom demand was for $3.2m. Getty said he didn't have that sort of money, which was true. But his father, J. Paul Getty I, the legendarily rich and mean oil billionaire of Sutton Place, could certainly afford to pay – and refused. The kidnappers sent the boy's ear to a Rome newspaper and said that other bits of his anatomy would follow unless the ransom was paid. In the end J. Paul Getty I lent J. Paul Getty II the ransom money – at four per cent interest – and Paul III was released.

In 1976 J. Paul Getty I died and, much to everyone's amazement, our Getty showed up for the funeral. (He was the only Getty son who did.) He was wearing white sneakers and smoking a cigarette and he had Bianca Jagger on his arm. Then he disappeared back to Cheyne Walk.

In 1981 his son Paul III was in the news again. Since the kidnapping he had become seriously addicted to hard drugs, but it was actually some disastrous mix-up of prescription drugs which sent him into a coma from which he eventually emerged blind, paralysed and speechless. Our Getty, his father, refused to pay his medical bills and his ex-wife had to take him to court for the money.

This was the Getty who was to emerge just four years later as Britain's greatest philanthropist. He gave £50m to the National Galley, £20m to the British Film Institute, £2m to build a new cricket stand at Lord's, and set up a £20m trust to support humanitarian causes. Mrs Thatcher rushed round to the London Clinic to convey the thanks of a grateful nation, the Prince and Princess of Wales invited him to dinner privately at Kensington Palace and, best of all, just one year after the National Gallery bequest, the Queen conferred on him an honorary knighthood. His acceptance into the bosom of the Establishment was rapid indeed.

I first spoke to J. Paul Getty in 1985. At the time he was known to be staying in the London Clinic (he stayed there for fifteen months, being treated for a circulatory problem in his legs and for cirrhosis of the liver) and I decided to try ringing him up. Amazingly, the first time I rang I was put straight through and a soft American man's voice chatted pleasantly for ten minutes about his love of Britain.

But everyone said afterwards, 'How do you know it *was* Getty you spoke to?' and I had to admit I had no idea. So I rang the London Clinic again. The receptionist said that Mr Getty never took calls. 'But I spoke to him just half an hour ago,' I wailed.

'Mr Getty *never* takes calls.'

Six months ago I started writing regularly to Mr Getty and to his lawyer, Vanni Treves, asking for an interview. Mr Getty never replied. Mr Treves eventually rang and asked me to come and see him in his office. He seemed to like me; I certainly liked him. He is about forty, looks like a typical pin-striped lawyer, but has a wickedly seditious sense of humour.

'Paul's really a sweetie,' he kept assuring me, 'but he does have this hatred of journalists.' He said that he occasionally agreed to speak to journalists on the phone, but never face to face. Meanwhile, I should submit a list of questions and he'd see what he could do.

Suddenly, after weeks of silence, Mr Treves rang one Tuesday to say that Mr Getty would see me that Friday at his flat. No photographer, no tape recorder and no questions other than those already agreed. Mr Treves would come with me to make sure that I didn't stray.

So on the Friday I met Mr Treves in a back street in St

James's, and he took me round to the block of flats where Getty now lives. It is a surprisingly modest-looking block with no mention of the name Getty in the porter's lodge – he lives, of course, under a pseudonym.

It was only when we got in a gold-panelled lift, so smooth it seemed motionless, that I caught the whiff of money in the air.

Getty's secretary opened the door, and we were in a dark and sumptuous hall. In a niche at the end of the hall was a spotlit painting which I recognized as a Gustave Moreau. Paintings by Moreau are so rare that I thought they were all in museums. The scent of money was by now overpowering.

Vanni Treves led me into the drawing-room, which, in contrast to the gloom of the hall, was light and airy with a wall of windows looking directly on to Green Park. The most striking object of furniture was an old-fashioned acoustic gramophone with a horn curling right up to the ceiling. But, of course, the focus of the room, for me, was a huge square-backed sofa with the back of a man's head just visible over the top. The man did not turn or rise as we entered; I had to walk round the sofa and into his eyeline before he acknowledged my presence. But his eyes remained glued to a colour TV set which was showing golf.

Vanni Treves said he was just going to wash his hands and I was not to say a word until he got back. So I sat there like a statue, lips firmly sealed, watching J. Paul Getty watching golf.

He was smoking a foul pipe and drinking beer. He had an enormous pillow behind his head. The sofa was big enough for a bed and, like an invalid's sickbed, had everything within reach – books, magazines, videos, letters, bottles of pills, a basket of fruit, a drinks trolley and, most important, the television remote control.

I had been half expecting to find Mr Getty with matted hair or fingernails grown round his hands, like Howard Hughes. In fact he looked perfectly kempt in a blue cardigan and striped shirt, with white socks and soft leather mules on his feet. I covertly examined his legs. The reason he stayed in the London Clinic for fifteen months was that his heroin addiction had left him with a circulatory problem which periodically made his legs swell up 'like slabs of raw beef'.

Actually, his legs looked fine. But he seemed to move with difficulty, and to suffer some discomfort. Only the great head – set like a bison's, thrusting forward from his shoulders – gave an impression of strength.

After ten minutes the strain of keeping silent proved too much for me. 'Is that a Moreau in your hall?' I blurted.

'Yes, and I've got another one in my bedroom,' he replied. Then he switched his eyes back to the golf.

At last Vanni Treves came back and, much to his and my amazement, Mr Getty greeted him by saying, 'Take Miss Barber to my bedroom.' Mr Treves just stood there gaping but Mr Getty, instead of explaining about the Moreau, said tetchily, 'You know where my bedroom is, don't you?'

So Mr Treves took me to the bedroom, where I duly admired the Moreau and an even lovelier Edward Lear landscape at the foot of the bed. The bed was a surprisingly camp Elinor Glyn job with a tiger-skin cover – the sort of bed much favoured by sixties rock stars. It did not have any of the bedside clutter of the sofa in the drawing-room; in fact, it looked unused.

Mr Treves decided to take me on a tour of the flat (was this interview never going to take place?) and we admired the many fine pre-Raphaelite paintings, the shelves of priceless books, the gorgeous Persian rugs, the vast collection of 78 r.p.m. records of great opera singers, and a gleaming kitchen which, like the bedroom, looked unused.

We went to the secretary's office, which is also the film and video library, so that Mr Treves could borrow a Bugs Bunny cartoon for his children. (Mr Getty seems to own every film ever made.) I noticed in passing that the guest's loo contained an old *Sunday Express* magazine announcing my award as Magazine Writer of the Year. Was that why he agreed to see me? I never discovered.

At last Mr Treves could prolong the tour no longer and we returned to the drawing-room. Mr Getty remained motionless with his eyes on the golf. I took out my list of questions; Mr Treves took out his. I coughed very loudly and read the first question from my list: why had he decided to give so much money away?

'I've always been interested in philanthropy, ever since I met John D. Rockefeller who handled the charitable side of the Rockefeller Foundation. But I couldn't give money away till my father died because I didn't have any.'

'Robert Lenzner says in his biography of your father . . .'

Mr Getty snarled, 'Never read it; they're all lies those books. Never read them.' (Actually this was a lie, because Mr Treves had already told me that Getty read the Lenzner book and hated it, but I was not disposed to argue with Getty's snarl.)

'You were saying you had no money . . .'

'I didn't have anything except my salary' (as an employee of his father's Italian oil company) 'until I was nearly forty. My father controlled the whole trust. Oh, I had a legacy of $50,000 when I was twenty-five. Bought a house with it. Slid down a hillside the first time it rained!'

'And when your name is Getty,' prompted Mr Treves, 'people can't believe that you don't have money.'

'Sure. If ten people go out to dinner, it's the one called Getty who's expected to pick up the tab.'

'So you've known what it feels like to be hard up?'

'Sure I have done. Many times. I was driving a Volkswagen till my father died.' (And living in Cheyne Walk. Mr Getty's idea of abject poverty is not yours or mine.)

When his father died in 1976, he inherited one quarter of the Getty Trust, which was then worth at least $1.3bn. But at that stage the trust's money was all tied up in Getty Oil shares. The real bonanza came in 1984 when Paul's brother Gordon sold out Getty Oil to Texaco and released all the cash. Since then Getty's *income* has been around a million dollars every week.

He started giving in about 1980, and his first gifts were

fairly small and capricious, often inspired by news items he had read or seen on television. For instance, he gave money to send some stranded seal pups back to their mothers; he read that John Ogden the pianist was so broke that he had had to sell his piano, so he told him to choose any piano he wanted and send him the bill (it was for £18,000). He gave money to the families of striking miners and then – when that hit the press – to working miners. He gave a million dollars to his old friend Claus von Bulow to pay his legal fees, when he was accused of attempting to murder his wife by injecting her with insulin.

'They were just instinctive things – things I saw or read and responded to. I like to do things other people won't do – I won't bother with the big charities because everyone does those.'

In the early days, people often didn't believe it when they had a phone call from J. P. Getty. 'Yes and my name's Rockefeller' was a common response. Diners Club tore up his first application. But gradually the list of his donations lengthened and in 1985 he made his greatest and most publicized gift – £50 million to the National Gallery. Mr Getty had arrived.

I started asking Mr Getty a question which came out, ineptly, as 'Since your sudden respectability . . .' Mr Treves jumped with alarm, but Mr Getty chuckled richly, 'Sudden respectability! Vanni, why did you let her in? What did she pay you?' But he laughed heartily and even stopped watching the golf.

'I meant, since your knighthood . . .' 'Yes, it's very flattering. It sums up all the history of England, which I've loved since I was a schoolboy. I've always been attracted to British culture and history.'

Not enough, though, to take out British nationality – why not? Mr Treves shot me a warning look (this was not on my list of questions) but Mr Getty answered forcefully that he preferred not to pay British taxes: 'I want my money to go on things *I* choose, not on Trident.'

But not having British nationality means that his knighthood is only an 'honorary' one – like Bob Geldof, who was knighted at the same time, he can't use his title. Did he find that frustrating?

'I do. Yes, I do,' he agreed, nodding his great bison head.

'You don't really, do you, Paul?' asked Mr Treves, obviously surprised.

'*Course* I do. It's like giving with one hand and taking away with the other. Anyway, where does it say I can't use the title? I've got the book of rules here somewhere' – and he started groping tetchily through the piles of books on the table – 'It doesn't say anything about not using the title.'

'Would you rather be a lord?'

'I'd rather be *king*!' he shot back.

'What about a duke?' said Treves, still not taking it seriously.

'They haven't created a hereditary dukedom since the 1800s – I've looked it up. They don't create a hereditary anything now if you've got children.'

It's an interesting thought: if £50m gets a knighthood, how much would one have to give to get a hereditary dukedom? Possibly more than even Mr Getty can afford.

I asked Mr Getty a question about begging letters, which was a terrible mistake because it suddenly reminded him that I was a journalist. 'Any time my name's mentioned in the press, I get a new sackful. It'll happen after this article. I do feel hounded by the press, indeed I do. Journalists are a damn nuisance,' he snarled.

After that, he switched his eyes back to the golf and we sat in silence for a while. I was interested to notice that Mr Getty could do this, apparently indefinitely, without showing any embarrassment whatsoever. He just switched his attention from me to the golf like changing channels. He has the manners of someone who has never had to put himself out for anyone and wouldn't know how to begin. Not bad manners exactly – rather, no manners at all.

Mr Treves suddenly got up and came back with a framed

photograph. It showed Mr Getty in a cap surrounded by soldiers and it was taken, Mr Treves said, at the SAS Headquarters in Hereford. Apparently Getty gave the SAS some money, and they helicoptered him up to Hereford for a visit. I think it was meant to prove that Mr Getty does go out. But when I tried to ask what Mr Getty was giving the SAS money *for*, Mr Treves suddenly whisked the photograph away and said, 'Forget it.'

Mr Getty seemed disposed to acknowledge my existence again, so I asked him why he had moved to St James's. 'Because Cheyne Walk is falling down. We're getting it repaired.'

He is hoping to move eventually to Wormsley, a 1,700-acre estate in Buckinghamshire which he bought in 1984. At the time, he said he had no plans to live there and was buying it purely as an investment, but recently he has had a tower added to house his priceless collection of antiquarian books. Would he like being a country squire?

'Yes, I shall walk around with a stick and a cap and milk cows. The staff will all be trained to touch their forelocks when I appear!' Again the rich, sardonic chuckle.

Rumour has it that one of the cottages at Wormsley has been adapted for wheelchair use, and that Getty's paralysed son Paul III has already spent some time there. Certainly he was in England a few months ago. There was a touching story in the papers that his father had wheeled him round the National Gallery at dead of night. Alas, Mr Treves told me it wasn't true. 'Paul saw his father, and he visited the National Gallery, but not together.'

Still, there are signs that Getty is beginning to play the dutiful father, which will certainly make a change in the Getty family history. He himself barely saw his own father from the age of four, when his parents divorced. He was brought up by his mother in California, and he recalls writing to his father when he was twelve and getting the letter back with all the spelling mistakes underlined. He in turn rarely saw his four eldest children, Paul III, Aileen, Mark and Ariadne, after he divorced their mother, in 1964.

When his second wife, Talitha Pol, died, he handed their three-year-old son Tara Gabriel Galaxy Gramaphone over to her parents, and saw the boy 'for maybe twenty minutes a year'. This was during his Cheyne Walk withdrawal in the 1970s. But recently, he has begun seeing his children again, especially Mark, who is a student at Oxford, and Tara, who is going to train as a farmer at Cirencester Agricultural College. Perhaps he hopes to end his days at Wormsley, surrounded by his children, like a conventional paterfamilias.

I asked him about his books and paintings and his collection of 78 r.p.m. records, and he talked very happily and enthusiastically, as if to a fellow connoisseur. He showed me how he played his 78s on the huge horn gramophone, using bamboo needles which have to be sharpened before each play so as not to damage the records.

When I asked him what he most liked doing he said, 'Watch films, television, listen to records. Read. And I play with girls!' he added, twinkling.

This emboldened me to ask whether he had a girlfriend and he immediately switched off the smile.

'Yes,' he said shortly. But his intimates believe that he remains faithful to the memory of Talitha. 'The pain does not evaporate,' he said, thirteen years after her death.

Getty is so well-read, so erudite, so obviously intelligent, it seems a waste that he has never had his own career.

'I did have a career once, in the oil business. I hated it.' What would he have preferred? 'Oh, to be an oceanographer. Or a librarian. Or a movie star!'

By now, he seemed to have forgotten the golf, Mr Treves had stopped policing my questions, and we were getting along famously, I thought. But then Christopher Gibbs arrived (he is a Bond Street antique dealer, and Getty's best friend) with a book dealer in tow.

'Hello old fruit,' cried Mr Gibbs, 'still doing the interview?' 'Yes,' said I.

'No,' said Mr Getty, 'we've finished.'

'Look,' I said, in a last-ditch stand, 'you've said that all the books and articles about you are full of lies. This is your chance to set the record straight.'

Mr Getty gave me his most terrifying snarl so far. 'No, no, no, NO. It just gives you a chance to print the damn lies all over again.'

Much to my surprise, Mr Treves and Mr Gibbs suddenly moved together to my defence. 'Go on, Paul. Say it. There is one thing you particularly hate.'

Mr Getty only shook his head like a cornered bull. Mr Treves and Mr Gibbs exchanged looks, Mr Gibbs nodded, Mr Treves said, 'That he's a recluse. He hates people saying that.'

'No!' roared Mr Getty, absolutely furious. 'Be quiet.'

Mr Treves and Mr Gibbs shrugged sympathetically at me and both retreated to look at the book dealer's book.

I thought to soothe Mr Getty by changing the subject. 'What's the best thing that's ever happened to you?' I asked.

Staring me full in the eyes for the first time, he said: 'The best thing? The best thing? It's hearing a journalist saying, "Thank you, Mr Getty. I must go. Goodbye."'

He said it with such quiet venom, I leapt immediately to my feet, said, 'Thank you, Mr Getty. Goodbye,' and bolted for the door. He was speaking to Mr Gibbs about the new book before I had even left the room.

Mr Treves said afterwards, 'I'm sorry he was grumpy, I'm sorry he was rude. He really does hate seeing journalists; it's a total ordeal for him. He is a very very sweet person really and I am sorry you didn't see that side of him.'

Actually, I did a bit, just in glimpses, when he was talking about books and records and paintings. And I was impressed by the fact that he inspires devotion from two such obviously good characters as Mr Gibbs and Mr Treves. I liked his dry wit and the way he roared with laughter when I spoke of his 'sudden respectability'. I suspect he himself is quite amused by the way the Establishment has suddenly taken him to their bosom, after having been an outcast for so long. In fact, I suspect he is still an unrepentant sixties hippie at heart – only now a hippie imbued with wealth beyond the dreams of avarice.

I was forcibly reminded of this right at the end of our interview. As I said, there were all these piles of books, magazines, letters round the sofa, and I was aware of a pile of transparent plastic envelopes on the floor by my legs. When I stood up to leave, I happened to glance down and saw what all these transparent envelopes contained: money. Oodles and oodles of brand new £50 notes in sealed wads fresh from the bank. The rich *are* different. And J. Paul Getty is richer and differenter than most.

Reproduced by permission of the *Sunday Express*

BOB GUCCIONE

18 September 1983

Bob Guccione sits in New York in the Georgian panelled room he bought in London and had shipped over, and settles down to talk about the past. The past, for him, started at 9.45 a.m. one Monday morning in 1965 when he drove from his home in Chelsea to a cul-de-sac in Brixton and parked his Cadillac convertible outside a bank. He climbed into the back seat of the car, which was piled high with envelopes, and began ripping them open. They all contained money. He put the cheques into one paper bag, postal orders in another, cash in a third and at 10 a.m., when the bank opened, there he was on the doorstep clutching his three paper bags. An international publishing empire had been born.

At the time Guccione was an expatriate American painter living in London with a wife and four children (five, if you counted the one from his first marriage) to support. He worked as a cartoonist, dry-cleaning manager and mail-order pin-up photographer. He also distributed the *London American* news-sheet and in his tours of the news-stands he noticed an odd thing – *Playboy* magazine had no British rivals. There was *Playboy*, doing very nicely thank you, and there was *Health and Efficiency*, and nary a nude in between. He decided to start his own rival. To raise money he planned a mailing shot – and sent out one million brochures to selected affluent British males telling them that if they would send in their subscriptions, they would receive twelve copies of a great new magazine called *Penthouse*.

Till then he had no money – he had not paid the rent on his house for six months. But he had a good address, and a flash Cadillac (he always had a canny appreciation of the value of 'props') and a printer who agreed to print the brochures and send them out on tick. The mail-out day was fixed for Thursday. On Thursday the printer phoned with 'a slight problem, Mr Guccione'. He explained that it was his company's policy not to pay for postage on the mailing shot: Bob would have to buy the stamps. 'Of course,' said Bob, 'come round and collect my cheque at 3 p.m. But meanwhile, buy the stamps and mail the stuff out.' The printer did; Bob managed to delay the meeting till 3.30 p.m. when the banks were closed; he knew the cheque could not be banked until Friday and cleared until Monday, and on Monday, he *knew*, all the subs would come rolling in. And they did.

Bob loves reminiscing about those early days – the paper bags full of money, the sprints round the pillar-boxes to post his brochures, the police waiting outside his house to serve a writ for indecency in Her Majesty's mails, and timing his appearance in Wells Street magistrates court for the maximum possible publicity effect. It was all fun in those days: one senses he is a little uncomfortable, or at least bored, with his present respectability. 'Yes,' he said sadly, when he finished reminiscing. 'I've come a long way from Ifield Road.'

I worked for him in Ifield Road, in fact I worked for him for seven years, from 1967 to 1974. Ifield Road, SW10, was Penthouse's first office, a horrifically squalid cramped terraced house looking out on to West Brompton cemetery, piled high in every room with dirty books (The Penthouse Book Club) and flimsy underwear (Penteez Panties). Later, when we moved to 'huge new offices' they were an ex-sausage-factory off the North End Road. Needless to say, outsiders were not encouraged to come to the offices and important meetings were eventually held at the Penthouse Club, a scene of particularly Stygian gloom crouched in a Shepherd Market backstreet. The girls, 'Pets', were dressed as sort of naughty French housemaids. People were always keen to go there *once*: I remember taking Auberon Waugh there and he was shocked to death when one of the Pets started chatting happily about how she'd managed to get her dad on to a new kidney machine and he was getting much better, thank you. The girls were always too *real* to be proper sex objects.

Anyway, that is all in the past. In 1969 Bob launched an American edition of *Penthouse*, moved to the States, and made a fortune, later starting a highly successful glossy science magazine called *Omni*. He is still the sole owner of *Penthouse* and all its offshoots, and is reckoned by *Forbes* magazine to be worth between $200m and $300m. He lives in the largest private house in Manhattan, nine floors of prime real estate, surrounded by his 'museum-quality collection of artworks'. He shares the house with Kathy Keeton, vice-Chairman of Penthouse, President of Omni, ex-stripper from South Africa, and his mistress for the past eighteen years.

The house is pure Citizen Kane. You go in through wrought-iron doors that once belonged to Richard Nixon, past a burly armed security guard watching your arrival on closed-circuit television, and into a vast marble hall with glimpses between pillars of a Roman mosaic swimming-pool alongside. The reception area at the end features assorted Old Masters ('Deposition from the Cross', 'Pietà', 'Agony in the Garden', 'Martyrdom of the Saints') and a wall of Jacobean linenfold panelling which slides away at the touch of a button to reveal a cinema screen. The whole house is infested with dogs, Rhodesian Ridgebacks – horrid bristly things the size of zebras. Bob said later there were only five of them, but there seemed to be fifty thundering to and fro.

My appointment with Bob was for 3 p.m. but I turned up

at 3.15 with no sense of haste. In the old days in London the office at going-home time was always littered with businessmen slumped wearily on banquettes saying, 'I'm Bob's two o'clock appointment' or 'I'm Bob's lunch.' Time worked differently for Guccione. He was an insomniac, never went to bed before 4 a.m., never got to sleep before seven, snatched a couple of hours, made a few hundred phone calls, and then ambled into the office around 2 or 3 p.m. to start on his ten o'clock appointment. So I was very surprised indeed, when, ten minutes after my arrival, a secretary announced, 'Bob will see you now.' Good grief – perhaps he had changed so dramatically, I wouldn't recognize him?

But no, there he was, same old thing, dressed in his usual absurd style – powder-blue suede trousers, blue silk baseball jacket opened to reveal the usual tonnage of gold chains and medallions. He had done something funny to his hair – had it tinted or woven or both – but otherwise he looked exactly the same, at fifty-two, with the same magically compelling gravel voice.

He took me into his study, and started reminiscing happily about Ifield Road. I kept wondering what was different about him and eventually realized: he wasn't smoking. He used to smoke five packs a day; one never saw him without a smouldering fag. 'Yup, I quit. Don't know why. Don't feel any better. Can't taste or smell things any better. May live longer but we'll never know.' And then he dropped another bombshell – 'Went on holiday last year' – and I duly fell off my chair. Bob has never in the history of the world been known to take a holiday; he did once go on someone's yacht for ten days but that was a business contact and they spent all their time doing deals. But last year, he swore, he went on a real holiday to South Africa to see Kathy's family, for two whole weeks. And how did it feel? 'It felt . . . extraordinary,' he said, still awestruck at the strangeness of it all. 'For the first time in my life I was getting something like eight hours sleep – normally if I get four, it's pretty good. I slept. I thought I would suffer some kind of withdrawal symptoms, being that far away from things, but you know, I really enjoyed it.'

In fact, Bob's aides had told me, it was getting more and more difficult to drag him out of the house at all. He always works from home and often whole weeks go by without him venturing outdoors. He has never swum or even paddled in his own pool; and he has certainly never set foot in the basement gym.

He still photographs many of the girls for the magazine, and always makes a point of doing the Pet of the Year. The photographs have become more explicit over the years (in 1970 *Penthouse* 'went pubic' and *Playboy* followed three months later) but Guccione's style hasn't changed one iota. He favours soft-focus pink tones and lots of flowers in the foreground, which once led Paul Raymond, his English rival, to remark, 'That guy is a failed florist.' Bob is very proud of his photos: 'Now here's something you don't see in any other men's magazine,' he told me, opening a recent issue of *Penthouse*. 'You see, we throw away a whole double-page spread just on a head shot, something artistic. The pictures are very sensual, but they're not crude in any way, not vulgar.' He attributes his success to the fact (don't laugh) that he is a prude: 'I *am* a prude, which means that if I do something saucy or sexy, there's a need to justify it by extremely good elegant production values and incisive editorial. It's not something I think out intellectually – it's a need, and a need I share with the readers. I cannot allow a piece of unjustified sex to go out. But most publishers of girlie magazines don't have these personal problems. They are really ebullient, outgoing, healthy-attitude types with no problems about sex and the result is their material looks that way. It's not thoughtful, sincere.'

Bob can be extremely witty in casual conversation, but once he starts talking seriously 'for the record' about *Penthouse* he can get terribly boring, so I thought to jolt him on to a new tack by asking if he is, as so often rumoured to be, a member of the Mafia. The two dogs under the table growled,

and Bob growled too, saying I should know him better than
to ask that and it was very tiresome that anyone with a
Sicilian name was automatically assumed to be 'involved in
organized crime'. Anyway, to cut a long story short, he told
me that he had been investigated exhaustively by the FBI and
everyone else in connection with his Atlantic City casino-
building project, and found to be innocent of any involvement
with 'organized crime'.

The Atlantic City project is the thing that currently keeps
him awake at nights. For three and a half years he has had
$74m of his own money tied up in the attempt to build a
Penthouse Casino-hotel complex in Atlantic City, but as
successive funding operations have fallen through, the casino
remains half-built and costs him several million dollars a year.
Why bother, I asked. All those hassles, and he doesn't even
like gambling. 'When it's built,' he said soberly, 'it will
produce an income of around $55–60m a year, and I need
the cash-flow to finance my Atomic Project.'

'Your *what*, Bob? You're not building a bomb, are you?'
He smiled, but that was the last smile I got for the next hour
while he very slowly and seriously explained his Atomic
Project. Briefly, he is financing research into a form of atomic
fusion (not fission) which he thinks, if successful, will revolu-
tionalize the energy industry overnight and, incidentally, send
the price of plutonium plummeting through the floor. The
Russian, American, and some European governments all have
their own atomic fusion projects, but Bob has the only one in
private hands and it will make him, if he succeeds, bigger
than Getty, bigger than Ford, bigger than all the multimillion-
aires in history put together. He is so worried that the US
government might nationalize it that he is considering setting
up a parallel project in Israel.

It sounds, of course, like complete raving madness but Bob
has raved on about apparently lunatic projects before and
some of them came off – he once did a deal with President
Tito to start a Penthouse Casino resort in communist Yugo-
slavia. (It was on the island of Krk, pronounced crook, and it

failed in the end because the local staff could never be taught to serve customers at anything faster than one drink per hour, but still it was an achievement just to launch.)

After about two hours in the study, Bob decided to take me on a tour of the house. A secretary had already shown me the pool and gym and sauna and hairdressing salon and dining-room and patio downstairs, and countless bathrooms with their toilet bowls all 'carved out of one solid block of finest Italian Carrera marble', their gold swan-necked taps, and lapis lazuli mosaic tiling, but Bob was keen to show me the paintings himself. He has so many paintings that half of them are still stacked on the floor and leaning against chairs because he hasn't found space to hang them. It is a fairly staggering collection – Van Gogh, Matisse, Rouault, Soutine, Chagall, Renoir, Vlaminck, Picasso. He pointed out a Degas of a girl drying herself after a bath. 'When I was a kid, the first art book that I ever owned had that in it, so when I saw it for sale, I couldn't resist.' (He rarely talks about his childhood: it was pretty ordinary, one gathers, in New Jersey.) Then he showed me a 1905 Pink Period Picasso of a 'Boy with White Collar' and said wonderingly, 'That's the most expensive single painting I own – two and a half million. Doesn't look it, does it? It's got about six bob's worth of paper in it.'

Finally I whispered the inevitable – 'But are they all genuine?' – and he looked really hurt that anyone could ask. 'Sure – I'll kill the dealers if they're not.' It wasn't that they didn't look genuine, but I couldn't see how anyone could buy so many top quality paintings in so few years. But then he pointed to all the rows of well-thumbed Christie's and Sotheby's catalogues in his bookshelf and said that, actually, he had a man out at that very moment bidding for a Rouault for him, and it all seemed more plausible.

Suddenly there was a great woofing and wooshing of dogs around the house and we heard Kathy's voice in the hall. Bob first met Kathy Keeton in 1965 when he went to interview her for the second issue of *Penthouse*. She was a dancer at the Pigalle at the time, having moved to London from her native

South Africa, and Bob was instantly struck by the fact that her dressing-room was knee-deep in financial magazines. He asked why, and she said she was passionately interested in business. So he asked her to leave her £150-a-week starring role at the Pigalle and work as a £45-a-week advertising sales-woman for *Penthouse* instead. She said yes, and thus was born a partnership as formidable as Antony and Cleopatra, Romeo and Juliet, Héloïse and Abélard, Marks & Spencer.

In the London office, she was always known as Miss Whiplash because of her icy manner and five-inch spike heels, though it was often rumoured that she had a heart of gold really. Since she never spoke more than five words at a time, it was hard to know. She always addressed me as darling, which with her South African accent came out as 'dollink', and I sometimes wondered if she actually knew my name. Anyway, I awaited her arrival at the top of the stairs this time with some trepidation.

'Hello dollink,' she said, offering me her long cheek to kiss. 'Gosh, Kathy, you haven't changed at all,' I said wonderingly. She looked me critically up and down. 'No, I haven't,' she said.

The degree to which she hasn't changed in all of eighteen years is really staggering. Perhaps she is Countess Dracula. She always had long, peroxide hair and dark suntan and still does; she always wore tight trousers, wasp-waist belt and low décolletage, and still does; she always favoured pastel-coloured silks and suedes and still does. Since her style owes nothing to fashion, it is no more unfashionable now than it ever was. 'Haven't your tastes changed *at all*, Kathy, over the years?' I asked. 'No. I still like the same things I liked as a child.' Such as? 'Walking, funfairs, science fiction, music, art.' 'But what about things you didn't have as a child like, oh, say – caviare?' 'I liked caviare from the first time I heard of it.' It is an odd vision: a poor South African miner's daughter dreaming throughout her childhood of caviare, gold bathtubs, Cartier watches and wall-to-wall Mongolian goat-hair car-pets, but in a peculiar way it makes sense.

I tried to ask her age but she said, 'Oh come *on*, dollink' (she must be forty-two or forty-three) and whisked me off to see her bathroom with its 'twenty-four-carat gold mosaic step-in whirlpool tub' and her clothes closet the size of a bedroom with about a thousand pastel-coloured silk and suede numbers on rail after rail. Then she showed me her and Bob's bedroom which featured the by-now-familiar Penthouse décor of pillared bed, fur counterpane, assorted French Impressionists, but it did have a quality all the other rooms strikingly lacked: it did feel, just faintly, like home. At the end of the fur-covered bed was a purely functional non-marble, non-onyx, non-antique table supporting a whole clutter of television, video recorder, video games (Kathy's current favourite is Pacman), with the inevitable spaghetti of wires trailing unglamorously out the back. How curious that at the very heart of the Penthouse empire one should find the wherewithal for a nice cosy evening of telly in bed.

I asked Bob if, at fifty-two, he ever felt old and he said, yes, sure, he did: 'I've been doing the same thing now for eighteen years.' It is quite possible that, if left to his own devices, he would put away the gold medallions and suede trousers and become a perfectly normal middle-aged man. But he has Kathy to live up to. They have no plans to marry (although three years ago Bob finally got a divorce from his English wife), but they obviously have a very special relationship – Bob talks of Kathy with protective fondness and when I asked her if her feelings for Bob had changed at all over the years she said, 'Yes, I love him more and more and *more*.'

It was time for me to go and Bob and Kathy kissed me affectionately and said it was so nice to see an old friend and I must come and stay with them next time I was in New York. I suspect they don't really have any friends, so that an ex-employee seems as much like an old friend as anyone. But to me, though I saw them almost daily for years, they still seem as strange and exotic and mysterious as Martians. They are an oddly private, self-enclosed couple. They live and breathe and talk Penthouse twenty-four hours a day and so have trouble communicating with anyone who doesn't share their obsession. When I arrived in Bob's house, he asked me: 'You married, honey? Children? Yeah? Huh.' And I realized it was the only personal question he had ever asked me. Such lack of curiosity could be put down to monomania, of course; but I believe in their case it is also a symptom of acute shyness.

I will be very curious indeed to see what Bob is doing in ten years' time. If you had told me ten years ago that in 1983 he would be worth at least $200m and would be heavily into atomic fusion, I would have said you were joking. So if I say now that in ten years' time it is just possible that Bob Guccione will be supplying all the world's energy from his own atomic fusion reactor, and that in fifty years' time there could be a Guccione Museum in New York to rival the Guggenheim . . . 'Well, honey,' as he said himself, 'I've come a long way from Ifield Road.'

Reproduced by permission of the *Sunday Express*

RICHARD HARRIS

1 July 1990

Richard Harris is a surprising man in many ways, and he has a very surprising habit. I'm not quite sure how to describe it, and prudish readers had better skip the rest of this paragraph . . . Schoolboys call it playing pocket billiards. He puts his hand down inside his tracksuit and sort of rearranges things – King, Queen, Knave; Knave, King, Queen – or sometimes doesn't rearrange them so much as just hangs on for dear life. I have seen shy small boys do it at playgroup, but I have never seen it in an adult before. He did it the whole time I was with him.

He cuts a pretty odd figure anyway, sitting in the Savoy foyer at noon in a tracksuit, when everyone else is wearing suits. It isn't even as if he jogs: the reason he wears tracksuits all the time, he says, is because he finds them comfortable. *Comfortable for what*, I wonder darkly, but his conversation is so enchanting it soon distracts attention from what he is doing with his hands.

He is staying at the Savoy (he lives in the Bahamas) while he plays Pirandello's *Henry IV* at Wyndham's Theatre, and the play is such a hit they have now extended the run from July to October. Very few people are rich enough to be able to stay at the Savoy for months but he is one of them: 'I was very *wise* when I was young. Amazingly for a man who is supposed to be as *mad* as I am, and as irresponsible as I am, and as crazed and Rabelaisian as I am, I also have a sensible side. I realized at the height of my career that one day it would all stop and I did not want to dwindle into looking for work on television and playing small parts – because my temperament wouldn't allow it, I have to *lead* – so I went to live in the Bahamas, which is tax-free, and with the 50 or 60 per cent I saved in taxes, I bought land – estate after estate after estate in California. Then I sat back and forgot about them. And of course they've doubled and quadrupled and whatever the other words are – one house I bought for $400,000, I've just sold to Barbra Streisand for $6½m.'

So he is canny? He bridles at the word canny, but admits, 'I suppose I am . . . shrewd.' He hasn't always been: in the sixties he went bankrupt twice. But that, he explains, was because in those days he was prone to renting Lear jets and taking parties to Paris and picking up bills for eighteen suites at the George V. 'I was *very* wild. But eventually I got wise, just around the beginning of the seventies. My mind went back to my father and mother being broke, so I took care of it. And I *did*; I was very clever.'

When he was born, in 1930, one of eight children, the Harrises were rich. They were the biggest flour millers in the south-west of Ireland, and their house had nannies and upstairs maids and governesses and gardeners. But they were ruined when Rank millers – 'the *English!*' – moved in and undercut them till they were forced to give up. 'So we went from being rich to being poor. I saw it all dwindle; I saw it all go to nothing. And I could see my mother having to scrub floors and wash sheets and shirts for eight children, and that left a *fantastic* impression. I still see her like that. The old psychological tapes still go on in my head and I say, "I don't want to be like that." I'll *never* be like that, in fact, I know that now, because I couldn't spent my money in five lifetimes.'

As he talks, his accent becomes increasingly Irish; he doesn't *quite* say 'begorrah' or 'at all, at all', but you feel he might, and he did actually say 'Bejayzus' at one point. He is an entrancing, beguiling storyteller; he loves talking about himself and he does it brilliantly; the temptation is just to sit back and enjoy it and stop asking questions. But is any of it true? Early on, I quoted something he was supposed to have said in an interview, and he roared, 'You mustn't believe *anything* that I say in the press, even what I'm telling you now.'

Yet his interviews over the years show a certain consistency. Not one goes by in which he doesn't say he has no regrets, but as the years pile up (he turns sixty this year) the reasons for regret become glaringly apparent. He wasted at least a decade of his life in heavy drinking; he had a great career in the fifties and sixties but he threw it away. In 1965 *Nova* magazine proclaimed him 'the next of the big international stars. He could be the biggest of them all.' But somehow he never was – and in the seventies he was reduced to appearing in films such as *Orca – Killer Whale*.

In fact, what *is* remarkable is that he has somehow managed to retain a great reputation, while having so little to show for it. A list of Richard Harris films is, with one or two exceptions, a list of films you wouldn't want to see even on a black night in Doncaster. The first exception is *This Sporting Life*, directed by Lindsay Anderson in 1963, in which Harris played a rugby-league footballer and won the Best Actor award at Cannes. But commercially, the film was a failure, and he turned down a Hollywood contract in order to return to the London stage. A supposedly starring role in Michelangelo Antonioni's *The Red Desert* ended prematurely when he fell out with the director, and he also had rows during the making of *Mutiny on the Bounty* – in one scene, Harris refused to lie down when Marlon Brando hit him because, he said, Brando's hit was so feeble. Directors found him difficult because he had such strong views on acting. Or, as he said himself in 1964, 'I have a reputation for being troublesome on films. They say I'm not cooperative because I will ring the director at two in the morning to discuss something, because

I will turn up on set on the first day of shooting with twenty pages of notes.' Troublesome, in a word.

But in 1967, he had his second (and last) great film success as King Arthur in *Camelot*. Suddenly he was big box office – he even made a pop album, *MacArthur Park*, which sold five million copies, and was invited to read his poems to the New York Poetry Society. But unfortunately this success coincided with the break-up of his first marriage to Elizabeth, the mother of his three sons, and he was too busy drinking to capitalize on it. Thereafter his career went steadily downhill and the films he made in the seventies are without exception dire. He was always stupidly cast in action roles and 'loincloth parts' – *The Bible, Heroes of Telemark, Hawaii, Man in the Wilderness* – when what he wanted to be doing was *Wuthering Heights* or *Hamlet*, and he complained bitterly in 1965, 'I don't regard myself as an action star. That's my calvary, this is where I am crucified as an actor, and this is why there is the actor's burden when making a picture. You'll find it drives you mad, drives you to drink . . .'

The drinking – or 'hell-raising' in the journalese of the time – was a feature of his image from his début onwards, and may have eventually made it difficult to insure him for films. By the beginning of the eighties, 'I grew to hate making films because the standard of the films I was making was so bad. Finally, nine years ago, I was making a movie with Bo Derek, called *Tarzan the Ape Man*, and it was a forty-four-day shoot and I remember on the first night before I went to bed, I opened my diary and wrote, "forty-three days left". And I thought *why*? Why am I willing away my life? I'll never get those forty-three days back again; I don't need the money; I'm very rich. So I said, "That's it," and stopped making movies.'

He also stopped drinking for good. He had always been a binger rather than a steady drinker, with stints of sobriety interspersed by massive, public benders often accompanied by fisticuffs. But on 11 August 1982 he sat down at the Jockey Club in Washington and drank two bottles of their best Château Margaux 1957 and never touched alcohol again. He is evasive about why this happened – 'I just decided' – but he once admitted that a doctor warned him he was becoming diabetic, and that his drinking blackouts were actually comas. He was also sobered by seeing Richard Burton on the wagon when they made *The Wild Geese* together in 1978: 'The courage of that guy! But there was agony and pain in his abstinence. I thought, "Well, I'm beyond that stage. I was as bad as him in 1970, so why carry on and get that way again?"'

With the end of film-making and the end of drinking, he embarked on a stage tour of *Camelot* which eventually lasted six years and took him all over the United States. It sounds like an actor's nightmare, but he insists that he enjoyed it. He liked the travelling, and he needed the therapy of constant working while he got used to not drinking. 'And what it did was, it really consolidated my voice. Because to make it work I had to do vocal exercises every day for two hours and now everyone who comes to see my Pirandello says, "There's not another voice in England like it."'

As far as he is concerned, his Pirandello makes up for all the wasted years. He wanted to do it all his life – it was the first play he ever saw as a child – and it was he who persuaded Duncan Weldon to produce it, and drove it on through all the traumas of the pre-London run when actors, directors, designers were falling like ninepins and the start date had to be postponed three times. He was – is – obsessed with the play; he had all Pirandello's notes and journals translated into English and sacked two directors when he felt they hadn't done their homework. And now he feels triumphantly vindicated – 'It's the *best*! I can't *wait* for eight o'clock every evening. I'm the happiest man in the world because Irving Wardle and Jack Tinker and all those critics acknowledge the work. And I'm *back*. I'm probably where I should have been for years, but there we are. Never look back in regret: I'm here now.'

He is putting all his energy into the work and allows

himself no distractions. He gets up at twelve, has lunch, rests in the afternoon, goes to the theatre at 6.30, does the performance, goes to bed and reads till 2 or 3 a.m. Next year he hopes to do *King Lear* or *Macbeth*.

Even his film career may be about to revive. He admits wryly that when he announced his retirement from movies eight years ago, 'Hollywood didn't go into a state of depression; there was a general shrug of indifference', but now his phone has suddenly started ringing again. The reason is *The Field*, a film set in Ireland which he made earlier this year, which will be premièred at the New York film festival in October. Is it good? 'Good?' he shouts, 'It's *wonderful*. It's a *great* script with a *brilliant* director. It's mon-u-mental.'

He is so obviously so blissfully happy with his return to the London theatre, it seems a shame he didn't do it ten years ago. Why didn't he? 'Because ten years ago I was living that fine life of madness. I didn't have the discipline to do it. But then I made the choice [presumably when he gave up drinking] that I was going to spend the rest of my life fulfilling certain dreams, and this was a dream. *Lear* is a dream, and I'll do it. It's not too late. Never say never. Never look back on your life as a kind of mistake because *nothing* is a mistake in my life. The only mistake I made in my life is that I never got round to playing *Hamlet* – and I know I could have been superb.'

But why has he waited till sixty to sort himself out? Why has it all taken so *long*? It is not the sort of question he likes, and provokes another busy burrowing in his tracksuit. He once said that 'the worst thing about being a film star is the introspection and, in Hollywood, the involvement with psychiatry ... It neutralizes you, psychiatry.' Yet he admits that he has a friend who is a doctor of psychiatry, with whom he will occasionally talk things over – not his *own* problems, you understand, but theories of madness, of schizophrenia.

He seems to have a hang-up about women. He once boasted in an interview that he had slept with more women than Simenon (who slept with over 10,000) but he laughed when I quoted it. 'Ten thousand? Is that so? I just thought it was a wonderful quote – journalists love it.' His wild days as a ladykiller coincided with his drinking and 'you don't function very well when you're full of beer'.

Now, he says, 'my sex life is in reverse, it's like an old car that's come out of gear somewhere. You can't survive – *I* can't survive – without having women around. But it's the permanency of it that's something else – whether you want someone *continually* in your life, that's the question.' His parents, he says wistfully, barely knew each other when they married; they were put together by a matchmaker and told to get on with it. 'But they *grew* to love and *grew* to companionship, and when my mother died, my father died within the year of a broken heart. They loved each other to *death*.' He envies their fidelity, but could not achieve it in either of his own two marriages, to Elizabeth Harris (daughter of Lord Ogmore) in the fifties and sixties, and to Ann Turkel, the actress, in the seventies. He was unfaithful to both, he says, and they to him, but he was never disloyal, and he remains good friends with them today. Indeed, his friends sometimes speculate that he might remarry Elizabeth – who reverted to the name Harris by deed poll after she divorced her second husband, Rex Harrison – but he seems to think not: 'I'm not the easiest man to be married to.'

His public image – loud, rumbustious, apparently extrovert – is, he admits, largely an act. 'My life is full of sort of quiet, silent giggles, because I'm very difficult to get to know – my wives will tell you that – because I appear to be upfront, but I'm not at all. And because of that it's very difficult for me to have relationships and friendships, very difficult, because eventually to be penetrated – not that I fear having it penetrated – but I do believe there's a large portion of me that belongs to me and nobody else. I couldn't even share it with my wives.' (Is that the portion which his hand is even now nervously clutching?)

He has just two friends, one a doctor of music in Wales, and the other an international banker, and they've been friends for thirty-five years. Both men, he says, are more intelligent than him and that is why he values them. He fell out with one of them for a whole year, but eventually rang him up and apologized. He says he has no friends at all in the Bahamas, and never mixes with anyone there.

He likes to be alone; he often spends weeks on end without seeing anyone except the servants. 'By myself, I'm the *best*! I don't mean that arrogantly – or maybe I do. I find myself the best company in the world. I read prodigiously, I listen to music prodigiously and my tastes are extraordinary – everything from Gregorian chants to opera to Mahler to Frank Sinatra. I often wonder: how can I love Sammy Davis and love Mahler and Delius? I think there's probably three or four of me inside and whoever wakes up first that morning functions.'

But then his periods of silence and solitude give way to a restless urge, when he hops on a plane looking for excitement and action. The trouble with the Bahamas, he says, is that 'although it's beautiful and the people are gorgeous, I, however, having a very active mind, and a challenging mind, find there are no challenges there, intellectually or artistically'. So then he takes off to London, to Dublin (he still has a house in Ireland) or to California (where his eldest son, Damian, lives) or to New York to see theatre. 'I'm very restless. I live on a whim. I'll just wake up one morning and say I'm bored and leave.'

This curious alternation between intense solitude and intense socializing may have started in his teens when he had tuberculosis for two and a half years and was confined to hospital. He once said, rather bitterly, that he always thought he had lots of friends until he was in hospital, when remarkably few came to see him. On the other hand, 'I wouldn't change it. I found myself at the mercy of my imagination. I began making conversation with pillows and light bulbs.'

As soon as he recovered, he jumped on the boat to England and presented himself at RADA, sleeping many nights on friends' sofas or even in doorways because he could not afford to pay rent. His TB gave him the courage and determination to become an actor.

He says he has no friends who are actors. Not even Peter O'Toole and Albert Finney? 'No, not at all. Peter and I were friends in madness when we were much younger, but we never had a tremendous closeness. He's the greatest actor of our generation, and he wrote me the most beautiful letter the other day; Finney, too – we're all overjoyed with each other's successes. But friends? Not really.'

I'm surprised by him saying that O'Toole is the greatest actor of his generation, because I assumed Harris thought *he* was. But no, he says soberly, he is good, but O'Toole is better. This is a rare note of modesty in his conversation, and an indication that he takes acting too seriously to lie about it.

On other subjects, he is content to boast, though with a little counterpoint of irony that suggests it is all part of the interview performance. But, he insists, 'I am terribly confident, unashamedly confident of myself. *Very*. And I suppose if you ask am I arrogant, I will have to say yes I am. Arrogant with my work, and arrogant also with my *life*.

'I know what I want. I'm not confused at all. I know precisely what I want, and I know what I am doing from day to day. It may seem aimless, but it's deliberately aimless. And if I waste my time, it's because I want to waste my time.'

Goodness, say I at this point, he is obviously a very wonderful person. Doesn't he have any faint little faults or flaws at all? His eyes flash in recognition of the sarcasm, and he grins appreciatively: 'Oh, of course I've got millions of faults. But I'm not going to tell *you* about them. I wish I could control, when my temperament *does* explode, I feel very guilty. I have literally *days* of horror and guilt and remorse.

'I know it can be frightening when I blow – it's *Lear*, it's huge, it's volcanic – and then I go home and feel *terrible*. I mean I still remember how badly I behaved to Lindsay Anderson on *This Sporting Life* – I behaved with such ruthlessness – and that still torments me, I still sometimes phone him up when I feel dreadful.

'I impose standards on people that are very difficult. I didn't speak to one of my friends, one of my two friends, for over a year. I am full of horrendous faults.'

Vanity, for instance? He readily admits that he dyed his hair for years because 'it looked good. It used to be auburn, then I dyed it blond for *A Man Called Horse* in 1967 and I liked it, so I kept it. I liked to wear my hair blond, then tint my beard a bit darker.'

But isn't that vain? 'No, I am totally unvain. I am not the slightest bit vain. Look at the way I walk around. I've never owned a hairbrush, I've never owned a comb. Look at my clothes – I always wear a tracksuit – how can I be vain?

'I've got a coat upstairs that cost me £40 in the King's Road years ago that I wear all the time, lying on top of an $1,800 Versace leather coat that I never wear. *Look* at me. If I was a Hollywood star now, I'd have my eyes done, and my face done, and the wrinkles removed and these droopy eyelids gone – but that's not me. Are you going to say I'm vain in your article?'

'Yes.' This is clearly the moment he has been waiting for; it is as if someone has shot him full of adrenalin; it is the moment in the Dublin pub when someone swings the first punch and all hell breaks loose.

He gleefully starts thumping the table and shouting: 'That's what you're saying because that's what you want to write about! This is where you journalists are all so cock-eyed! Why have an interview at all? You've written it all before-hand. You can't understand me – obviously you can't because you've got a female mind. I'm too bright for you altogether.'

The best voice in London, at full belt, has immense carrying power, and virtually the entire Savoy grinds to a halt while everyone listens. Harris enlists all the businessmen at nearby tables as witnesses: 'Did you hear what she said? She says that I'm vain. *Look at me!*'

As an attention-getting exercise it is peerless: at one point the manager comes over to tell him to stop thumping the table, but the exchange has a half-hearted feel because it has obviously happened many times before. He *loves* it, he loves 'having a discussion', and I realize that his conversation beforehand – which had seemed lively and interesting to me – was a poor pale thing in his view compared to the joys of a good shouting match.

Alarmed by the noise, the shouting and the thumping, I try to change the subject, but he is like a boxer who props his opponent up so he can hit him again: 'Go on, go on,' he urges. 'I want to hear how you rationalize things, how you justify yourself.' *I* want to know what he imagines he means by a female brain, but he is less excited by that topic because it takes the conversation away from him.

'It's a fact. You have a woman's body, what's wrong with having a woman's brain? I mean I've got a cock and you haven't . . .' (Oh, *that* old thing again – he really thinks I'm trying to steal it.) 'Come on, boys,' he shouts to the next table, 'You're my witnesses. You jump to my defence.'

It is an exciting, disturbing madness; it *is* 'hell-raising'. He wants a happening; he wants everyone to join in, shouting, arguing, with perhaps a spot of fisticuffs and himself at the centre of it all.

But, of course, the foyer of the Savoy is not the most congenial environment for a happening, and the more excited he becomes, the more people turn away and pretend to resume their own conversations. I too am suddenly eager to get away, thinking yet again how very *tiring* actors always are. I wanted to provoke him but I got more than I bargained for and now I am looking at my watch and mumbling about the parking meter running out.

He walks me to the door, not so much walking as sort of gambolling through the full Thespian repertoire of antics, still shouting to passers-by: 'She says I'm *vain! Look at me!*'

As I leave, he is already picking up a new audience, a girl at the flower stall, who looks alarmed. 'You've got a great tape there!' he shouts after me. He means a great perform-

DAVID HART

11 March 1990

Never underestimate the power of the old school tie. When I first asked David Hart to do an interview he was reluctant. He said he had been ridiculed and hurt by journalists and he doubted my good intentions. Happening to mention this to my husband, he said, 'Oh, I knew him at school. His nickname was "Jewy"' Next day when I relayed this information (not the 'Jewy' bit but the school connection) to David Hart's office, he was on the phone in a flash, saying, 'Come and see me on Monday.'

This was odd because David Hart always tells everyone he hated school; in the recent Channel 4 documentary about the miners' strike, *A Strike out of Time*, he said the reason he became a 'libertarian' was because he was so unhappy at Eton, where he believes he was a victim of anti-Semitism. My husband – who is also half Jewish – says that although there was anti-Semitism at Eton, none of the other Jewish boys was ever called 'Jewy' or – Hart's alternative nickname – 'Spiv'. (Incidentally, David Hart denied knowledge of either of these nicknames, and said stiffly, 'My usual nickname is Diehard.') Nevertheless, it was Eton that got me my interview. The only proviso was that I had to read his novels first – he biked them round – 'Because I *am* a novelist after all.'

'David Hart, novelist' was not quite the article I had in mind, but I enjoyed reading *The Colonel* and *Come to the Edge*. Both deal, rather portentously, with the subject of the outsider versus society; both have heroes who are rich, Jewish, well-endowed and misunderstood. One of them takes over the government; the other ends up in a loony-bin. *Come to the Edge* begins: 'This book is dedicated to you, Citizen.'

However, I was more interested in David Hart's political role – if any – and the question of whether he is or is not a secret guru to Mrs Thatcher. On the phone he told me: 'There is one question you must not ask me. About the lady. I will not answer so there is no point in your asking.'

During the miners' strike David Hart acted as unofficial adviser to Ian MacGregor and financial backer to the National Working Miners' Committee. While Peter Walker, then Energy Secretary, wished to reach a settlement with the NUM, Hart strongly urged MacGregor not to compromise: he saw the strike as a political showdown with the forces of Marxism. His personal style throughout the dispute was high-key; he whisked round the coalfields by helicopter, or by chauffeur-driven Mercedes, and summoned working miners to meetings in his suite at Claridge's. Peter Walker at one point shouted at him on the phone, 'You cannot run this strike from Claridge's,' and Hart told him, 'I seem to be doing all right so far.'

More recently, he has bobbed up again as chairman of the Committee for a Free Britain – a right-wing lobby group mainly noted for the lavish parties it throws at Tory Party Conferences. It also gives money (David Hart has plenty of money; his father founded a bank) to 'libertarian' causes, such as students' unions who wish to disaffiliate from the NUS. It puts out very glossy pamphlets on the liberty of the individual and the need for less state interference. One 1988 pamphlet was a strong attack on Sir Geoffrey Howe's Foreign Secretaryship; it may or may not be significant that Mrs Thatcher fell out with Howe and sacked him shortly afterwards. Hart says the committee consists of himself, Baroness

Cox, Lord Harris of High Cross and Christopher Monckton, a political journalist on the London *Evening Standard*. I was hoping Monckton would give me lots of 'background' on David Hart, but in fact he couldn't slam the phone down fast enough.

David Hart also has interests in Eastern Europe and the Soviet Union; he runs a *samizdat* agency to publish Russian dissidents' work in the West. He writes occasional political articles in *The Times*, whose editor, Charles Wilson, is a friend, as was his predecessor, Charles Douglas-Home. (During the miners' strike, Hart got into miners' meetings by saying he was a *Times* journalist; more deviously still, he used a *Daily Express* photographer to serve a writ on Arthur Scargill at a NUM conference.)

According to the *Guardian*, he also has clandestine involvement with the CIA, various American right-wing groups, and with one Charles Elwell, formerly of MI5's 'domestic subversion' division. All this makes him seem powerful and sinister: but according to my husband and other friends who know him socially, 'Nobody could possibly take David Hart *seriously*.' Could Mrs Thatcher? 'Oh well, yes, maybe she could.'

Anyway, I went to see him at his home, Coldham Hall near Bury St Edmunds. At the station, a uniformed butler in morning coat and striped trousers stood beside a glossy Range Rover to meet me. He was surprisingly chatty, asking if I'd seen the recent Channel 4 programme about the miners' strike in which Mr Hart appeared. He told me that his brother was a miner and supported the NUM, 'so it's just as well I didn't work for Mr Hart when all that was going on!' He worked before for the Duke of Northumberland, which was 'very nice' but working for Mr Hart was more fun. 'I do everything for him, drive, buttle, valet, help on the farm, load on shoots, clean all his hunting gear, cook his breakfast and his lunch. The only thing I don't do is groom: I hate a horse.' He said Mr Hart was the best boss any butler could ever wish for.

Then we arrived at the house, a beautiful Elizabethan (1574) rose-brick manor but set in a rather dull, featureless park with plenty of lawns but no gardens. In *The Colonel*, David Hart says of his hero, 'His taste was heroic rather than subtle,' so I was curious to see what heroic taste might be: it seemed rather conventional, chintz and Tudorbethan. The house was spotlessly clean with lovely waxed floors, but quite dauntingly cold. His friends call it Colditz.

David Hart bounded out to greet me. Heavily built, forty-five-ish, he exuded energy and obviously didn't feel the cold. He questioned me closely about my husband; only when satisfied that I really *was* married to an ex-schoolmate did he allow me to switch on my tape recorder.

I asked what he thought of the portrayal of him in *A Strike out of Time*. He said it was accurate on the whole, but he never said that he wanted to 'crush' the miners. 'I *loved* the miners, I stayed in their houses and even once shared a bed with a miner. The idea that I would ever want to crush them is nonsense. I wanted to *save* them from Scargill.' He also didn't like the fact that the actor playing him in the dramatization sat with his legs apart and wore a Biggles flying jacket. 'I wore half change throughout the strike. That's an Eton expression – ask your husband what it means.' (It means jacket, shirt and jeans.) But did he turn up at miners' houses in a chauffeur-driven Mercedes? 'Well yes, but we parked down the street. And he was only a *driver*, not a bodyguard.' And did he stay at Claridge's throughout? 'I didn't have a London house at the time so of course I had to stay in a hotel . . . Yes, it was Claridge's.'

We adjourned to the kitchen for lunch – a frugal affair, consisting of tinned tomato soup, a small piece of Brie and sliced bread, washed down by one glass of champagne. Throughout, the butler stood silently against the wall, like a stick of furniture, which I found distinctly odd considering he'd practically told me his life story in the car. Surely you either have a butler who chatters away to guests like a normal human being, or you have one who pretends to be part of the furniture, but not one who fluctuates between the two?

There is always a suggestion with David Hart that he is not

quite *comme il faut*. He is too obviously, ostentatiously, rich. In restaurants, he will toss his car keys to a waiter and tell him to fetch his cigars, which are the size of cucumbers. At school, he wore those incredibly expensive silk socks which are so thin as to be almost transparent. 'Flashy,' my husband said.

The hero of *The Colonel* is a Jewish immigrant from central Europe who 'determined to train himself to be a member of the English ruling class . . . until he could so exactly imitate this society . . . that it would forget his sudden, unexplained arrival in its midst'. I wondered if this was true of David Hart himself? 'No, of course not. I mean, I went to Eton; I was brought up as a member of the English ruling class; I didn't need to disguise myself. I was brought up to hunt, to shoot, to fish; to sit at excellent tables with wonderful food and very good conversation; to see beautifully cleaned silver; to know what proper table service was; to expect the tablecloths to be spotless; to have linen sheets on the bed; plenty of maids; beautiful light streaming in the windows. That's the life of the English aristocracy − or what it used to be. Nowadays of course most of them haven't got the money to keep it up.' Precisely. He has camouflaged himself in the pelt of an extinct species and therefore stands out a mile.

Perhaps *The Colonel* was based on his father's experiences? 'Absolutely not. My father was very English, he went to Westminster. He was born in England, as was my grand-father.' The family were originally distinguished rabbis in Padua; they came to England during the Napoleonic Wars. His father was brought up as an orthodox Jew, but he married an Irishwoman, a Gentile. David Hart was even baptized into the Church of England, though he still seems keen to present himself as Jewish.

His father, 'Boy' Hart, was a stockbroker and then founded a successful bank, Henry Ansbacher, in the 1940s. He was a brilliant water-colourist but he repressed his artistic yearnings in order to be a financier. 'He was a shy man, rather uncomfortable in some ways, to me. He was very non-demonstrative, like that generation were. He adored me and I adored him but there was this terrible barrier between us because he was so shy. He was also a very very strong man and, for us children [he has a younger brother, Tim], a rock-like figure. Rather formal – I never heard him swear in his life – and very correct in his relationship with my Mum, which didn't always work too well but he would never *dream* of admitting that.

'He had an extremely tough personal morality . . . very difficult for a child to live up to. I'll give you a good example. During the Cuban missile crisis, we were all in London and I was scared. I was old enough to understand and I thought "My God, we're all going to be nuked!" And we were sitting listening to the radio and I was fidgeting about and being very nervous and my father said, "I'm beginning to feel ashamed of you. However frightened you may be – and it's natural to be frightened – you've jolly well got to face it with courage." It's tough, isn't it? But he was *right*; the only way to face that sort of thing is to face it with courage. You have no option, otherwise you just fall to pieces and you're useless.

'I remember another thing – and it makes me fond of him to think of it. I used to get my shirts laundered by a particular Jewish laundryman in London and one day he was rather insistent on seeing me. I thought perhaps I hadn't paid his bill. But he said, "I just wanted to tell you something about your father. He's a very great man." I said, "Oh – thank you very much – but why?" He said, "Well, in the war I was in his unit in the Fleet Air Arm and I was very scared. He called me into his office and he said, 'Look. You're a Jew. I'm a Jew. I'm scared; you're scared. But we have simply not to allow ourselves to show to other people that we're scared. We've jolly well got to face it with courage.'" And this *so* impressed this bloke, the laundryman, that it completely solved his problem and in fact he had rather a good war.'

As he says, a hard father to live up to. Hart *père* must have grieved when his elder son left Eton prematurely ('I was *not* sacked') immediately after O-levels, and became a film-maker, rather than a banker or lawyer. His 16mm film short, *Sitting Quietly, Doing Nothing, Spring Comes and the Grass Grows by Itself*, won a certain *réclame*, though more for its title than its action. Then in 1972 he went into property, made several millions, spent slightly more, and went bankrupt in 1974. 'Two years to make it; one year to lose it. They were extraordinary times.' His father had thoughtfully informed his bank when David first went into business that he took no responsibility for his son's affairs so rescue was not forthcoming from that quarter. In any case, Hart insists, 'I didn't *want* to ask anybody to bail me out. I made a mistake; I took too many risks and I had to pay the price.'

The price was high: he lost his huge country estate on Exmoor, his London house; even his watch and fountain-pen. He moved to a small rented flat and took a job as an estate agent. 'It was jolly good for me; made me put my feet firmly on the ground. It's just *good* to have to face the realities.' In 1978 he was discharged, his father having died in the interim. He is now 'in property' again and clearly not short of money, though it is impossible to discover how much of his fortune is his own creation and how much inherited. Coldham Hall itself is in trust for his sons.

He has three: one, aged eighteen, from a youthful affair, and two, aged fifteen and nine, by his ex-wife, Christina. 'We get on perfectly well; it's a perfectly friendly, sensible, relaxed arrangement.' He also has a girlfriend, Hazel, with whom he has lived for ten years and whom he says he now plans to marry, 'If she'll have me.' Why did it take him ten years to get round to it? 'I don't like discussing my private affairs.'

His life altogether seems extraordinarily complicated. Sometimes he describes himself as a novelist and playwright (he has just written a new play called *Ask Machiavelli* which he is hoping to put on in London), sometimes as a farmer (he farms three hundred acres) and sometimes as a property developer. He works three or four days a week in London, travelling up by helicopter, while his butler takes the car; he hunts one day a week, and has large house parties most weekends.

A feature of Colditz weekends used to be Saturday night
roller-disco at Bury St Edmunds – Hart was a passionate
roller-skater – but he broke his ankle and had to give it up.
He describes his friends as, 'You know, the usual play people,'
and mentions Sir Tatton Sykes, a wealthy landowner, Christopher Logue the poet, Anthony Blond the publisher and Eric
Clapton the guitarist (with whom, he says, he used to play
the flute) – but he also has many working-class friends. 'I
don't like the English aristocracy, and I don't like the
bourgeoisie. I am very happy and relaxed with working-class
people and I've spent a lot of my life with them.'

One of David Hart's most attractive qualities is his roman-
ticism. He believes that 'The thing is not to be afraid of one's
dreaming.' Where most people only fantasize, he acts. At
Eton, when he was told off for walking out of bounds with
the sweetshop owner's daughter, he argued so persuasively
that he was allowed to take the girl out after all. Other boys
could only gnash their teeth. Later, falling in love with the
actress Elsa Martinelli in a film, he wrote and said he would
like to meet her and, 'To my astonishment, she rang me and
we met and had a *wonderful* romance, really lovely.' She was
thirty-four, he twenty-two.

Perhaps because of his wealthy background, he tends to
feel that anything is possible, and he does not suffer from the
fear of ridicule which inhibits most people's dreaming. He
said he would not help me to define him because, in defining
him, I would belittle him; and he read me a passage from
Come to the Edge which he said summed up his personal
philosophy: 'Members of a crowd are only ready to consider
a free spirit a success after he has surrendered his individuality
to them. Only when his most heroic actions, his extraordinary
taking of risks, have been restrained by them, defined by them
and brought within their understanding, only then will members of a crowd let him speak. That is why a free spirit is
always mocked.'

But what is this free spirit about? Is he just an eccentric
playboy with grandiose delusions or is he really, as he claims,

a political fixer? The hero of *The Colonel* has a 'mind usually stuffed with schemes for advancing himself either in society or in public life'. David Hart claims, 'I work a great deal, at weekends, all the time really,' and says that half his working time is devoted to politics. The day after I saw him, he was off to Poland, Hungary and Czechoslovakia 'just to try and see if there is anything we can do to help. They need advice on how to organize themselves and they asked me to come and talk to them.' Who did? 'Various people.'

He is now thinking of putting himself forward as an MP because Sir Eldon Griffiths, the sitting member for Bury St Edmunds, is retiring. 'It will be principally because I want to help people. I had dinner with Enoch Powell the other day and he said what he really missed about retirement was not the House of Commons, but his surgery. Helping people is very exciting.' And if he becomes an MP, will he hope to become Prime Minister? 'No, I don't think I do really. It's a horrible life, with terrible stresses and strains. To be PM is really making an enormous personal sacrifice.'

So what are his political beliefs? He describes himself as a libertarian, which he defined to me as someone who wanted to see greater freedom for the individual and less state interference – education vouchers and privatizing public services. I said it sounded like a rich man's version of I'm-all-right-Jackism, and he responded furiously, 'Madam. If you think that about me, why did I get involved in the miners' strike? Why did I get involved in any of the things I do? I work *really* hard, politically, for nothing. It costs me a lot of money, a lot of time and I get absolutely zero reward except the satisfaction of trying to do my bit for other people.' Then he reeled off a long quotation from Nietzsche about how people who tried to help others were always misunderstood.

But it is hard to find anyone who has benefited from David Hart's activities. Chris Butcher, aka 'Silver Birch', the organizer of the Notts Working Miners and therefore someone whom David Hart was theoretically helping, told me, 'That man did more damage to the working miners than anyone in

the industry. I've more contempt for him than I have for
Arthur Scargill.' It is hard even to find anyone who admits to
associating with David Hart, and he himself says he would
not 'embarrass' his political friends by citing their names.

What about his supposed CIA and MI5 links, as detailed in
the *Guardian*? Hart is dismissive. Yes, he says, he knew Bill
Casey, the late director of the CIA, very well, but only by
pure chance, because he was a friend of a mutual acquaintance. As for Charles Elwell, the mysterious MI5 anti-subver-
sive connection: 'He retired *years* ago. It's typical *Guardian*
nonsense.'

Does David Hart have any political influence at all? It all
depends on whether he has the ear of the Prime Minister, but,
as he warned me beforehand, he refuses to answer any
questions about 'the lady'. According to *Private Eye*, he once
told a friend that he didn't need to sign the Official Secrets
Act because 'Thatcher's told me so much I could blow her
out of the water in five minutes', but he told me he never said
any such thing. He is a close friend of Sir Alan Walters
(Walters's name appears frequently in the Coldham Hall
visitors' book) and of Tim Bell and Charles Powell, all of
whom are Thatcher intimates.

Hart claims that he has sometimes helped her with her
speeches, for instance by suggesting the phrase 'soul politic'
to contrast with 'body politic'. He mentioned that he was a
friend of Kenneth Clarke, the Health Minister, and that he
knew 'most' of the Cabinet. But Kenneth Clarke said that he
had no recollection of meeting Mr Hart, and no Cabinet
names appear in the Coldham Hall visitors' book. I put it to
David Hart that he was just a political groupie who liked to
delude himself and others that he had political clout. At this
point he invited me for a drive around the estate, without my
tape recorder, during which he said he would 'steer' me on
the real situation.

In my experience, people generally tell you things off the
record to get you to print a fib or two.

The gist of David Hart's revelations, as we bounced over

his acres, was that, yes, he knew Mrs Thatcher, and sometimes offered her advice. She had particularly welcomed
outside advice during the last days of Sir Geoffrey Howe's
Foreign Secretaryship, when she was unhappy about the
Foreign Office's attitude to, for example, South Africa. (One
of the CFB pamphlets has a picture on the cover of Sir
Geoffrey Howe giving what appears to be a Black Power or
Marxist salute to a crowd in Mozambique. According to Hart,
when Mrs Thatcher ticked him off about it, Howe said he was
just swatting a fly. Sir Geoffrey Howe refused to comment.)

When we got back to the house, David Hart said that was
all off the record; and I said, 'Oh don't worry; I won't
remember a word of it.' He looked displeased. Perhaps the
fact is, he wants people to believe he has influence with the
Prime Minister, without actually saying so himself?

I suspect that, along with Sir Hector Laing, Lord Rayner,
Charles Saatchi and other passing gurus, he may have had the
ear of the Prime Minister at one stage, but his stage is now
over. She likes meeting new people (particularly if they are
dashing, unconventional, rich and male) and hearing their
ideas, but having heard them, she passes on to gurus new.
This was no more than a suspicion until I said goodbye to
David Hart, and the butler drove me to the station. He was
in chatty mood again, and said he was so pleased Mr Hart
had shaved his beard off this morning 'for your photographer'. Oh, did he have a beard? I said, not really listening.
'Yes, he always grows one every August when we go deer-
stalking at Montrose, and then he shaves it off the first time
he goes round to No. 10.'

It took me a long time to register the import of this but
finally I did. It was now February. 'You mean he hasn't been
round to No. 10 since last August?'

'I suppose he hasn't, no.' I think we can all sleep easier in
our beds.

Reproduced by permission of the *Independent on Sunday*

BARRY HUMPHRIES

20 September 1987

Listen, possums, we will try to forget Dame Edna Everage, Housewife Superstar, for a moment, and concentrate on her creator, Barry Humphries. He is a deeply elusive creature. Even people who have known him for years throw up their hands in horror when you ask them to describe him. 'Well, *mad*, obviously . . .'

I will skip, for a moment, the twenty-odd, *very* odd, phone calls that preceded our meeting, and arrive on his substantial doorstep in north London. Although it was the appointed day, time and place for our interview, I had no very high hopes of finding Barry at home. In the end, it was his wife, Diane Millstead, who answered the door – a pale, ill-looking blonde in a grey dressing-gown, all too obviously roused from bed.

'Uh, Barry must have forgotten. Come in, though, I'll make some tea.' She said she was glad I'd got her up because she'd spent all week in bed with mouth ulcers. 'What sort of milk do you prefer, soya or goat?'

She told me to explore the house while she made the tea, so I did. I was staggered by its size, its grandeur, its quite intimidating formality. Even Dame Edna would be silenced by it. The drawing-room is a vast salon of grey silk sofas and black lacquer tables, art nouveau glass and important French and Belgian symbolist paintings. No trace of children in the house, though the Humphries have sons of six and four. They must be exceptionally well trained. When I admired the paintings, Mrs Humphries ('Aw, call me Diane') said, 'Yes, but we've made a resolution: no more dead artists.'

In the kitchen, I noticed a newspaper cutting pinned up on the wall – the only non-immaculate thing in sight. It was about a baby with a terrible skin disease. Diane saw me reading it and said, 'I cut that out because I can tell that what the baby is *really* suffering from is a food allergy, so I'm going to ring the parents and tell them.'

Did she often do things like that? 'Whenever I see a possible case of food allergy that the doctors have missed, yes.'

Then we went through to the imposing drawing-room and sipped our soya-milk tea while she talked about food allergies. Many, many people, she believes, suffer from food allergies without realizing it. Her own children had asthma until she trained them, from the age of three, to recite, 'I am allergic to milk and all milk products, to food additives, preservatives and colourings,' whenever they went to other people's houses.

Her own sister, she went on, suffered from ulcerated colitis ('where you defecate the bowel lining') because she didn't realize her own allergies. 'I myself am allergic to salmon and bananas,' she said proudly.

When I mentioned that I had a friend who suffered from colitis, Diane said, 'Well, what's her name, what's her number? I'll ring her up right now.'

Too embarrassing, I said, so Diane made me promise to make my friend ring her instead. I was touched by her unselfish concern.

After half an hour of food allergies, and still no sign of Barry Humphries, I asked Diane to tell me about herself. She is thirty-seven, married Barry seven years ago, and is basically a painter and sculptor, though she gave up her own work for three years while she co-wrote and produced Barry's film *Sir Les Patterson Saves the World*, raising all the $7½m budget herself. 'I loved doing the deals. I loved talking about money.'

Now she is back to painting again and she took me up to her studio at the top of the house to see her work in progress. It was a very brightly coloured, almost hallucinogenic, nude with wispy hair standing in the sea. She told me it was a portrait of a psychiatrist friend in Sydney.

Then we went back to the drawing-room and talked about food allergies some more until Barry Humphries walked in. 'Don't feel *too* guilty,' cried Diane. 'Don't apologize *too* abjectly.' In fact, he didn't apologize at all; he had obviously clean forgotten our appointment and the twenty or more daily phone calls that preceded it.

'But how very nice that you're here *now*,' he said smoothly. 'I expect you'd like me to tell you about Dame Edna's plans . . . Well, she is appearing in her own show, *Back with a Vengeance*, which will tour the country before coming to the Strand Theatre, London, in November. And, of course, she's currently presenting her own chat show on LWT, *The Dame Edna Experience*.

'This seems to me the first chat show with a female presenter in this country if you don't count Gloria Hunniford, and Dame Edna is inclined not to. I think Gloria was the John the Baptist to Dame Edna's Jesus.

'Dame Edna's show consists of . . . confrontations, I think is the word . . . between herself and celebrities. Inevitably, they are all *fearless* celebrities. Dame Edna is at the height of her powers. Never has she been more incisive, compassionate, pivotal and seminal . . .'

Barry seemed more than happy to rattle on about Dame Edna, *as* Dame Edna, for ever, but in our many phone conversations beforehand he'd insisted that this wouldn't be a 'Dame Edna' interview but a 'real Barry Humphries' interview. The trouble was, though, that the real Barry Humphries got seriously annoyed whenever I tried to ask him any questions. For instance, was he still attending Alcoholics Anonymous?

'Well, if I *were*,' he said sarcastically, 'I wouldn't be able to tell you, would I? Because that's what the word anonymous means – it's from the Latin, you know.'

Then I asked why he and Diane had decided to get married again (without getting divorced in between) earlier this year in Sydney. Was it, as friends reported, because they'd been unofficially separated and wanted to mark their reconciliation?

'How did you know about that?' he snapped. 'It wasn't in the papers.'

'Yes it was. Dame Edna herself wrote a report.'

'No she didn't. It must have been completely fabricated by a journalist – which I think is rather *rude*, don't you? Anyway, we just believe in occasionally remarrying. It's rather *nice*, especially for the children, who were not, after all, around to enjoy our first wedding. And I was rather keen to be married in church. Our first marriage was in a registry office but I'm more interested in going to church now, as I approach death.'

Approach death? He is fifty-three. Could this be a symptom of the famous Humphries hypochondria?

'I am not a hypochondriac. My urine is a very bright colour due to the number of vitamin pills that I take, but that is all.'

A friend of mine once went out with Barry Humphries, after his second marriage and before his third (to Diane), and said it was like going out with two people. As Barry Humphries, he was terribly serious, agitated and glum, talking endlessly about pollution and suchlike topics, then he would suddenly flip into Dame Edna and become wild, anarchic and outrageous.

I suggested that 'some people might say' that his desire to dress as a woman might mean that he was sexually mixed up, and he (quite rightly) jumped down my throat.

'Might they say that? I can't say that I've heard them. Any more than I've heard them say that there must be something strange about Antony Hopkins wanting to play an old man, King Lear. Or that Michael Caine must have murderous tendencies, because he plays a murderer. If they *do* say anything so foolish, then they don't know anything about acting, *do* they?'

Of course, there's a difference: Antony Hopkins and Michael Caine are playing scripted *roles*, they're not making up the character as they go along. There is a lot of Dame Edna in Barry Humphries, not least the wicked glint in the eye as you say something foolish and he prepares to pounce.

But one important way in which Barry Humphries differs from the Dame is that he is an intellectual and, like all Australian intellectuals, jolly well makes sure that you know it. In programme notes, he describes himself as 'a landscape painter of distinction and an authority on late-nineteenth and early-twentieth-century art and literature'.

In conversation with me, he talked about Gauguin, Dickens, Trollope, Mark Twain and, at length, about Oscar Wilde. I think he possibly models himself on Oscar Wilde. He wants to be known as a 'wit' and spends a lot of time choosing his words ('Do I mean illumined? No, irradiated') and honing his epigrams. Your role as an interviewer is merely to record his *bon mots* for posterity.

Humphries decided to be an intellectual at an early age. Growing up in the genteel suburbs of Melbourne, his father a builder, he dreamed of a Europe full of coffee-houses where people would endlessly discuss books and paintings, and never venture to the tennis-courts or the beach. He wore his hair long to show that he was a 'Bohemian', dropped out of Melbourne University without taking his degree, and came to London in 1959. He described himself as a 'Dadaist' in those days, though he made his living by drawing Barry Mackenzie cartoons in *Private Eye* and playing Fagin in *Oliver!*

He married twice, had two daughters and was an often-drunken figure on the London party scene. Dame Edna did not appear in public until the early seventies and Sir Les Patterson ('the Australian cultural attaché') a little later.

He still divides his life between London and Australia, but he talks about Australia with increasing bitterness, especially after the disastrous critical reception of his film *Sir Les Patterson Saves the World*.

'It was felt to be subversive,' he explains, 'and a deterrent to immigrants.' But the truth is that Australia, in its new mood of cultural nationalism and confidence, has no sympathy for 'deserters' who have spent most of their lives in Europe. The film is undergoing re-editing, and will not be released here until early 1988.

Meanwhile, what of the real Barry Humphries? He remains as elusive as ever. In a way I feel I came closest to knowing him in the bizarre three weeks before we met, when I spoke to him almost every day on the phone. Every time I rang there would be this sort of keening noise on the other end of the line and then, 'Well I can't talk *now*. Why don't you ring again in an hour?', or two hours or tomorrow or whatever the case may be. Often he would spend as long as fifteen minutes explaining why he couldn't talk *now*. Once he told me to ring him later at his wigmaker's and gave me the telephone number. When I rang there, he said, 'But I'm at my wigmaker's. Obviously I can't talk *here*.' Another time, ringing him at home, I got his wife saying, 'Well obviously he can't talk *now*, he's in bed' – at four o'clock in the afternoon.

When I finally pinned him down to a date, he said, 'Come to LWT.' I said I'd rather interview him at home. 'At home? What a charming idea! Where do you live? Give me your address.' Of course, he knew perfectly well that I meant at *his* home, but I gave him my address and waited at home all morning while he failed to show up.

From these phone conversations, I concluded that Barry Humphries was a gibbering wreck, a man teetering on the brink of a nervous breakdown. But people who have worked with him assure me that he is always like that. And, indeed, while I was with him, the phone rang and I heard him saying, in the same hysterical tones, 'Well obviously I can't talk *now*. Ring me back this afternoon.'

I think he is much more of an actor than people realize and even the mythical 'real Barry Humphries' is a well-studied pose. He himself may sometimes be confused by all his roles. And as he warned me when we met: 'The aim of an interview is to throw obscurity where light shone before, to cast picturesque shadows where formerly all was irradiated. The aim of the interview is to obfuscate the truth.'

Reproduced by permission of the *Sunday Express*

WILLIAM HURT

8 April 1990

To meet William Hurt, the American actor, is to be enfolded immediately in the sort of tender, caring and professional attention provided by a nurse. His greeting is 'Hi, Lynn. You all right?' He fusses around, arranging my chair, plumping cushions and saying, 'Just *wait* till you see what I've ordered for our lunch.' We are in the Halcyon Hotel in Holland Park, west London, in a beautiful rooftop conservatory which is part of his suite. Shortly after my arrival two waitresses come in bearing plates of smoked salmon sandwiches, scones, strawberries and cream: tea for lunch. 'This is the *best* meal in London,' he raves. 'You're gonna *like* this.'

The concern for my comfort is continuous. As the sun moves over the conservatory, he several times moves my chair, re-plumping the cushions, and draws the blinds. At one point he leaps up and says 'Here, let me get you some ice', and scoops a handful of cubes out of an ice bucket and puts them in a cup. 'This is a *clean* cup. Don't worry, my hands are *really* clean.' I'm sure they are. But I don't know what I'm supposed to do with the ice. The effect of all this attention, however well-meant, is to make me acutely aware that my face must be red and sweating. Normally, this wouldn't bother me, but he, who is so cool and clean and dry, is clearly upset. And his ministrations are just too much. The image which keeps popping bizarrely into my mind is of Christ washing the disciples' feet.

He is in London as the guest of the British Association of Film and Television Arts. He has spent the morning at his computer, writing notes and studying flight regulations (he has a private pilot's licence), and will spend the afternoon picnicking with his wife in Kew Gardens. On Monday he will return to Paris, where he has started work on a film for Wim Wenders called *Until the End of the World*. His choice of roles is determined by the axiom 'Go for good projects, never good parts' and in consequence his filmography is impressive: *Altered States*, *Body Heat*, *The Big Chill*, *Kiss of the Spider Woman*, *Children of a Lesser God*, *Broadcast News*, *The Accidental Tourist* – all good films and good performances. He won an Oscar for his portrayal of the transvestite in *Spider Woman* and was nominated for *Children of a Lesser God* and *Broadcast News*. He is an actor whom other actors admire.

As a person, though, he carries a big question mark. He rarely gives interviews and the few that exist make him out to be a fruitcake. His PR has warned me beforehand on no account to mention 'The Case'. The case was a palimony suit brought last summer by his one-time girlfriend, Sandra Jennings, a ballet dancer who lived with him from 1981 to 1984 and is the mother of his seven-year-old son Alex. She maintained that he was constantly drunk and violent. Her evidence was supported by testimony from Alex's babysitter, Linda Patrick, who said that Hurt also abused Jennings's successor, the deaf actress Marlee Matlin. 'She told me Bill beat her and kicked her and did it in front of Alex.' The trial was shown day after day on American television and, although Sandra Jennings failed to prove that they had ever had a common-law marriage, the image of Hurt as a violent, paranoid, woman-beating drunk will not easily be erased. I suspect his appearance at the BAFTA awards and this interview – which was offered to us, not solicited – might be by way of testing how bad the image damage is: an English dress rehearsal, as it were, before facing the press back home in the States. He has clearly given thought to how he will make me like him.

He is beautiful in a WASPy American way – tall, clean, freckled, wholesome. He wears a T-shirt saying, 'I fish therefore I am' (yes, he says, he does fish) and spotless, knife-creased jeans. The creases to me betoken a life ministered by servants and indeed he grew up in affluence: his father was a government officer in charge of foreign-aid programmes and his stepfather was Henry Luce III, the son of the founder of Time Inc. Hurt went to expensive private schools and grew up in beautiful houses. When he was offered a scholarship at Juilliard (his drama school) he turned it down on the grounds that he didn't need the money and other students did. 'Mr Nice Guy, huh?' he adds, afraid I will misconstrue it as boasting. His fear of saying anything nice about himself is quite a serious handicap throughout the interview.

'Are you really forty?' I ask, and he puts his head in his hands and groans alarmingly. 'Leave me *alone*! I've been going through a lot of *anxiety* about that, the last few months, but now I'm just *pleased* about it, pleased that I made it.' Did he have a big party? 'I've been having a sort of low-level party but your heart can only stand so much. I feel I'm living on borrowed time.' Seeing my serious, sympathetic expression, he grins, only joking. 'This is a real good time in my life. I'm having a good time.' He keeps fit and 'works out' – two dumb-bells lie beside him on the table, and he tells me he ran six miles before breakfast. 'I'm trying to stay in some kind of shape.' Did he go through a typical mid-life crisis? 'I don't know. I don't know what's typical. The cadences of my life have not necessarily fallen into the proper, normal stages. A few years ago, some wonderful things happened in my life and since then I've been seeing everything very differently.'

'You mean you gave up drinking?' There is a flash of sheer panic behind his eyes, a sudden 'Where's the exit? Let me outta here', but he gets a grip on himself to answer cautiously, 'Well, around that time, yes. And finding out some things about myself, really important things, and beginning to face them and get help with them, and get a real hold on some wonderful *joys*, you know? It's great.'

His style of speech is very American, and hard to convey on the page because it depends a lot on emphasis and speed. He uses many of the terms which are generally dismissed as psychobabble, although I am rather fond of psychobabble myself and welcome this chance to practise it. Some of his tussles with the language give the impression of a man trying to fold a balloon into a matchbox: 'The generosity of spirit required to be an artist is often misconceived and turned into a *flagrante delicto* of some sort; a perversion of recalcitrancy will turn the exuberance of expressiveness into the image of something dirty.' But it is not true that he has no sense of humour: he makes several good jokes and sometimes breaks off some of his more knotty attempts at self-expression to laugh wryly, 'Oh *God* – what am I *saying*? Help me. I'm roaming.'

He has the actorish ability to change mood in the middle of a sentence. Asked if he is close to his family, he says yes, he has good friends 'and they're family. And my wife is my friend.' What about parents? 'My parents are . . . are . . . I don't spend a lot of time with my parents.' He is frowning, then suddenly laughing, 'My mother's *dead* so I don't spend a lot of time with her' – then suddenly serious again, 'Though you can spend a *lot* of time with a dead parent, I tell you. You can spend more time with a dead parent than you spend with yourself.' This is a heavy thought and he spends a lot of time shaking his head but suddenly he is sunny again – 'But I don't.'

More disconcerting is his habit of bringing God into the conversation when you least expect him. For instance, I asked if he was a workaholic, if he got fidgety when he was not working. He said: 'No, I'm the opposite: I can wait. The only thing that makes me nervous is I can wait for ever. I feel that I have a right to *live*, even if I'm not working. God has a purpose for me, and that's all I need to know.' He was brought up a Presbyterian and 'I was very serious about my spiritual life from a very early age. What was true for me then is true for me now: that what a lot of people know as God was the most important thing in my life, and I'm glad about that, I'm glad.'

He started college as a theology major, and was once quoted as saying he did it to impress his stepfather, who was religious. But to me he said, 'People have made too much of that. You know, I was *young*, and I needed to explore. I went through a period of my life where I wanted *saving*, you know? But you don't have to be a minister to get saved.' After college, during his drinking years, he lost his faith to some extent: 'I was not in a good mood with God for a long time, and, like all children, I was angry and petulant. I was labouring under a popular misconception: that God is standing there with a baseball bat just waiting for you to screw up. He's not. He doesn't *want* you to screw up: he'd like to be able to help you.' Recently, Hurt and his wife have become members of their local Presbyterian church in New York State, so he has returned to his childhood fold.

He met his wife, twenty-eight-year-old Heidi Henderson, by whom he has one child and another on the way, when they were both inmates of the Betty Ford Center (a drying out clinic) in 1986. Before that, he was an alcoholic, full of violence and self-loathing. His brother Jim told *People* magazine, 'Deep down inside, Bill is a very good guy, but his fame has made him paranoid over questions of control. After *Altered States* [his first film, in 1980], his drinking problem became very bad, and continued to be very bad for a long time.' Sandra Jennings told the court that he would drink huge bottles of Soave Bolla followed by vodka, and also took lithium (a drug for manic depressives). 'His personality would change completely. He was a classic alcoholic.'

The turning-point came, Hurt recalls, one day in Atlantic City. 'I was just walking down the street in Atlantic City at four o'clock in the morning, and I *hate* Atlantic City, you know? I never in my life liked gambling, it always kind of scared me and I was just walking down the street and . . . I don't know. I can't explain it, but it was then that I decided:

I've had it. It's gonna change now. And it was then that I started looking, and finally did something, about a lot of things. But the problem is, when you're discussing a nadir, often people misconstrue it as the *cause* of the change, but it was just that I happened to be there, in Atlantic City, on the day when it – whatever it was – happened.'

Was he drunk at the time? 'Not really. No more than – it was just a bad day. I was having a bad day. You can't pile it all on drinking because there are a lot of things you can use to avoid your life. You can use work – which a lot of us do – that's a temptation too.'

Why was he trying to avoid his life? 'Well I think I, like perhaps a few billion other people, tried to delay my adolescence for way too long. I tried to postpone adulthood.' His parents split up when he was about six; according to his brother Jim, 'Bill is still living through some kind of childhood pain, a sense of rejection that has always coloured his life.' Sandra Jennings said he was insanely possessive and suffered 'terrible separation anxiety. He said that's because his mother or dad was always leaving.' His real father was often stationed abroad in the course of his foreign-aid work and Hurt spent much of his childhood travelling: he mentioned to me that his favourite activity as a child was 'sitting in airports looking at people'.

When he was ten his mother remarried and his life thereafter seems to have been dominated by a need to impress his stepfather. 'When I started to act,' he has said, 'I was desperately trying to find something that I could respect about myself. I didn't feel I was worth very much.' He was also self-demanding: 'I tried very, very hard. I was perfectly fine the way I was, but I just didn't know it. And so – I scarred myself.' Lawrence Kasdan, who directed him in *Body Heat*, *The Big Chill* and *The Accidental Tourist*, says: 'He was so hard on himself that sometimes he would be very hard on other people too.'

He is reluctant to talk at length about the reasons for his alcoholism. 'Oh, I'm not getting into that. I'll share with you to some extent, but really the place for me to talk about that is with other people who seriously want help.' And does he do that? 'Yes.' By addressing AA meetings? 'No. That's grandstanding, or it would be for me. I work with people one to one. Like in New York, you know you get a lot of panhandlers [beggars] these days? I've found a solution to the guilt of walking by a guy asking for something. Because in your head you're thinking, "What's the point of giving this guy a quarter or a dollar if he's just gonna drink it down or shoot it up?" You're just helping to kill him. But on the other hand, you're thinking, "Who am I to be so self-righteous? If he wants it, give it him. Maybe he's gonna bottom out and the sooner he gets to his bottom the better for him." So nowadays I take him to a McDonald's or somewhere and buy him a meal. I say, "You're hungry? OK, let's go. Let's go get a burger, a hot dog. You want some food? I'll buy you food." It *works*. Or sometimes they just walk away. Saves you $3.50.' And do they talk, these panhandlers? 'Oh, sure. People talk if you talk to them. I have my best conversations with trees, mountains and strangers.'

I am a stranger. But our conversation is hampered by his distrust of journalists, and mine of actors. Inevitably, he soon embarks on a discussion about the meaning of reality, the falsity of media attention, the mendacity of image-creation, etc., etc. He worries about whether I will be 'judgemental', and whether, for instance, I will mistake the glass of apple juice in his hand for whisky. (It is apple juice; I sniffed it.) He says that sometimes when he reads articles about himself, he thinks: 'How on *earth* could I have given that idea? I mean, I'm a *sweet* person. How *can* they have written that stuff?' More interestingly, he explains that the reason he rarely gives interviews is because 'I try to resist the temptation to typify, to generalize. In my work, I'm constantly trying to be *specific*: I've noticed that the largeness of your imagination, your comprehension, really depends on the ability to be specific.' Hence his fear of being trapped in some generalization about actors or alcoholics.

Then the photographer comes and the paranoia that has occasionally flickered behind his eyes comes rampaging out into the open. He tells the photographer: 'I don't pose. I'm not going to pose for you.' (Though he changes into a shirt because for some reason he doesn't want to be photographed in his fishing T-shirt.) The photographer says he'll just shoot as we're talking, but Hurt can't talk with a photographer around. 'I'm sorry, I'm getting confused; I can't concentrate. Every time you hear a camera going off, something in your brain says "Freeze!", like if someone pointed a gun.' Surely this is strange for an actor? But Hurt's alarm is real; he is almost frantic with fear. In the end, we pretend to converse while the photographer takes pictures, and resume when he stops.

But the fragile trust that we have established has gone and Hurt keeps worrying about the fact that I am a journalist. 'I recently did a play-reading for Greg Mosher at the Lincoln Center,' he explains, 'an Arthur Miller play called *The Archbishop's Ceiling* and the play is about the question: is there a microphone in the room and, if so, who is listening? Who are we talking *to*? I wonder if journalists ever considered, when they were in Tiananmen Square and showed the faces of all those people on American television – did they consider that all the Chinese government had to do was send a guy over to an American motel with a video recorder and they'd got all their rebels? So: who are we talking *to*? Who has the right to steal our intimacy? *Nobody* has that right.'

At this point the BAFTA man comes to take Mr Hurt for his picnic. 'How'd it go?' he asks. 'I don't know,' William Hurt says, turning to me, 'how'd it go?' I don't know. What with my deep distrust of actors and his deep distrust of journalists, *my* belief that he might be putting on an act, and *his* belief that I might be misrepresenting him . . . how do you know if the native you meet in the jungle is a cannibal? Given all that, I'd say it went OK.

Reproduced by permission of the *Independent on Sunday*

JEREMY IRONS

30 July 1989

This is not an objective article. I don't want to give a cool appraisal of Jeremy Irons, or even to be snide. I just want to boil him in oil.

A month ago I had no strong views on Jeremy Irons. He was a tall, handsome English actor who was good in *Brideshead*. Then a nice PR asked if I'd like to see a preview of *Danny, the Champion of the World*, starring Jeremy and his ten-year-old son Sam Irons, with a view to interviewing him. I saw the film, I liked it, I said yes.

My diary thereafter has scratched-out appointments with Jeremy Irons on practically every day. I was supposed to meet him in the Groucho Club, at home, in a photographer's studio. One day I was supposed to have lunch with him but he cancelled at a few hours' notice because he 'didn't like to eat and talk at the same time'. The PR was often almost sobbing as he delivered these messages to me.

This continued for three weeks or more. Finally there came a morning when I had a 10.30 a.m. appointment with Jeremy Irons at a West End hotel and the PR didn't phone to cancel. I assumed this was mere oversight, but went along anyway. Who should be waiting for me: not Jeremy Irons, not the PR, but Theo Cowan. Now Theo Cowan, I should explain, is the doyen of film publicists and a much-loved and respected figure on the showbiz scene. Finding him waiting to babysit a Jeremy Irons interview was a bit like going to the passport office to renew my passport and finding Sir Geoffrey Howe behind the counter.

''E's late,' said Theo Cowan. We sat and waited. At 10.50 Jeremy Irons sauntered in. He didn't apologize for his lateness, he didn't say hello or shake hands, he said: 'Well, we all know who we are and why we're here – let's get on with it.' But Theo Cowan drew him aside. 'I'd like a private word, Jeremy.' Afterwards, he ushered us into a side room and said, 'I think you'll be all right now,' and left us to it.

Jeremy Irons threw himself back on a sofa and lit the first of many cigarettes, not offering me one. 'Well?' he said. I started to ask him a question, but in the middle he suddenly got to his feet, walked over to the window and started fiddling with the curtains. 'I hate things to be done *wrong*,' he announced. 'For instance, this tieback' – and he took the curtain tieback off its hook and turned it over – 'was designed a certain way and somebody went to all the trouble of making it that certain way. So it would be *quite nice* to have it hanging the *right way up*. There!' And he put the tieback back on its hook and resumed his seat.

'Have you ever read *Zen and the Art of Motorcycle Maintenance?*' he asked, and I confessed that I had (back in the sixties when it was compulsory hippie reading – I wouldn't recommend it). 'Well, that is the way I enjoy life. I enjoy doing things the best way, the most craftsmanlike way, the efficient way.'

A waiter comes in with coffee. Alas, he has obviously not read *Zen and the Art of Motorcycle Maintenance* because, in pouring the coffee, he spills some. Jeremy Irons points this out. He watches, eyes glittering, fingers drumming, while the waiter mops it up. The waiter, who had entered the room a confident and happy man, slinks away, broken.

Is Jeremy Irons, I wonder aloud, the sort of person who would watch someone doing the washing-up and then tell them they were doing it badly? 'Yes,' he agrees. 'I'm imposs-ible. Intolerant, impatient and impossible. I'm *appalled* by sloppy work and if I see something done badly – props, for example – I say so. It's what *I* call professionalism.'

Professionalism, bah! How often I have heard actors trot-ting out that tired excuse for their own behaviour. What professionalism actually means is doing one's own job well: it does not include telling other people how to do theirs.

I wouldn't like to be a *tea boy* on a Jeremy Irons film, let alone a fellow actor. What on earth must it have been like for his son working with him? Sam, to be fair, seems perfectly happy in the film, a natural actor with limitless unforced charm; it is Jeremy Irons as his father who seems awkwardly miscast.

Why did he make *Danny, the Champion of the World*? He admitted that as an acting role it was not exciting and he 'played it like a £30-a-day actor' but he'd been 'acting his socks off' in *Dead Ringers* so he didn't mind.

The appeal of *Danny*, he explained, was that he could do it with his family (Sam, and also his father-in-law, Cyril Cusack, the Irish actor) just ten minutes from his home in Oxfordshire. And also it was a great vehicle for Sam . . .

But wasn't it rather dangerous, I suggested, putting a child into the hothouse atmosphere of film-making? Mightn't it turn his head, and make it hard for him to settle back at school? Jeremy Irons sighed: 'You're sounding very much like my wife' (the actress Sinead Cusack). 'She was very unsure about it. She is much less sanguine than I am. She argued and argued about it, saying it was dangerous.' So why override her objections? 'Because it's a *wonderful* experience for a child to go to work with a parent. It means they're part of the parent's *life*. So that was the positive side, and the fact that I was there to keep a close eye on him. When he finished, two things he said stick in my mind. Someone said to him, "I expect you want to be an actor?" and he said, "No. But I'd quite like to be a lighting cameraman." And then I asked him a few weeks later, "Do you miss it – the filming?" and he said

"Yes I do. I miss the attention." And I thought, "Well that's quite good because, of course, that's the main thing you get – attention – and he sees it very clearly."

His younger son, three-year-old Maximilian, he says, is 'at the moment a great attention-seeker and certainly, compared with Sam, seems much more set to become some kind of performer'.

Anyway, Sam has now resumed his schooling and Jeremy Irons is off to America to make a film with Glenn Close about the Claus von Bulow trial. Last year he made four films on the trot: *Dead Ringers* (in which he gave an excellent performance as twin doctors), *A Chorus of Disapproval* (an Alan Ayckbourn comedy), *Danny*, and *Australia*, a love story with Fanny Ardant. The range is typical: he has always avoided being typecast.

He realized at the beginning of his career, when he did *Brideshead* and *The French Lieutenant's Woman*, that he was in danger of becoming 'Hollywood's resident Englishman', so he went off to do a Polish film, *Moonlighting*, and seasons at Stratford and on Broadway.

He believes in chasing hard after parts he wants. He wrote to the producer of *Brideshead* offering himself for Charles Ryder, and he moved heaven and earth to try to get the Robert Redford part in *Out of Africa*. 'I rang Meryl, I wrote to the producer, I worked really hard for that part. I knew that Redford was bored with acting and that he was absolutely wrong for the role – too old and American – but Redford was a friend of the producer and that was how the deal was set up.'

Right at the beginning of his career he went to read for a BBC play with Judi Dench. After half an hour's reading he suddenly threw down the script and said, 'I'm going. I'm getting much too fond of this role and I'm actually not right for it. I'm too tall and I'm not foxy enough.' So he went off on a delayed honeymoon with Sinead Cusack to Greece. The director telegrammed him that he'd got the part. 'But why?' said Jeremy Irons. 'Why did you cast me?' And the director said, 'Because you wanted to do it so much and that is something money can't buy.' So now he chases parts all the time.

He turned forty last September but sighs irritably at mention of his age. 'I don't *feel* forty. I feel twenty-eight and always will. But I think the forties are a wonderful decade for a man. I see them very separately from my thirties. When I was thirty I made a big career decision. I told the company that was trying to screw me over, to stop me making *French Lieutenant's Woman*, to get lost, and I won that battle. So at thirty I thought, "Right, you're your own man." And I went through my thirties with great vigour and pushed hard for my career. Now maybe that youthful arrogance is settling a bit . . .'

I told him he was 'still very good looking' and he beamed. He adores compliments. If you mention that you liked his performance in so and so, he says, 'Oh, how exactly? Tell me more.' It is a trait all actors share but I have rarely encountered it in such an insatiable form. But to get back to his looks . . .

'I've never thought of myself as good-looking, which I think is useful. If I'm shot at the right angle and with the right lens, I can look all right. And yes, I know the angle and the lens. You see,' he says turning his right profile towards me, 'you don't want to look at this too often. It's all right in three-quarters, but not full profile. My right cheek is hollower here' – tracing a line down his strangely flat cheek – 'the bone is higher, the jaw not so square. It's just not such a good profile.'

Did he tell directors that, or leave them to work it out for themselves? 'I tell them. The left profile is the one to use if you want me to look creamy. The other profile looks more vulnerable.'

When he has to bare his body for a part, he spends weeks in the gym beforehand, pumping iron. 'It's really my back muscles that I have to work on: I have very strong arms and legs. I hate going to the gym but it's necessary sometimes.'

Would he mind the advent of grey hairs? 'No. I actually found the first one the other day. I was *rather* pleased. Enough people have said to me, "You're going to be *wonderful* as you get older," for me not to worry about it.'

One of the odd things about him is that, although he has the right looks and the right sort of ruthlessness, he has never been a great ladykiller. He married his first wife when he was just twenty-one, at Bristol Old Vic. That was 'a total disaster' and lasted a year, but he soon fell for Sinead Cusack and went to considerable pains to get his first marriage annulled, so that they could marry in a Catholic church. The marriage went through 'a sticky patch' in the early eighties, but now seems steady.

Jeremy agreed that he could have been a Lothario but wasn't: 'It's terribly tiring, I imagine. And I've never needed to do that. I mean, the logic seems to me that if you find someone you love, you want to stay with them, and that means marriage. Also, I believe you have to make a commitment to get joy. It's the old Puritan ethic: you have to put something in to get something out.'

He also values security. When he was fifteen his father made him take a vocational guidance test. One of the options was the theatre but the report said: 'Not right for you because you need too much security.'

'But I think it's the security that my family gives me that enables me to take risks in my profession,' he explains. 'The analogy is with a castle, and I ride out on my white charger, but I know I can always come back to the castle.'

Nevertheless, he admits that he's intrigued by open marriages where both partners have affairs. 'I find those rather interesting. I'd love to know how they work behind closed doors.' 'Rather badly, I suspect,' I said firmly, and Jeremy Irons gave me a sharp look – perhaps I was sounding just like his wife again.

Like most people, probably, I first saw Jeremy Irons in *Brideshead Revisited* and formed my image of him on the basis of that role. This was to underestimate his considerable powers as an actor. He is intelligent and articulate, like Charles Ryder, but he is not, like him, wet and ineffectual. On the contrary, he seems ruthless, arrogant and generally contemptuous of other people. He can still, he claims, 'turn on the creamy *Brideshead* charm' when he wants to, but nowadays he seldom bothers. At no point in our conversation did he say anything kind or generous about anyone else.

And at the end, when he still hadn't mentioned, let alone apologized for, our two dozen cancelled appointments, I raised the subject myself. 'Oh that,' he said airily. 'It was the publicity people's fault. They just can't do their jobs.'

Reproduced by permission of the *Sunday Express*

SIR JOHN JUNOR

4 February 1990

Unwary readers of the *Mail on Sunday* must have been rather surprised the other week to find their new political columnist recommending that the Archbishop of Canterbury take himself off to the Lebanon. Sir John Junor – for it was he – admitted that this might result in the archbishop falling victim to a terrorist's bullet, 'but even if he did, would there not be for him the enormous personal consolation of knowing that in death he was achieving more, much more, for the Anglican faith than ever he has done in life?' *Sunday Express* readers, of course, would have recognized this as a typical bit of Junor bishop-bashing, but after thirty-five years JJ's column no longer appears in the *Sunday Express*. His move to the *Mail on Sunday* represents the greatest act of treachery – and even Junor uses that word – that modern journalism has seen.

Junor is, above all, the journalists' journalist, the one whose column is compulsory reading throughout the Fleet Street diaspora. His fans include not only the predictable right-wingers (Richard Ingrams, Auberon Waugh) but also left-wingers like Paul Foot. All who have ever worked for him remain obsessed by him, and cherish his bizarre pronouncements. ('Only poofs drink white wine.' 'Never trust a bearded man.') Alan Watkins and Peter McKay – two former Junor employees, now respectively political columnist of the *Observer* and columnist of the *Evening Standard* – talk of starting a luncheon club whose sole purpose would be the swapping of John Junor anecdotes. Opinions differ as to whether he was a great editor, but everyone agrees that he is a great columnist. The *Private Eye* parody, Sir Jonah Junor, written by Peter McKay, was a bowdlerization of the real thing. The real JJ is bigoted, racist, sexist, coarse, funny and always unpredictable. He boasts, truthfully, 'No one ever knew what I was going to say – including myself.'

It is his hatred, his rage, that gives his column its appalling fascination. His daughter, the journalist and TV presenter Penny Junor, describes his rage as 'quite unique. He makes very personal, virulent, attacks on people.' There is no JJ column in which someone does not get badly hurt: Lord Denning, for instance, 'unctuous old humbug'; Jonathan Dimbleby, 'bumptious little twerp'; Sir Richard Attenborough, 'ancient, affected, side-whiskered trendy'. JJ nurtures this rage and values it. He always carries a tape recorder, 'because then if I see something in the paper or on television which angers me, I can dictate it there and then. If I made a note to write it later, I would lose that anger.'

I saw the rage in action at lunch with him in Dorking, when I tried to argue that his view of Aids as appropriate punishment for sodomy was wrong-headed and cruel. Immediately, the eyes bulged, the skin mantled – it was as if someone had shot purple dye into his veins – the voice curdled into a snarl. His first assumption was that, if I were defending gays, I must be a lesbian. 'You seem to have an extrrrrrra-ordinary sexual attitude yourself if I may say so, *Miss* Barber. No doubt you approve of lesbianism yourself?' I found myself gabbling that I was happily married, with children. But why did he hate homosexuals so much? 'Unhappily,' he intoned, 'some men are born in a certain way and with those people I have great sympathy. It's the proselytizers I object to; the people who flaunt their homosexualism and try to subvert and convert other people to it. These are the people I have an utter hatred for, because I think they are spreading filth.'

By now the voice was booming round the walls of the genteel Dorking restaurant, the face was deep indigo, and an unfortunate waiter who had come to collect our plates stood paralysed like a rabbit in a car's headlights. '*Filth*, Miss Barber. I regard buggery' – he paused to savour the word – 'buggery as the putting of a penis into shit. Don't you, Miss Barber? Don't you?'

Had he suffered, I asked, some personal assault by a homosexual, a childhood fumbling from a scoutmaster, perhaps? 'Absolutely not. Absolutely not. Absolutely not. Absolutely not. But it may of course have something to do with my generation. Homosexualism was virtually unknown in Scotland.' A long pause. 'Anyway, what would you do with the problem, Miss Barber? Stick it all under the carpet, never mention it?'

'Oh no. I have several gay friends. We talk about Aids.'

'Gay friends! Where do you meet them?'

'Well, at home.'

'And do you tell your dinner guests, "This is John. He's homosexual"?'

'Well, not like that. I might say, "This is John, and this is his boyfriend, Hugh."' JJ goggled at me, completely purple, eyes popping, but silent. Eventually he managed to croak, 'I find that idea most . . . *unusual*. It does not happen in Auchtermuchty.'

Auchtermuchty is the small town in Fife that he has made his personal Brigadoon, 'where there is human decency and morality and the old standards to act as a touchstone against modern life'. Or so he says in interviews. But in his column, Auchtermuchty emerges – perhaps more accurately – as a place of vicious surface respectability and seething passions, where 'the kilted laddies of the Auchtermuchty Curling Club' eternally chase the tweedy wives of the Ladies' Bowling team. In any case, he doesn't actually *know* Auchtermuchty. He

only drives through it, very fast, on his way to the Royal &
Ancient at St Andrew's. He comes from Glasgow and his
feelings about Scotland are altogether ambivalent. Selina
Scott, who knows him well, describes him as 'a professional
Scot who once told me with a tear in his eye that, like the
salmon, he would always return to his native land'. But he
has managed to endure half a century in London without
showing any inclination to return, and he recently told a
Scottish interviewer, Kenneth Roy, that the Scots nowadays
were 'a bunch of whingeing third-raters'.

He claims he is still a Calvinist, and uses this to justify his
hatred of homosexuals. But there is nothing Calvinist about
his attitude to adultery, which he appears at least to condone,
if not endorse. He has consistently defended Cecil Parkinson,
while attacking Sara Keays as a 'vicious, vindictive, scheming
bitch'. His views on divorce are as follows: 'I don't like
divorce, but I don't condemn people who get divorced. In the
Church of Scotland, marriage is a contract, not a sacrament.'
He is still married, though his wife stopped living with him
some years ago. Colleagues from the *Sunday Express* recall
him as 'always having an eye for the ladies'. Yet a golfing
crony who perhaps knows him better than most insists: 'He's
not a *lover* of women. He's a plunderer of them.'

He is unrepentantly sexist. Trying to work out whether he
is also racist is more difficult. When I went to his house, he
pointed proudly to a photograph of him and Edward Heath
standing on either side of a tiny black man. It reminded me
of Noël Coward's joke about the King of Tonga – when
asked who the black man next to the king was, Coward
replied, 'His lunch.'

But JJ said: 'You asked me if I had any black friends, Miss
Barber. There is one. The President of the Gambia.' JJ goes
golfing once a year in the Gambia and produces this as
evidence that he is not a racist. But his column often *seems*
racist. He once referred to a news story of a Hull hospital
doctor who had turned away a dying tramp. And what was
the name of this doctor? he thundered. 'It was Dr Falih Abed

Ali Al-Fihan. What was his nationality? I do not know. But I
have a sneaking suspicion that he does not wear the kilt.' JJ
was duly reprimanded by the Press Council. The following
week he was unrepentant. 'I tell you this. Even if Dr Falih
Abed Ali Al-Fihan spends the rest of his life turning away
dying tramps, I think I will still have more respect for him
than I have for the po-faced, pompous, pin-striped, humourless twits who sit on the Press Council.'

The Press Council is one of his regular targets, though it is
not top of his hit list. That honour must go to the bishops.
All the current bishops, in his view, are 'trendy old women':
it is then a nice point whether he hates the Bishop of Durham
or the Archbishop of Canterbury more. Dr Runcie is 'about
as much good as a glass eye at a keyhole' and single-handedly
responsible for bringing down the Church of England; the
Bishop of Durham is a 'vain old fool' and 'fat old humbug'
whose ordination, Junor notes seriously, elicited a lightning
bolt from God to burn down York Minster. After bishops, he
hates all homosexuals or, as he would call them, poofs,
pansies, powder-puffs and queers. Of course, he hates all
pinkoes, Commies and 'Greenham Common sluts', though he
rarely wastes much breath on them. Neil Kinnock is a 'weak,
wet, Welsh windbag' and JJ's opinion of him was further
lowered when Glenys revealed he sometimes helped her with
the washing-up. Among foreign politicians, George Bush is 'a
neutered old tabby' and Bob Hawke of Australia 'a third-rate
tear-jerker'. Australia, incidentally, is 'swamped in cocaine
and corruption'. But this is as nothing compared to Ireland.
'Wouldn't you rather,' he wrote after the Brighton bombing,
'admit to being a pig than to being Irish?'

The list of his likes is much shorter. It starts with the three
goddesses – Mrs Thatcher, the Princess of Wales and Selina
Scott – who can do no wrong. Among men, he admires David
Owen, Sir Geoffrey Howe (a bit – though his suede shoes are
a black mark), Enoch Powell, the late Manny Shinwell, and
nearly all golfers. He is surprisingly keen on the French,
despite the fact that they are foreigners. He likes all birds and

often writes about his bird-table. Some of his most maudlin and embarrassing paragraphs are devoted to 'the miracle of the swallows'.

JJ's sense of humour is an elusive animal. He believes he has one and points to the 'funny' which usually closes his column. The 'funny' is almost invariably coarse, and about flatulence. For instance: 'It is fascinating to learn that in order to make themselves go faster through the water, some Romanian lady Olympic swimmers are injecting air into their bottoms.

'*Into?* Are they quite, quite sure?

'Could it just be possible that for all these years members of the Auchtermuchty Ladies Swimming Society have been doing things the wrong way round?'

However, according to one long-serving associate: 'The one thing all people who know JJ agree on is that he has absolutely no sense of humour.' Peter McKay puts it differently: 'He never found anything funny if everyone else found it funny. I remember one occasion at the *Sunday Express* when he'd suddenly scrapped some terrible war serial and decided to run a story about a polar bear trapping a man on an ice floe instead. This was late on Friday, and everyone was saying, "But we can't get the artwork done in time." But he said, "Well, just send down to the library, they're bound to have some pictures of polar bears." So someone went haring down to the library and came back with a picture. It was a picture of a performing bear wearing a grass skirt and riding a unicycle. We all fell about, but JJ was furious. "I don't know what you all find so funny." And the laughter died.'

His daughter Penny explains: 'He doesn't have much of a sense of humour about himself, I don't think, but he has a very lavatorial sense of humour, a very basic, schoolboy's sense of humour. He loves stories about people slipping on banana skins. Other people's misfortunes are pure delight to him.'

Perhaps because he is so quick to laugh at others' misfortunes, he never discusses or refers to his own. Nobody knows

what he felt when his wife left him, or when his daughter
Penny lambasted him in the *Sunday Times* 'Relative Values'
series. Sir John himself gave a conventional interview, saying
that 'the greatest happiness that can come to anyone, the
greatest wealth in the world, is children'. But Penny's account
of their relationship was devastatingly frank. 'We don't
actually talk a lot . . . When I was a child I sometimes didn't
want to be alone with him because he unnerved me . . . He's
a very dominating man, he would like to have everybody
jump when he presses the button . . . I don't think he's
happy.'

When I tried to ask him about Penny's interview, he cut me
off sharply. 'I'm not really responsible for what my daughter
says. All I can say is that when the children were young [he
also has a son, Roderick], I never had people to dinner, no
matter how important, without the children being there too.
They were always treated as equals.' A good father, then? 'I
think so, yes.' But later he rang me especially to say, 'Of
course, if Penelope says I was not a good father, she must be
the judge.'

His house – a low-beamed pseudo-farmhouse in Surrey – is
densely decorated with photographs of his children and
grandchildren, though it is noticeable that the biggest, blown-
up photographs are of JJ in full editorial fig – interviewing
LBJ, meeting various astronauts, accepting an honorary doc-
torate from a Canadian university. The house feels a bit like
a pub. He is proud of it, pointing out 'my land, fifty acres, all
the fields down to the stream there, my woodland'. He always
says he lives near Dorking, though the house is nearer
Gatwick. It is hard to imagine what he does there, alone. In
the evenings, with a glass of whisky, he apparently studies his
bird-table and ponders the meaning of life.

He is reluctant to talk about the past. He lives for the
present and the future – which is probably why he seems
younger than seventy-one – and cannot be drawn into reminiscence. Even writing his memoirs, as he has been, has not
given him any curiosity about the past – 'That might simply

be, of course, because they're no damn good.' He describes his father, the foreman of a steel roofing works, as 'very orthodox in his views', and his mother as 'a hard-working business lady, ambitious for her children, [who] sacrificed everything to get them a good education'. He was lazy at school but got into Glasgow University to read English. Then came the war – 'It was fun' – which he spent in the Fleet Air Arm. I said he must have been very brave, flying from aircraft carriers. 'That's very far from true. I was a devout coward. In fact I spent my time editing the Fleet Air Arm magazine, which was a damn sight safer than flying areoplanes.'

After the war, he stood unsuccessfully as a Liberal parlia-mentary candidate, while making his living from journalism. Lord Beaverbrook spotted him, and made him assistant editor of the *Daily Express*. Eventually, Beaverbrook told him he must choose between politics and journalism. If he chose journalism, said Beaverbrook, 'I will put a golden crown on your head.' Junor chose the golden crown and became editor of the *Sunday Express* at thirty-five.

Peter McKay says that 'the moment he was hired by Lord Beaverbrook, he stopped leading an ordinary life. He tried to over-compensate. He would go to the Savoy Grill for lunch but take the bus there. He'd come up by train from Dorking and tell himself he was an ordinary chap. But it wasn't true. He's a very rich man and he's had more than thirty years of uninterrupted power.'

Everyone attests to his kindness to people when they're down. He has been known to find jobs for out-of-work journalists and to 'put in a word' for people here and there. On Christmas Day he takes a hot meal to his golf-club caddy, Curly, who sleeps rough in the bunkers.

He is sentimental. For years he always sent a Valentine card to his daughter Penny. He recently rang Selina Scott to tell her that the Terrazza Est restaurant, where they first had lunch together, was closing down and would she lunch with him again there on its last day?

But he likes people in their *place*. They are either superiors or inferiors, never equals. As editor of the *Sunday Express* he was an absolute tyrant, liable to call employees in at any time to tell them that their work was 'piss-poor' or to make some personal remark. He told one leader writer: 'You grow a lot of hair in your ears.' He told me, when I visited him at home: 'I notice you keep scratching yourself, Miss Barber. Could it be a flea? A flea in a pair of tights must be a terrible thing.'

Peter McKay believes it's a conscious imitation of Beaverbrook. 'Beaverbrook used to question people about small, banal things and make a mountain out of a molehill. It's a habit of tyranny, isn't it? Because it unbalances people.'

He took a nosy, personal interest in his employees and heaped them with alternate praise and blame. One long-serving employee, Michael 'Inspector' Watts, recalled: 'The thing we used to dread from him above all was praise – oh *God* it was awful. Because you knew that after praise, within a week or fortnight, would come the lash. He felt that, having been praised, you would become uppity so it was important to slap you down.'

All employees attest to his alarming carrot–stick routine. But it had one good effect. Michael Watts: 'What was good was that there was never any in-fighting or office politics. We were all in the same boat.' Peter McKay confirms this, and adds, 'There was a sense, in working for Junor, of entering a sort of childhood. He would take all these people – many of them middle-aged – and reduce them to the status of children. We were enfeebled by his tyranny – but rather happy with it. Nobody ever wanted to leave. I think that is why he has so caught the journalistic imagination.'

The long-term effect, though, of having this court of middle-aged children was harmful to the *Sunday Express*. Although JJ is always referred to as 'a great editor', the truth is that the circulation of the *Sunday Express* actually halved (from four million to two million) under his editorship. After great success in the fifties and early sixties, he presided over twenty years of steady decline. The paper became a sort of fossil, still with its 'Cockleshell Heroes' stories illustrated by line drawings, its jokes about Picasso and Henry Moore and 'long-haired' pop stars, well into the eighties. It was, until recently, a profitable paper with a doggedly loyal, diehard readership, mainly remarkable for its gluttonous consumption of garden sheds. But the paper's contact with the real world became increasingly slight.

Perhaps every enduring editor is a one-off, a king without an heir. Junor is the last survivor of the Fleet Street generation which came to prominence under Beaverbrook. He believed that great newspapers were made by great editors and great proprietors working in harmony, and he looked in vain for a proprietor he could worship as he once had Beaverbrook. The end, when it came with Lord Stevens, was sudden. Stevens appointed a new editor, Robin Morgan, without even consulting JJ. 'It was like a slap in the face with a wet cod.'

Will he now enjoy an Indian summer on the *Mail on Sunday*? Will he convert a whole new readership to a passionate hatred of bishops and bearded men? He once, in his column, quoted 'a beautiful young lady' (probably his daughter Penny) explaining the attraction of an old boyfriend: 'He made me laugh.'

'Could anyone,' asked JJ, in full maudlin bird-table mode, 'say anything nicer about anyone? Wouldn't it make a wonderful epitaph?'

Reproduced by permission of the *Independent on Sunday*

BARRY MANILOW

21 August 1983

Nineteen-year-old Noell Jagielski arrived at the First Great Barry Manilow Fan Club Convention in Chicago clutching a very large sheet of ordinary brown cardboard. O sacred cardboard: it hath touched the bottom of Barry Manilow. It happened on 12 November 1982. Noell had driven two hundred miles to Barry's concert at Charleston, West Virginia, wearing, as usual, her Barryshirt, Barryneck-lace, Barrybaseball-jacket, with her white jeans and white Adidas tennis shoes (which she wears because He wears them) and clutching the 700-dollar Minolta 35mm camera with zoom lens that she bought to get better close-ups of Barry at concerts. ('You can always tell the real fans from the amateurs by their cameras,' she told me.) She also carried the large photograph of Barry that she takes with her everywhere, and a banner proclaiming PITTSBURGH WANTS TO DO IT WITH BARRY.

And it worked! After the concert, a man came and said Barry wanted to meet her backstage. He shook her hand and autographed her photo, and then he put his arm round her and she put her arm around him, and the cardboard that she had been using to keep her photograph flat was in her hand, and so it came to rest *against Barry's bottom*. So thát is why

Noell's cardboard is sacred, and why all the other fans queued up to touch it.

The convention was held at a brand-new motel on a motorway forty miles out of Chicago. When the fan club first tried to book the hotel back in January, the manager told them he had four hundred rooms and how could they possibly fill them? Ha! In the event, 1,500 fans came – including 120 British fans who had paid £750 to get there – and overspilled every hotel for miles.

The average age of the fans was about thirty, though there were children and grandmothers too; the average *weight* of the fans was about 13 stone. (Odd that the world's thinnest singer has the world's fattest fans.) Most of them had begged, borrowed or stolen in order to get to the convention. Sue Richardson, a secretary from Caterham, said that she had sold all her jewellery; Linda Campbell from High Wycombe had starved for six months; and Noell, the cardboard-carrier, said she had spent all the money she had saved to go to nursing school so now she wouldn't be able to fulfil her ambition to become Barry's private nurse.

The convention was billed to start on Friday, but many fans arrived early to catch his Thursday night concert. Nineteen-year-old Lynette Pascal from Iowa arrived with a strategy. There is a moment in every Manilow concert (Manilovers know it well) when he asks for a volunteer from the audience to sing 'Can't Sing Without You' with him. Naturally, Lynette fought and clawed her way to the front, as any self-respecting fan would. But Barry chose someone else. Then Lynette held up the T-shirt she had had specially printed. It said, 'I was SUPPOSED to sing with Barry Manilow.' Barry saw it, laughed, and invited her to sing with him too.

When she got back to the hotel, all the other fans were waiting for her report: 'Oh,' she said, 'he has the most gorgeous crowsfeet I've ever seen. His hair is a tiny bit coarse, but he has the softest skin. I slipped my hand inside his shirt – incredible!' The other fans all cried and sighed and said they were glad for her. That is the nice thing about Mani-lovers: they rejoice in one another's successes.

On Friday morning all the fans stood in line to collect their convention kits. These cost $65 and contained a Barrybadge, Barryhat and Barrypic, together with a flashlight for waving at concerts and – most important – a ticket for the Saturday-night concert. Opening the tickets was a real nailbiter. Some fans burst into tears when they found they were back in rows 13 or 14. Michelle Lanier from New Orleans found herself in row 4 and when she wanted to enrage her friends (who had all drawn row 14) she just held up four fingers and wiggled them gleefully.

When the fans had finished queueing for their convention kits, they went and queued at the fan-club shop to buy everything from Barryshoelaces at $3 to gold Barrynecklaces at $150. All the Barryproducts have the Barrylogo, which is a line drawing of him in profile with wavy hair looking surprisingly like a Greek god, or at least watersprite. I felt it would be in poor taste to tell anyone my Manilow joke, viz: Q: How do you make Barry Manilow's nose four miles long? A: Fold it in half.

The official activity for Friday was the Barryexhibition in the main hall of the hotel, when all the individual local fan clubs put up tables displaying their Barrynewsletters and Barryartefacts. The newsletters all had poems, such as this from Pittsburgh's *Cloudburst*:

> Where are you my beloved:
> Are you in the garden
> Amongst the flowers
> Who quiver in your gentle hands?
> Or are you amongst the books
> Seeking human knowledge?

The Pittsburgh Fan Club publishes twenty-four pages of this stuff every month; multiply that by about a hundred for the number of local fan clubs and add in another twenty-four pages of the quarterly *Barrygram*, the official organ of the BMIFC, and that adds up to quite a heap of Maniliterature every year. In addition, there are all the Barry *objets* – statues and models and dolls and blankets and embroideries. Sallie Papp from Denver was wearing her Barryshirt – a huge denim jacket covered with exquisite embroidery detailing all Barry's concerts, and Diane Steed from St Louis, Missouri, was wearing her clown suit with cross-stitch titles of all Barry's 104 songs.

And everywhere, of course, there were Barrypix. Barrylovers collect and swop photographs of Barry with the eagerness of schoolboys trading postage stamps, and they have a special way of looking at Barrypix. They flick through several dozen fairly quickly and then find one which captures 'their' Barry and they gaze at it for about an hour and go into a trance. Most of them own more than five hundred Barrypix; several of them own more than five thousand. Bottom shots are always in demand. There was one whole wall of pictures of Barry's bottom at the exhibition captioned, 'Behind every great man . . . there's a cute tush.'

Officially, Barrylovers like his eyes best, but when you ask them to describe his eyes they just burst into tears. They burst into tears all the time anyway. In one of the hotel lounges they showed twenty-four-hour-a-day videos of all Barry's concerts, and the only sound you could hear in there, apart from the Barrymusic, was a gentle continuous sobbing. I learned to carry a box of Kleenex round with me throughout the convention so that whenever I asked a fan some searching question like 'What does Barry mean to you?' I could start doling out tissues.

A lot of fans' speech consists of quotes from Barry's songs, but it was only when the tenth woman had told me that she 'made it through the rain' that I recognized this. The song they quote the most is called 'All the Time' and it sums up everything that Barryloving is all about. The gist is: I thought

I was crazy, a freak, the only person in the world who felt this way . . . till I met you. The fans' ambition is to be 'Lonely together', which is also a quote.

As Friday wore on, a rumour rustled and buzzed round the halls of the hotel – 'Barry is coming *here*. Tonight!' The organizers said definitely not: Barry was not coming and had never said he would. The English fan-club organizers, forty-three-year-old Mollie Baldwin and thirty-seven-year-old Lynn Killick from Epsom, said they sincerely hoped he wouldn't come. 'He'll be eaten alive, torn to pieces,' they said. They were shocked by the goings-on and overt sexuality of the American fans. 'The difference is,' Mollie said, 'that the American girls think they *own* him, whereas *we* think Barry owns us. They're so demanding. At the concert last night, a girl practically dragged him offstage – my heart was in my mouth.' Lynn said: 'It would worry me to death if he came here.'

But all the other fans said they were hoping, longing, *praying* for Barry to come, and all day long they eagerly recited signs and portents. 'Barry has no concert tonight. There's a banquet planned for us with a surprise. They're unloading tons of audio equipment in the ballroom. And Barry wouldn't – couldn't – let us down,' said twenty-two-year-old Beth Lyster from Windsor, Canada. I asked her friend, Joan Fries from Michigan, what *she* thought. 'I believe Barry will come. I believe he has *already* come. He is in the hotel now. But in disguise.'

In disguise!!! It was several seconds before I could winch my jaw back into position to say, 'But look, mmm, Barry has quite a *distinctive* sort of face. I mean, not to put too fine a point on it, his *nose* is kind of unmistakable. And there are so few men here, *any* man is bound to attract attention.'

'What makes you so sure he'll disguise himself as a man?' she replied, unanswerably.

Naturally I spent the rest of the day looking out for a six-foot rake-thin woman with a nose the size of a cucumber, but by 7 p.m. it was obvious that Barry, in some form, was coming anyway. The hotel was knee-deep in security men and the fans were all shooed out to wait in a one-mile-long queue round the car park. When they finally filed into the ballroom they groaned at the realization that many of them would have to stand, but they were sweet about letting people in wheel-chairs (there were at least two dozen at the convention) through to the front.

Then Rosie Cowan from Michigan and Faye Klapman from New York, the co-organizers, made lots of speeches, and then a grizzle-haired heavy-set woman called Roberta came on-stage and the fans all screamed in delight. Roberta Kent is Barry's 'creative consultant': some say she is his girlfriend, though size- and age-wise it looks improbable. She said Barry had told her to tell them he wished he could be with them tonight, and a heart-wrenching sob rolled round the room. 'But,' she said, 'it was Barry's birthday last week and I knew you'd all like to wish him a Happy Birthday' – and at that point ten burly security men staggered in under a giant birthday cake. I hoped Barry would erupt through the icing, but he didn't. Instead, when Roberta said, 'So let's all blow out the candles,' a voice suddenly boomed, 'I'll blow my own candles out, thank you,' and there he was. Barry Manilow. In person.

While I was registering his orange skin, candyfloss hair and startling resemblance to Pinocchio, all the fans were scream-ing and fainting in coils all around me. It was at least ten minutes before Barry could make himself heard, but when he could, he explained that he proposed to answer some ques-tions from his fans.

The big news was that his current favourite video game (he is keen on video games) is Donkey Kong. The big tragedy was that his beagle, Bagel, had gone blind. 'Ohhhhh!' went 1,500 fans, breaking into sobs. 'But you know,' Barry went on, shushing them, 'it's true Bagel is now *blind* and that's *awful*. I thought I'd never get over it. But, you know,' and here his voice sank to a hypnotic whisper, 'she *survived*. She is carrying on. So if you ever hear me do a song about carrying on, you'll know it's for Bagel. It's kinda inspirational.'

One of the questions was whether Barry had any special rituals he went through before a concert and he said, 'Yeah, I whirl a chicken round my head.' Whereupon Anne Carole Butler of the Detroit Beagle-Bagels threw a rubber chicken on-stage. (Afterwards, when I asked her why she happened to have a rubber chicken with her, she said, 'For the same reason I have these,' and clapped a pair of Mickey Mouse ears on her head.)

After about an hour, Barry said he had time for only one more question and he read it out from his list. 'What do your fans mean to you?' As he opened his mouth to deliver a sincere and moving reply, someone to the right of the audience shouted out, 'Money in the bank.' Well! The soppy smiles vanished in a moment, and a tornado of boos swelled and rumbled round the room. Realizing a lynching was about to begin, Barry moved fast. 'I want you to know,' he said chokingly, 'that I would not exist if it weren't for you. I feel like I am blessed because I have all of you. You are the kind of supporters that artistes dream of.' And then the loudspeakers blared out 'One Voice, Singing in the Darkness' and a choir of fans came onstage and Barry disappeared.

The fans filed out so quietly I assumed they had been disappointed. It *had* been a fairly boring evening, I thought, despite all the riveting news about Bagel. But next day, they told me unanimously that they had been numbed, overcome, with emotion. 'I wouldn't have missed last night for *anything*,' said thirty-six-year-old Denise Robinson from High Wycombe. 'The tears were falling down my face. I just couldn't believe he was there in front of me.'

Most of the fans spent Saturday going over their memories of what Barry had said, and writing it down in notebooks. By the end of the day, they could all recite his monologue word for word. When they got home, they would copy it all out to send to those of their unfortunate Barryfriends who had not been able to make it to the convention. Most Barryfans write at least three Barryletters a week – some write three *a day* – to their Barrypals around the world.

After all the emotional dramas of Friday night, there seemed a danger that the Saturday night open-air concert at Poplar Creek would come as an anticlimax. But no. Although Barry's voice, as Jean Rook once memorably said, sounds like a bluebottle caught in the curtains, his *show* is pure magic. And it is the fans that make it so. At Poplar Creek they put on at least as good a performance as Barry himself. Applauding the intros, humming the harmonies, clapping and leaping for the hot numbers, sobbing quietly in the slow numbers, and finally waving their flashlights in unison for the anthem 'One Voice', they could not have done it better if they had rehearsed it for months.

On the way back, the coach I was in got lost and when I finally trudged into the hotel, a fan from one of the earlier coaches asked me what happened. 'The driver got lost,' I said, and *then* I heard myself saying, 'but we made it through the rain.' It was not raining in Chicago and never had been. I had simply succumbed.

What is it about Barry Manilow? Apart from hype and gross sentimentality and general rubbish, what else is it that makes it different from any other hysterical crowd scene? It is not Barry Manilow himself, that is for sure. He is a bad singer of banal songs. It is his following, not him, that is special. Sue Robinson, a Caterham secretary who helps organize the London Marathon, defined it best: 'I think we're nice people, gentle, sensitive people – not in an arty-crafty sort of way, but our emotions are closer to the surface than most. We're very much into sharing.'

This was borne out by twenty-year-old Tina Pryke, who told me what being a fan had meant to her. Tina has been blind since the age of five. Many times she has been to Moorfields Hospital for various operations. But last time she went it was different. She had just joined the Barry Manilow Fan Club. When she arrived at Moorfields, her room was already full of flowers and letters and photographs, and her new Barryfriends visited and wrote to her every day. The operation worked for two weeks: for two weeks she could see. And then her eye rejected the grafted cornea and she was blind again. 'If I ever do get my sight back, the first thing I'll do,' she told me, 'is get on a plane and come and see Barry.' But at least she has been to Chicago, her first flight in an aeroplane, helped and escorted throughout by her new Barryfriends: 'It's been wonderful, the whole thing.'

The promise Manilow puts out in his songs is that if you love him, your life will change. From being lonely, unappreciated, a misfit in society, you will find a kindred soul and achieve that Barryapotheosis of being 'lonely together'. The odd thing is that, in a way, the promise is fulfilled. I talked to dozens of women who had been stuck at home, depressed, friendless, prospectless, when they first heard Manilow's music. They dreamt that Barry would come through the door and make everything all right. He didn't. But what happened instead was that they joined their local fan club, met like-minded sentimentalists, shared their problems, attended Barrybashes, set off to conventions, concerts and places they never would have believed they could reach: in short, their lives *were* changed, and for the better. They made it through the rain, all thanks to one voice, singing in the darkness. Manilow magic indeed.

Reproduced by permission of the *Sunday Express*

SIR YEHUDI MENUHIN

16 December 1990

Sir Yehudi Menuhin has been revered as a great violinist for most of the twentieth century. But in recent years, he has become something more – a guru, a wise man, a musical Laurens van der Post, a priest of the order of Prince Charles. His wife calls him the Bodhisattva, the Hindu messenger of the gods. Transcending nationality, religion and politics, he speaks for a higher moral universe, above and beyond this workaday world. He practises yoga, cares for the ecology (even as a child, he has said, he worried about car exhausts), he admires the Animists of Senegal because they can see souls in trees.

One of the few international honours he has not yet been awarded is the Nobel Prize, but it may come. 'One of my earliest dreams,' he told the publisher Naim Attallah, 'was to bring peace to the world.' He has become a sort of head of state for art. Wherever the great and good assemble to promote international brotherhood and cultural understanding, Menuhin is there.

His wife says, 'He isn't a man, he's an institution.' And of course when a man becomes an institution, he invites the attention of an iconoclast, someone to throw a brick through his window. It came last Sunday, devastatingly, in the shape of Tony Palmer's television documentary *Menuhin – A Family Portrait*. The film started gently enough, recording Menuhin's childhood triumphs, with early newsreels of the boy prodigy, 'Mozart the Second', rather tubby and greedy-looking in those days, posing with his parents and younger sisters Hephzibah and Yaltah. Then the picture gradually darkened. Yaltah recalled how their childhood was sacrificed for the sake of Menuhin's career, how their ambitious mother controlled every minute of their days, made them read their private letters aloud, chose whom they should see and what they should read. Menuhin never crossed a road alone till he was eighteen. There were Menuhin's own children, now middle-aged, complaining of his failures as a father and Menuhin's wife, Diana, jeering and sneering at him. Finally there was Menuhin's mother – formidable at ninety-four – greeting Menuhin with rapture, while poor Yaltah complained that she was not allowed to see her mother, because she wanted to save all her energy for her son. It was almost a textbook illustration of how, in a family, the success and happiness of one member can sometimes be bought at the expense of all the others.

So how did the film go down *chez* Menuhin? I presented myself at Chester Square, Belgravia, on Tuesday to find out. Lady Menuhin greeted me by saying that she had 120 Christmas presents 'to wrap, with a friend, personally' before lunch. She is a tall, thin, dramatic-looking woman, with a voice that could carry across continents. As for the Tony Palmer film, 'W*ell!* I think he's a *brilliant* film-maker. His *Walton* was sad but then Walton did have sad things in his life. But I feel somehow – it may be that nowadays you've got to bring out – oh! – any underside you can find, and I was worried because it didn't show what a *marvellous* father he has been in *all* circumstances. *So* generous, you know, always giving his children whatever they needed. And all *that* is on the cutting-room floor, along with me. But I went to Simon Jenkins's party and to my delight everybody – well, nearly everybody – had seen the film and thought it wonderful. And that's all that matters.'

At this point, tiny Sir Yehudi comes into the room and greets his wife with rapture – 'Purple suits you so well! And the Missoni hat!' Lady Menuhin tells him she must go, but gives me one parting observation: 'You know, the *awful* thing I've discovered is that *if* you're efficient and devoted, according to the media, you're called dominating. Nice translation, isn't it? If you're a wimp and lie in the background and do nothing, I suppose you're called wonderful!' And so saying she sweeps out.

Sir Yehudi seems quiet and small and restful by comparison. He apologizes for being tired and explains he gave a concert last night in Strasburg for the Sakharov Foundation, with parties and speeches before and after, went to bed at two, got up at five and by lucky chance found Yeltsin's representative on the same flight to London, so he explained his views on Russia's future to her and she tape-recorded them to relay to Yeltsin. He got to Belgravia at nine, answered his mail, is now seeing me before attending a lunch party, and will catch the 5p.m. flight to Glasgow. A full life. At seventy-four, he says, 'I feel younger than ever before.'

But he soon interrupts himself to say urgently: 'I don't know how *you* felt about the Palmer film. What was your feeling?' I explain that I found it damning. It made a plausible case that his success had been bought at the expense of many. Disarmingly, and very sweetly, he immediately agrees: 'Well, yes. The way you put it . . . I often feel that – that I *have* been so marvellously supported, and I'm very grateful for it. But whether it was at the expense . . . My sister Hephzibah died of cancer, so I don't believe *that* can be put at my door. She had a most unfortunate marriage, terrible, it went the whole gamut from heaven to hell.'

Then he settles into a passionate diatribe about Tony Palmer. 'Like many people in the media, he has his own particular professional deformity, which is the desire to present something new, unexpected, perhaps sensational.

That is a temptation for everyone who is not creative in the highest sense. And, as well, he has something that makes him unable to acknowledge happiness, love. I'm afraid that may arise from his own private experiences – because, after all, people are describing themselves, aren't they? And as one of my secretaries said, "But there's no *love* in the film." Which is extremely irritating, because my life is full of love, absolutely.'

What about Yaltah's evidence, though, about the cruelty of their childhood, their mother's sternness and lack of compassion, the way she controlled every facet of their lives? Yaltah had said movingly, 'We were really not living the life of children at all' and 'One didn't cry, one didn't get upset . . . It was like a prison door; you could knock and knock and just hurt your knuckles . . . No one was ever there.' But Sir Yehudi feels that Tony Palmer was wrong to take Yaltah's word for things. 'For instance, Yaltah tells this story about my mother cutting her hair off – she presents it as an act of barbarity. But if you want to know the facts: Yaltah always loved her hair, she would sit in front of the mirror and comb her golden tresses. She *still* can't be separated from them, even though they now look ridiculous on her rather wizened face. But anyway, we came back one day to find she'd been experimenting with hair tongs, and had made great patches in her scalp. Whereupon my mother said, "Well, there's only one way to cure that, and that is to cut all your hair off." And having done that, she said to my sister and me, "It would be nice if you two would do the same, to keep her company." Now that is the whole story, as it happened.

'But you see Yaltah and my mother,' Sir Yehudi goes on, 'didn't see eye to eye. She feels that she suffered at my mother's hands and that of course creates a resentment. But in fact my mother is one of the most remarkable and wonderful women in the world, selfless to a degree, having given herself completely to her children, and a woman of great pride, integrity, of absolute honesty, a strong and wonderful woman. And never compromising. Now obviously to a mentality which is rather – shall we say? – *ordinary*, she could seem forbidding, formidable, because people of ordinary size cannot cope with people of extraordinary size. And so Yaltah makes this kind of superficial, stupid accusation. My mother is, and remains today at ninety-four, one of the greatest women I know and I love her deeply. So did Hephzibah. Yaltah was a special case. True, she had a childhood that was suffering. Not that she was *denied* anything, but she suffered from the fact that she didn't, in my mother's eyes, measure up to Hephzibah and to me. Maybe that's a fact.'

And was it true, as Yaltah said in the film, that their mother refuses to see her? 'Yaltah is a difficult girl in that she continually writes my mother the most adoring letters and says, "When can I come and see you?" and my mother is very wise and says, "Look, I love you dearly, but I really think it would be wiser if you did not come because I know within five minutes there'd be recriminations." But Yaltah writes these continuing letters because, poor love, she's probably longing for my mother's love.'

Poor Yaltah. Still, the fact that his sister doesn't get on with his mother is hardly Sir Yehudi's fault. A more serious criticism of *him* in the film is that two of his sons, Krov from his first marriage, and Gerard from his second to Diana, say that he was a bad father who never gave them any attention. Krov recalled that when he wrote as a young man and asked to see his father, he said No. Gerard said, 'It wasn't much of a family . . . Overall, the word I would use to describe the atmosphere would be one of careful formality,' and 'I was extremely lonely, left out.' Sir Yehudi reacts with unusual anger: 'Yes, well, look. Gerard was shown sitting in *my* house, which he's been occupying for years – my wife has already given him half her capital. I'm sure he has his frustrations because he would like to be successful and make a lot of money. He is a young man – well, I say young, he's forty-two – of great honesty and integrity, but very like my mother – uncompromising. I have a great respect for him. I am the one who looks for compromises and solutions. I love to bring

people together. He doesn't bother about that. And to see this
young man, charming, personable – he can be sometimes very
beastly – who is enjoying his parents' hospitality at the age of
forty-two . . . I think if one wanted to be hurt, one *could* be
hurt by that.'

Is it possible that Menuhin gave his children money, or
houses, instead of time or attention? Menuhin insists, 'I've
given them – or Diana has given them – an enormous amount
of time. Sometimes she would have to leave them for a while
to be with me but she would always write the most wonderful
letters. You know, sometimes I think you can give *so* much
that it is taken for granted, and not necessarily appreciated.'
How much time *did* he spend with the children?' 'Well, look.
What happens to the children of sailors? This idea of a
"normal" child – there are various kinds of normality.
England used to have a marvellous attitude to children, that
they lived in their own world, so they didn't have to share a
depraved adult world. The children had a real childhood.
There were whole months every summer when we were
together.'

In fact Krov is now on good terms with his father again,
having written to his stepmother, at Menuhin's suggestion,
'the *sweetest* letter saying he didn't realize how silly he was
to trust Tony Palmer and apologizing for the pain he must
have caused her'. The pain was caused, not so much by Krov's
complaints about his father, but by his statement in the film
that Menuhin only really found happiness in his first marriage
(to Krov's mother Nola). Menuhin says this is nonsense, 'My
first wife was a very atttractive girl – especially to a young
man – and she happened also to be very wealthy. Not that
that affected me – in fact nothing cost me more than the
divorce because I was eager to get it at any price, and I gave
her half my earnings for about fifteen years. And that's to one
of the wealthiest heiresses in Australia. And she went off, as
soon as I left to do my war work, with a string of men. And
so, to say that that was the one glowing period of my life –
it's inexcusable. And Diana is played down. There is no

reference to our passionate, devoted relationship for *forty-five years*!'

The underlying theme of the Palmer film is that Menuhin has spent most of his life in the grip of two powerful, manipulative women – first his mother, and then his second wife Diana. His first marriage to Nola was his brief bid for freedom, but it didn't work and he submitted again to the maternal yoke. While he *was* married to Nola, his mother still ran their lives, telling Nola when they should eat and when they should have sex, rushing round to rub his back at the first hint of a cold. And then Diana took over – in the film she is shown telling Menuhin what to say and what not to say, combing his hair and even at one point wiping his nose.

But Menuhin insists: 'Look, I don't feel overpowered. I lead a full life. I have a huge correspondence and I don't bother Diana with it – my correspondence with Margaret Thatcher, for instance, with the Queen of Spain – Diana doesn't read my letters. I am very much an independent man. Diana will say, "Oh that hat doesn't suit you," and will get me another hat, or if we have to face officials – which I absolutely detest – *little* people like immigration officers, she will say, "Now you be quiet, I'll handle this," because she knows how to do it, whereas I just fume and fluster. But I'm not being *bossed* in any way whatsoever.'

Nevertheless, there is no question that *the* woman in his life is his mother – 'a remarkable woman, a marvellous, passionate and deeply feeling woman, but totally unsentimental. You know, I've never seen my mother cry. People don't realize what a strength that is. I remember even when she lost her own mother, her sacred idol, she didn't cry. Her mother must have been a sweet woman, quite different to her, warm-hearted and gentle.'

His mother still lives alone, in Los Gatos, California, where Menuhin grew up. 'She's in good condition, has a very good diet, very frugal, very clean,' he says. 'In fact she has almost no what we used to call garbage. She uses cloth, she doesn't use those disposable tissues, and she washes them herself. She is still very attractive, as you can see in the film. She dressed up for the occasion with all her coquettish ways – she was *wonderful*, don't you agree?'

Yes, wonderful – but terrifying. She was a proud woman, who kept her children apart from the common herd. She 'didn't want the family to be subject to the curiosity of outsiders – and there was a *lot* of curiosity, people wanted to show us off socially, wealthy people wanted me to play in their salons. But my parents kept them at bay – they would have cheapened our lives.'

Hence Menuhin's élitism – his habit of castigating 'little people'. Yaltah's husband Joel Ryce says in the film that even as a child Menuhin saw ordinary people 'as something to be shunned and avoided for ever as meaningless . . . There are very few people who actually interest Yehudi Menuhin.' He never went to school, and only made friends with companions his mother chose. But he gets terribly upset at being told that he had an abnormal childhood – 'It was *different*. It was different from being dragged up on the street, from going to school every day – and American schools always smell. They smell of feet.'

Menuhin no doubt realizes that criticism of his upbringing is actually criticism of his mother, and criticism of his mother is simply not allowed. My faltering attempts to explain that it was unusual to have such a very close filial relationship in one's seventies got absolutely nowhere: his mother is such a special woman that, naturally, people who have ordinary mothers cannot understand. He has nothing but contempt for psychiatrists and all their fancy notions. Yaltah's husband is a psychiatrist. 'If someone comes into a room,' Menuhin explains, 'and falls over a step and shouts wildly, the psychiatrist says this must be because of some childhood trauma he suffered thirty years ago. But it takes no notice of the fact that he is shouting wildly because he has just broken his toe.'

At the end of our interview, Menuhin begged me to be fair,

to answer Tony Palmer's criticism, and to proclaim the truth. But what is the truth? Unquestionably, the film accentuates the negative, but this is a healthy counterweight to all the years of hagiography. Even Menuhin doesn't claim that the film *fakes* anything. Sir Yehudi is a sweet man – I found myself charmed by him, despite my reservations – who invites protectiveness. His late sister Hephzibah once said that all the sweetness and tenderness she and Yaltah received as children came, not from their parents, but from Yehudi. But perhaps his innocence demands a high price in terms of other people's guilt. His wife Diana put it best: 'He doesn't believe in evil, which is nice for him, but not so nice for those of us who have to keep the evil away, which is there.'

RUDOLPH NUREYEV

19 August 1990

I have never seen Nureyev dance, and now I doubt I
ever will. But I am old enough to remember the furore when
he defected to the West in 1961. He was the first of the ballet
defectors, and he seemed unbelievably exotic – not just a
Russian, but a *Tartar*, whatever that was. He could jump
further and higher than anyone else; he was *farouche* and
temperamental; above all, he was beautiful. Once, in about
1966, I went to a party in London and he was there. I didn't
even speak to him but I boasted to my friends about it for
weeks. It was as good as meeting John Lennon or Mick Jagger
or Jackie Kennedy. He was that big a star.

And now I am to meet him, in Orta, a resort on the Italian
Lakes near Stresa, where he is performing his show *Nureyev
and Friends*. Stresa is the equivalent of, perhaps, Paignton.
Once a year it holds a music festival which attracts an
international audience, but it is not festival time now. The
theatre last night was three-quarters full; this evening it will
be barely half-full. This morning Nureyev's manager made
him get up early to receive a formal welcome from the Mayor
of Orta, in hopes of a paragraph in the local press. Tomorrow
he will drive an hour to Milan, fly ninety minutes to Naples,
drive three hours to Paestum and perform outdoors in the

evening. He has always said he will 'fly anywhere' to dance, and now, schlepping around the resorts of Italy to play to half-empty audiences of bored tourists, he is proving it.

Why does he *bother*? He is fifty-two, and practically crippled. He has a growth on his heel, a calcium spur, that gives him constant pain. He can't need the money. He has no wife or children to support (though he does subsidize a sister in Russia, and some of his nephews and nieces), and he still has a salary as resident choreographer of the Paris Opéra-Ballet. He also receives royalties from the many classic ballets he has re-choreographed: every week a Nureyev ballet is performed somewhere in the world. He has always invested his money wisely in property. His friend Maude Gosling recalls that when he first came to her house – an elegant villa in Kensington – he said, 'I will have a house like this,' and she thought, 'You'll be lucky.' But now he has homes in Paris, Monte Carlo, New York, a farm in Virginia and an island off Ischia, and is thinking of buying another in the Caribbean. He owns several great paintings, many valuable antiques, an important collection of textiles. He doesn't *need* money – and in any case it is doubtful whether his performances now make a profit. They are the indulgences of a rich, eccentric man who has dedicated his whole life to dancing and perhaps fears that stopping will mean death.

When we arrive at the hotel in Orta, Nureyev is still upstairs having a massage, so we sit on the terrace talking to his manager, Luigi Pinotti. A talkative bear of a man in his mid-forties, he first joined Nureyev as his masseur in 1963 and accompanied him and Fonteyn on all their great sixties tours – triumphal progresses when they would receive 40, 50, 60, even 80 curtain calls. Now Luigi has graduated to manager, not only of Nureyev, he boasts, but of many '*étoiles*', and when I ask if he still sometimes gives Nureyev his massage, he replies disdainfully, 'No. We hire someone.'

As a manager, he says, his forte is 'provoking' business: he goes out selling the Nureyev package. Planes are good for this; the other day, on a plane, he met a businesswoman from Bangkok and told her all about *Nureyev and Friends* and gave her the video, and now, he hopes, they will get a booking in Bangkok. Will that be profitable, I wonder, flying eight dancers – all *étoiles*, as he keeps saying – out to Thailand? 'Maybe yes, maybe no. Sometimes we can do a deal on the hotel, on the flights.' The scene is so doomy, so end-of-the-roady, I find myself shivering in the Italian sun.

And when Nureyev eventually appears, I seriously want to run away. He resembles one of those dolls in national costume, but the very tacky sort that don't stand up properly. He is wearing a maroon velvet cossack shirt, green velvet jodhpurs which may once have been tight-fitting but now hang in wrinkles, a silly sort of Tyrolean short jacket, a green tweed beret stuck with brooches and a plaid thrown over his shoulder. The clothes are all seedy and shabby but it is his boots that really make me want to weep. They were once Cuban-heeled Mexican cowboy boots, but now the heels are wonky and the seams splitting; there are great holes in the toes; you couldn't give them to a tramp.

He says that we are going to lunch on an island: Luigi will arrange it all. Meanwhile he signs autographs for a group of businessmen who have just emerged from their sales confer-ence. Some of them clearly have no idea who he is and look at him doubtfully. Then a boat takes us over to the island restaurant where we sit under a vine pergola, and Nureyev signs more autographs for the waitresses.

I am relieved to find he speaks much better English than I expected – heavily accented, not always grammatical and sometimes eccentric, but the sophisticated English of an intelligent man. He says he speaks 'many languages badly' but English is the one he mainly reads and thinks in. He started learning it even before he left Russia: 'I was shamed into it. I was on tour with the Kirov in Beirut and one evening in the hotel a young man came up to me, "Do you speak English?" *Niet!* "Parlez-vous français?" *Niet!* "Sprechen Sie

Deutsch?" *Niet!* So as soon as I went back to Russia, I found a teacher. I really wanted to learn French and there was an old lady in Leningrad who said she would teach me. But, she said, "The only thing is you will have to carry every morning the bucket of dirt downstairs" – because there were no toilets. And I thought, "No. I am too grand, I am a dancer." So of course I never learn French. But *now*, I tell young people, "If you want to achieve something in life, you have to carry the bucket of dirt."'

For the past decade he has lived mainly in Paris, where he has a very beautiful apartment, filled with his favourite antiques, and a magnificent harpsichord. But this year he had a row with his employers, the Opéra-Ballet, which ended with Nureyev being sacked as artistic director but retained as choreographer.

So will he now sell his Paris apartment? 'No. I don't have to. Not yet. Things are not *that* bad.' How many houses does he own exactly? Suddenly his eyes flash, his nostrils flare: 'Are you *that* kind of journalist? Then forget it. Margot taught me that very early. She said, "When someone asks you something you don't want to answer, say, It's none of your business."' This is my first taste of the famous Nureyev temper and it takes me by surprise – but I also recognize its justice. It *was* a lazy question – I was actually thinking about what food to order – and he spotted it immediately.

Meaning to placate him, I ask what ballets he has seen lately, but he says none. 'When I don't dance, I can't bear to watch any ballet. To go and see the Kirov dancing *Swan Lake* – I can't think of worse torture. In the theatre I feel pinned down, like butterflies. There is some kind of false, hateful atmosphere. I can't watch. I'm not meant to be a spectator: I'm meant to be a performer.'

He is also meant to be writing his autobiography. He signed the contract ten years ago and now really has to deliver. 'But chewing all that fat and regurgitating it . . . Pah!' For him, the past is – literally – another country, and one he hates to recall. When he thinks of his childhood – the cold, the hunger,

the nine people crammed into one room – it seems 'as strange
to me as it would to you. Like it never happened; like I read
it in a book. When I went back to Russia last year . . . people
speak the same language, but it doesn't match.'

He cut himself off deliberately when he came to the West,
by refusing to read Russian, speak Russian or befriend any
Russians for all of seven years. It sounds almost paranoid,
and he admits, 'There was that, too. You must have read that
Khrushchev put out a writ on my life. And even now they tap
my phone in London. But no, I thought, "What's the point of
coming to the West? I *wanted* to be in the West. Why still
wallow in Russia?" I think it was my salvation.' Nor, he
insists, has he ever subsequently felt nostalgic. 'Never. *Never!*
Though I had quite a lot of hideous moments in the West, I
never, even in my basest moments, wanted to go back. I
gained infinitely by being in the West.'

But in the past few years he *has* been back, to see his dying
mother (alas, he left it too late, and she could barely recognize
him) and last year to dance with the Kirov. He wanted to see
Leningrad again, and his old partners – 'I had eleven partners
in three years! A big career!' – and at his performance he
found them all sitting abreast in the front box. 'I couldn't be
nervous because I went to Leningrad with an injured foot and
then the regret was I tore the calf of the other leg, so I had no
leg to stand on. It was all bandaged and plastered. But I
thought, "Well I can still show some style." And to cancel
would be too disappointing. I didn't come to show anything.
It was really a kind of caprice, a desire to be on that stage
once more.' And how was it? 'Terrible! The smell. It's sort of
run down. And still the same old babushkas sitting in every
exit.' He says nothing about his performance, but the *Soviet
Ballet* magazine critic wrote: 'Everything became strangely
muddled; we tried to look through time to see the dance as it
would have been thirty, or even twenty years ago. Our
ovations were addressed to the past – to one of our own who
was unfamiliar to us.'

*

I asked about his home town, Ufa, and his sister who still lives there, but he said furiously, 'No! I don't want to speak about my sister, or Ufa, all that.' But later he relented and said he had revisited Ufa and found it 'not too ugly – nice wide streets, a lot of trees, still some of the old wooden houses'. He also talked of his early love of music. Even at six, he would sit glued to his father's radio – 'that terrible little thing, but we could listen to funerals. When someone died, they played Beethoven and Tchaikovsky all day. There was a Schumann trio I remember, and *Nutcracker* transmitted from the Bolshoi.' He asked his father if he could learn the piano, 'but he said, "My son, you can't play the piano. You can't carry it on your shoulders and we have no place to put it down. Why don't you learn accordion?" But I say, "No. I don't want accordion." Even then I knew this is ugly music.' Now he owns pianos, harpsichords, organs – at least one in each of his homes.

He saw his first ballet on New Year's Day 1943, and knew immediately it was for him. His father was scornful, but his mother encouraged him, and let him go to folk-dancing classes with the Young Pioneers. Then, when he was eleven, an old lady called Udeltsova who had danced in Diaghilev's *corps de ballet* volunteered to teach him, and eventually got him an audition with the Kirov School when he was seventeen. He entered the next day.

From ballet school, he was whizzed straight into principal roles, bypassing the *corps de ballet*. The company's leading ballerina, Natalia Dudinskaya, chose him to partner her (he was half her age) and even invited him to share her one-bedroom apartment – 'But I always sleep on the sofa.' And even in these early days, he always *thought* like a star. 'I was always very conscious of box office. When a performance of Dudinskaya was announced, she sold all the tickets in one day. I sold in three! I was aware that ticket sales mattered. But of course we didn't have any publicity at all. I knew I had become superfamous when there was a photo of me and Dudinskaya in *Pravda*, a little photo with a line of text, but

Pravda is only two pages and in Russia that was enormous! And the second time, when I went to Vienna with the Kirov, I fall down in a big *manège* because the stage was so slippery, and then somehow from the floor continue my jump, and *Izvestia* wrote a paragraph about it. That meant I was *really* famous – two mentions like that in three years.'

And then, in 1961, he came to Paris with the Kirov Ballet – and defected. It was a spur-of-the-moment decision, but 'a very good move. Like the saying, you follow your nose.' The Kirov was due to go to London for the next leg of the tour, and everyone was given tickets except Nureyev. He was told he was flying back to Moscow for a special gala, but he knew it meant he would never be allowed to leave Russia again. He quietly walked over to the airport police. It was the first major Russian defection in years and attracted enormous publicity. 'That was frightening; too much. I thought, "Why do they write all this? Why? Why?" And every word – whether it was praise or criticism – was agony to read. Now I don't believe it. Anyway, it's too late.' He gives a strange, humourless laugh. 'It's too late!'

The hardest lesson he had to learn in the West was to take responsibility for his own life. 'In Russia, you know, you grew up with an absolutely in-built instinct that somebody older, taller, bigger, dictates your life. He decides what you are going to do – the authority, the father, you know? You are trained in submission. And so to make decisions and learn to act on your own is a very painful process – and very long. You have to tell yourself you cannot wait. But at the beginning I was waiting, waiting, and no big Daddy comes.'

His ambitions in the West were, first, to dance for Balanchine, and second to train with the teacher of Erik Bruhn, the great Danish dancer. But Balanchine rejected him: 'He took me to lunch at the Russian Tea Room and said, "You know I don't have *pas de deux* in my company. My ballets are very dry – but I like them dry! No," he said, "you go off and dance your Princes, get tired of them, and then come back." Well. I never got tired of Princes, and Princes never got tired of me.'

Then he went to Denmark to find Erik Bruhn's teacher but that was disappointing too because she was a Russian, Vera Volkova, and 'just like my old teacher, Pushkin. But he, Erik, was excellent and I watch every one of his performances, and learn from that.' Erik Bruhn was his first close friend in the West – ten years older than Nureyev and considered, before him, the best male dancer in the world, he was generous in befriending the Russian newcomer who would soon eclipse his fame.

His first English friends were Margot Fonteyn and Maude and Nigel Gosling. Maude (née Lloyd) was a former prima ballerina; Nigel was the *Observer*'s art critic, and also its ballet critic under the pseudonym Alexander Bland. Nigel died, much mourned, in 1982, but Maude remains Nureyev's closest friend, and he stays with her when he is in London. She is eighty-two, but as lithe and eager as a schoolgirl.

She recalls the first time she ever saw him, dancing with the Kirov in Paris. The Kirov was coming to London the following week, but Nigel decided to see them first in Paris to prepare his review. 'And we went to the theatre and *Sleeping Beauty* began and when the Prince came on, we sat up. Just the way he walked on, even before he danced, was enough to make you feel, "This is somebody quite extraordinary." We looked on the programme but the name wasn't Nureyev. Apparently he'd been such a success as the Bluebird the night before, they put him on again. We didn't meet him that night but we came back and told everyone, "You wait. You wait till this new dancer arrives next week – you'll be bowled over." But of course he didn't arrive.' After he defected, he joined the de Cuevas ballet in Paris for six months, then went to Denmark to train with Vera Volkova.

A few months later Margot Fonteyn was arranging a charity gala, and the Goslings told her she should try to get the new young Russian dancer, whom she had never seen. She rang Vera Volkova in Denmark, who said, 'I think he is a genius. He has the nostrils.' But he didn't have the fare to come to England. So Nigel Gosling persuaded the *Observer* to pay.

Those early months in the West were terribly lonely for him, Maude recalls. 'He was nervous and very much on his dignity, so he wasn't going to allow people to realize how lonely he was.' Margot gave him £5 a week for steak and bananas and Tube fares, and he went to every party he was asked to in search of free food. He talked dancing to Margot and Maude and 'everything else' to Nigel – 'Which is what he preferred,' Maude says. 'Later, when he was touring, he'd ring up at two in the morning from all over the world, and talk about the art galleries he'd been to or the buildings he'd seen. Nigel always said he had an amazing eye.'

Nureyev always used to say he had just four friends: Nigel and Maude Gosling, Margot Fonteyn, and Douce François. The latter was a Chilean heiress who looked after him in Paris for thirteen years – one of many socialite ladies who attach themselves to him – but he apparently dropped her a few years ago. Nigel died (and Nureyev conquered his fear of hospitals to visit him on his deathbed). Now his two remaining friends are Maude and Margot, and Margot is in poor health. I said something about 'when Margot dies . . .' and Nureyev was outraged: 'Why? Why should we speak about it? She looks very well, the English doctors gave her not one week, but she had the operation, kept her chin up and chewed up the cancer, and there she is.' Maude told me he had rung her afterwards to complain, 'Oh! She asked me about Margot. You don't *say* things like that!'

His private life remains mysterious, as he wants it to be, but there is no partner in his life. His first love is and always has been the ballet. His colleagues at the Kirov used to tease him, 'When will you marry?' till one of them answered, 'He's married already – to the barre.' 'Which was true,' Nureyev added, 'I was absolutely a virgin till I came to the West.' Really? 'Not quite. Almost. But that's how it was. Nothing could disrupt my dancing. I was obsessed with dancing.'

Although he was enthralled by the sexual freedom of the West, he once told Margot Fonteyn, 'The trouble is, I do not have the courage to be as wicked as I want.'

He fell in love several times. 'But then . . . everything flourishes, and then peters out, you know? But when it develops into friendship, then it is blessed. Friendship is the highest form of love, I think.' He has never lived with anyone. 'I'm too problematic, too independent. One *wants* to, but then, it's too painful, too dangerous. One cannot share, a dancer cannot share life with anybody. No go . . .'

And besides, he rarely stays anywhere for more than a few weeks. He was born on a train (his mother was returning from visiting her husband in the army) and says, 'I don't know if such a thing exists as a vagabond soul, but I travel always.' Yet when I ask what is the most glamourous thing he can think of, he says, 'Home. Home is glamorous, to have around you the things that you like, not to go out.'

He is essentially a loner, and self-reliant. He has always refused to put himself in the hands of agents or mentors, believing that no one can look after his interests as well as he can himself. He has no secretary and consequently never replies to letters – Maude Gosling says she has boxes and boxes of his fan mail unopened at home – nor does he employ the retinues of assistants which are the normal lumber of celebrity. He travels alone, lives alone, sleeps alone. Maude recalls an occasion when she was with him in Venice and they went to supper at Harry's Bar after his performance. Nureyev, as usual, was carrying two enormous bags and Maude heard a passer-by say, 'That looks awfully like the dancer Nureyev,' and his companion's reply, 'Couldn't be. He's carrying his own bags.'

When he first came to the West, there were endless press stories about his temper tantrums. A typical one described how, at a party, someone handed him a plate and told him to serve himself at the buffet, whereupon he exclaimed, 'Nureyev does not serve himself!', smashed the plate and stormed out. I asked if he was still temperamental. 'Of course any artist must have temperament. They are exigent, no? They make demands. They demand of themselves superior performances and that creates great stress, but they demand from *themselves*, not others. Of course, a person not in the shade of art will not understand. When they try to bring their own norms, they don't match.' So it's true that he shouts at people? 'What does it matter to you? I never shout at *you*. Yes, I shout when it can save situations. When it cannot, I don't.'

He is difficult to read because he is so un-English. His personality is mercurial, alternately arrogant and shy, trusting and suspicious. It is the *speed* of the emotions that baffles – the way he can be rude one minute, friendly the next. He has enormous willpower, exemplified by the fact that he flies so much though terrified of flying. He is canny rather than wise, instinctive rather than thoughtful, but he has learnt to use his instincts shrewdly. Above all he is a man who knows himself – 'centred', as the Americans say – and who has always been totally clear about his priorities, which begin and virtually end with dancing.

Which brings us finally to the great question, the question I have been warned never to ask: *why* does he go on? In the end he raises it himself. Talking of his work as a choreographer, he says, 'But the main thing is dancing, and before it withers away from my body, I will keep dancing till the last moment, the last drop.' And how will he know when the last moment has come? 'When it becomes unpleasant to be on-stage. Till then, I go anywhere. I like performing. It makes me feel good, physically, mentally.' Maude Gosling and Luigi Pinotti both confirm this; that often he will seem dead beat, exhausted, finished, but as the hour of performance draws near, he suddenly charges into life. Performing now has nothing to do with money, with fame, with ambition; it is something he *needs* for its own sake and he hates to go for more than ten days without it. He is delighted that the American choreographer Flemming Flindt has created a new ballet for him, *The Overcoat*, in which he plays a fifty-year-old man – he reckons he can hobble through it for a good many years.

But what does he fear will happen if he stops? The question provokes a terrible sulk but eventually he mutters, 'I might become very fat.' Is that so awful? 'If it is inevitable . . . but I manage to ward it off for quite a while, no? Let's say, fifteen years.' In fact, in 1966 *Nova* magazine said, 'He has only two, perhaps three, more years of dancing ahead.' When I quote it, he flashes his arrogant flared-nostril smile, 'And where is this *Nova* magazine now?'

'Extinct.'

'You *see!*' he crows. 'You see!'

Some of his friends believe that he would almost be relieved to break a leg, to be forced to give up. But till then, as Maude Gosling says, 'Why stop? He still gets an audience, he still gets paid, he's still happy doing it. He doesn't read the critics. Look at Callas. They dragged her down, they killed that woman. Nobody tells a writer or a painter to stop. Whereas everybody keeps asking Rudolph, "When are you going to stop?" and it drives him *frantic*. He really loves to dance, it's his life. And he's still got something to give – look at the fans at the stage door. Why should he stop?'

After lunch, he gets the boatman to take us for a spin round the lake, urging 'Faster! Faster!' He is relaxed and happy, and as we get off the boat I tease him about his terrible boots.

'I always wear,' he tells me.

'But what happens when they fall apart?'

He laughs, recognizing that the question is not really about boots. 'I mend again with Elastoplast. I *always* mend again.' And he smiles his proud smile, and hobbles away, soles flapping.

Reproduced by permission of the *Independent on Sunday*

KEN RUSSELL
15 September 1985

Everybody knows that Ken Russell is the man who makes sexy, sacrilegious films about nuns, Nazis and nymphomaniacs. Well, not quite *about* those things – the subjects are usually perfectly respectable Lives of the Great Composers and so on – but the nuns and Nazis will start creeping in. He summarized his life of Tchaikovsky (*The Music Lovers*) as 'the story of a homosexual who marries a nymphomaniac' – he has a strictly *Sun*-headline view of history. His latest film, *Crimes of Passion*, is a lurid tale of sex'n'violence with Kathleen Turner as a prostitute and Tony Perkins as the inevitable mad priest.

One therefore expects Ken Russell to live in some kind of hotbed of perversion. In fact he lives in the Lake District, in Borrowdale. 'Oh good,' I said rashly when he invited me up there, 'we can climb a fell.' I should have remembered that Borrowdale has the highest rainfall in England. The weather was fine all the way up to Keswick, but the minute the car turned into Borrowdale, the heavens opened and the rain came bucketing down.

Still, there was Ken Russell in his little cottage by the roadside positively champing at the bit. He looked like a rather cross gnome who had been forcibly dragged down from his airy mountain and rushy glen. No sooner had I entered the front door than he was inspecting my feet. 'Where are your boots?' he barked. 'No boots? You can't walk in *those*. I know! We'll go to the boot shop in Keswick and get you some.' 'But, er,' I stammered feebly, 'couldn't we just wait until it stops raining?' Of course it never did stop raining – it never does in Borrowdale – so we didn't go for our walk. I regret it now. I would have liked to have seen the fifty-eight-year-old wild man of British films hurling himself up a Lakeland fell in his plus-fours and climbing boots, trusty Wainwright in hand. I just wouldn't have liked to have seen myself trying to keep up.

Instead, he led me to the upstairs sitting-room with its panoramic view of rain beating against windows. His American wife, Vivian, brought tea, while their seven-year-old daughter, Molly, danced in carrying her new baby brother Rupert, and chattered away in her broad Cumbrian accent. Ken Russell gave me a guided tour of the room – walls of books and records, carved statues of saints, Victorian harmonium, enormous light-up gnome in the window and, best of all, his map of the Lake District with flags stuck in the peaks he has climbed.

There is barely a peak he *hasn't* climbed, and many of them he has climbed with a film crew in tow. He used the Lake District as Norway in his life of Delius, as Iceland in Rossetti, as Bavaria in Mahler. Most recently he used it as the setting for a new Cliff Richard video, and Keswick Drill Hall became the audition centre for thousands of females aged from eight days to eighty. He first discovered the Lake District in 1967 when he was looking for locations for Rossetti. He arrived at night, booked into a hotel, opened his curtains in the morning and there it was – 'the spot I'd been looking for all my life!' For several years, he made do with staying in hotels, but one day he went into an estate agent's in Keswick and found this cottage. It was terribly small when he started – though he has since extended it – and bang on the road, about as public as any house could be in Lakeland, with troops of hikers peering in the windows, but still he loves it. His wife Vivian is a gardening fanatic and grows amazing lilies.

It is all as far as possible away from Hollywood, but that is how Ken Russell likes it.

Still, Ken Russell's pose as the Hermit of Borrowdale should not be taken *too* seriously. Last year, for instance, when he finally married Vivian, six years after the birth of their daughter, he did it in the full glare of Hollywood razzmatazz. The setting was the old *Queen Mary* moored at Long Beach, California, and the three hundred guests were told to wear nautical dress. Russell himself wore the uniform of an RNVR lieutenant as he was fully entitled to do, having been one, but the other men all pranced round as admirals. Tony Perkins conducted the wedding service: he had sent off $25 to a mail-order ad and been made a minister of the 'Universal Life Church'. His two sons, Elvis and Osgood, were pages, while the bride and groom's daughter Molly was bridesmaid. It was all in outrageously bad taste and not at all the sort of wedding they have in Borrowdale.

Earlier this year, Ken Russell was headline news again when he made a rude gesture to the first-night audience of his production of *Faust* at the Vienna State Opera. 'Assholes' he called the audience, which is not what opera-goers like to hear. He is famous for his terrifying rages at opera rehearsals and on film sets. I got a slight taste of one when I happened to mention that I had seen the American (heavily cut) version of *Crimes of Passion* instead of the (less cut) British. While he beat his forehead and gnashed his teeth I decided that it would be imprudent to remark that I wouldn't have minded if it had been cut even more.

Watching any Ken Russell film inevitably leads to speculation about the state of its maker's psyche. The images seem to come boiling straight from the subconscious; they are like a Technicolor encyclopaedia of Freudian symbols. It is therefore tempting to suspect that Ken Russell might be mad. Not that he *seems* mad, here in the Lake District, but perhaps he has been mad in the past. Now how to raise the subject tactfully?

'Have you ever been certified insane?' I finally ask, when we have moved on to the Secret Garden Bar of the Borrowdale Hotel for drinks. 'Yes,' he says without batting an eyelid, 'once. It was when I got back from my one trip in the Merchant Navy. Although the war was long over, the captain made me stand on a spot the size of a beer-mat for eight hours a day staring at the Pacific looking for Japanese submarines, while he, naked, stood on his hands and looked up my shorts. He said: "Russell, put on long trousers. Your legs are too good in shorts." I didn't know what he was talking about, but I knew I wanted to get out. So I went to a psychiatrist and he gave me a certificate.

'Yes,' he continues, 'I was a bit off my head then. I sat around the house for months like a zombie till I heard Tchaikovsky's Piano Concerto No. 1 on the wireless and that somehow got me going again. Since then I'm as sane as the next man!'

He says he is still haunted by extraordinarily vivid memories of his childhood in Southampton – 'this road that nobody ever came along, never seeing another soul, playing alone in the garden'. His brother was six years younger and never became a soul-mate – he now runs a car-hire firm in Southampton. Their father worked in a boot shop which *his* father owned; their mother was a shopgirl who married the boss's son. 'We had a maid, which was every shopgirl's dream, but it meant my mother had nothing to do. So she'd take me to films, and to tea dances and fashion shows.'

Then, when he was ten, he got a film projector and a job-lot of films from a bombed-out chemist's and he was hooked. He attended Pangbourne Naval College and got all his schoolmates to act (in drag) in an amateur film. When he was invalided out of the Merchant Navy, certified insane, he went round all the British film studios begging for a job but the studios were in decline and wouldn't look at new talent. National Service followed and he joined the RAF and there met a ballet dancer who persuaded him to try dancing. He worked as a dancer for five years, till a string of injuries forced him to leave.

It was, he recalls, a strangely sexless youth. 'I look back in total amazement at those years – amazement that I survived intact. I was always being picked up by young gents and somehow missing the last train and having to share a sofa but nothing ever happened. I was so innocent. I knew I wanted to fall in love and get married and lead a sort of normal existence, but at the same time I knew I had to be doing something creative. In the end my father paid for me to go to Walthamstow Art School and I met my first wife there, and started taking photos and that was the beginning, really . . .'

His first wife, Shirley Russell, was the costume designer on all his films; they remained married for twenty-one years and had five children – 'like spots before the eyes,' he says now, 'too many, too close together'. He was a Roman Catholic convert at twenty-seven; lapsed ten years later. Meanwhile, his career took off. He made three short films on spec and showed them to Huw Wheldon at the BBC. 'It was, you know, that moment when your luck turns and a door opens. I remember Huw saying, "Okay then, we'll take you on," and my scalp sliding back and thinking, "Heck, this is it!"'

The forty arts films he made for the BBC between 1959 and 1970 are now considered classics. His lives of Elgar, Delius, Debussy, Prokofiev, Rousseau, Bartok, Isadora Duncan were universally admired and they pushed forward the boundaries of television biography. But gradually his films grew more extravagant, and his life of Richard Strauss (heavily infested with nuns and Nazis) brought down the full wrath of the Whitehouse brigade. So Russell sailed off to Hollywood and a string of successes – *Women in Love, The Music Lovers, The Devils, The Boyfriend, Mahler, Tommy* – until 1977 when *Valentino*, starring Rudolf Nureyev, fell to earth with a crash. Part of the trouble was that Ken Russell's marriage was breaking up – Shirley Russell found Vivian Jolly (Russell's present wife) sitting in Ken's chair on set. But also, as Russell admits, 'I got a terrible performance out of Nureyev. He kept wanting to talk more and dance less, but his English was unintelligible.' Alexander Walker, the *Standard* film critic, said that *Valentino* was a film 'bursting with hate . . . a callous exercise in humiliation', whereupon Ken Russell hit him over the head with a rolled-up copy of his review during a television chat show. At all events, the film was a disaster.

From then on, Russell was branded with the Hollywood curse – 'unbankable'. He might have redeemed himself by directing *Evita*, as he was meant to do, but typically he refused to do it with Elaine Paige in the lead ('She looks like a cross between Princess Margaret and Barbara Windsor') and Tim Rice refused to do it without. Then he spent years trying to set up a film about Maria Callas with Sophia Loren but La Loren eventually got cold feet. By the early eighties he was saying, 'Films are a dead medium. It's a false world and I'm sick of it.' Instead, he embarked on a second career as an opera director, whizzing round the world stirring up whole new storms of controversy – *Madame Butterfly* as an opium-smoking prostitute, *La Bohème* as a heroin-addict punk. He heralded his latest production, Gounod's *Faust* at the Vienna State Opera, by saying: 'The plot is worthless and the music is not too much either so you have to do something drastic.' On with the nymphomaniac nuns.

The great virtue of opera, he explains, is that 'When they say, "Will you do this opera for us on 12 October 1999," you know that as long as you're still alive, it will happen. Whereas so many film projects fall through. You get terribly excited writing scripts but then it's just sitting around waiting and promises, promises. It's terribly frustrating *not* making films.'

Any director with half an eye to his future would have made a nice safe film for his comeback. Ken Russell, typically, chose *Crimes of Passion*, which was loaded with censorship problems from the start. 'I don't *try* to be controversial,' he wails, but one can't help suspecting he would be jolly disappointed if he wasn't. His next project is *Moll Flanders* (a prostitute again) for Bob Guccione of Penthouse, which is hardly likely to restore him to the bosom of Hollywood bankability.

But at least, in his precious Lake District, he is happy. 'Even if I *am* out of work, I can always climb a mountain!' He asked me to stay to supper and we had a very cosy family meal in the kitchen, with Molly asking me if I knew what the vegetable dish was called and then telling me 'Ratatouille!' in her best Borrowdale French accent. Vivian and I talked about babies, breast versus bottle feeding, while Ken Russell beamed at the head of the table like a kindly paterfamilias. And then the phone rang. It was the record company saying that they thought Russell's new Cliff Richard video was too controversial. Something about a scene with a ball they didn't like. Russell suddenly turned from a benevolent gnome into a furious troll, rolled his eyes and beat his forehead and howled into the phone: 'Controversial? *Controversial!*' He came back from the phone looking shaken. But one couldn't help suspecting that deep down inside there might be a tiny nugget of glee. Making Cliff Richard controversial — now even for Ken Russell that is quite a feat!

Reproduced by permission of the *Sunday Express*

SIR JAMES SAVILE
22 July 1990

Sir James Savile is absolutely knocked out, over the moon, tickled pink, and thrilled to bits with his knighthood, and still reeling from the excitement of it all. Ooh, but it has played merry hell with his diary. 'The Queen deciding to give me this tremendous responsibility – I mean, you go to bed one minute without a care in the world and you wake up the next morning with this gi-normous responsibility come through the letterbox. Do you want to see the gear?' he asks, burrowing under the put-u-up to find his briefcase (we are in his London flat) and eventually producing a transparent plastic folder. 'Read it all,' he urges. 'Go on. Have a little dwell on that. That folder encapsulates it all.'

The folder encloses the letter from the Prime Minister offering him a knighthood, the envelope it came in, some bumf about keeping it secret till the proper date and then – proudest of all – telegrams of congratulation from Charles and Diana, from Prince Philip, a handwritten letter from Angus Ogilvy and a very sweet home-made card with a stuck-on snapshot of Princess Bea, from the Duchess of York. He is almost bursting with pride as he shows them off.

'I was lying in bed here,' he recalls, 'when I heard the little clink on the door and an hour later, when I got up, I picked up the letter – there was only one letter on the floor – and it said "OHMS", so I thought it was from the Income Tax. And I thought, "That's unusual" – because I get my tax stuff up in Leeds. But what I got was: "OHMS. Urgent. Personal. From the Prime Minister's Office" – and there it was.'

The letter from Downing Street enclosed a form which he had to sign to say he would accept the knighthood, and, rather than trust it to the post, he hopped in a taxi and delivered it himself to the policeman at the end of Downing Street. The policeman said 'Congratulations,' but Jimmy (he was still Jimmy in those days) said, 'I don't know what you're talking about.'

He didn't tell a soul. It was 'thirty-six days of agony' between hearing of his knighthood and its public announcement. 'Ooh, I can't *tell* you the agony, because the ramifications of not telling were just phenomenal. People would say, "Now next week . . ." and I'd go, "Hm?" For the first time in my life I *appeared* to be indecisive, because I'm always totally positive.

'And all my people, at Leeds Infirmary, at Broadmoor, Stoke Mandeville, were all ringing each other up saying, "Here. What's wrong with the Godfather?" They thought I was sickening for something. The last forty-eight hours was the worst – grind, grind, grind. When it came out at midnight – radio and teletext the same time – it was such a relief.'

Since then he has had nine hundred letters, seven hundred phone calls of congratulations, and he promises he will reply to them all in the fullness of time when he has recovered from his daze.

He is still undecided whether he wants to be Sir James or Sir Jimmy, and looks at me a bit carefully ('Is she taking the mickey?') when I call him 'Sir James'. But he certainly wants to be called one or the other: he is intensely proud of his honour. Alone among television stars, he has always insisted on having his OBE after his name on the programme credits.

The only surprising thing about his knighthood is how long it has taken him to get it. He has been raising money for charity for at least twenty years – over £30m at the last count – and Stoke Mandeville's National Spinal Injuries Centre is almost entirely a result of his efforts. The day after I met him, he was going to open yet another £2m donation to the hospital – a new magnetic resonance imager which for the first time will enable surgeons to see the spinal cord as well as the spinal column, with no side effects to the patient. He raised the money, negotiated with Hitachi and the Japanese government to deliver it at unprecedented speed, and meanwhile got the hospital to knock down walls and rebuild areas to make room for it.

His official title at Stoke Mandeville (and at Broadmoor, and at Leeds Infirmary, where he performs similar benefactions) is 'voluntary helper' – but his help is quite breathtaking in its scope. In 1988 the Department of Health suspended the whole management board of Broadmoor and put Savile in charge of running the place, which he is still doing with every apparent success.

He raises money and also gives his own money, channelling nine tenths of his income into two charitable trusts. He earns a BBC salary as presenter of *Jim'll Fix It* and the World Service radio programme *Savile's Travels*, and is a paid consultant to Thomas Cook, the travel agents. But most of his income comes from personal appearances, for which he charges a minimum of five figures. 'I don't even get out of bed for less than £10,000,' he says, explaining that if he charges a lot, the event is well-organized, whereas if he doesn't, it isn't.

'I went to a thing recently in a field with some lovely people but when I got there, there was no raised platform and no microphone, so how was the audience meant to see me? And they all go, "Oh yeah. We never thought of that." Now if they'd paid the ten grand, they'd have set to work with a great to-do, you see.' This makes sense, but sometimes comes as a shock to people who imagine that because Savile is charitable he is also unworldly. He isn't.

Many businesses and organizations use him as a conduit to the Royal Family; he can pick up the telephone to most of them and has long worked with Prince Charles ('the most caring fellow I've ever met – oh, unbelievable') on the problems of the disabled. He is an habitué of Highgrove and Buckingham Palace, of No. 10 and Chequers, where he often spends Christmas or New Year – though he carefully points out that he has been friendly with *all* the last four Prime Ministers because Stoke Mandeville is Chequers' local hospital.

Anyway, he is very very well connected; many multinationals use him as a consultant and not just for PR purposes but for marketing advice. To the public, he remains the silver-haired tracksuited jester, but those who have worked with him take him very seriously indeed.

Still, his jester image may have made his knighthood slower than it would otherwise have been. 'I would imagine that I unsettled the Establishment,' he agrees, 'because the Establishment would say, "Yes, Jimmy's a good chap but a bit strange . . . a bit strange." And I think maybe in the past I suffered from the vulgarity of success. Because if you're successful in what you do, you can become a pain in the neck to a lot of people, especially if you're doing it in a voluntary manner, right?'

Right. So being awarded a knighthood was a joy and an honour. More interestingly, he says it was also a relief. For the past several years, tabloid journalists have been saying that he must have a serious skeleton in his cupboard, otherwise he would have got a knighthood by now. 'Ooh ay, I had a lively couple of years, with the tabloids sniffing about, asking round the corner shops – everything – thinking there must be something the authorities knew that they didn't. Whereas in actual fact I've got to be the mot boring geezer in the world because I ain't got no past, no nothing. And so, if nothing else, it was a gi-normous relief when I got the knighthood, because it got me off the hook.'

What he says about tabloid journalists is true. There has been a persistent rumour about him for years, and journalists have often told me as a fact: 'Jimmy Savile? Of course, you know he's into little girls.' But if they know it, why haven't they published it? The *Sun* or *News of the World* would hardly refuse the chance of featuring a Jimmy Savile sex scandal. It is very, very hard to prove a negative, but the fact that the tabloids have never come up with a scintilla of evidence against Jimmy Savile is as near proof as you can ever get.

I wasn't sure whether Sir James actually knew what the particular skeleton in his closet was supposed to be, though I notice that he told the *Sun* five years ago that he never allowed children into his flat. 'Never in a million years would I dream of letting a kid, or five kids, past my front door. Never, ever. I'd feel very uncomfortable.' Nor, he said, would he take children for a ride in his car unless they had their mum or dad with them: 'You just can't take the risk.'

Still, I was nervous when I told him: 'What people say is that you like little girls.' He reacted with a flurry of funny-voice Jimmy Savile patter, which is what he does when he's getting his bearings: 'Ah now. Sure. Now then. Now then. First of all, I happen to be in the pop business, which is teenagers – that's number one. So when I go anywhere it's the young ones that come round me.

'Now what the tabloids don't realize is that the young girls in question don't gather round me because of *me* – it's because I know the people they love, the stars, because they know I saw Bros last week or Wet Wet Wet. Now you, watching from afar, might say, "Look at those young girls throwing themselves at him," whereas in actual fact it's exactly the opposite. I am of no interest to them, except in a purely platonic way.

'A lot of disc jockeys make the mistake of thinking that they're sex symbols and then they get a rude awakening. But I always realized that I was a service industry. Like, because I knew Cliff [Richard] before he'd even made a record, all the Cliff fans would bust a gut to meet me, so that I could tell them stories about their idol. But if I'd said, "Come round, so that I can tell you stories about *me*," or "Come round, so that you can fall into my arms," they'd have said, "*What! On yer bike!*" But because reporters don't understand the nuances of all that, they say, "A-ha".'

This seems a perfectly credible explanation of why rumour links him to young girls. It still doesn't explain the great mystery of his non-existent love life. His name has only ever been linked to one woman, his mother, whom he called the Duchess.

He was devoted to her – the more so, perhaps, because as the youngest child of seven, he'd had a fairly scant share of her attention. 'I wasn't her favourite by any means; I was fourth or fifth in the pecking order.' But when he became famous, he laid his fame and money at her feet, and they had sixteen years before she died in 1973 where she had 'everything'. He once told Joan Bakewell: 'We were together all her life and there was nothing we couldn't do. I got an audience with the Pope. Everything. But then, I was sharing her. When she died she was all mine. The best five days of my life were spent with the Duchess when she was dead. She looked marvellous. She belonged to me. It's wonderful, is death.'

(Incidentally, he has an enthusiasm for dead bodies in general which can be quite unnerving. The first time I ever met him, eight years ago, he raved on about all the bodies that came his way in the mortuary at Leeds Infirmary and how he wished he could take the healthy eyes from one and the good bones from another to repair his living patients. He sounded like Dr Frankenstein.)

But back to his love life. 'You must have had *some* sex at *some* time,' I tell him, and Sir James looks pained.

'Well. I would have thought so. But it's rather like going to the bathroom. I've never been one to explain to people what I do when I go to the bathroom and I'm not a kiss-and-tell punter. All I can say is that I've never ever got anybody into trouble; I've never knowingly upset anybody; and I've always been aware that in my game there is a clear line between infatuation and actual, genuine liking. Other than that, you must draw your own conclusions.'

Well. One safe conclusion is that people who equate sex with going to the bathroom don't like it very much. His views on sex and love are altogether cynical; he said in passing that 'sex was like what they say about policemen – never there when you want one' and that 'it so happens that it is illegal to have sex on tap – unless you happen to be married, in which case you end up with a wife having a headache'.

He says that he has never been in love, never had a live-in girlfriend, never been even within shouting distance of getting married. He claims that he decided this as early as his twenties, soon after he was injured in a mining accident and became a disc jockey around the Mecca ballrooms of the North.

'I was too busy for that. The pop business was a tremendous lively business and each day was a mushroom – there was only that day and there was only that night. It's a very peculiar lifestyle but I realized that, in order to succeed, I would have to actually *live* the business. And I couldn't do that and live a normal human-being life as well – it doesn't work. Look in any of the papers – well-known people who try to lead normal lives, it invariably doesn't work out.

'Now bearing in mind that I'm not particularly paternal, and that I wasn't yer actual relationship-type person that *must* get married, *must* go through the normal thing, I thought: "Because I choose to be in this business and because the track record of the business is that marriage doesn't work out, therefore I won't even think along those lines."

'Now that makes you *different*, it makes you *strange*, and people then try to stick their theories on you to account for the fact that you're not married. But what they don't take into consideration is the awesome *logic* of it all.'

But surely this is the awesome logic of cutting off your nose to spite your face? It is logic carried to the point of insanity. Isn't it better to have even an imperfect relationship than no relationship at all?

'No! I don't agree. My life is the greatest life in the world. *The greatest life in the world!* You go to bed, you haven't a care in the world; you get up, you haven't a care in the world. It's *fun* – do you understand? So why should I spoil a lot of fun?'

His six siblings are all married – 'they're all nice and normal' – and he has whole tribes of nieces and nephews, about forty-seven of them at the last count.

When I ask if he is a good uncle, he immediately starts talking about money: while the Duchess was alive she was his sole beneficiary; when she died, he made his brothers and sisters his beneficiaries, and if any of them die he may, or may not, include their children in his will.

He says he speaks to most of his siblings most weeks, but it's physically impossible to keep up with all their children and grandchildren. 'We're a close family, but we're a very commonsense family. Our commonsense is not to everybody's liking, but that's all there is to it.

'I quite envy people who have been in love,' he admits, 'and I would be perfectly happy to fall in love today. But how could I, with my lifestyle? I don't have girlfriends because it's not fair, the same as I don't have plants because I'd never be back to water them, and I don't have cats and dogs, and I don't have kids because I'd never be there to see them.'

This is true. His lifestyle is unique and really unsharable with anyone else. In the week I met him, he'd been to Crewe to open a school for children with learning difficulties, to Liverpool to visit Broadmoor's sister hospital, Ashworth, to Leeds Infirmary to attend their gala, to Newcastle to do some radio programmes, and on to Glasgow to run an exhibition race for charity.

He'd come back to London overnight on the sleeper in order to meet me in London at 9 a.m. and was then going on to a business meeting and to Stoke Mandeville to 'open' their new machine.

He rarely spends two consecutive nights in the same bed, and he has beds – you can hardly call them homes – two in Leeds (one at the Infirmary) and one each in London, Scarborough, Peterborough, Bournemouth, Stoke Mandeville and Broadmoor. The London pad, a service flat near the BBC, is probably typical or slightly more luxurious than most: it is a one-room cell with a fold-down double bed, a large television tuned to Teletext, a closet full of tracksuits, a blown-up photograph of the Yorkshire Dales, and a completely empty kitchen.

'But where do you keep your *things*?' I asked him. 'What things? I have seven toothbrushes and seven telephones, one in each place.' 'But you must have *some* things. Souvenirs, ornaments.' 'Yeah, there's one,' he says, pointing to a huge, staggeringly ugly silver-gilt trophy on top of the television. 'That's the Male Jewellery-Wearer of the Year Award from the British Jewellery Association. I have souvenirs in all my places.'

He seems genuinely delighted with the trophy, both as an *objet* and as an award. He enjoys a bit of a flash, like his Rolls-Royces (he is now on his seventeenth) and the gold and diamond Rolex watch on one wrist and the gold and diamond name-bracelet on the other. But all these he regards as tools of the trade – 'I'm in a flash game. People like a bit of glamour, a bit of pizazz. They wouldn't like me to come on the bus.'

He is not an aesthete, not a gourmet, not a sensualist. His idea of relaxation is running in marathons and half-marathons, usually for charity. He eats whatever horrible snack or sandwich is most quickly available; he never drinks alcohol; he never wears anything other than tracksuits.

The only glimmers of self-indulgence are the fat Havana cigars he smokes regularly and the annual cruise he takes by way of holiday.

But even on holiday, according to the Cunard PR Eric Flounders, who has often travelled with him: 'He gives all his time to other people. He is quite wonderful, actually. He never tells anyone not to bother him, and if he sees someone he thinks needs some particular attention, he goes out of his way to do it.' Like his hero, the Prince of Wales, he tends to make a beeline for people in wheelchairs, though he

himself insists he doesn't: 'I talk to *everybody* because I'm
gregarious.'

He works incredibly hard but he says this is only because
people ask him to: 'Left to meself, I would never move out of
the chair. I'd smoke cigars, look out of the window, watch
the Teletext, see if I can make a few quid, listen to some jazz
on the radio. But the phone rings, and somebody says, "Can
you? Will you?" and the mail comes – I get five hundred
letters a week – and being an obliging type of punter, I say
"yes", if I can. So I finish up having a very hectic life, but
that's at the diktat of other people – I don't look for it. Left
to meself, I'd just be wandering about.'

Incidentally, his business organization consists of himself,
his diary and the telephone. He has no agent, no manager,
and never writes letters. Yet if he says he will open your fête
on 14 July 1992, you can forget about it for two years and
know that he'll be there on the day.

It is a life of self-punishing austerity that seems like a long
expiation for some lasting sense of guilt. His accountant,
Harold Grumber, who has known him for thirty years, once
said: 'The most important thing for Jimmy is peace of mind.'

It is a constant theme of his conversation – his need to go
to bed with a clean conscience, to feel that he has done his
best. He says he is like a surgeon who can do five operations
in a day and eight patients turn up: the trick is to do the five
he can, and not allow himself to worry about the three that
he can't. But he obviously *does* worry about them, hence his
inability ever to refuse a request if he can possibly fit it in.

He is a prickly man, a self-righteous man who cares for
humanity but not much for individuals. He has 'thousands'
of acquaintances but no confidants. He is very keen on reason,
very distrustful of emotion: he boasts often of his 'logic' and
his membership of Mensa. He has total recall – 'I can
remember *everything*.' His image – the dyed hair, the tracksuits, the flash jewellery and above all the patter, which I
would say is the most irritating thing about him – is a
deliberate smokescreen designed to make stupid people think

he is stupid. Once he knows you well enough to drop the patter, he talks like the exceptionally hard-headed Yorkshire businessman he is – albeit a businessman with a social conscience.

But his conversation is all facts, all specifics. He has no time for speculation, for introspection, and especially not for self-analysis, which he regards as 'soft'.

He became seriously annoyed when I kept asking about his childhood and snapped: 'We had no time for psychological hang-ups. We were just survivors, all of us. None of that "Oh, I was ignored as a child" – what a load of cobblers! I don't know whether I was or I wasn't. All I know is that nothing particular wrong happened and I had a good time.'

I asked whether he ever suffered from Bob Geldof's 'compassion fatigue' and he said no, he wouldn't let himself, because that would be illogical.

But he admits that 'I'm constantly taking stock of what I'm doing so that I do it – hopefully – for the right reasons. I can't *guarantee* I'm doing it for the right reasons because nobody can guarantee that. But I do it by instinct and instinct tells me I've no reason to believe I'm doing it for the wrong reasons, therefore I just carry on and do it.

'And thank goodness, having no wives, no homes, no kids, no dogs, no plants to water, at least you've got blinkers on and you can attend to what comes in on the rag and bone [phone].'

Why do so many people find him so insufferable? Partly it is a class thing: he operates at a folksy level designed to please little old grannies in Scunthorpe, which goes down badly with the middle classes. Many showbiz stars can turn on the man-of-the-people stuff and then turn it off again when talking to journalists, but Savile never turns it off because it is entirely genuine.

It means, though, that he rarely talks to people as equals; he is either the licensed jester, as at Chequers or Buckingham Palace, or the patron, the glittering bestower of gifts. He spends a lot of time with people *in extremis* – the recently bereaved at Leeds Infirmary or, more harrowing still, the patients and their families at Stoke Mandeville. (An awful lot of the patients at Stoke Mandeville are young people who have been disastrously injured in riding or sports accidents and now face the rest of their lives as paraplegics.)

Touring the Stoke Mandeville wards with him is a disconcerting experience: when he coos over a young woman paraplegic, 'A-ha, now I can have my way with you, my dear!' one can only pray that she appreciates the joke. I remember the most frightening thing anyone ever said to me was when I was being wheeled in for a back operation and the junior doctor remarked cheerily, 'We'll have you walking again in two weeks – and if we don't we'll send Jimmy Savile to visit you.' Much as I admire Sir James Savile, he is someone I never ever want to be visited by.

'You do seem to be almost saintly . . .' I tell him. 'No, no, no, no, no,' he exclaims, horrified. 'Why don't you, instead of saying "saintly", say "You do seem to be totally practical"?' But perhaps that is true of saints, too.

Reproduced by permission of the *Independent on Sunday*

MURIEL SPARK

23 September 1990

Mrs Spark – one does not call her Muriel – has a set
routine for receiving journalists. You take the plane to Pisa
and the train to Arezzo, and walk a few yards to the Hotel
Continentale, where she will meet you at the appointed time.
She will have dressed for the occasion in one of her smart silk
frocks, with high heels and a piece of good jewellery. Miss
Jardine, whom she calls Penelope but you call Miss Jardine,
will be with her, dressed more comfortably for Tuscany in a
loose shirt and espadrilles. They will order drinks and sit with
you for a hour and if you pass muster, the drinks will be
followed by dinner in the hotel (which is very good), but at
that point the tape recorder must be switched off.

Mrs Spark will answer your questions politely, gamely, but
with her mind clearly elsewhere. Many of her answers are
very tentative, even daffy, but occasionally she hits a subject
she has thought a lot about, and then she becomes almost
aphoristic in her certainty. For instance, I told her of a mutual
acquaintance who had lost a lot of money, and she said
firmly: 'Oh, that's a *pity*. You should become richer as you
get older, not poorer.' She knows what she knows very surely,
but there are whole areas of life, including her own life, in
which her interest seems woolly, at best. One of her heroines

has the habit of silently reciting the Angelus at noon every day, regardless of what she is doing, even answering the phone, and it occurs to me now that Mrs Spark probably recites something silently whenever she encounters journalists – perhaps the Book of Job. She makes it very clear in *The Girls of Slender Means* that she despises journalists, though she is too polite to say so to me. She is elusive in the way her novels are elusive: she is the magician who makes you concentrate on the egg in his right hand, while all the time manoeuvring the dove in his left.

One of the great mysteries that emerges from the cuttings file is the way her looks have changed dramatically over the years. The first publicity photographs in the 1950s, when she was in her thirties (she was born in 1918), show a sturdy, bun-faced woman with tight, ugly curls and mannish clothes. Then when she moved to Rome, in her late forties, she suddenly emerged as a startling beauty – svelte, slim, elfin, dressed in couture clothes and chattering away about her jewellery. (She had the habit then of buying herself an 'important' piece, a Cartier watch or a diamond brooch, to commemorate each novel. She doesn't any longer, because 'there's no call for it in Tuscany. It just stays in the bank.') The late sixties and early seventies were her Roman Spring: she moved in high society and occupied a flat as big as a football pitch in the centre of Rome. A friend who knew her then, Eugene Walter, said that the transformation happened quite suddenly: 'I saw her off on the plane to New York one day, a dumpy middle-aged Scottish woman, and met her off the plane two weeks later, a teenager in a full-length mink coat.'

How did she suddenly become a beauty in middle life? 'Oh, really?' She gives a fluttery sort of feminine-genteel laugh. 'Well, I don't know. I had hairdos and all sorts of things. I think I was quite pretty when I was young, and then I went through a very bad period in my thirties. And then in my forties it sort of cleared up. But I was never a great beauty. A lot has to do with having a bit of money, to buy some clothes and have my hair done.' But in your thirties, you were . . .? 'I was fat, yes, I don't know why: I just was. I went up and down a great deal. Then I lost weight and I felt very much better and looked very much better.' Success obviously suited her. 'It suits everybody,' she says with sudden firmness. 'If it's deserved; if they've worked for it.'

Her life story seems full of odd disjunctions. There was her childhood in Edinburgh, which we can picture from *The Prime of Miss Jean Brodie* – the bright, enthusiastic child, precociously good at English, winning fiction prizes and having her poetry published in magazines. She was Muriel Camberg then – her father was Jewish – but, although she says she takes after him more than her mother, she says she doesn't feel Jewish: she feels Scottish (and sounds it still). She wanted to go to university, but her mother, a music teacher, opposed it. Money may have been a factor: her father was an engineer in a rubber factory and the family was not well off. They paid for her to go to private school ('There was that little effort'), but university was beyond their means. So she upped and married, very suddenly and very young (nineteen), and went with her husband to Rhodesia, where she had her only child, a son.

This is the period of her life that is absent from her books and interviews. All she will say is that it was her worst experience. 'I don't like talking about it – he's still alive, poor thing.' At all events her husband's character changed, and she fled with her baby to South Africa, and then eventually (the war was on) to London. She sent her son to be brought up by her parents in Edinburgh, while she worked for the Foreign Office, in one of those hush-hush intelligence places. Motherhood is a theme that barely surfaces in her fiction. Was she a good mother? 'Oh, *I* think I was a good mother, but I'm sure my son wouldn't think so. I had to work, so my mother really took the role of mother for him. I'm not extremely maternal, but I think of him always – still do.' Is he all right? 'He lives in Edinburgh.'

After the war, she worked as a publisher's copy-editor, and as secretary of the Poetry Society, in the rather seedy milieu she describes so vividly in *A Far Cry from Kensington*. Money was a perennial problem. She knew she wanted to be a writer but there was no money in *that*, and though her parents looked after her son, she still had to support him – she had no alimony. The obvious solution would have been to get married again, but 'I didn't find anyone I wanted to marry. I didn't meet the right person. And I think I was too anxious, too worried. You know, I was a girl but I wasn't a girl: I had too many anxieties.'

Instead she became the prematurely middle-aged, sturdy and dependable Mrs Spark who appears in her first publicity photographs. She published poetry and well-received biographies of Mary Shelley and Emily Brontë, she edited the *Poetry Review*. In 1954 she converted to Roman Catholicism 'because it made more sense', and at the same time decided to give up all publishers' hack-work to concentrate on writing novels. She seems to have had some sort of breakdown, brought on by slimming pills, and had hallucinations in which, for example, the word 'lived' would become 'devil'. 'I suppose it was a real breakdown,' she says dismissively, 'but it didn't last very long, maybe three or four weeks. As soon as I stopped taking the pills and started to eat again I was all right.' Graham Greene came to the rescue, offering her £20 a month while she wrote her novel: the only conditions were she shouldn't meet him and above all shouldn't pray for him. So she wrote *The Comforters*, the first of an astonishing six novels in four years, culminating in *The Prime of Miss Jean Brodie* in 1961. That book was something of a watershed. Turned into a play and then a film, it made her financially secure and famous throughout the world. But it drove her from London, first to New York and then to Rome.

She once told Philip Toynbee that she left England to avoid her old friends, because she'd outstripped them and they couldn't cope with her success: 'It was painful to be with them, simply because I felt like a sort of reproach to them – and they to me.' But when I mention Toynbee, she replies with vigour: 'What I told Philip Toynbee and what he printed are two different things, I can tell you *that*! However,' she concedes, 'I did cut myself off rather because . . . well, it was terribly awkward. Some people were charming but some were really very resentful and said the most awful things. So I thought: "Why should I put up with it? Off I go."'

'In particular, one old friend [she told me his real name but I can't use it for fear of libel – not a famous name anyway] with whom I had a long, *long* affair, behaved in the most extraordinary way. He was so jealous. For a man who had been really, well, very keen on me, put it that way, he turned very, *very* strange. He writes memoirs about me, lies, but I haven't see him since 1952 or 1954, or maybe once in 1960 – that's thirty years. So he doesn't know much about me, you know. And he's become a mythomaniac, so that the more I take no notice of him, the more he invents new things.' Was he a writer? 'He wanted to be. And would have been. I used to help him with his work; I would read his poetry and say: "Take out all those adjectives." I really helped him a *great deal* with his work. And he was terribly upset when I became successful, absolutely furious. He didn't think I would make a literary success and he didn't think I deserved it. He didn't understand creative work and he didn't think mine was anything. And he hated me having money. But why didn't he ask me for money if he wanted it? I'd have given it gladly.' He is presumably the original of Hector Bartlett, the *pisseur de copie* in *A Far Cry from Kensington*. She talks about him a lot, obviously still baffled and bothered by his treatment of her.

She moved to New York in the early sixties, and although she wrote arguably her greatest novel there, *The Girls of Slender Means*, it was generally an unhappy period. 'I was getting very dry, you know, dried out. My friends were mostly academics and other writers, so that was all right, but I just didn't like the material. It was too distracting and rather arid towards the end. And most of all, a play of one of my books, *The Prime of Miss Jean Brodie*, opened on Broadway. It had already opened in London, which is why I went to New York, to get away.' Why did she need to get away? 'Because I'm temperamentally unable to cope with theatre people, or film people. Not that they're not nice – they're awfully nice – but they're a different kind of creature. They don't know what they've said before. There's no continuity in their lives. And it's very difficult – *I* find it difficult – always to be called "Darling" the minute they see you. It's an extraordinary world.'

Anyway, when *Jean Brodie* opened in New York she fled to Italy. 'It was a great relief to go somewhere where nobody knew a thing about me, to be just a *Signora* in society. At that time I was very well-known in England and America. I'm still well-known, but I know how to protect myself a bit.' Fame obviously flustered her. At first she seized it avidly, believing it was the proper reward for her years of work and poverty, but then she was upset when the spotlight of attention turned elsewhere. Every time she published a book, 'there would be a big fuss, lots of fun, and then everyone would sort of go home, and you were all on your own. Nobody. Now it's different because I've got it more steady, and I don't *care* so much. I used to care quite a lot when I was a young writer.' She was – and I imagine still is – very competitive; she wants to be the *best* writer of her generation, and she thinks in terms of posterity rather than, say, coming top of the best-seller list. Although she doesn't say so, she must wonder – as anyone must – why she hasn't been made a Dame.

In Rome she met Penelope Jardine, who has been her companion for the past twenty years. She is a tall, big-boned woman with fine straight hair who could be absolutely any age from late thirties to early fifties. She sat listening – or dreaming? – throughout our conversation, occasionally putting a word in. At one point, when I was asking Mrs Spark how many languages she was translated into, Miss Jardine interposed, rather tartly, 'Not as many as you used to be,' but on the whole she remained a quiet, restful presence in the background. She is a painter and sculptor. I asked if she was 'one of the fabulously rich Hong Kong Jardines' and she said no, she didn't think so, though her grandfather went to China. In fact, she said, she 'lived on the poverty line', but I was not convinced: she has that unconcerned-about-money air you only get from having plenty of it.

They met in 1968, when Miss Jardine was studying at art school in Rome but needed a part-time job. She heard from a friend that Mrs Spark was looking for a secretary and was told to find her in the hairdresser's, which she did. Her great fear was that Mrs Spark would ask which of her books she most enjoyed – at that stage she hadn't read one – and they both laugh at the memory. 'I was not a great secretary but I'd done a typing course and knew you had to keep your left little finger on the *q*' (you don't, in fact, you keep it on the *a*) 'so Muriel took me on.' She proved, if not a great secretary, then at least a great organizer. She runs their household now, keeps the files, answers correspondence (they have had their telephone converted to fax so there are no phones to answer), does the driving, and keeps a 'character list' of Mrs Spark's work-in-progress. Since neither of them enjoy cooking, they mainly eat out. Mrs Spark once tried to make a bed, and slipped and broke her ribs, so now she doesn't attempt such things: she is not domesticated.

Miss Jardine looks after Mrs Spark but she is not like an employee. Mrs Spark is careful to tell me several times that the house they both live in (a converted rectory) belongs to Miss Jardine. I ask Mrs Spark whether, if Miss Jardine were ill, she would abandon her work to look after her, and she says, oh yes, in fact it happened not so long ago, when Miss Jardine fell off a ladder and broke both her legs. 'Muriel was *marvellous*,' says Miss Jardine gratefully, 'she managed everything.'

They like travelling together, by car or ship (Miss Jardine doesn't fly), and describe how, a couple of years ago, they both gave up smoking by dint of driving non-stop across Europe with no cigarettes in the car. At night Mrs Spark would leave a bag of sweets beside Miss Jardine's bed to stave off the pangs, and in consequence, says Mrs Spark, Miss Jardine gained eight kilos, while she herself gained three. Their life in the Tuscan countryside is very self-contained. Mrs Spark has her writing, Miss Jardine her painting; they have several cats and dogs, and 'enough' friends, though few Italians because the Italians 'don't know about entertaining'. Their worries seem to be the usual Tuscan ones – forest fires and water supplies and what to do if their plumber decides to retire. Miss Jardine sometimes starts sentences 'We think . . .' and then corrects herself, '*I* think. Muriel hates me saying we.'

Mrs Spark once told John Mortimer that the reason she never remarried was because she didn't have it in her to be a good wife. But why? Was she flighty? 'No. Sexually, probably, I could be faithful: that's not the point. The point is I couldn't concentrate on the job, I really couldn't. I'm too interested in my writing: I couldn't *work* at a marriage. And, you see, my experience of men is that they resent it if you are successful – and I never had the slightest intention of not being as successful as I could be, and why not? If I married a man who was better than me at writing, *I* wouldn't like it, and if I was better, *he* wouldn't like it.' But couldn't she have married someone who wasn't a writer at all – a successful industrialist, say? 'But you still have to do *something*, entertain people, offer something. You can't just be the writer who never puts in an appearance, it just wouldn't *do*. No, I'm not cut out for marriage at all. Love affairs, maybe – but *marriage* . . .' Did she have many affairs? 'No, nothing very much. Here and there. Generally speaking, I didn't want to get in too deeply. The only person I would have married was the man I told you about, because I got used to him, but I'm glad I didn't because I wouldn't be married to him *now*, I'm sure of that.'

I remark that she seems to have a rather old-fashioned idea

of the wife's role, and the conversation suddenly turns into a sort of women's consciousness-raising group, but a very primitive one, *circa* 1970, for absolute beginners. Mrs Spark opines: 'I'm sure I do. But I'm sure most *men* have a traditional idea of the wife's role. I dare say some modern marriages are different, but basically there's always the woman mopping up. All I say is, you're only half a person if you've got to go along with someone else. I mean, I can share – I *do* share with Penelope to a certain extent – but marriage is a different thing, a kind of obligation of being with them for a lifetime.' Marriage doesn't *have* to be like that, though, say I: it can mean being looked after yourself. 'Can it?' – she is unconvinced – 'I've never met anyone who'd be willing to do that, and you'd still have to look nice or something. I don't think I'd like it.' Miss Jardine: 'I think you have to be a sort of tyrant woman to have a marriage like that.' Me: 'Manipulative, perhaps.' Miss Jardine: 'Or a *malade imaginaire*.' Mrs Spark now asks me – as one might ask, Have you got a fax machine – 'Have you got a husband?' 'Yes. Mine's all right.' Miss Jardine: 'I've had friends who've been very women's lib and made their husbands do the washing-up – which is fine – make the beds, which is not so good, and even wash their own socks, which is *frightful*. They just put them in some kind of soap powder and leave them for a month.' I struggle to explain that what men do with their own socks is really their own business, but Mrs Spark and Miss Jardine both cling to the idea that marriage is, for women, servitude and therefore better avoided. Mrs Spark concludes: 'Maybe I've got a hysterically panicky, gloomy view of marriage.'

The fact is that although she wrote on Mary Shelley and Emily Brontë and other approved feminist subjects long before women's lib was heard of, and although her novel *The Abbess of Crewe* – a sort of Watergate set in a nunnery – was hailed as 'a dream come true for the women's lib movement', she is not really a feminist at all. Her maternal grandmother was a suffragette who marched with Mrs Pankhurst, but her mother believed that once women got the vote, the battle was over – 'And I think so too, in fact. Somehow women's lib, the movement, has defeated itself because more and more they tend to clump women together and I don't quite like that.'

Although she is critical of the present Pope, she has no doubts that she will die a Catholic. Death holds no terrors for her; nor does she particularly fear infirmity, as long as she can keep on writing.

Her latest novel, *Symposium*, is published this week, and she is already at work on her next book, an autobiography. 'I'm doing it in vignettes, flashes of memory, kind of as Proust wrote, because I value Proust's writing. Anyway, that's how memory works – little flashes. I've also gone into all sorts of things, like where butter came from and what one wore, because people like that, details. I have to be totally honest because I couldn't write otherwise; the pen just wouldn't write.' Unfortunately, the book will not elucidate the mystery of those missing years in Africa, because she plans to stop when she leaves Edinburgh: 'I don't want to involve living people: one shouldn't hurt their feelings.' And anyway, she says, 'I've got no startling revelations to make; it's more reflections on human nature.'

She reckons she will write three more novels. The reason is typically Muriel Spark, both down-to-earth practical and mildly loopy at the same time. She has an absolute 'fetish' – her expression – about *how* she writes: in longhand with a fountain pen, straight on to the page, and rarely correcting anything. She always starts with the title, and recites it to herself as she goes along – her publishers tried to persuade her to change the title *Symposium*, but she flatly refused. She writes with special fine-point pens, and is so superstitious that if someone else uses one of them, say to write down a phone number, she throws it away. And she writes in the seventy-two-page spiral-bound exercise books obtained from the stationer James Thin of Edinburgh that she has used to write in since she was nine. One notebook equals about 10,000 words, so seven make a novel. But now the notebook manufacturer has gone out of business and, according to Miss Jardine, they have only twenty exercise books left, barely enough for three novels. (She is writing the autobiography in a different sort of notebook, keeping the 'proper' ones for fiction.) She will, it goes without saying, continue writing till she drops, but the day when she fills the last page of the last notebook will be a nervous one. She *thinks* she could probably adjust to another sort of exercise book, but it would be a shaky business.

She writes, she says, from a desire 'to make people smile – not laugh, but smile. Laughter is too aggressive.' It sounds a very modest, almost *too* modest, ladylike ambition, though it could apply equally well to Jane Austen. And Mrs Spark has the ruthlessness of the great artist. Nothing matters to her except her work. 'I'd give up *anything* for my work. Otherwise I don't care, about my goods or anything. I'm careless about material things really. I don't care what I spend or what I do provided it's in favour of me getting down to write.'

Reproduced by permission of the *Independent on Sunday*

LORD AND LADY SPENCER

8 February 1987

Lady Spencer said she couldn't possibly give an interview to anyone without her husband. 'We do everything
together.' This sounded like pure affectation to me, but I
didn't have any choice in the matter, and anyway I assumed
that Lord Spencer was a more or less gaga old buffer who
could just be parked in the background somewhere like a
piece of furniture. How wrong I was.

In fact, my visit to Althorp was full of surprises from start
to finish. I was not due to meet the Spencers till two o'clock
but, arriving early, I found that Lady Spencer had made
elaborate and efficient arrangements to provide me with lunch
in the tea room, and for her housekeeper, 'wonderful Joyce',
to give me a guided tour round the house.

The house came as something of a surprise, too. Much
derided by the snooty heritage lobby for its fake coal fires,
modern carpets and sparkling new paint everywhere, it
actually looks smashing – warm, colourful and very inviting.

Lady Spencer also looked warm, colourful and inviting
when she came dashing up to me in the gift shop, thrust a
bottle of Althorp wine into my hands, and said, 'That's just
to thank you for coming here to see us.'

Lord Spencer drove us back to the house and then we all

sat in the drawing-room while I asked them questions. The ritual was as elaborate as a Japanese tea ceremony and took quite some getting used to.

I would address a question to Lady Spencer, something perfectly straightforward like 'How many visitors a year do you get here at Althorp?', and she would say to me, 'Oh, how *sweet* of you to ask,' and then, to Lord Spencer, 'Isn't it sweet of Miss Barber to ask?' Lord Spencer (basso profundo): 'Most kind.' 'Well, now let me see. Oh, I'm so bad at figures – Johnny, how many was it last year?' Lord Spencer: 'About forty thousand.'

This ritual accompanied any question at all, but a question which revealed some prior knowledge of the Spencers produced a positive paroxysm of politeness. For instance, I asked Lady Spencer about an episode back in the fifties when she complained about dirty teacups at Heathrow Airport.

'Oh, how *sweet* of you to remember! I'm always terribly touched when people remember these little things about me. Isn't it kind of Miss Barber to remember . . .' etc.

You have to get the hang of the vocabulary, too. For Lady Spencer everyone is either 'perfectly sweet' or 'absolutely charming' unless they are a 'very, very dear friend', in which case they are perfectly sweet *and* absolutely charming. She never seems to say anything nasty about anyone, except that she does occasionally say that someone is 'frightfully, frightfully clever', which one gathers is not such a nice thing to be as 'perfectly sweet' or 'absolutely charming'.

I suspect that her antennae about people are not very sharp and that she basically divides the world into PLUs (people like us) and not PLUs. The reason I suspect this is that she asked me three times who my father was.

Right at the beginning, she said, 'Do tell me, because we've both been wondering – haven't we? – are you by any chance related to that wonderful well-known journalist, Noel Barber?'

'No.'

And a little later: 'Are you by any chance related to Lord Barber, the former Chancellor of the Exchequer?'

'No.'

Finally, over tea, and no longer with any pretence that the matter was relevant to anything we were discussing at all, 'What *does* your father do?'

'He's retired.' I was tempted to leave it at that, just to drive Lady Spencer mad with curiosity, but I had succumbed to her charm by that stage so I generously added the information, 'He was a civil servant.'

'Oh, how *fascinating*! What kind of civil servant exactly?'

Now I like nosey people (being a particularly nosey person myself) but to be nosey about someone's parentage means only one thing: snobbishness. She was asking me, quite crudely, what class I came from, whether I could be counted as a PLU, and was evidently disappointed to find that I couldn't. But, having said that, I must add, in fairness, that there was nothing else the least snobbish about her dealings with me: in fact, Lady Spencer treated me more hospitably than anyone else I have ever interviewed.

At first we talked about Althorp and its paying visitors. Lord Spencer's father reputedly greeted visitors with a shotgun, but Lord Spencer said, 'Only metaphorically. He particularly liked connoisseurs coming here, he liked to show museum people around the place, and art experts.'

The present Spencers have embraced the paying public with enthusiasm: not only do they open the house every day, but they have 'functions' in the evenings and try to be present to greet the guests whenever possible.

'We enjoy that, we really enjoy it,' Lord Spencer said. 'We meet some absolutely fascinating people here, all sorts of interesting people who we would never normally meet at all.'

He added that many people came to the house originally 'to see Di's Dad', but the nice thing was they returned, and brought their friends, because they fell in love with the house.

'A lot of people come here, too, because they know I've been ill – I have had trouble with my head – ' (actually a brain haemorrhage in 1978 which kept him at death's door for four months) 'so they bring their husbands or their wives who have had the same trouble and they say, "Here's Lord Spencer: *he* managed to get over it and you can do the same." That's very nice, being an encouragement to other people. A lot of ladies bring their husbands here, and they look a great deal more decrepit than I am!'

Lord Spencer now seems far less decrepit than when he first appeared on television, weaving an uncertain path up the aisle to give away his daughter's hand in marriage to the Prince of Wales. He still walks a *little* nervously, and he still has trouble reading because his eyes sometimes jump the lines, but he is absolutely not gaga. He told a terribly funny anecdote about a party of American ladies who came to Althorp having done a whistle-stop tour of Europe. 'They obviously hadn't a clue where they were, so I said to one of them, "Madam, would you like to step outside and see the Taj Mahal?" and she answered, "Aw, just wait till I have taken my medication."'

Recently, he said, they had not been home at Althorp much because they had been whizzing round the country doing book signings for his book *Japan and The Far East*. They had been to Leamington, Sheffield, Gateshead, Chichester, Windsor, Farnham, and had done several separate sessions in London.

'Gosh, how *awful!*' I exclaimed, thinking nothing could be worse than sitting in a bookshop being gawped at.

But 'We love it,' they raved together. 'It's such *fun*. We went to Boots in Nottingham, and we were at the top of the escalator and all the people sort of *surged* up towards us. Oh, it was such fun.'

I asked at one point whether they telephoned each other a lot when they were apart, and they both looked rather puzzled. 'We do everything together,' said Lord Spencer.

'But you must sometimes spend the odd week apart.'

'*Week?*' they chorused in amazement, 'No, we never spend a week apart.'

Lord Spencer said fervently, 'Never away for a night, not a night. A day perhaps, might be away somewhere for just a day.'

But what if, I asked, Lady Spencer had to do something

for, say, the British Tourist Authority, of which she is a (paid) committee member?

'I'd tag along behind,' said Lord Spencer.

'Oh, darling, you are *sweet*! I'm trying to think. I *did* once spend a night away when I had to go to Glasgow for a meeting, but I hate being without him, I miss him terribly, I worry about him. We like to be together.'

They obviously delight in each other's company and stick together almost like two Babes in the Wood. But after we had been talking for about an hour and I was asking Lady Spencer about her career in local government, Lord Spencer suddenly erupted: 'I want to go. You've been talking about yourself *endlessly*.'

'Oh, my darling!' Lady Spencer looked really alarmed and stricken. 'Sorry!'

So then we adjourned to another room to take photographs and Lord Spencer confided, 'I enjoy her prattle really. It's just a question of *when* she talks, but I like her prattling on, I really do.'

After the photographs, Lord Spencer had to go off on business so Lady Spencer had a chance to prattle on uninterruptedly over a delicious tea in the library. She talked about the members of her family and her rather strange, lonely upbringing. Her two brothers are very much younger than her, so she was virtually an only child and spent all her time, it would seem, reading. She was educated by governesses until she was eight, and then (it being wartime) she was evacuated to Canada and went to school there.

Her mother, Barbara Cartland, was not then 'really *famous* as a novelist as she is now'.

'I mean, I remember Mummy constantly writing books but maybe just one a year at that time. But, of course, one always knew she was sort of special and different and clever. Do you know Mummy? Oh, you would absolutely love her – she's very, very funny and clever and quick. She makes me seem like a *snail*.'

Lady Spencer herself published two short stories in her teens, 'But then I thought: Well, I've proved myself, now I don't have to do it again.' Instead she got married, at the tender age of eighteen, to the Hon. Gerald Legge (later Lord Lewisham, later Lord Dartmouth), had four children, and remained, to all appearances, happily married until 1976 when she suddenly upped and divorced and married Lord Spencer, whom she had met on a heritage committee. 'My fault was that I fell madly in love when I was forty-five,' she explained.

Her whole life nowadays seems to be completely bound up with her husband. One gets the impression that she has few close friends to call on, certainly no confidantes.

I put this to her and she said, 'I think that's *so* perceptive of you, and, of course, you're absolutely right. But if you're very close to one person – I mean, I regard my husband as my husband and my lover and my best friend – you don't really have time for anyone else. I sometimes say to John, "I'm so busy I never see any friends," and he says, "*I'm* your best friend" – which is rather lovely, don't you think? But I do see that perhaps a woman needs a woman friend, too, do you find?'

While we were having tea, I kept admiring a lovely small painting on the wall opposite of a small boy on a beach. Lady Spencer told me it was painted by William Nicolson and was of her husband when he was ten. 'I always think he looks rather a sad and lonely little boy, don't you? I don't think that living in a big house particularly brings happiness. People tend to forget the loneliness you may suffer if you're a child.'

The Lady Dartmouth of LCC days was once described as an 'iron hand in a wrought-iron glove' and everyone who worked with her commented on her iron self-discipline, efficiency and determination. Obviously, she is still a very efficient lady, self-disciplined and most determined, but there is a softer side, too – the side that clings passionately to her husband, and looks stricken if he rebukes her.

'Yes, I have changed,' she agrees, 'and I think John's taught me a tremendous lot. He's so wonderful with people – I'm sure you've noticed that – there's something special about those big blue eyes that makes people stand up and tell him all their problems. And he's taught me to see that everyone has their interesting side which before . . . well, it wasn't that I wasn't interested, but I sometimes felt I didn't have the time. But you've got to *find* time to appreciate people.'

A happy marriage then, the marriage of a good talker and a good listener, and the marriage of two formerly rather lonely people who are now inseparable. But I was left in no doubt about who was boss in the partnership.

After tea, Lady Spencer asked me if I would like to see round 'the private bits' of the house, and she was just showing me into her private sitting-room when Lord Spencer emerged from his study. He gave her a look of thunder, and she asked meekly, 'Do you mind, darling, if I just show Miss Barber my sitting-room just for a *second*?'

He grunted assent, but there was no question that we could not have entered if he had said no. Lady Spencer has found her lord and master.

Reproduced by permission of the *Sunday Express*

FREDDIE STARR

19 April 1987

The first time I met Freddie Starr I thought he was mad. And I don't mean mad as in zany or whacky, I mean mad as in screw loose or tonto. It was in a photographer's studio where he was doing publicity shots for his forthcoming cabaret tour and, as soon as I produced my tape recorder, he patted his pocket and said darkly, 'I know your game.' What? 'You've got your tape, I've got mine. I've learned about the press. They can be very sly.'

Then he laughed and said, 'Anyway, I ate all the hamsters before you came.'

This was an allusion to the *Sun* headline of 13 March 1986: 'FREDDIE STARR ATE MY HAMSTER. Comic put a live pet in sandwich, says beauty.'

In the story, model Lea La Salle claimed that Freddie Starr was staying with her and her boyfriend Vince McCaffrey and came in late one night and demanded a sandwich. 'Get it yourself,' she said, and the next thing she knew, 'He'd put my hamster between two slices of bread and started eating it.' The hamster's name was Supersonic – alas, poor Supersonic.

Next day's *Sun*, predictably, had Freddie Starr all over the front page again proclaiming that the story was 'absolute garbage. I love animals – and I'm a vegetarian.'

All good knockabout stuff and only the most brain-
damaged *Sun* reader could have seriously believed that Freddie Starr ever ate a hamster. The only question, really, was
where did the story originate? Who made it up?

Freddie Starr denied that he did and said it was 'absolutely
disgusting the way the press made things up'. But then he
boasted several times that it was 'the headline of the century'
and that he'd 'got two front pages out of it'. He said his
helicopter pilot had suggested printing it as a T-shirt, and
he'd told the *Sun* to do it, and he'd spotted Bruce Springsteen's
guitarist wearing the T-shirt on stage.

All of which he seemed to think was an entirely good thing
– though he didn't like it when his children came home from
school crying because their classmates told them, 'Your daddy
ate a hamster.'

So his relations with the press seem intricate, to say the
least. For instance, it was he who started a great spate of
stories three years ago saying he used to be a drug addict but
had now reformed.

'Yes, I went to the press about that,' he admitted, 'but it
wasn't, "Give me £20,000 and I'll sell you a story." I don't
need that. I would rather go to a friend of mine and give *him*
the exclusive, so he gets the money. Like, if I knew *your*
phone number, Lynn, I'd phone you up and say, "I've got a
story. I'd like to give it to you for you to earn a few bob."'

Well (sort of) thanks. I mean I'm sure he meant it as a favour.
But it seems a weird kind of journalism, if stars and writers col-
lude together to do each other favours and pay the mortgage.

The other problem with Freddie Starr is that he never
actually answers a question. Instead, he switches easily into
the sort of half-baked sentimental patter that passes for
thought in papers like the *Sun*. Here, for instance, word for
word, is his answer to my question: 'Did you stay with Vince
McCaffrey and Lea La Salle as the *Sun* story claimed?'

'I'm writing a book and it's all in there – what I think
about the press and their motives, the way they get stories,
the way they lie, the way they pay people off. They've got no

respect for our Queen. A person I would die for is my Queen and country but they've so humiliated the Royal Family – for God's sake give them a break, leave them alone for once, leave Diana out of the papers, please, please, *please*, I request it. And please leave Prince Charles alone. We all know he's going thin at the back, but we all love him. We all love Diana and we all love our Queen.'

He did this every time I asked a question – launched into some mad harangue on a completely different subject. For instance, when I asked him about his spiritualist beliefs, I got a ten-minute diatribe on 'Page Three girls who are little better than prostitutes'.

There was a *very* weird and nasty moment when he was talking about a recent *Sun* story that he was having an affair with ex-model Mrs Joy Dutton. They weren't having an affair at all, said Freddie, but they were old friends and when he saw her in a restaurant on the Costa del Sol he naturally went over to say hello. And two journalists who were also there leapt up and took a photo – 'And one of them was you,' he suddenly announced. 'Don't go "Oooo". You know *exactly* what I mean.' Huh?

That was one occasion, he said, when he didn't grab the photographer's camera and 'put it where the sun don't shine' but he wanted to warn photographers who came to his house, 'I do a lot of shooting; I carry a shotgun, and if I see someone at the window, he's got to take the consequences.'

Some of his best friends, he adds, are criminals: 'But they're the equivalent of superstars – they're not petty crooks.'

Did he mean, I asked aghast, sort of gang leaders like the Kray twins? 'The Kray twins should have been out of prison years ago. They never hurt anybody out of their environment. The authorities made an example of them, which I find very unfair when someone can go into a vicarage and rape a woman and get four years.

'Most of the people I know that are real top villains are the first to give the word in prison if a child molester gets through. They kick the shit out of them. And so it should be, because anyone who hurts children or who rapes a woman, should be castrated. I think drug pushers should be hung and they should bring the death penalty back.'

He says all this with an expression of great piety as though beating up child molesters is a more than adequate atonement for a few little crimes like murder.

He also stammers a lot. Stammering is usually the result of an over-strict, over-authoritarian upbringing, and Freddie admits that his father, a Liverpudlian bricklayer, was 'very Victorian, very strict. He said to me once, "Keep your friends close to you and your enemies even closer." He put me on a table and said, "Jump and I'll catch you," and I jumped and he took his hands away and I fell on the floor. He picked me up and stroked my hair and said, "Never trust anybody in your life. Not even your own father." '

Not, one would have thought, the most lovable of fathers, but Freddie said he was a great man and the night he died (when Freddie was seventeen) was the worst night of his life. He was less forthcoming about his mother. According to his ex-wife, he once had her barred from a club he was appearing in for being drunk. He himself has been a teetotaller all his life.

At this point, Freddie's manager came to whisk him away for 'a meeting with Lord Delfont. Write that down. He likes a mention.'

If I had not met Freddie Starr again, I would have written him off as a thoroughly nasty thug. But by chance he asked me to join him on Monday at Windsor Races and there I saw a completely different side of him. He seemed far more relaxed. I think he had probably checked me out and decided I wasn't a *Sun* photographer. Also he was surrounded by his friends.

The racing was all off-stage. We spent the afternoon in a private pavilion near the paddock, being served delicious food and drinks, and only occasionally casting an eye at the races on television. Once in a while someone would venture out into the cold to place a bet and everyone except me won lots of money. Ten-pound notes were being passed round like Kleenex.

The party consisted of Freddie and his wife Sandy, Leon Fisk, his manager, and his wife Mary, Voila Paulton, a large jolly lady greengrocer, and her husband Les, who organized the betting. Then there were various racing types in Barbours and trilbies, one of whom turned out to be ex-England footballer Mike Channon. Adrian, Freddie's helicopter pilot, had his nose deep in Anthony Burgess's autobiography ('He's a bit of an intellectual,' Leon told me) until tempted out by Elaine, Engelbert Humperdinck's 'travel assistant', who was there to arrange flights for Freddie and Engelbert's forthcoming three-week stint in Las Vegas. Sandy Starr – looking wonderfully unhorsey in a white fluffy sweater and high-heeled boots – introduced everyone and passed round snapshots of their children, eleven-year-old Donna, seven-year-old Jodie and baby Stacey.

Naturally I was on the lookout for all the criminals Freddie had said he knew and, sure enough, one man introduced himself as 'Harry from the Underworld' – but later someone told me he was 'Windsor's whelk king'. More interesting were the two or three sharply suited men who slid quickly past when introductions were being made, and one who did a smart about-turn and was never seen again when I said I was a journalist.

Freddie was happy to talk about racing and teach me how to read a race card and look out for all the 'dodges', like horses being held back in a race. He owns eight racehorses and bought the first one at Windsor on a whim three years ago, after a selling race.

'God said to me, "Go and bid," and I did. Next thing I knew I was wandering round the paddock holding a horse.'

Racehorse owning is expensive so where did he find the money?

'I've always been highly paid, I've always invested it well. And don't forget I've been in the business, at the top, for twenty-five years.' His only *real* extravagance, he says, is travelling by helicopter.

I asked him what was the best thing that had ever happened to him and he said simply 'Sandy' – his wife. 'She's grown spiritually over the years, she's grown really lovely.' And then, he said, his 'three lovely children'. But, in fact, he has four children, three by his present marriage, and a twenty-year-old son Carl by his first marriage. But he is on bad terms with his first wife, especially after she sold her story to the *Sun*, saying that he beat her, beat Carl and indulged in 'kinky' sex.

At one point we wandered out into the cold to watch the Freddie Starr Challenge race and for Freddie to present the trophy. However, most of my afternoon consisted of Freddie's friends coming up to me, staring deep into my eyes and saying things like, 'I can see through you.'

Then they would launch into long accounts of Freddie Starr's psychic powers. Voila Paulton, the greengrocer, told me that she first met Freddie soon after she lost her daughter, and Freddie said, 'I can see you've suffered a bereavement.' And then he described her daughter with total accuracy, even though he'd never met her.

Many people, too, told me about Freddie's acts of kindness and generosity – how, appearing in a seaside town, he'd heard of an old acquaintance down on his luck and staying in a hotel there, and he slipped in and paid his hotel bill without a word. And how, at a charity auction to raise money for a cancer-stricken singer, the bidding was going slowly and Freddie suddenly leapt in '£500 – no make that £5,000' – and went on bidding against himself until he ended up writing a cheque for £20,000.

While we were at the races he slipped £100 to the gents lavatory attendant. Why? 'Oh, because he's such a nice old man. You can't be happy with money unless you help people along the way.'

As the afternoon wore on, all the men except Freddie became loudly and hilariously drunk and more and more people kept pouring into the pavilion. It gradually became apparent that the races were over and everyone else had gone home. I thought I would go home, too, but Voila, the psychic greengrocer, took me in a vice-like grip and said she needed me and we were all going to Freddie's. So then we drove off in a convoy ('Just follow the red Roller!') through winding back lanes to a long, low manor-house floodlit as if for a football match, and Freddie and Sandy (who had whisked back by helicopter) and their children welcomed us into their home.

Sandy and her girlfriends went upstairs to bath the baby and everyone else crammed into the snooker-room where, Freddie explained, the children were forbidden to enter so we could swear and drink as much as we liked – but nowhere else in the house. When the men started fooling around playing snooker Freddie suddenly slapped a wad of banknotes on the table and said '£100 a frame' – which sobered them up.

After that, memory becomes hazy. But as I was leaving, I found Freddie alone in the kitchen watching television. 'Got what you want?' he asked.

'Yes thank you,' I said – 'though on second thoughts, I wouldn't mind knowing the truth of the hamster story.'

'The truth of the hamster story' – and he almost howled with irritation – 'is that I didn't eat the hamster for chrissake. And no, I didn't make it up. The only time I stayed at Vince McCaffrey's was in 1979 when Lea La Salle would have been a child of fifteen.

'But just remember, next time you read some Freddie Starr scandal in the papers – you've met me, you've met Sandy, we're a close family, we've got friends, we've got feelings. I'm an entertainer, not a gangster.'

Reproduced by permission of the *Sunday Express*

JACKIE STEWART

16 October 1983

Bang bang. Three thirty p.m. Friday in a splashy marsh on Lord Montagu's estate at Beaulieu and the last pheasant spirals to the ground in a shower of feathers. The dogs are whistled in, the guns leave their stands and splash back to the high ground where the Range Rovers and Land Rovers are waiting. Jackie and Helen Stewart sit on the tail of their four-wheel-drive Mercedes G-wagon, pulling off muddy boots and dripping oilskins. Gerry, the chauffeur, hands them clean Gucci shoes and helps Helen out of her husky and into her Saint Laurent cloak.

Jackie, as always, is consulting his Rolex watch, thinking about the schedule. A private Cessna is standing on the tarmac at Southampton Airport waiting to spirit him off to Edinburgh (e.t.a. 5 p.m.) for a formal dinner. But saying goodbye to Lord Montagu and the other guns, collecting his brace of pheasants and tipping the gamekeeper and beaters, all take time. So it is 4 p.m. by the time we leave the Beaulieu woods to drive to Southampton, and there is one more essential delay. 'Mars Bars!' Helen Stewart suddenly exclaims passionately, and Gerry is told to stop at the first sweetshop we come to, where Helen dashes in and emerges with armfuls of Mars Bars and Twixes and Banjos and

Maltesers. These, it seems, are things that millionaire tax exiles really miss.

Now we are running very late indeed and Jackie, sitting in the back with me, orders Helen, sitting in the front with Gerry, to stop talking to Gerry so that he can concentrate on his driving. Jackie then starts issuing a non-stop stream of instructions: 'Down into fourth, pull out a foot, hold the centre, we can overtake this lorry – now, *go*. Okay, up into fifth. Come on, we can take this car too, come on, Gerry, *go*. I said go – what are you doing?'

'Too near the corner,' Gerry mumbles, 'I couldn't see.'

'You had time *before* the corner,' Jackie says, grieving. It goes on like this all the way to Southampton – an extraordinary display of back-seat driving, but driving carried to the millisecond, to the inch. It is a vision of driving as an exact science that I'll never forget, and a reminder of why Jackie Stewart is special. He is special because he was three times world champion racing driver and possibly the greatest driver of all time.

Up till then it had been Jackie the businessman and Jackie the wheeler-dealer, and Jackie the PR man – above all, Jackie the PR man. Even when he was shooting with Lord Montagu, supposedly having a day off, one sensed there was a PR angle too. You can meet useful people at a shoot, one could imagine him thinking – after all, it was shooting that made him so chummy with Princess Anne and Captain Mark Phillips. I asked him about the etiquette of shooting and he explained it punctiliously – not to shoot low birds, not to 'poach' from the next gun, and not to hit every single bird because it made the other guns feel bad. Jackie was a European champion trap-shooter before he ever became a racing-driver, so it is not easy for him to miss pheasants, but he managed a few times in the interests of good form. These are things he cares about – getting it right, assessing the situation and obeying the unspoken rules, delivering what is required. And he always *does* get it right, that is what is so daunting, so that everyone who meets him comes away saying 'What a nice

chap.' His own favourite term of praise is 'together', as in
'He's very together', and of course he is supremely together
himself. The only slight flaw in the performance is that it is
liable to make other people feel untogether to the point of
disintegration.

The shoot was my second meeting with Jackie Stewart. The
first was a couple of months beforehand, when he was in
London on business. (He lives in Geneva, but works all over
the world, flying an average 400,000 miles a year.) The idea
was that I should tag along to witness what he called 'a
typical working day'. This particular day started for him at
the Grosvenor House Hotel with his usual 7 a.m. breakfast
of All-Bran and a quick jog round Hyde Park. Then he had a
business meeting in his suite with representatives of Mark
McCormack, his agent, plus his European corporate lawyer
and ditto ditto banker to discuss forthcoming deals. At 9 a.m.
promptly he phoned his secretary, Ruth Kinnear, back in
Geneva, as he does every day of the year. At ten, Gerry the
chauffeur came to collect him in the Britax-owned Ford
Granada, number-plate JYS 1 (John Young Stewart), that is
at his disposal whenever he is in England.

It is important to realize that almost every minute of Jackie
Stewart's time is *owned* by someone. Goodyear, Ford, Britax,
Simoniz, Rolex, Moët et Chandon and several other com-
panies all pay him a retainer to act as their 'PR consultant'
for so many days a year. At forty-three, he earns reputedly
over three-quarters of a million a year – more than he ever
did as a racing driver. He also quite possibly works harder.

This day was to be the property of Goodyear, and we were
off to Solihull, Birmingham, for lunch with a convention of
tyre dealers. Gerry drove and Jackie spent most of the journey
making phone calls on the car phone.

Soon after noon we arrived at a roadhouse hotel outside
Birmingham where fifty or so Goodyear tyre dealers were
waiting. They were all wearing brown suits and broad shiny
ties and two 'hostesses' went round lighting their cigarettes
and laughing at their jokes. Jackie strode in with his peculiar

tiptoe walk and started greeting people by name, shaking hands and slapping backs. After a sit-down lunch of grapefruit and chicken salad, he got up and made a speech. It was given without notes, and it included plugs for the Ford Sierra and for Britax seatbelts and of course for Goodyear, as well as several good jokes which had the tyre men rocking in their seats. Afterwards, they all said what a good speech it was. Even so, they might have been surprised to learn what Jackie charges for making a speech. He charges £5,000.

After lunch, all the tyre men trooped back to the bar for liqueurs. Jackie doesn't drink. He doesn't even drink tea or coffee. He doesn't eat much either. As far as I could tell, he also doesn't seem to pee. Perhaps he is fuelled by petrol. While the tyre men grew louder, Jackie Stewart quietly signed hundreds of photographs of himself for the tyre men to give their children. 'To Donna', he wrote, 'to Darren, to Jason, to Sharon, best wishes, Jackie Stewart.' In his book *Faster!* (1972) he recounts, how, as a young man, he spent many hours practising his signature. He knew he would be signing a lot of autographs in the years ahead; he knew they would be preserved; and he did not want them to be a discredit to him. He was mildly dyslexic as a boy but he wanted his signature to be right.

At three we left the hotel and drove back through pouring rain to London, Jackie making phone calls all the way. We got back to the Grosvenor House in time for him to go to his room to change, from navy blue suit into navy blue cord trousers, navy blue sweater, navy blue shirt and navy blue slip-on shoes with stacked heels. He changed because we were going to visit a boys' club of which he is president and he wanted to look casual. If he hadn't had time to change in his hotel room, he would have changed in the car – he took the clothes with him to Solihull just in case. It might seem a lot of effort to go to in order to look casual but that is what perfectionism is all about.

Up in his hotel suite, he offered me a drink then found the drinks fridge unaccountably locked. A similar accident had

befallen him in Solihull when he had offered Gerry money for
his lunch then found he had come out without his wallet. He
had to borrow a tenner from a Goodyear man, who said, 'I'm
still waiting for the last tenner you borrowed.' Money seems
to be a bit of a problem with Jackie Stewart, for all he earns
so much of it. He admits that however much he has, he never
feels he has enough, and he takes pride in being 'a canny
Scot'.

'Do you mean mean?' I ask.

'What is mean?'

'Well, like J. Paul Getty installing a pay phone for his
guests.'

'Oh no,' Jackie says, shocked. 'I'd never do that. I'd just
leave them to pay whatever their conscience dictated.'

What is Jackie Stewart like? Well, he is short, about five
foot seven, and, like many short men, he walks on his toes
and carries his shoulders high to make himself taller. He has
a barrel chest and a very thick neck. A racing driver drives
lying down but with his head slightly raised, so the muscles
of his neck need to be strong. He has a long face with hooded
eyes, one more hooded than the other, and set close together.
He speaks, of course, with a Scottish accent and he talks very
articulately indeed. He has considerable insight; one feels he
is a man who knows himself well, so no Freudian skeletons
are going to come popping out of the closet. He is highly
competitive, and can be aggressive and irritable. He got very
irritable later when, on leaving the Grosvenor House, Gerry
almost hit another car in Park Lane and then got lost. 'Why
didn't you look it up in the A to Z and memorize it?' Jackie
asked crossly. If he were a chauffeur, he certainly would have
done.

We drove deeper into the East End, through pouring rain,
and finally drew up outside a small building labelled Springfield Boys' Club. Inside, there were lots of black boys playing
snooker and table tennis. They looked at Jackie Stewart
without interest, either not recognizing him or recognizing
him and not giving a toss. The club chairman, Anthony

Marsh, came to greet him but he was more interested in having a row with the club coach about football fixtures. Jackie tried to act as peacemaker and kept slapping the club coach – a huge black athlete – on the back but the coach shook him off irritably. Jackie suggested a game of table tennis with one of the boys. 'Oh you want your photograph taken playing table tennis?' said the chairman. 'No,' said Jackie, peeved. 'I want a game of table tennis.' So one of the boys was volunteered and Jackie beat him 21–17.

Then it was time for the committee meeting. The Springfield Boys' Club was originally launched by racing driver Graham Hill in 1968 and Jackie Stewart took over the presidency on Hill's death. He attends nearly all the committee meetings and never misses the December bunfight when 'we have some really impressive people along – Prince Michael of Kent, Daley Thompson, people like that'. During the committee meeting, Jackie went into fairly lengthy reminiscences about what he was like at sixteen – serving an apprenticeship (in his father's garage), itching for responsibility. 'There aren't any apprenticeships nowadays and our boys aren't itching for responsibility,' one of the committee members said sourly. It was a far lower level of appreciation than Jackie Stewart is used to but he took it extraordinarily well. Mr Marsh told me afterwards that Jackie is an active and energetic club president, and has taken boys from the club to stay with his own sons in Switzerland.

We left Springfield at about 8.30 and Jackie said he was going back to his hotel to make a few more phone calls, have a sandwich, do twenty minutes of exercises which he had not had time for that morning, and go to bed. He asked if I wanted to come to Solihull with him again the next day for another Goodyear lunch but I said no, it was too dull. What about the glamorous Jackie one was always reading about in the gossip columns, the one who went shooting at Gatcombe and partying with George Harrison and Roman Polanski? What about a *fun* day? I said. 'Fun day,' Jackie said grimly and started leafing through his diary. Tyre testing at Akron, car dealers' convention in Las Vegas, Ford commercials in Detroit, recording dates with ABC television, another meeting with tyre dealers – we looked through several jam-packed weeks in vain for any sign of fun. Eventually he dug out a day two months ahead – shooting with Lord Montagu and dinner in Edinburgh – would that be fun? Yes, I agreed. It would also be a chance to meet Helen, his wife, who would be joining him.

The next time I saw him he was standing in Lord Montagu's marsh shooting pheasants as fast as his loader could load, and Helen, his wife, was beside him. I had heard a lot about Helen meantime. For one thing, I had heard that she had left him, and gone to live by herself in New York. That was clearly not true, since there she was – a slim, slight, blonde figure, still with those sixties' model-girl looks. Impossible to believe she could be forty-one. In some ways, she looks rather like Jackie – the same long face and slightly hooded eyes, the same slight but erect carriage.

'Do you like going on shoots?' I asked her as Jackie banged away being Dead Eye Dick.

'No.'

'Oh,' I said, nonplussed. 'Why not?'

'Well, it's very wet, isn't it? A bit boring.'

In cold print, it probably sounds rude or hostile but it wasn't at all – just unusually truthful. That is the thing about Helen Stewart. She isn't 'shy' as newspapers often say she is: in fact, she is perfectly self-possessed and can be very articulate when she wants to be. But she doesn't gush, she doesn't flannel, and if a question can be answered with a straight yes or no, she leaves it at that. That is no doubt why she is friends with Princess Anne, who has the same direct manner of speech. Gossip columnists made great play of Helen Stewart, humble little baker's daughter and ex-bank-clerk, becoming godmother to Princess Anne's daughter Zara, but as usual they got it wrong. Helen Stewart's father was the owner of a chain of bakers' shops, and she was brought up in Helensburgh, one of the most affluent suburbs of Glasgow. She is well educated and upper middle-class. More to the point, she is deeply religious (a Presbyterian) and a conscientious god-mother to four other children besides Princess Anne's.

After the shoot and the drive to Southampton, we flew in a Ford-owned jet to Edinburgh. Jackie promptly and efficiently fell asleep while Helen talked quietly, sometimes inaudibly, about her life and plans. Her main problem is the familiar one for many women of her age – boredom. Her two sons, Paul, seventeen, and Mark, fifteen, are away at boarding-school, and Jackie is on the road constantly. She finds herself alone in their large house outside Geneva most of the time. Now Jackie has bought her an apartment in New York so she can go to art classes and dance classes, which she loves, when none of her family need her. She wants to 'do something', to make a role for herself apart from being Mrs Jackie Stewart. She is not cut out by upbringing or conscience to be a member of the idle rich.

The dinner that night was a formal do at Hopetoun House, an eighteenth-century stately pile a few miles out of Edin-burgh. Jackie wore a kilt; Helen wore a billowing silk skirt and brocade jacket. Walking up the steps to the house as a piper skirled them in, they both looked beautiful but oddly small and fragile, and they were squeezing each other's hands for reassurance. Inside, there were lots of big burly people talking loudly. The dinner was given by the Motor Racing Journalists of Scotland to present an award to Jackie Stewart for 'services to motoring in Scotland': though actually it was another PR stunt funded by Ford. I sat next to an old and distinguished sports journalist, J. B. McLaren, who told me how he first recognized the young Jackie's talent. He, McLaren, had been lent a souped-up Austin Healey and he drove it over to the garage in Dumbuck, near Dumbarton, which Jackie's father owned, because he wanted Jackie's brother Jimmy to try it. Jimmy was already a well-known racing driver. Jimmy drove it, and then noticed his kid brother drooling over it. Jackie was then about fifteen. 'Let him drive it,' he said to McLaren, 'he's a good driver.' So McLaren drove Jackie to a private road in the country and then let him take the wheel. 'I knew immediately he was special,' he recalled. 'There was confidence and accuracy and speed. He was the greatest natural driver I've ever come across.' And then he added: 'Jimmy was a great driver too.'

Jimmy. Everyone I talked to who had known Jackie in the early days talked about Jimmy, often in the reverent tones of Sherlock Holmes fans talking about Mycroft. Jimmy is eight years older than Jackie; he was a famous racing driver while Jackie was still a schoolboy. Jackie's only claim to fame then was that he was Jimmy Stewart's brother. At fifteen, Jackie took up shooting (his grandfather was a gamekeeper) and went on to become British champion at nineteen. Even so, Allan Jones, whose father coached Jackie at his shooting estate in North Wales, recalls: 'Whenever I went to stay with his family in those early days, I always thought Jackie was totally overshadowed by his brother. The conversation was always Jimmy this, Jimmy that. The sideboard was covered with Jimmy's trophies. I think that made Jackie more competitive. He wanted a slot on that sideboard.'

In 1954, Jimmy had a crash at Le Mans and the next year, on his second race back, he had an even worse one at the Nurburgring, when he was trapped under the car for twenty-five minutes. He retired from racing, and Jackie swept him off the sideboard for good. Jimmy took over his father's garage but then sold it. His marriage broke up. Jackie lent him money to start a business in Florida but it wasn't a success. 'Jimmy didn't really make anything of himself,' Jackie told me and a whole tableful of tyre dealers at the Goodyear lunch.

At the Hopetoun dinner, someone told Jackie that the Edinburgh Motor Racing Club – one of his old haunts – was having a disco that evening, and Jackie insisted we should all go on there. It was after midnight when we arrived and there was no tumultuous welcome – everyone was too busy dancing and drinking. A very drunk man, about Jackie's age but overweight and balding, came up to me and said: 'I'll tell you the truth about Jackie Stewart. I'll tell you the *real* story.' Yes, I said, go on. But he was too drunk and all he could do was repeat, like a stuck gramophone record, 'I'll tell you the real story.'

What *is* the real story about Jackie Stewart? Is there a hidden skeleton in the cupboard? Actually I don't believe there is. Drivers who drove with Jackie remember him as an unusually 'clean' driver. He was tough and competitive, certainly, but he never did anything underhand. His present life is also clean. He earns a lot of money but he earns it by working exceptionally hard. The only trouble is that he earns it by doing PR, an activity the value of which is often difficult for the outsider to discern, and the commodity he is PR-ing, basically, is himself. Goodyear and Ford and Britax and the rest all pay him to promote their products because of his name and reputation and because they know he will always behave impeccably. He can never be anything other than a nice guy because that is his profession. This is fine but it makes one a little reluctant to add to the chorus of praise saying what a nice guy he is. I found I wanted to go round the Goodyear tyre dealers saying, 'Do you realize he is *paid* to slap you on the back and remember your name and ask if your wife has recovered from her operation?' Jackie would say I was motivated by envy as, he would say, all journalists are.

There is a striking passage in his book *Faster!* where he recounts walking in Hyde Park one sunny day in the middle of a hectic season and seeing all the people milling about and thinking, 'It was all part of another life, totally remote from the way I live, and more than anything it made me think about what a candyfloss world I live in, just how removed I am from the way most people live and think.'

I brought this up rather diffidently on one of our interminable car journeys, thinking that he would probably not remember something he had written ten years ago, but he picked it up immediately. 'Yes,' he said, 'I was thinking about that just the other day. I was thinking how nice it would be to go to Speaker's Corner but I never made it. I still feel that I'm in a cocoon. I am, yes, sure I am. I still feel I'm ... packaged ... in a way.' The odd thing was: he said it seriously, but without regret.

Reproduced by permission of the *Sunday Express*

BARON AND BARONESS THYSSEN

28 May 1989

Lugano is a small and sleepy Swiss town where elderly hausfraus seem to spend the whole day window-shopping for cakes. It is sweet, bourgeois and, frankly, dull.

The Villa Favorita, though only a mile out of town, is something else entirely. It is one of the many homes of Baron and Baroness Thyssen and it has the whiff of international jet-settery about it. It is an eighteenth-century Italian *palazzo* housing the world's second-richest private art collection – second only to the Queen's. Last year there was a great hoo-ha when Mrs Thatcher tried to get it for Britain, and dispatched Prince Charles to Lugano to woo the Baron, but alas, he had already signed an agreement with Spain.

Not surprisingly, the villa is surrounded by serious security – policeman on the gate, gatekeepers at the lodge, endless guards with walkie-talkies along the drive. They had to find a 'personal bodyguard' to take me to the Baron's private quarters – but when we got there, the bodyguard disappeared as if in a puff of smoke, and left me to wander alone among the priceless paintings.

I finally found the Baron in a dark, panelled study, eating his breakfast – yoghurt and apple – off a silver tray. He was wearing his customary yachting blazer and gleaming cuffs, but his hands were shaking badly and he said he'd been up until two the night before. I was pleased to notice that, at sixty-eight, he has nice new white teeth; when I saw him in London two years ago, his teeth were horrible to behold.

He said the Baroness would join us in a minute. Talking to him while he had his breakfast was uphill work; he is taciturn by nature and his English is far from fluent. His mother was Hungarian and his father German, but he never lived in either country; he grew up in Holland and then became Swiss. His German grandfather founded the family fortunes (iron and steel), which now provide him with an income in the millions.

I was relieved when the Baroness, 'Tita', whirled in, chattering nineteen to the dozen, and even he began to come alive. She is Spanish and fun; as warm and friendly as he is cold and reserved. She is like a puppy who comes and jumps on your lap – even if you *want* to resist, you can't help but be charmed.

She told me that she knew she was 'destined' to marry the Baron. (She is a great believer in destiny and fate, hexes and omens.) She first saw him at a party when she was still married to her first husband, Lex Barker, the Tarzan actor, and she felt, 'I don't know, very nervous, and I thought, "If I were not married I would say this is the man of my life." It made me feel so nervous. I say to my husband, "Can we go? I am very tired." So I left without speaking to Heini. I knew it wasn't right for me to talk to him then.'

Then came meeting number two, by which time Lex Barker was dead, her second marriage to a film producer ('the biggest mistake of my life') had been and gone, and she had a baby, Borja. This time, when she saw Baron Thyssen, 'I knew immediately I was going to be his.' She was staying on a yacht with friends on the Costa Smeralda, Sardinia, and was due to fly home to Spain that day, but there were no seats on the flight – 'fate, you see' – so the friends asked her to stay another day and come to dinner with Baron Thyssen.

Another woman had been asked as his dinner partner, but he had eyes only for Tita. 'And during dinner he looked at me, and our eyes met, and I felt – I don't know – shock. It was so romantic.' He asked her to lunch the next day and told her to bring her friends. 'And we arrive on a small boat and he was waiting on the dock, and as soon as we land, he put his arm round my shoulders. Then we had lunch and went swimming . . .'

At this point, the Baroness collapses in giggles and asks the Baron, 'Shall I go on?' He nods. 'So we were in the water and we were kissing, and it was so funny because there was this friend of ours who is a great windsurfer. She is so good she wears all her jewellery on her surfboard because she never falls in. But when she saw what we were doing in the water . . . splash!'

So their courtship, for want of a better word, lasted just one day. Marriage, however, had to wait while he divorced his fourth, and longest-serving, wife Denise Shorto. (He has since sued her for the return of some jewels he gave her – he lost.) The wedding to Tita finally took place in 1985. He then formally adopted Borja. The Baron also has four natural children – Heini, Francesca, Lorne and Alexander.

It seems to be a happy marriage. He said he liked her immediately for 'her friendly eyes, and all the emotions she shows in her face'. He also likes the fact that 'when I start a row, she keeps quiet, she doesn't answer back, so we never have any fights'. She agrees that she is a docile wife. 'He wins, always, because I am an old-fashioned girl.'

Many women might quail at becoming wife number five, but the Baroness points out that she was also Lex Barker's fifth wife, and that marriage certainly worked. Her eyes still mist with tears when she speaks of him – his death from a heart attack was the worst shock of her life. 'He was like my father, my brother, my lover, my friend. I felt very protected when I was with him.' Would she say the same of the Baron? 'He is like my brother, lover and friend, but not father – I am older now.' The age gap is about the same, but she was only twenty when she married Barker. Now she is forty-four.

*

Lex Barker would never let her have a child because he already had three by his previous wives and said he never saw them. But she regretted it bitterly after his death. Hence, perhaps, Borja.

I asked the Baron which of his previous wives the Baroness most resembled and he said, surprisingly, Nina Dyer. She was his second wife, a bisexual English model, and the marriage lasted only ten months. In fact, he told me, by the time he married her, their affair was already over, but her mother had just died and he married her for consolation. Later, she committed suicide.

Or did she? When I mentioned Nina Dyer's suicide, the Baron said, 'Yes, but you can never tell, when someone takes sleeping pills, whether they took them of their own free will or whether someone made them.' This was odd because, just a few months ago, he caused a great furore in America by casting doubt on *another* suicide – that of his fourth wife's lover, who died by dropping out of a Manhattan skyscraper window in his underpants. The inquest seemed satisfied that he jumped, but Baron Thyssen told a journalist that he thought he was pushed. But why? Does he go in for conspiracy theories? He certainly seems to have a dark imagination. He told me that Nina Dyer's troubles all began when she wore the Hope Diamond – 'which of course, as you know, is notoriously unlucky'.

Yet the Baron and Baroness's superstitions seem to work in curious ways. The engagement ring she wears all the time – a simple diamond the size of an adult fieldmouse – was previously given by the Baron to Nina Dyer. It disappeared on her death but later he found it in a saleroom and bought it for Tita. Didn't that seem unlucky? After all, Nina Dyer had an unhappy life, she killed herself. 'Yes, but she did not kill herself with this diamond!' the Baroness giggles merrily.

I asked the Baroness what was the Baron's worst fault and he said quickly, 'My drinking, no?' But she said, no, not his drinking but his perpetual movement, and the fact that he would never go to bed. 'He can't understand that other people need to sleep.'

He admits that he is a restless man: from the time he inherited the Thyssen fortune in his late twenties, he has never spent more than three days in any one place. They have homes in Lugano, in Madrid (where his Old Masters collection will be moving), in Marbella ('but that is only a beach house'), on the Costa Brava, in Paris, in London, in Jamaica and 'oh yes, an apartment in Barcelona, I forgot'.

Didn't it get rather tiring whizzing round all these homes? The Baroness shrugged. 'I am used to it. My first husband, Lex, was just the same.' There is an important difference, though – when she was married to Lex Barker, she didn't have a child. Eight-year-old Borja goes to school in Madrid: didn't she feel she should stay at home with him? 'Yes, but you see my son is younger and my husband is older. I feel I must profit from my time with my husband.'

Ironically, the Baron had already told me that he suffered an unhappy childhood – because he never saw his parents. He saw his mother for, at most, one month a year, and his father for a week. They divorced when he was eight, but he didn't even know it for another three years because they were never around anyway, and nobody bothered to tell him. His brother and two sisters were much older and already grown up. He lived with a governess in The Hague during term-time, and went with her to the seaside for holidays. The governess (who brought him up from babyhood) was German, but strongly anti-Nazi and left-wing. She killed herself when the Germans invaded Holland – 'but, of course, I was already gone by then'.

The Baroness also comes from a broken home – her parents divorced when she was five – but a much more 'normal' one. She lived with her mother and brother and saw her father, an engineer, at weekends. She spent all her time reading novels – 'you know, where the heroine is carried off by pirates, and then the hero comes and rescues her. I was a very romantic child, living in poverty, writing poetry. I would go to bed early so I could read my books and dream dreams.'

'She still reads, you know, books,' the Baron says, as though this is some incredibly rare and remarkable hobby like camel racing, or white-water canoeing. But, of course, now she has less need to dream. By all accounts, her big ambition now is to be a Spanish duchess – quite an achievement for a former beauty queen, because the Spanish aristocracy is notoriously strait-laced. But she has already persuaded the Baron to lend his Old Masters to Spain for ten years, and they have bought a house in Madrid to be near the collection. She told me she was doing it up 'in Indonesian style – but of course I am very nervous about the result because Heini, you know, has very good taste'. I would be nervous too. Baron Thyssen remarked, apropos of nothing, that he was brought up by the sea and always liked to look over water.

'And is your house in Madrid near the water?'

'No.'

She told me that she was hoping to train him to travel less frenetically and to settle down more. But he told me, when she was out of the room, that all his wives said that. But why *did* he keep moving so much? After all, he has already handed over the business to his eldest son, Heini Jr; he is officially retired. 'Yes, but I have so many important meetings around the world.' While we were talking, his youngest son, Alexander, rang from Rome and I heard the Baron saying, 'I am in a meeting right now.' I longed to call out, 'Don't worry, it isn't important; talk to your son.'

My appointment with the Baron and Baroness was supposed to be for one hour, from ten to eleven, but at one thirty I was still there, while other people – presumably their eleven, twelve and one o'clock appointments – piled up in the salon outside. By the end, I was anxious about missing my plane and kept asking them more and more risqué questions (Is the Baron insatiable in bed?) in the hope that they would throw me out, but they never did. (The answer, by the way, was 'Well of course at the beginning, but not so much now.')

But why? Why are they so desperately keen on publicity? It must be the Baroness's doing because, before she arrived on the scene, he never gave interviews at all. Does she hope it will help to make her a duchess? If so, it seems misguided. Another weird thing was that after they agreed to see me, but before I arrived, they sent me an incredible pseudo-legal form to sign, saying they could check every word I wrote and alter it to suit themselves. I wrote back a snooty letter about 'the cherished British principle of freedom of the press' and they said, in effect, all right, forget the form – come anyway. But it was like the business with the bodyguard – a lot of flummery and fuss, and then nothing.

Reproduced by permission of the *Sunday Express*